SAVING MARTHA & MOLLY

Saving Martha & Molly

Ghosts of Casco Bay

Cary Vajda

M·P·P
www.MissionPointPress.com

Mission Point Press

Published by Mission Point Press
www.MissionPointPress.com

Cover illustration: Jeff Bane
Book design: Deirdre Wait

Hardcover ISBN 13: 978-1-965278-86-4
Paperback ISBN 13: 978-1-965278-85-7

LCCN: 2025915108

Printed in the United States of America

"The eye is the lamp of the body.

If your eye is good, your whole body will be full of light.

But if your eye is bad, your whole body will be full of darkness!"

— Matthew 6:22-23 HCSB

PROLOGUE

*S**ave Martha and Molly.*

"What?" I cried out. "You can't be serious."

Hannah, you forget who I am.

"Forget?" I shook my head. "God, help me," I muttered.

I am.

"By giving me an assignment which makes my blood boil? How could You, Lord?"

A silly question.

I continued my rant, "Martha and Molly have lived despicable lives. During my life they treated me with disrespect. In fact, many times I was the brunt of their mischief. They were born into wealth and enjoyed the trappings of the privileged class. On the other hand, in their eyes, I was a member of the lowly class meant to serve them. Although I tried—You know how hard I tried—I could not convince myself to like them. Tolerance of their behavior, which is far from affection, was the closest I ever got."

Do not challenge my patience.

"I'm sorry, God. But I'd rather not accept your assignment. I say, let Hell have them."

Free will is My gift to mankind. It is the ability to choose one path over another, to decide which direction to take in your life, as well as the afterlife. Hannah, my dear child, what have I taught you about this gift?

I sighed. "Free will is forever subservient to God's will."

Therefore, your appropriate response to My request should be …

"Thy will be done."

Thank you, Hannah. To begin your mission, you must bear witness to an event which triggers all that follows.

With a slight bow, I said, "As you wish, my Lord."

CHAPTER 1

I am Hannah. I was born in Portland, Maine, in 1853. My parents, John and Sarah Phillips, were good people; they showered me with their love and protection. My father was a master ship's carpenter, and my mother managed our family's shop selling ship fittings and fishing gear. I could not have chosen better parents to raise me.

At twenty, I married Samuel Clarke. He was my childhood sweetheart who I met while walking the shoreline of the Portland peninsula when I was ten. He was gathering driftwood for his father to carve. I was collecting sea glass to add to my mother's collection. Soon after our chance encounter, we began collecting our treasures together. Years later, when Sam and I married, our vows did not include "until death do us part" for we pledged to be together, forever.

Sam lost his life at the age of thirty-five when his ship sank during a storm off the coast of North Carolina. Unfortunately, his death occurred just before he learned I was with child. My death came during childbirth. God took us both before we could be parents to our only son. It has been difficult to forgive Him, the Lord God Almighty.

Although cut short, I lived a wonderful life. Do I wish I could've lived to a ripe old age alongside my husband? Without a doubt. However, it is God's plan for me to help others during my afterlife. I do not protest because it would do me no good. Besides, to whom would I complain? God?

When given an assignment by God, I am blessed with the knowledge I need to fulfill His request. Everything connected to the people I'm required to help fills my head. I know their past and I see and hear their present. Not only am I aware of an unfolding situation involving those connected to my mission, but I also have an awareness of thoughts held by them. Whether they are just thoughts or thoughts which lead to action, I know them. This peculiarity is often distracting as I often hear a thought, then I hear it again when it is said.

However, the future of those I must help is left unknown. In other words, at the time of my interventions, I can't be certain if my efforts will result in a positive outcome. Why? Free will. Those I try to guide are free to decide whether to accept my help. Thus, for better or worse, they choose which path to take.

Per His command, I must take a temporary absence from Heaven. I leave it with the thought I should be watching Jacob McLellan. Within a blink of an eye, my thought takes me to my destination, Earth.

CHAPTER 2

November 1892. Hannah found Jacob McLellan in the second-floor library of his grand home. Sipping a hot cup of coffee, he is formally dressed in preparation for another day as the mayor of Portland, Maine. She watched as he took a measured bite from a sweet pastry, still warm after being delivered by a servant minutes ago.

Hearing the cold wind batter the mansion, Jacob shivered with the thought of venturing out into the crisp New England weather for another meeting with the city council. Today's important topic was the need to cobblestone more of the city's streets.

Jacob placed the pastry back down on a plate. With no one observing his next move, at least the living, he licked the icing off his sticky fingers. He took another sip from his cup and savored not only the coffee flavor, but also the calming solitude he found only when his daughters were asleep.

He leaned back into his chair, eyeing the framed pictures hanging on the walls of the room. Some were paintings of pleasant, tranquil scenes, others were photographs of special moments in his life. The photograph he was most proud of is a group of men he commanded in 1863 when he led them on a side-wheeled steamer, the *Chesapeake*, to a victory over the Confederates. Jacob stood in the center of the photograph with his good friend, John Phillips, beside him. John was Hannah's father.

Jacob took another sip of brew and looked to the wall on his right where a wedding photograph was hung. This picture was taken on Christmas Eve, 1873, of Samuel Clarke and his bride, Hannah. Although a pleasant reflection, the memory of his girls' behavior during the blessed event caused his smile to change to a frown.

Jacob shook his head and thought, *what was Hannah thinking when she chose my daughters to be her bridesmaids?* Before her entrance, the twins shamefully sashayed down the aisle in their exquisite gowns, blowing kisses to *their* adoring audience. Later that evening, when Hannah threw her bridal bouquet, they created another embarrassing incident. After shoving the other women aside, both caught the bridal bouquet and savagely ripped it apart.

Jacob had the foresight to ask the photographer to take two shots of the newlyweds. The first photograph was presented to the wedding couple. The second he kept as a reminder of the goodness he saw in Hannah and desperately wanted for his girls.

Continuing to reminisce, he thought of the many embarrassing moments his family had endured. One such occasion occurred after Sam and Hannah died. His daughters tried to take the orphaned baby from their grandparents by suing them in court. In his reverie, a grin spread across Jacob's face. Unbeknownst to all, it was he who paid for the grandparents' lawyer.

A blood-curdling scream pierced Jacob's brief serenity thus halting his pleasant recollections. Coffee spilled onto his lap. Another scream followed. The twins were awake; another day had begun.

As Jacob rose from his seat to deal with the ongoing battle between his daughters, he felt lightheaded and dropped back into his chair. Discomfort spread throughout his arms, back, and chest. A cold sweat swept over him.

His cup fell from his hand onto the floor. No longer could he hear the earsplitting shouts coming from down the hall. His thoughts were now of the peace and quiet he was finally enjoying. Jacob smiled as he took his last breath.

Some said Jacob McLellan's death was due to the weight he had gained over the past twenty years. Most, however, suspected the cause of death were his daughters. A day in the McLellan mansion never went without drama caused by Martha and Molly.

Soon after their father was found dead by a servant, the twins called for their family's carriage to take them to their favorite boutique. After all, two stylish black gowns ruffled with black French lace were required. Draping strands of black pearls were also necessary to draw attention to their ample cleavage.

Three days later, a funeral was held at Whispering Woods Cemetery for Mayor Jacob McLellan. Hundreds of Portland's citizens came to honor him, a man dearly loved by many *outside* his home. While condolences were offered to Minnie, no one took the time to offer their sympathy to the twins.

As their father was lowered into his grave, each twin held a smirk behind a lacy black mourning veil. The McLellan fortune had just moved one step closer to their greedy grasp.

*   *   *

It was late spring in Portland, six months after the mayor's death. Roses were in bloom, normally a sign of a new beginning. For the twins, it would be the beginning of their end.

Martha and Molly felt a rainbow of hope when they imagined the possibility of their mother soon joining their father in eternity. Both looked forward to the pot of gold at the end of that rainbow, the McLellan fortune. But they couldn't help but wonder, how long would that be? Both agreed, "The sooner the better."

The natural progression was to ponder a way to assist their mother to an earlier, rather than later, death. As they considered how to end their mother's life, the notion of killing her came to a screeching halt. They just couldn't do it. They shouldn't do it. Both realized the dastardly deed would not have the desired result.

After their mother's demise they would inherit the family fortune, causing it to be split in half. "No!" cried Martha. "No!" cried Molly. "Half is not enough!"

"What could be done?" asked Martha. "What should be done?" asked Molly. To solve the dilemma both came to the same conclusion; my twin sister must die before my mother.

Death by hanging, death by stabbing, death by gunshot, death by drowning, or death by suffocation with a pillow … the twins just couldn't decide. Then, it happened … inspiration.

Martha was in the sitting room while her sister was upstairs in the library. Both were sipping tea while reading the newspaper. Within the folds of the daily news, each found a story about Dr. Thomas Neill Cream who had been convicted of several heinous crimes. The doctor, also known as the Lambeth Poisoner, had, on at least four occasions, used strychnine to poison prostitutes in and around the London neighborhood of Lambeth. After being found guilty Dr. Cream was executed on November 15, 1892. Just before the hangman's noose was placed around his neck he confessed to being Jack the Ripper. But, as the writer of the news article later found, he couldn't have been that serial killer for the doctor had been sitting in an Illinois state prison at the time of the Ripper killings.

Within the article, the writer also noted it was not common for a man to use poison to murder. Women usually preferred this method. "Hmmm," grinned Martha. "Hmmm," grinned Molly.

Which poison does one select when one wants to kill her twin sister? There were so many from which to choose. Where does one begin to find the right one for a loved one?

Time was of the essence, since there was no way of knowing when their mother would naturally pass. Unknown to each other, the twins made separate trips to the library to discover the best way to execute the execution of the other.

✳   ✳   ✳

It was around ten on a Tuesday morning when Martha called for their family's coachman.

"Where is it you wish to go?" he asked.

"Public Library," she snapped.

Ten minutes later, the carriage pulled in front of the library. Hustling from his perch, the coachman helped Martha down from the carriage. With determination, she promptly marched towards the entrance of the stately building.

Sitting on the steps were an elderly couple. Both were dressed in rags and smelled like the garbage they had just foraged in. As Martha passed by the old man, he reached out and touched the sleeve of her coat. "Please madam," he pleaded, "we're hungry and ask for a small donation to quench our thirst and hunger."

Martha was appalled. *He touched me! The gall of that grubby dreg?* She brushed aside his dirty hand and deliberately pushed him into his partner. Both rolled down the steps. Martha scrunched her nose. "Filthy leeches! How dare you touch me?!" she said.

The man looked up. "Sorry, ma'am. Just askin' for a coin or two. My wife and I haven't eaten in days."

She spat at the old couple. "You are not my problem."

With her nose in the air, Martha climbed the remaining steps to the library's entrance. Impatiently, she waited for her coachman to open the door. Once inside, she demanded assistance from the librarian.

Martha found aconite, which is derived from the plant monkshood. It is also known as wolfsbane. This was an untraceable poison. It could be absorbed merely by touching the leaves with bare hands. Rapid heart arrhythmia, asphyxiation and finally the victim would experience suffocation.

On the very same day Martha visited the library, Molly did the same around two in the afternoon. She found belladonna, also called nightshade. At the time, it was used in small doses as a pain reliever and muscle relaxer. It was also used in cosmetics to create a blusher. If ingested or too much was applied to one's skin, it was known to be lethal. The poison caused severe hallucinations, rapid heartbeats, breathing difficulty, as well as terrible seizures.

✳   ✳   ✳

Having discovered her choice of poison before Molly, Martha was the first to arrive at The Apothecary Shoppe. "Do you have wolfsbane?" she asked.

The shopkeeper chuckled. The woman was obviously trying to look like an older man. She was stooped over with a walking cane, and her voice clearly sounded like a woman trying to speak like a man. And the clothes she was wearing … he hadn't seen such vintage clothing hanging on a man for quite a while. The funniest thing is he could smell the strong scent of the woman's perfume.

The shop owner replied, "Yes, I do. But I must warn you; do not touch it with your bare hands."

Two hours later, Molly had her coachman stop one block from her destination. After he helped her down from the carriage, she bent over and began her charade. Molly hobbled to The Apothecary Shoppe and stopped before the entrance. As she reached for the doorknob, an old woman dressed in tattered clothing reached out to her.

"Sir, if you please …" She pointed to her husband who was in the middle of a coughing spell. "My husband is ill. Can you help us? Just a few coins will buy the medicine he needs. If we must, we'd be glad to work—"

Molly's nostrils flared as she knocked the woman's hand away with her walking cane. She growled, "Out of my way, you old hag."

Molly turned, took a deep breath, and pushed the door open. Seeing a man working at the shop's counter, she shuffled over to him. "Do you have nightshade?" she asked.

The shop owner looked up and thought the customer looked familiar. Except for the apparent change into a different vintage man's suit, her mannerisms were much like an earlier customer. Instead of asking if both patrons were the same person, he replied, "Yes, I do."

As she paid for the herb, the man said, "I must warn you, be careful—"

"I will be sure to use this sparingly," she said with a grin.

"You are wise for it will do great harm to you if used in large doses."

With a twinkle in her eye, Molly nodded.

✳   ✳   ✳

Martha arrived home to discover Molly was not there. *How considerate of my sister,* she thought. Being extremely careful not to touch the wolfsbane, she ground the leaves into a fine powder. Then she went into Molly's bedroom and sprinkled the dangerous herbal powder into her sister's face cream jar. After a quick mix, Martha placed the jar in the exact spot where she had found it.

Molly returned home to find no one in the kitchen. She searched for a tea ball infuser, found it, and filled the small vessel with a mixture of tea leaves and nightshade. Before leaving the kitchen, she slipped the poisoned infuser into her pocket.

Martha came down the stairs to see her sister coming out of the kitchen. Both abruptly stopped and gave each other a curious look. They chuckled to themselves. Each one knew the other twin would not have much longer to live.

✳   ✳   ✳

That evening, after the servants left the mansion and her mother had retired for the night, Molly set her evil plan into motion. She knew her sister enjoyed sipping a hot cup of chamomile tea before retiring to bed. This helped Martha with digestive concerns, and to relax after a day of fighting with her sister.

Molly intercepted Martha as she was making her way into the kitchen. "I want to tell you something."

Martha snapped, "What is it now?"

"I wish to apologize for the harsh things I said to you earlier today."

This is new and very suspicious. Just what is my sister up to? Martha scrunched her nose and curtly replied, "Apology accepted."

"Let me make it up to you," said Molly. "May I prepare your nighttime tea?"

Martha couldn't remember the last time her sister did anything nice for her. "Why not, I was headed into the kitchen for that very reason."

Martha watched with curious interest as her sister poured water into a teakettle and placed it on the stove. While it was coming to a boil, Molly took a tea ball infuser from a drawer and filled it with tea leaves. When the water boiled, the teakettle whistled, thus causing Martha to take her eyes off her sister. This moment of distraction was all Molly needed to switch infusers. She placed the contaminated infuser into a teacup and poured hot water over it.

Molly smiled. "I hope it's how you like it."

As Molly took the stairs to her bedroom, Martha thought how ironic it was that her sister's last act was to do something nice for her. She then followed her sister up the stairs.

When Molly walked into her bedroom, she found it very warm, and was pleased a servant had opened the window when turning down the bed. After putting on her silk nightgown, she sat at her dressing table and applied her face cream. All the while, complimenting herself on her outstanding performance in the kitchen.

At first, it sounded like a drum beating in the distance. But it got louder. Felt louder. It was as if a mad drummer was inside Molly, and he was beating her heart into submission. Suddenly, she was clutching her throat and gasping for air. Shortly after Molly fell to the floor, both her breathing and heartbeat stopped.

Meanwhile, Martha had put on her nightgown, which matched the one her sister was wearing. Sitting on the edge of the bed, she sipped her tea and marveled at the thought of how easy it had been to poison Molly. She snickered. *The entire McLellan fortune will soon be mine.*

Martha's little celebration abruptly ceased when the seizures began. After a minute or so, the convulsions slowed; hallucinations then took hold of her mind. She was an angel and needed to spread her wings. She stood, then raced towards the window, flung it open, and leaped through the wire-mesh screen. Martha had taken flight into the night.

✳　　　✳　　　✳

Minnie woke when morning came, expecting to face another day of conflict within her home. Because her maladies were becoming more debilitative with each passing day, an attendant helped her up and out of bed, then dressed her.

Once she was ready to meet the day, Minnie was helped down two flights of stairs and into the dining room. During this difficult trek, she noticed how quiet it was in her home. The only sounds she heard came from the kitchen as breakfast was being prepared. *My daughters have not yet woken from their sleep,* Minnie thought to herself. She muttered, "Thank you Lord for giving me this blessed peaceful moment."

Minnie's breakfast was promptly served, hot tea and one smashed hardboiled egg swimming in warm butter. A slice of lightly buttered toast with strawberry jam completed her morning feast. As she took a sip from her teacup, the gardener disrupted her pleasant morning when he rushed into the dining room.

Perturbed by the interruption, Minnie barked, "What is it?"

"Madam!" he cried out as he tried to catch his breath. "I have dreadful news. I found Martha below her bedroom window lying in a bed of roses." He wailed, "I believe she's dead!"

Minnie's teacup fell from her fingers and crashed onto her plate of food. *This cannot be true.* "Show me!" she commanded.

The gardener and her attendant helped their employer from her chair, out of the mansion and down the front steps. Then they carefully led her to the side of the house where Martha had flattened a bed of roses. She stared at her daughter's still body for a moment, tears falling down her cheeks. Minnie leaned down and touched her; the body was cold, and her daughter's neck was broken.

With her attendant's assistance, Minnie struggled to stand. She said, "Help me back into the house, then tell the coachman to notify the police at once."

Minnie's next thought was to tell Molly her twin sister was dead. With the aid of her attendant, she climbed the stairs and moved towards Molly's bedroom. She entered the room without knocking.

The servant gasped at the sight of the dead body. Minnie fainted and joined Molly on the floor. Instead of immediately helping her employer, the domestic shooed the flies away from the dead twin. She then closed the window.

Meanwhile, the gardener found the coachman in the carriage house and informed him of Martha's death. He said, "Madam has requested you to summon the police at once."

With haste, the coachman prepared the horses for the short trip to the police department. Just as he was about to snap the horses into a speedy trot, Madam's attendant ran out of the mansion. He heard the woman shout, "Molly's dead, too!"

CHAPTER 3

"Big John" Murphy, Portland's city marshal, was feared by all who disobeyed the law and respected by those who appreciated a peaceful city. When a crime occurred within his authority, Big John had no problem unleashing his men to find the perpetrator. Once a suspect was apprehended, harsh interrogations were employed. Confessions from the guilty, as well as a few from the innocent, assured that justice would be quickly served.

Big John, who was fighting a summer cold, took a bite from his pastry and sneezed. "Shit," he said as he brought the sleeve of his uniform up and wiped his nose just as the door to his office burst open.

"Don't you know how to knock?" Big John yelled.

The detective leaned on the door frame. "I do Big John, but we need to go."

He took measure of Detective Bevis and chuckled to himself. Bevis was a slender man of medium height who fashioned himself after Sherlock Holmes. Although he was not a smoker, the detective was usually seen with a pipe in his mouth to complement his inquisitive look.

"Get rid of that damn pipe."

"Yes, sir. But we need to go, now."

The city marshal reached for his mug of coffee and took a gulp. "Bevis, I don't have time for this. I've an important meeting with the city council. Can't you manage it by yourself?"

The detective cleared his throat. "Sir, we have two dead bodies at the mayor's mansion."

Big John jerked his mug, hot coffee splashed onto his desk. "Which mayor?" he asked.

"What do you mean which mayor?"

Big John sighed. "The one who died last year, or the one who's sitting in his place."

"Ah, the one who's dead. I should've said the dead bodies are at the deceased mayor's wife's home."

Big John had hoped the bodies would've been found at the new mayor's home. He truly despised the man. *Perhaps next time.*

"Well, Bevis, I guess that trumps the city council meeting."

The city marshal shoved the remaining pastry into his mouth and gulped the rest of his coffee. Pushing away from his desk, he rose from his chair to a full height of six-foot-six. He straightened his tie. "Let's go. We shouldn't keep the dead waiting."

On the way out the door, Big John grabbed a burly policeman headed out for an early lunch. Without objection, his subordinate immediately fell in line with the detective as they paraded out of the police station towards the carriage reserved for the city marshal.

The coachman opened the door of the carriage. The driver asked, "Where to? City Hall?"

"Nope." Big John climbed into his seat. "Change of plans. Take us to the McLellan mansion."

With a quick snap of the reins, the horses broke into a speedy trot. During the short ride to the former-mayor's home, Big John thought, *somehow the current mayor and the nine-member city council will twist the blame on me for anything which causes embarrassment to the city.*

When they arrived at the mansion, Big John barked an order to the policeman, "Stay here and guard the house from all gawkers and news reporters. Say absolutely nothing about why we're here."

He turned to Bevis. "You, my deaf detective, I told you to put that silly pipe away."

With a compliant nod, Bevis slipped the pipe into his coat pocket.

Big John turned, hitched his pants, and took the steps leading to the entrance of the stately home. The detective followed close behind. When he reached for the brass door knocker, the door suddenly opened.

"Good day, sir," said the butler with his torso as straight as a high-back wooden dining chair.

Surprised, Big John took a step back, placing the heel of his size fourteen shoe onto the tip of his detective's shiny right shoe. Bevis gasped.

"Madam is expecting you," the butler said. With a white gloved hand and a slight bow, he motioned the visitors to enter the home.

Just as Big John took a step forward, an elderly woman abruptly appeared. Mrs. McLellan looked up at the big man. As she took measure of Big John, he felt her regal status. He could swear he was shrinking before her eyes. Although she was far more than a foot shorter, he knew he was 'Little John' within her presence. In that moment, his power waned into subservience. "I'm, I'm City Marshal John Murphy."

When she didn't respond, he added, "Assisting me with this investigation is Detective Bevis."

The detective tipped his hat.

Mrs. McLellan looked at Bevis's attire. As she gazed at the costumed detective, a slight smirk entered the corner of her mouth, disappearing as quickly as it came. She said, "Thank you for coming."

"Yes, ma'am," both replied.

She snapped, "The mess my daughters have caused must be cleaned up immediately."

"Madam, the mess you call is a crime scene," Big John said. "It cannot be *cleaned up* until we have completed our investigation."

The old woman winced. "Crime scene?"

Bevis stepped forward. "Yes, ma'am. That's what we call them until we figure out what happened."

The old woman ignored the detective. "City Marshal Murphy, I like my home to be tidy. Do not defile it anymore then the dead have already done."

The marshal nodded. "Where are the victims?" he inquired.

"My daughters are where we found them. Their bodies have not been moved. They lie where their mischievous deeds have left them. Martha is outside resting in a bed of roses and Molly is on her bedroom floor."

"Madam, after we have a look at the crime scenes, my detective and I may have questions for you."

"Well, when you are ready to question me, I'll be sitting in the courtyard having a cup of tea. Until then, my servants will assist you."

Big John and his detective stepped through the mansion's main door and into the entrance hall. With their mouths agape, they were overwhelmed by the opulence of the home. Following the maid up one flight of the grand staircase, the men were led to a closed door.

She choked back her tears. "Madam and I were the ones who found Molly. The poor dead woman. … Flies were devouring her. So, I shooed them out of the room and closed the window and door."

Bottle flies. It was amazing, thought Big John, *how they could detect a dead animal from a mile away.* When he placed his hand on the doorknob, the maid turned and scurried down the stairs.

The two officers stood in the doorway, taking in the essence of the crime scene. Dressed in a nightgown, the body lay sprawled on the floor. The maid had not shooed all the flies away for many were busy laying their larva in the victim's mouth, nose, and ears.

Scanning the room with their eyes, they saw a pile of clothes tossed over a chair. Likely, they were what the woman had worn before changing for bed. Another chair next to the woman's makeup table was toppled over. The bed had been properly turned down, perhaps by the maid who ran away.

Big John sauntered into the room and knelt next to the body. After brushing the flies away, he touched the pale, cold flesh. Looking up, he challenged his detective. "Bevis, tell me what you know about rigor mortis."

Detective Bevis stepped forward. Speaking through his handkerchief, he responded as if he was reciting from a medical book. "One to two hours after death, rigor mortis starts to occur in the eyelid muscles and then moves to the lower jaw, head, face, and neck muscles. At four to six hours, rigor forms in the trunk of the body, six to eight hours to the larger joints, and eight to ten hours to smaller joints."

The marshal took hold of a cold finger and was unsuccessful when he tried to bend it. He looked up at his detective again. "Time of death?"

"Last night, possibly between eleven and midnight."

Big John studied the body. "Since the hands of the victim are clutching her throat and her lips are blue, it appears she was choking to death."

"Sir, there is dried froth on and around her mouth. That suggests—"

Big John grunted as he stood. "It's too early to make assumptions. Let's go meet the other woman."

Murphy stepped out of the room, followed by his detective. Coming down the stairs, he spied a man at the base of it with his hat in hand. He was pacing back and forth muttering to himself.

"Who are you?" Big John bellowed.

The man stopped in his tracks and looked up. "Gentlemen, I am the gardener. If you would, sirs, please follow me to the other body." He smirked as he turned towards the door. "Martha is waiting for you."

Big John and Detective Bevis followed the man out the front door and to where rose bushes graced the side of the mansion. The gardener pointed to the body. "I was the one who found Martha. I didn't touch her." A slight smile briefly appeared on his face. "I didn't even make an effort to shoo away the flies who were making a feast of her."

"Leave us," Big John said.

Both officers stood over the second body and gathered their thoughts. This woman looked very much like the other woman and was also clad in a soiled nightgown. However, unlike the other woman, this one's head was uncommonly positioned. With her hair flattened on one side, she was imbedded into the smashed roses. It was a tragic floral arrangement.

"Appears to be a broken neck," the detective surmised.

"Damn it!" Big John snapped. "The window is open above us and the screen is torn out. We'll have to make another trip up the stairs to search the room."

After they finished examining the second victim, the two officers reentered the home and climbed the stairs once again. When they reached the second floor, Big John was breathing heavily.

The door to the room with the open window was closed. When they entered, everything they saw in the room was as they had expected. The clothes the victim wore prior to putting on a nightgown were tossed onto a chair. The sheets on the bed were turned down as if they were waiting for the victim to slide in for the night. However, there were two things out of place, the teacup and saucer. Both were lying on the floor, broken.

Big John chuckled. "Well *Sherlock*, what do you suppose happened?"

"The teacup will tell us, sir."

"That's a fair assumption. Other thoughts?"

The detective opened his mouth as if to add something but did not.

"Don't be shy. Let's have it."

Bevis said, "The gossip I've heard is the twins, Martha and Molly McLellan, loved each other as much as they hated each other. From the looks of it, hate won out and they may have killed each other."

"Or someone killed them," the city marshal suggested.

The detective shrugged. "Whatever you say, boss."

Big John sighed. "It's time to have a talk with the old woman."

The city marshal led his detective into the courtyard behind the McLellan mansion. Minnie McLellan, who was sitting at a small round table, took notice of the men who had just entered her sanctuary.

Marshal Murphy asked, "May we join you?"

Minnie nodded and turned to the servant who was waiting patiently to serve her. "Lucy, we'll require two more settings for these officers."

As they took their seats, teacups and saucers magically appeared in front of them. Tea was poured. Once the task was completed, Lucy backed away from the table and became part of the courtyard scenery.

The marshal cleared his throat. "Madam, I'm sorry for your losses."

Minnie dabbed her eyes with an Irish linen handkerchief. "Thank you. Now that pleasantries have been exchanged, what questions do you have?"

To counter the old woman's possession of the moment, the marshal leaned in towards her. Without any sign of emotion in his voice, he said, "Please tell us where you were last night, what you did this morning, and how you came to know your daughters were dead."

Minnie took a sip of tea and sighed. "I went to bed at my usual hour and awoke around nine this morning. After I got dressed, I came down for breakfast. Except for sounds coming from the kitchen, the house was noticeably quiet. I remember being pleased with the tranquil notion my daughters must still be fast asleep in their beds. Little did I know …"

With shaking hands, Minnie brought her teacup up to take another sip of tea but did not. Placing it down, she continued, "As I sat down to enjoy my breakfast, the gardener burst into the dining room and announced he had found Martha lying dead in the rose bushes. After I saw my daughter's body, I went upstairs to my other daughter's bedroom."

The detective asked, "Why did you go there?"

She shot him a displeasing look. "I think you already know the answer to that question, *detective*."

The city marshal interceded, "Madam, we must hear it from you. We cannot assume anything."

"Well," she said, "Molly needed to know her sister was dead."

"What did you find when you entered the room?" the detective inquired.

She told them, which matched their image of the crime scene.

Marshal Murphy asked, "How soon after you discovered the bodies did you report the deaths?"

"Immediately. I sent my coachman who sped to your headquarters with the news. And here you are … before lunchtime." She offered, "If you're hungry, I can have Lucy bring food out for you."

Detective Bevis smiled. "That would be nice—"

"No need, madam," the marshal interjected. "We must quickly move to the next step in our investigation."

"And what would that be?" Minnie asked.

The detective explained, "The coroner will examine the bodies to determine the cause of death, as well as the estimated time your daughters died. Armed with that information, our investigation will proceed to discover motives, opportunities, and means for the deaths to occur."

With as much firmness as she could muster, Minnie said, "Before you share your discoveries with the public, please provide the courtesy of first telling me."

Marshal Murphy nodded. "As you wish, madam."

✳   ✳   ✳

On day two of the investigation, the coroner informed the marshal and his detective of two important findings. He said, "First, the time of death occurred between eleven and midnight. Secondly, the cause of death was poisoning, perhaps from an herb."

Already believing he knew the answer, Murphy asked, "Where would you go to find an herb which can poison a human being?"

The detective replied, "The most convenient place: The Apothecary Shoppe."

✶   ✶   ✶

Marshal Murphy and Detective Bevis entered The Apothecary Shoppe located on Center Street. At the counter was a short, balding man in his mid-fifties using a pestle to grind a substance into a fine powder.

"Welcome," greeted the shopkeeper with a smile. He then poured the powder from his mortar into a glass jar.

The detective asked, "What are you doing?"

"Now and then I receive a new herb or, in this case, a seasoned armadillo shell to add to my inventory." He explained, "There's a tribe in the Southwest that believes, when this powdered shell is added to food or drink, their women become more open to men's needs."

"Hmm," Bevis reflected.

After capping the jar and placing it on a shelf, he asked, "Is there anything in particular you are looking for?"

"Yes," Marshal Murphy replied as he and his detective displayed their law enforcement shields. "We're looking for answers."

The smile left the shopkeeper's face. "Herbs will cost you. Answers are free."

Detective Bevis took the lead in asking the shopkeeper his name. After that, he explained they were investigating the death of two women who were poisoned two days ago. He also described the victims and both crime scenes.

The shopkeeper rubbed his chin. "Yes," he chuckled. "I do remember them and what each had purchased."

"What's so funny?" the detective asked.

"Some customers come into my shop wearing disguises to hide their identities. I assume they do this because it's embarrassing to be seen purchasing an herb to counter a malady, such as baldness, facial wrinkles, or deficient amorous activity."

The detective found himself thinking more about his own conditions rather than the investigation at hand. He asked, "You have herbs to address these—"

"So," interrupted the marshal, "were these customers wearing disguises?"

"That's what I found funny about these two women. It was as if they were each trying to look like an older man. They were stooped over with a walking cane, their voices clearly sounded like they were trying to speak like a man. The clothes they wore … I haven't seen such vintage clothing hanging on a man in quite a while. The funniest thing was I could smell the strong scent of a woman's perfume." The shopkeeper laughed. "I must say, they both put on quite a comical performance."

With an air of condemnation, the marshal asked, "And yet you served them?"

"Of course. That is how I stay in business."

Pushing the questioning further, the detective asked, "Did they come in together or separately?"

"Separately. After the second one left, it came to me who they were."

"And who were these two women?" Marshal Murphy barked.

The shopkeeper chuckled. "The McLellan sisters."

The two crime fighters nodded their heads in acknowledgment.

"Here's a funny story," the shopkeeper offered.

The marshal asked, "Does it relate to this case?"

Desperately wanting to share his story, the shopkeeper replied, "I believe it may."

Marshal Murphy signaled him to continue.

"A little over twenty years ago, shortly after I took over the shop from my father, the mayor's wife came into my shop with her twin daughters. I remember her saying, 'I need something to help me cope with my two headaches.' I prescribed an herb, which must have helped her because every month or so after that she'd purchase another jar of it."

The shopkeeper paused to collect his thoughts. Detective Bevis prompted, "And …"

"Then, I had the pleasure of meeting the mayor when he later visited my shop. He said his wife had suggested he come to me because, as I recall him saying, 'The two little shits are causing my severe headaches.' Well, I thought he meant his headaches were caused by being bound up, constipated. So, I gave him an herb to deal with this problem. Three days later, he came back into my shop. He was angry and demanded his money back. He said the herb was causing him to spend a great deal of time in the water closet."

The shopkeeper laughed. "It was then I explained why I had prescribed the herb, and he clarified the two little shits causing his headaches were his daughters. So, free of charge, I gave him the same herb his wife was using. After that, the mayor was pleased with my service."

✳　　　✳　　　✳

Following their visit to The Apothecary Shoppe, Marshal Murphy and his sidekick returned to police headquarters and found a woman waiting patiently to see them. After introductions, she said, "I have information you may wish to hear regarding the McLellan twins."

Marshal Murphy smiled. "You are?"

"My name is Ruth Cummings."

"Well, Madam Cummings, please follow me to my office. My detective and I want to hear what you have to say about this case."

Once seated, she said, "I heard about the deaths of the two women. There are rumors floating around on how they died."

"Damn coroner," Murphy mumbled.

The woman leaned forward. "I'm sorry?"

"Nothing, ma'am. Please continue?"

"Well, a few days ago, the two women came to my place of employment, which is the Public Library." She explained, "I've been a librarian there for over twenty years, helping our patrons find whatever they are looking for within our collection. Both women were researching poisonous herbs."

The men's eyebrows were raised. The detective asked, "Madam, did they come together or alone?"

"They came separately." She sighed. "I never enjoyed waiting on those two pompous women. If you ask me, the world is a better place without them."

"Thank you for coming forth with this information," the marshal said. "I believe it may be crucial to solving the crimes."

After the woman left, Detective Bevis said, "Motive, the inheritance. Opportunity, plenty of them. The means, we have them."

"Let's go back to the crime scenes," commanded his boss.

✳   ✳   ✳

Upon their return to the mansion, the two crime fighters re-examined both crime scenes. When they walked into the first bedroom, the detective picked up a tea ball infuser lying on the floor next to a broken cup and saucer. In the second bedroom, because remnants of face cream were found on the victim, the face cream jar was collected.

Both pieces of evidence were taken back to The Apothecary Shoppe, where the shopkeeper found wolfsbane mixed with tea leaves and ground belladonna mixed with face cream. The shopkeeper also confirmed which herb was sold to each woman.

After they walked out of the shop, the detective exclaimed, "Just as I thought. A double homicide!"

Marshal Murphy thought about his detective's appraisal and the political repercussions which could come from it.

✳   ✳   ✳

Marshal Murphy sat across the courtyard table from Mrs. McLellan. She coughed. It was a wet cough which caused him to push his chair back a bit. He thought: *Soon, she will join her daughters.*

Minnie muttered, "They're both dead."

Not hearing the woman, the city marshal asked, "Ma'am?"

"I said they're both dead."

"Yes, I know that ma'am."

"They're gone. My husband's gone …" She looked up at him with tears in her eyes. "Who am I to leave my fortune when I die?"

"Well, ma'am, there's me," he replied with a smile.

She gave him a puzzled look and he saw her eyes were portholes into a soul filled with hurt, loss, and sadness. Oh, how Big John wished he could take back what he said. The old woman deserved compassion, not jest.

"Madam," he said, "please accept my apology for an inexcusable lack of professionalism. I made light of a situation when I should have not."

Minnie folded her arms. "City Marshal John Murphy. I ask you where has your investigation taken you?"

"Madam, without a doubt, this was a double homicide. They each willfully, deliberately and, with much premeditation, poisoned each other on the very same night."

Minnie gasped. "What proof do you have?"

"The day of their deaths, Molly purchased nightshade, which was found in Martha's face cream. On that same day, Martha obtained wolfsbane, which was blended into Molly's tea."

Minnie sniffled. "Why would they do such a thing?"

"Although I cannot be sure, greed was the motive. Your estate was an inheritance each did not wish to share."

Minnie put her head down in her hands and wept. After a long, uncomfortable moment for the big man, she looked up with tears rolling down her cheeks.

"It was a suicide pact between two sisters who loved each other," she said. "This is a more palatable finding than a double murder by two people who hated each other. Don't you agree?"

Marshal John Murphy nodded his head. "Good day, madam."

✴   ✴   ✴

A joint funeral was held for Martha and Molly, and they were buried next to their father. The twins had come into this world together and had left it together. Martha and Molly are now resting forever, together.

Minnie McLellan was alone and knew her time to join her husband and daughters was growing near. Except for one estranged brother, she had no siblings to bequeath her fortune. As she pondered what to do, a thought occurred to her: *He has a son.*

CHAPTER 4

Ihave returned to my afterlife home. Although most spirits call it Heaven, I prefer a different name, God's House. I like 'house' because the word feels cozy and can be tantamount to 'home.' Whereas the word Heaven suggests a vast, endless place with no boundaries.

God's House is a place brightened by billions, no trillions of stars or more. It is where I can imagine anything I've experienced with all my senses heightened to the point where I feel alive. I think Hell would be just the opposite. Empty, devoid of taste, sight, smell, sound, and touch. The thought of this hollow place makes me shudder.

Now that I am home, I have the desperate need to confront The Lord God Almighty. This mission he has given me seems impossible for me to complete, even before I have had a chance to do anything about it.

"Oh God!" I cried. "They killed each other! Did you know this would happen? Of course you did. How could you let this happen?"

God was silent.

"Oh, I get it … free will. Now that the twins are dead, may I stop being just a watcher and help Minnie. After all, she was nice to me when I was alive. Shouldn't I return the favor?"

No. Three months will pass before your intervention begins.

"What will I do in the meantime?"

You should use this respite to visit the lives Martha and Molly have lived.

✳ ✳ ✳

As I await my return to Earth, I will feed my guilty pleasure. God forgive me for I love to eavesdrop. Although in life this indulgence was not held in high regard, during an afterlife it is expected. How can I explain it? It's like going to the theatre to watch *Hamlet* or *The Pirates of Penzance*.

While in this moment of confession, I'll add another one: I have the desire to share what I know. It's like a gossipy itch which I must scratch. Thank God it was not my nature to do this when I was alive for it could've caused hurt to others.

I return to my desire to eavesdrop on the lives Martha and Molly have lived. Because they are dead, it is their memories I must visit.

A funny thing about memories … they're like photographs. As time passes their clarity fades. So, when I visit a memory, it is an event shrouded in a misty haze. It's best because a sharper image can be seen as a harsh reality.

So, where do I start? With so many choices to choose, I've decided to begin at the time when the twins were barely into their teens. Their father, bless his soul, had to deal with their mischief in Boston. This was quite a while ago, so I expect the memory to be hazier than most.

✳ ✳ ✳

It was February 1868. Mayor Jacob McLellan was at home sitting at his desk in the library. He was staring at a stack of envelopes, the one on the top had grabbed his attention. Marked URGENT, it was from The Enlightened Academy for Girls. His hand shaking, Jacob reached for it. Taking it from the stack, he slapped it several times on the desktop, hoping what it contained would magically be altered.

Jacob sighed, then sighed again as he took hold of a letter opener, silver with an ivory handle. He sliced the top of the envelope open and fearfully peeked inside. The hope he had vanished from his mind for the request he didn't want to see had not gone away. It read: *McLellan, a delicate situation has arisen. Your presence is required. Immediately!*

"Oh, my god. What have they done now?" he grumbled.

This was not the first time Jacob had received an urgent letter from the headmaster, and he knew exactly what would be required to resolve the matter. It was always more money. A substantial cash donation was the only way to persuade the headmaster from expelling Martha and Molly and sending them home.

Jacob leaned back in his chair and stared up at the ceiling, praying for God to speak to him. He wanted a message that would offer him an alternative to what he must do. When no answer came, Jacob rose slowly from his chair. With letter in hand, he stepped out of the second-floor library in search of his dear wife.

After coming down the grand staircase, Jacob found Minnie in the sitting room sipping a hot cup of tea. She was wearing a simple, yet elegant yellow dress with white lace, a thin strand of pearls graced her beautiful neck. Jacob paused his approach and wondered what in God's name he had done to deserve his wonderful wife.

"My love," he said as he waved the letter in his hand. "I must go to Boston immediately."

Minnie looked up and frowned. "Our daughters?"

"Of course. What else could it be?"

She tittered. "Are you traveling by train, ship, or carriage?"

"Are you teasing me? The round trip by train will take one day. Whereas, by ship it would take several days. Carriage? It would take two weeks to travel to Boston and back. Minnie, the day after next I have business with the city council. As much as I would love to put off my encounter with the headmaster, I can't afford to do so. The train is what I must take."

"Give my regards to the headmaster. I do hope it will not cost us a king's ransom to keep them at the academy."

He nodded. "That is also my wish."

✳　　✳　　✳

At 5:15 in the morning, the coachman helped Jacob into his carriage. After a short ride to the station, he arrived in plenty of time to board the 5:45 train to Boston. Without a word to his driver, which was uncommon, the mayor stepped down from his transport.

The day was yet to dawn. Lanterns brightened the darkness and shined on those waiting on the platform to board the train. Jacob cautiously stepped around other passengers as they said their goodbyes to loved ones. *It would have been a nice gesture for my wife to see me off this morning,* thought Jacob with an air of self-pity.

Sounds and smells from the train being readied to depart filled the air. Rising smoke from burning coal heated the water, changing it to steam. Soon, it would propel the train towards its destination.

Prior meetings with the headmaster had never taken more than an hour, so no luggage was required. And, if all went as expected, Jacob would catch the late afternoon train back to Portland. Carrying only an umbrella, he stepped onto the train, plopped into a vacant seat, and closed his eyes. Images of what was yet to come on this day floated into his mind.

"Welcome aboard Mr. Mayor!"

Jacob snapped open his eyes to the sight of the train conductor, smartly dressed. "Thank you, Charles," he said. "You're looking sharp this morning."

The conductor grinned. "My wife would have it no other way. Enjoy the trip, Mr. Mayor."

Mr. Mayor. Jacob loved the sound of his title, and he loved serving the citizens of Portland, his quaint seafaring community of 30,000 people. Yes, he was the owner of a large shipping business which allowed the McLellan family to enjoy a life full of wealth and prominence. But it was his position as mayor of this God-fearing and patriotic city which gave him his true fulfillment in life.

Other passengers boarded the train and moved towards their seats. Jacob vaguely wondered why they were catching the early train. Each face wore a different reason for doing so. Some appeared tired or to be carrying a heavy burden, while others were driven by a potential business deal or the anticipation of joining a loved one.

With a loud blast of power, the train jerked forward. Smoke from the coal-fired steam engine filled the air. As the train gathered speed, hot embers blew out of the engine stack. To avoid errant cinders, passengers quickly closed the train car's windows. His journey had begun.

Jacob gazed out the window. The sun was just peeking above the horizon, causing the sky above the harbor city to turn reddish orange. *Red sky in morning.* A warning to all sailors of pending inclement weather. Jacob shook his head. *Indeed, it will be a stormy day in Boston.*

Jacob turned his attention to the morning newspaper. He stopped reading when the train crossed the bridge over the Kennebunk River an hour later. Looking out the window, he saw the small community of Kennebunkport and admired its quaintness. He smiled. Then he thought about all the other times he'd made this very journey. A frown appeared on his face.

Minnie believed in the division of responsibility between parents, so she never traveled with him to Boston. On occasion, she would deal with the twins' unruly behavior at home and, as always, he would deal with their troublemaking when they were away at the academy. Jacob didn't believe it was an equal division of labor.

He thought of the time the girls had been punished, for God knows what, by working an evening in the school's laundry. They'd been left alone for an hour and that was all the time they needed to perform their devilish deed. When the laundry was done, separated, and dealt out to their owners, the popular girls all found their underpants streaked with brown shoe polish.

"Little shits," Jacob mumbled. Then he thought *this new problem couldn't be as bad as when Martha and Molly found a few dead rats in the alley next to the school.*

The twins had decided their meals were not up to their lofty standards and hatched a plot to have the kitchen staff dismissed. When everyone was asleep, they tiptoed out of the building, retrieved the dead rodents, and took them into the kitchen. After removing the prepared cakes from covered serving trays, they carefully replaced them with the dead rats. When dessert was served the next day, utter chaos ensued. An investigation followed leading to the guilty parties. Cake crumbs were found beneath the twins' beds.

The train rolled onto another bridge, this one over the Piscataqua River. Once crossed, it entered the city of Portsmouth, New Hampshire. *Halfway there,* he thought.

The mayor was tired. He had had a fitful sleep the previous night and had rushed out of the house to catch the early morning train. Closing his eyes for only a moment, the movement of the train gently rocked him into a deep sleep.

He dreamt he'd arrived in Boston and hurried to meet with Mr. Bullard, the academy's headmaster. As he approached the building, he saw his daughters outside. Martha and Molly turned to him with innocent smiles, holding lit torches in their hands. "Stop!" Jacob cried out.

The headmaster was tied to a maple tree, its leaves not yet budded. Schoolbooks piled at his feet burned, the flames growing higher and higher. Behind the headmaster, children cried, their panicked faces pressed to the windows of the academy. All watched as his twins set fire to the building.

Mr. Bullard screamed, "You'll dearly pay for this, McLellan!"

"Wake up," he hears. "Wake up, Mayor McLellan."

Jacob's eyes shot open; the conductor was hovering over him.

"This is your stop, Mr. Mayor. My, my, you must have been having a terrible dream."

Soaked with sweat, Jacob breathed heavily. "Thank you, Charles. It was a nightmare."

Jacob rose from his seat, straightened his suit, and brushed the wrinkles out of his clothing as best he could. Stepping off the train into a chilly rain, he opened his umbrella and turned towards the location where his daughters were lectured and lodged, *The Enlightened Academy for Girls.*

"Enlightened, my ass," he grumbled when he saw the sign displayed on the front of the school.

Jacob stepped into the building and immediately came face-to-face with Mr. Bullard. The headmaster wore a crisp-looking suit and seemed to have already possessed the upper hand. Jacob lowered his umbrella to hide another effort to smooth out his rumpled suit.

Mr. Bullard shook his hand vigorously. "Mr. McLellan. I'm pleased you've responded so quickly to my message. Come. Come. Follow me to my office."

He paused, considering the headmaster's eagerness. *Was it due to the donation he was about to receive or, if not paid, the dismissal of his girls? Either way, if this were a game of poker, the man would certainly be holding the winning hand.*

Walking behind Mr. Bullard, he felt as he did when he was a boy being led by the headmaster to the office. He shook his head. *No good ever came from an encounter such as this.*

The two entered a private office. The headmaster went behind his desk and took a seat in a padded leather chair. Taking this as an invitation to sit, Jacob sat in a chair made only for discomfort and wondered if this was by design. Leaning back comfortably, the headmaster grinned.

Jacob cleared his throat. "Mr. Bullard, why is it you have requested a meeting with me? What is so urgent?"

The headmaster smiled. "Would you care for some coffee … some tea?"

"No," Jacob snapped. "I prefer to have my questions answered."

"As you wish," he said, leaning forward to take a slow sip from his coffee. "Answers to your questions will be found in the story I am about to tell."

It bothered Jacob that the headmaster was enjoying this conference. "Then, please," he urged, "tell."

The man tipped back again in his chair, tented his fingers, and looked to the ceiling. "The story begins two weeks ago, when one of my teachers, *Mrs. Bullard*, took the occasion to discuss a holiday of liturgical significance and romantic celebration."

Jacob cocked his head. "Valentine's Day?"

He nodded. "After sharing its origin with her class, which included your daughters, I might add, Mrs. Bullard, *my wife*, instructed her students to create a Valentine card."

Jacob squirmed in his seat.

"The directions were simple. Select a fellow student, who is considered a friend, to receive the card and mention one pleasant attribute. It was to be a good-hearted and creative exercise. However, that is not what happened."

Jacob's seat had become even more uncomfortable.

"To put it bluntly, *your* daughters couldn't complete the assignment because they have no friends to receive their cards. Simply put, their dispositions do not attract friends. Therefore, they received no Valentine cards. This was an embarrassment your twins could not bear."

"Mr. Bullard, you have not yet explained why you've summoned me."

"Oh, Mr. McLellan, my story has not yet come to an end."

He watched as the man took his pipe, packed it with tobacco, and set it to flame. Jacob stiffened. Under his breath he muttered, "You arrogant man."

After a long draw on his pipe, the headmaster continued, "A few days later, on Valentine's Day, cards were found by our students. Some were from my wife to Mr. Abernathy, our mathematics teacher, and some were from Mr. Abernathy to my wife. I must add that Mr. Abernathy recently gave your daughters failing grades on an assignment. He is also married, a father of three, a grandfather of eight, and is thirty years older than my wife. Hence, it was a scandalous surprise when these cards were discovered."

"I suppose it was," Jacob mumbled.

"Mr. McLellan, I have a question for you. What is difficult to regain once it is lost?"

Again, he squirmed. "Reputation?"

"Ah, yes, reputation. One could also say respect, standing, status, or even character." The headmaster took a few slow puffs on his pipe. "Well, as we discovered, the handwriting on the cards were not Mr. Abernathy's, nor my wife's. Can you guess by whose hands they were written?"

He muttered, "My daughters—"

The headmaster clapped his hands. "Again, you show your brilliance. Martha and Molly wrote the cards in a fit of revenge."

Jacob's mouth had gone dry. Sweat dripped from his forehead. "I'm … I'm sorry."

"Sorry?" Mr. Bullard leaned forward and looked directly into Jacob's eyes. "That is all you can say?"

He shrunk deeper into his ill-fitting chair.

"Mr. McLellan, this school will not tolerate such behavior! A remedy for your daughters' appalling conduct is required."

Finally, the moment had come to resolve this awkward situation, Jacob thought. He sat straight up in his chair and pulled out his wallet. "Would this be an appropriate time to make a sizable donation to *The Enlightened Academy for Girls*?"

"Ah, Mr. McLellan, you are indeed an enlightened man!"

CHAPTER 5

Mischievous pranks? Tomfoolery? No, I say. Playfulness did not guide the intent behind the twins' misbehavior. If one looked close enough, they would see the seed of evil had taken root in their souls; souls which God has asked me to save.

The next memory I will visit begins in May 1868, three months after Jacob visited The Enlightened Academy for Girls.

* * *

Anxious about his daughters' soon return home for the summer, Jacob hoped for a distraction from his worry. His prayers were answered when he was informed repairs were needed to one of his ships, the *Chesapeake*. Last night, the ship had returned heavy laden with cargo, but it did so while weathering a storm. Repairs were needed for the old side-wheeled steamer.

Normally, the ship's carpenter would make the fix, but an illness had kept him bedridden. Jacob immediately thought of his friend, John Phillips. He was one of the finest shipwrights in all New England.

The mayor called for his carriage. A short ride later, he arrived at his friend's shop, The Maine Sail. The shop is on the first floor of a simple two-story building near the docks. Managed by John's wife, Sarah, it is crowded with ship parts and fishing gear; most are used and some are new. Hannah's family resides above the shop.

John could occasionally be found making repairs to a small boat behind The Maine Sail. However, most of the time he was off to fix one of the many ships moored in Portland Harbor. On this day, Jacob is fortunate because he can hear the banging of a hammer and the sawing of lumber coming from behind the shop. He was pleased because he needed his friend's carpentry skills, and his advice.

"Greetings." Jacob called over the noise.

"Good afternoon, Mr. Mayor," replied Samuel Clarke. Sam, the shop apprentice, was also Hannah's boyfriend and future husband.

The mayor countered, "And to you, young man."

John put down his saw and brushed the sawdust from his hands. He asked, "What brings you here on this fine day?"

The mayor ambled up to John. "Well, besides visiting my friend, I'm in need of your excellent craftmanship." He explained, "During a storm last night, damage was done to the *Chesapeake*'s paddle wheel. Unfortunately, the ship's carpenter is ill, and I must have it repaired quickly. Can you help me?"

John nodded. "Sam can take care of things here while I go to the ship and take measurements. I should have the fix completed by tomorrow's end."

Jacob smiled. "I can't tell you how much this means to me for the *Chesapeake* is scheduled to depart in two days."

Before he walked away Jacob thought of the other reason for his visit but today was not the appropriate day to approach his friend. *Tomorrow,* he thought. *There's always tomorrow.*

★   ★   ★

The following afternoon, Jacob greeted his coachman and informed his driver where to go. He then climbed inside the carriage, and with haste, they were off in the direction to where the *Chesapeake* was moored.

As Jacob watched his regal mansion disappear from his view, he took in its opulence. *It is well deserved,* he thought. *After all, I am the mayor of Portland. With all the accolades I've received from being its strong and charismatic leader, I'm still just a man, a husband, and a father.* "Father," he muttered. *What is a father who can't teach his girls to be more like Hannah?*

The mayor wringed his hands together and was thankful the citizens of Portland could not see into his troubled soul. He gave a smile and an obligatory wave to those he passed along the way to the *Chesapeake.*

"Damn twins," he muttered. *Little do my constituents know of the problems I have to deal with at home.* He shook his head. "Who am I kidding? Everyone knows."

After arriving at the disabled ship, he found his friend working on the paddle wheel. Jacob asked, "How's it coming?"

Slightly annoyed by Jacob's visit, he replied. "Although the damage was more severe than you suggested, the repairs are going well. I've installed three new paddles and have one more to complete."

Jacob took a step closer. "This ship has seen better days."

"Yes, it has," he agreed, and turned his attention back to the job at hand.

Jacob sat on a crate and watched him work on the last paddle. After several minutes of silence, he asked, "Remember in '63 when we chased the Confederates with the *Chesapeake?*"

John stopped working. He replied, "I sure do. This ship received its fair share of battle wounds on that day. I must say the Confederates were no match for us."

The mayor shook his head. "What were they thinking sailing into our harbor in the dark of night? Did they not know we would retaliate after taking the *Cushing?*"

"Can't answer that," he said. "But I must commend you again for your quick action. As mayor of our fine city, you led our small armada of civilian ships to a victory over the enemy. I heard it's the only time during the entire Civil War where civilian ships won a sea battle with the South."

The mayor beamed. "It was a proud moment for all of us. What's most amazing is there was no loss of life during the entire battle."

Thinking the conversation had ended, John picked up the replacement paddle he had fashioned.

Jacob grinned. "Don't you think it's strange the captain of the Confederate ship, the *Archer*, and the Union captain of the *Cushing* were both from Georgia and attended the Naval Academy together before the war?"

John stopped what he was doing, then turned to his friend. "I don't believe you're here to reminisce about the battle of Portland Harbor. What troubles you, my friend?"

The mayor tried to grasp the words he wanted to say, but they did not come forth. John shrugged, then turned back to his work.

Jacob quietly sat. The only sounds heard were from seabirds calling to their mates, men on the ship loading cargo and provisions, and the ocean water as it lapped against the ship. After several minutes, he confessed, "I'm at a loss as to what I can do."

The ship's carpenter put down his tools and took a seat next to his friend. "About what?"

Jacob sighed. "My girls. No matter what my wife and I do, we cannot teach them to care about others. They don't have one ounce of compassion, grace, or humility. Lord knows they have far more than they need." He paused, then continued, "The only thing they fear is not having all they want. How can I teach them to be more like your daughter, Hannah?"

"By example," John replied.

Jacob, who had been staring at his shoes, looked to his friend for an explanation.

"Sarah and I show our daughter what's important in life by demonstrating it ourselves. As a result, love, sharing, and caring for others are attributes Hannah has acquired. This, I believe, is what God wants us to do." He chuckled. "If we can't teach them, at some point, God will. Heaven help them if they are unwilling pupils."

Jacob mulled over his friend's counsel. He professed, "Minnie and I have done as you suggested. But it is I who has failed them. Because I love them beyond reproach, it becomes my weakness. Consequently, it's difficult for me to deny them anything because I need their love in return. When I do meet their demands, it's never enough. What am I to do? Should I deprive them of their desires?"

"Wants and needs are two driving forces pushing us to change our behavior," John said. "I guess you could say, it's our nature to want more than we need. The trick is to learn how to love, share, and care for others while we pursue our desires. Along the way, we earn God's grace and are prepared to meet Him when our mortal life has ended."

The mayor slapped his friend on the back. "You should've been a preacher."

Shaking his head, John said, "No, my friend, that vocation is not for me. I prefer to work with my hands, not my mouth."

Mayor McLellan cocked his head. "Would you mind if Hannah joins my daughters on our trips to the library this summer? I pray what you have taught Hannah will rub off on my wayward girls."

John chuckled. "You have both my blessing, as well as my prayers. Now, leave me be so I can finish this job for you."

Jacob stood and shook his friend's hand. "Thank you, Father John."

John laughed again.

Jacob walked away deep in thought. *How is it that I, one of the richest men in Portland, cannot have what I want most, daughters who care for others as much as they care about themselves.*

CHAPTER 6

It was July 1868, two months later. The twins were home from boarding school and disliked venturing out among the common people. The weather was always blamed for their refusal to leave the family mansion. It was either too cold, too hot, too windy, too sunny, too gloomy, or too wet for a foray outside of their magnificent home.

Jacob often took a trip to the library on Congress Street. To entice his daughters to join him on this day, he promised to take them shopping before returning home. This pleased the twins because they saw it as an opportunity to get what they really wanted, the latest fashion and more jewelry to adorn themselves.

On this day, he decided to include a side trip while on their way to the library. With assistance from his coachman, the mayor and his daughters boarded the carriage. The twins silently sat with arms folded and steamed in displeasure at the thought of the guest who would soon join them. After a ten-minute trot, the carriage stopped in front of The Maine Sail. Looking in the direction of the simple two-story building, Martha and Molly unleashed their annoyance.

Molly whined, "Why does Hannah have to come with us?"

"Yes, father, why?" Martha added, "We just can't be seen with her."

"Daughters, it is important to do virtuous deeds."

As they often did in unison, the twins moaned. "Perhaps, but not for *her.*"

"Why so?" he questioned.

Martha scrunched her nose and pouted. "She is so uncultured."

Molly's nostrils flared; she mocked, "Not only that, but she also doesn't own a fashionable dress!"

Jacob took a deep sigh of annoyance; he pleaded, "For once, can't you have a bit of humility? Your arrogance simply does not become you."

Not understanding what exactly their father was talking about, Martha and Molly stared blankly at him. Their father's patience was wearing thin. With another sigh, Jacob explained, "We do this because she is less fortunate. That is the very reason we should include Hannah on our trips to the library."

The blank stares held by the twins did not waver.

Hearing the arrival of the mayor's carriage, Hannah rushed out of the shop to join the McLellans. She climbed into the carriage and sat next to the twins, giving both a big smile. In turn, they scooched as far as they could away from her insignificance.

"Hi Martha. Hi Molly," she greeted. "Isn't this a beautiful day for a carriage ride?"

In reply, the twins faced forward, crossed their arms, and expressed their discontent with an unabashed, "Humph."

After witnessing the exchange among the girls, Jacob quietly scolded himself for thinking his efforts would be fruitful. The twins were born into a wealthy family, but unfortunately, they assumed this also awarded them with royal status. Except for each other, they had no friends. Having Hannah join them on a carriage ride to the library was just another one of his attempts to expand his daughters' world beyond themselves.

Upon arrival, Martha and Molly trudged up the library steps, making sure to keep a wide berth between themselves and Hannah, the unwelcome interloper. A librarian met them at the door.

"Welcome to the Public Library," she said. "My name is Ruth

Cummings and I'll be happy to help you look for any book within our collection."

"Thank you, madam," the mayor said. "I've not seen you before."

She smiled. "Today is my first day."

"I hope it is a fine one. Madam, I'm Mayor McLellan and these two lovely young ladies are my daughters, Martha and Molly."

The twins looked at the simply dressed woman with an air of indifference, then ignored her. No acknowledgment was necessary for this creature was nothing more than a servant to cater to their selfish wishes.

"And this young woman," the mayor announced, "is Hannah Phillips."

Hannah smiled and gave her a slight curtsy. "A pleasure, madam."

Jacob thought, *why can't my daughters behave like Hannah?* He said, "Hannah is the grandniece of a very famous poet, Henry Wadsworth Longfellow."

Hannah's smile widened; the twins gasped. They were horrified by their father's disclosure. He didn't need to add that undeserved tidbit of information.

"Oh, my!" Ruth exclaimed. "It is such an honor to meet you."

Stinging glares of hatred from the twins were directed at the librarian who, after learning of Hannah's lineage, paid more attention to her during their entire visit to the library.

✴   ✴   ✴

Later that evening, after dinner was finished, the twins left the table to do whatever they wanted to do. For the time being, the servants serving the McLellan household would take the brunt of their foolish behavior. Meanwhile, their parents sought refuge in the sitting room.

Upon settling into cozy, plush leather armchairs, Jacob and Minnie enjoyed a glass of vintage wine. It was then that Jacob recounted his day with the girls. When he was done, he confessed, "I honestly don't know what to do. … I'm at my wit's end. Is it impossible to change our daughters' selfish ways?"

"Perhaps it is who they were born to be, the mold God poured their souls into."

Evidently not listening to his wife, he cried out, "Entitlement! That's the reason for their wretched dispositions."

"Of course. What did you expect?" asked Minnie. "The twins were born into a family of wealth and prominence; they attend a boarding school in Boston with children very much like themselves. They're waited upon by servants, and they're spoiled by their father."

"I do not spoil them," he snapped.

Minnie turned to her husband. "Yes, you do. When you want them to do something they don't wish to do, you entice them with shopping for extravagant clothing and jewelry. Although they may be clueless on several matters, they're not stupid. They know how to manipulate you."

"Well, what am I supposed to do? Swat their bottoms?"

"They're fourteen-year-olds. It's a bit late for that. Just continue what you've been doing but please pare back on enticing them with extravagant bribes in exchange for less than ill-bent behavior."

Jacob sighed, which had long become a part of his personal expression. "I will do as you suggest." The moment the words left his mouth, he thought how hard it would be for him to deny his daughters anything.

Minnie shook her head and chuckled.

Jacob noticed her disbelief. He knew she didn't believe him. When it came to the twins, he couldn't help himself. As much as he disliked their behavior, they were his precious little girls, and he dearly loved them. No amount of misbehavior could ever diminish them in his eyes. *Well,* he thought, *she should be happy that this is my greatest flaw.*

Jacob knew his wife was aware she was not his first choice for a bride. Before they met, he had pursued Hannah's mother, and she rejected his advances. Everything turned out for the better because this loss was eventually his gain, as well as Minnie's.

It was commonly known that the race to find love and improve one's status was not defined by where a young woman begins, but where she finds herself at the end of the race. It was Jacob's assumption that, in addition to residing within the McLellan mansion, Minnie's prize for coming in second place was being married to him—a man revered by all outside his home—the mayor of Portland.

Minnie inquired, "What are your plans for tomorrow?"

"I'm thinking about hiring a new tutor. Their present art tutor is not challenging them enough."

"Why do you say that?"

"The other day, I overheard the tutor lavishly praising the twins' artwork. I do not like it when undue praise is given. Frankly, our girls' artistry hasn't improved since they were eight. It's time for a change."

"Do what you think best."

"I always do."

He did not trust the tutor. The man was French and appeared to have an eye for young ladies. During a prior tutoring session, Jacob caught the Frenchie with his hand on Molly's shoulder. As he pointed out certain creative aspects of her painting, he was gazing down upon her cleavage. *A Danish tutor would've been a better choice,* he thought.

The pleasant chat the couple were having was disrupted by a scream. Another followed, both coming from the floor about them. Minnie picked up her glass of wine and smiled. "It's your turn, my love."

Jacob groaned. Rising from his chair he muttered, "My god, will it never end?"

At the base of the grand staircase, he heard Molly yell, "It's my dress!" His footfalls quickened as he climbed the stairs. When he reached the second-floor landing, he heard fabric ripping followed by Martha crying out, "But it looks better on me!"

"This has got to stop," he muttered. He heard another scream as he rushed into the room. Molly was tearing a dress off her sister, which had revealed one naked breast.

"Oh, my god! Oh, my god! Oh, my god!" he cried as he covered his eyes and stumbled out of the bedroom.

Jacob turned towards the stairs and tripped over his feet. Down he went onto the hallway floor. In his mind's eye, all he could see was a mound of forbidden flesh being clearly displayed. Blinded by this abhorrent vision of his own daughter, he scrambled off the floor and continued to stumble on his way down the staircase.

Returning to the room where his wife sat peacefully, Jacob plopped down into an overstuffed chair. He was red-faced and gasping for air.

Minnie sipped her wine and savored the moment. "Well?" she asked.

Jacob replied, "I do not possess the appropriate gender to deal with this situation. Please, Minnie, go to *your* daughters."

CHAPTER 7

The next memory I will visit is one of my own. The date is June 1870. Mayor McLellan has invited me to his home for a visit with his girls. Hopefully, his daughters would benefit from my moral character.

When the mayor's coachman arrived at my home, he helped me aboard the exquisite coach. Although I had misgivings about the invitation, I enjoyed the ten-minute ride to the McLellan mansion. Upon arrival, not waiting for the coachman's assistance, I bolted out of the carriage and bounded up the front steps of the mansion. A satin rope hung near the door; I pulled on the cord causing the doorbell to chime.

Robert, the butler, opened the door. He inquired, "Madam Phillips, I presume?"

"Yes," I replied with a curtsy.

He smiled. "Come in, come in. My master is expecting you."

As soon as I entered the home, my eyes opened wide and sparkled at what I saw. The McLellan mansion was a magnificent example of wealth and extravagance.

"Nice, isn't it?" Mr. Jacob McLellan said as he came down the staircase.

"It is," I replied. "I've never seen anything like it. You have a very lovely home."

"Thank you, Hannah." He turned to his butler. "Please fetch the twins."

Robert frowned. "As you wish, sir."

The mayor turned his attention back to me. He said, "My daughters are looking forward to your visit."

I smiled to myself thinking what he just said may not be true. "As am I," I said knowing that I was not being fully truthful.

Martha and Molly burst into the room. "Hannah!" They greeted me in unison. A quick glance at their father I'm sure was a reminder to him of the reward they expected to later receive.

Jacob looked at his elegantly dressed daughters and then at me. I was wearing a simple blue dress. He chuckled, which surprised me at first. Then, I thought it mattered not what I wore for my personal radiance could outshine any adornment. I forgave myself for that thought.

"I'll leave you three to enjoy your time together," he said, then quickly left the room.

We stood in awkward silence. Martha and Molly on one side, me on the other. While I took in the home's grandeur during this uncomfortable moment, the twins just stared at me, *their guest.*

I was tall and slender with red hair and green eyes. Whereas Martha and Molly looked very much like their mother from the shoulders up, the rest of their profile resembled their father. It was an uncommon blend between an apple and pear.

The twins' mother, Minnie, was a beautiful woman who possessed a classic look. She was small and slender with deep brown eyes and auburn hair. Although she enjoyed the trappings of wealth, at heart she was a practical woman with a quiet, regal demeanor. On the other hand, her husband was a gregarious man with a portly stature and receding hairline. With great fondness, many of his constituents compared his looks to Benjamin Franklin.

My gaze returned to Martha and Molly, who were now fidgeting with the jewelry hanging around their necks. They were mirror twins with asymmetrical physical features. Martha was right-handed and parted her hair on the left. Whereas Molly was left-handed and parted her hair on the right. Each had a mole on her cheek opposite their part. Confusing? A bit. There is another trait; both had facial tics. Martha often scrunched her nose, and Molly flared her nostrils.

But it was their dark brown eyes with red flecks which distinguished the pair from all the other children. They were cold, hard, endlessly searching for more than they selfishly needed.

I saw an olive branch was needed. "Please show me your wonderful home," I said.

The twins enjoyed every opportunity to show off what they had. After all, it is what I could never have. "Of course," they said in unison.

I followed the twins throughout the mansion. After touring the first level of their home, I saw it was five or six times larger than the apartment over the shop where I lived. The second level was next, followed by the third. What impressed me most was the cistern room containing a 3,000-gallon water tank which collected rainwater for the internal plumbing system.

During the rest of the hour, Martha and Molly entertained me in the drawing room. Sitting at the piano, the twins displayed the benefit of being tutored by a private instructor in music. This again was a luxury I would never have.

A servant entered the room. "Madams," she said.

"What is it now?" Molly snapped.

The woman cowered. "Lunch is waiting for you in the courtyard."

Martha scrunched her nose. "Better not be raining."

"It is not, Miss Martha," she said. "You'll find the cook has assembled a modest array of food for you."

Molly cocked her head, and her nostrils flared. "Modest?"

With a slight cringe, the servant took a sheepish step back. She explained, "Miss Molly, slices of smoked ham, cheese, crackers, a bowl of fresh strawberries, and an assortment of small cakes awaits you."

"I want cream for my strawberries," Martha shouted.

She nodded. "You'll have it, Miss Martha," replied the servant as she quickly backed out of the room.

I felt sorry for the servant and felt helpless for I could do nothing about the treatment the woman had received.

As promised a wonderful assortment of food and drink was prepared for us. We took our seats at a patio table, while two servants stood off to the side to meet our whims.

I said to them, "Thank you, madams."

Martha giggled. She whispered to her sister (loud enough for me to hear), "Perhaps Hannah should also be waiting on us."

Molly jabbed an elbow into her sister. She whispered back, "Remember what father said?"

Martha mimicked their father. "Treat Hannah with the respect she is due." She laughed. "Due?"

Molly joined her sister's laughter while I tried my best to ignore their banter.

After lunch and several belittlements delivered to the servants (and to me) by the twins, it was time for my visit to end. As I collected my things, the girls' tutor arrived for their two-hour painting lesson.

With my coat in one hand and a hat in the other, I moved towards the front door. With a Danish accent, the tutor called out, "Young lady, you are welcome to join in today's lesson." It was a surprise invitation from the man who just entered the mansion.

Never had I picked up a paintbrush and I was reluctant to accept the invitation.

Both girls cajoled me, "Please stay, Hannah. Please stay."

The twins' voices were tainted with insincere politeness; they truly did not want me to remain in their home, especially to benefit from a lesson not meant for a lowly person like me.

I hesitated at the door and considered the tutor's invitation. My disinclination became overcome by my dislike for the twins' condescending tone. I replied, "Kind sir, it is nice of you to offer me the gift of your instruction. I accept your generous invitation."

The twins gasped. I gave an innocent smile.

The afternoon lesson was on how to paint a seascape. I put my brush on the canvas and discovered something wonderful. It was as if my thoughts were flowing like a waterfall into my fingers. Down they went, spreading paint over the canvas.

The tutor appreciated my work. "My, my, Hannah. You have a special talent."

The twins, who were sitting in front of their easels and struggling with the lesson, jumped up from their chairs and rushed over to see the object of their tutor's appreciation.

I painted a beautiful seascape with a sailing ship in the background. Seabirds sailed overhead. The twins looked at each other and I'm sure shared the same question. *How can this be?*

"Oops," Molly said as she *accidentally* slipped, and her paintbrush slathered across my work. Both girls giggled.

The tutor tossed a sharp look at the twins, then turned to me. "Don't worry. I'll show you how to fix *mistakes*."

The lesson continued with the teacher bestowing most of his attention onto me, the poor peasant girl. Jealousy fumed within the twins who believed a social injustice had occurred. By all rights, they should've been the ones who had been gifted and, therefore, doted upon.

✳   ✳   ✳

Not having been witness to the following event, I must switch my memory to Jacob McLellan's faded memory. …

During dinner that evening, Mayor McLellan noticed his girls were in a fouler mood than usual. *Oh god,* he asked himself, *what have they done now?*

Minnie broke the silence. "Jacob, you wouldn't believe what happened today."

He mumbled, "I can only imagine …"

She continued, "As you know, Hannah visited our girls today. Before she left, they invited her to join them for their art lesson."

Martha and Molly rolled their eyes and grumbled.

"Terrific," Jacob said. "I wonder who got painted," he muttered under his breath.

"Well," she continued, "it appears Hannah has the makings to become an incredibly talented artist."

Jacob looked across the table at his girls. "At least the money I spent on the Danish tutor didn't go to waste."

CHAPTER 8

In the summer of 1871, Martha and Molly plotted to destroy my relationship with my beau, Sam.

For clarity, the memories I must visit are ones held by Martha and Molly as well as myself. Therefore, I must teeter between our recollections because some I have witnessed and others I have not.

I begin with Reginald Cunningham's twenty-first birthday party. Those in attendance have prominent pedigrees. In fact, Reggie himself comes from a wealthy family whose members had not worked a day in their lives for three generations. Two of his guests are the McLellan sisters. They were off in a corner whispering.

$$*\qquad*\qquad*$$

"Did you hear?" Molly asked. She giggled. "Hannah has a beau."

"A beau?" Martha snickered. "What is she? Eighteen? Dregs like her should already have three or four kids. Who's the suitor?"

Molly replied, "It's that boy who helps Hannah's father. His name is Sam."

"Humph," Martha grunted. "He'll never amount to anything. Probably stinks of fish."

Molly laughed. "More likely he tastes like a fish when she kisses him."

The two girls threw their heads back and let out a loud guffaw, everyone's attention momentarily drawn to them.

"We can't possibly let her be happy," Martha whispered. "Let's have some fun." She giggled. "Follow me."

The twins sashayed over to where Reginald was sitting and plopped themselves down, one on either side of him.

"Hi, girls," he greeted. "Got any juicy gossip to share?"

"Reggie," Martha said as she batted her eyes. "I understand you've written several poems."

"Yes," he replied. "Someday, I'll be compared to the likes of Mr. Longfellow."

Martha said, "We're going to help you."

"You write poetry, too?"

Martha laughed. "No, silly. But we know how you can meet Mr. Longfellow. Maybe he'll take you on as his protégé?"

Reggie leaned closer to Martha. "Please tell me more."

Molly played along, not sure if she cared about her sister's plan.

✳   ✳   ✳

Reggie just happened to be walking down near the docks where I was painting. I loved to paint life on the docks and around the harbor. Like other people who lived in Portland, this was very much a part of me.

Without making a sound, Reggie stepped up behind me. He said, "You certainly paint with passion!"

"Oh my! You startled me," I said.

He removed his hat from his head and placed it over his heart. "I apologize for my unforgiveable intrusion. I did not mean to cause you fright, but I couldn't help myself after seeing your artistry. You are an exceptionally talented painter!"

Rarely had I received such unsolicited compliments on any of my paintings. I thought *Sam had never said these words to me.* And I noticed this compliment came from a well-dressed, very handsome young man.

"Let me introduce myself," he said. "My name is Reginald Cunningham, but my friends call me Reggie. It is my hope, no, it is my sincere wish you will also call me Reggie."

During the following weeks, Reggie visited me several times while I painted. I learned he came from a wealthy family with old money. I also learned Reggie wrote poetry. He even shared some of what he had written. After listening to him recite his work, I couldn't confess that his poetry was dreadfully poor. I was too polite to hurt the feelings of a man who appreciated my artistry.

One month later, I was working in The Maine Sail with my mother while my father was repairing a small boat behind the shop. I was looking forward to this morning as Mayor McLellan would soon arrive to treat me to another carriage ride to the library, a ride where I could enjoy flowers and apple blossoms along the way.

I loved riding in the mayor's carriage because it was the finest in all of Portland. Everyone we passed stopped to see this majestic transport. Shamefully, I liked that they could also see me riding in it.

When the coachman pulled the mayor's carriage up to the shop, I heard the horses whinny as they pulled to a stop. A moment later, Jacob opened the door to the shop. Both my mother and I looked up to see him enter.

He greeted, "Good morning my dear Sarah. Good morning, dear Hannah. You both look exceedingly lovely today."

I giggled as I knew the mayor's compliments were more directed towards my mother rather than myself. Although he and my father have enjoyed a long friendship, my mother was Jacob's former love interest who, twenty years later, still warmed his heart when he saw her. Therefore, I knew his attentiveness would continue for a while longer. So, I gathered my hat and coat and stepped out to join the twins.

✷   ✷   ✷

Much to Molly's pleasure, Martha's plot to hurt Hannah's relationship with Sam was moving too slowly. Using this sluggish pace to her advantage, Molly encouraged her sister to change the plan. Hannah's embarrassment would be their new goal.

Martha took a small mirror from her clutch and held it up so she could see Hannah come out of the shop. Molly, with her nostrils flared, leaned over to grab the mirror from her sister. She whined, "You're not holding it so I can see."

"I am!" Martha cried as she pushed her sister away. "As planned, we must talk loud enough for Hannah to hear us before she boards the carriage." She snickered. "Eek! Here she comes now."

Hannah heard Molly say, "Wasn't the charity reception a few weeks ago so much fun? I couldn't believe how Sally, who was standing next to Reggie, misunderstood what we were saying about Hannah."

"Yes," Martha said in a louder voice. "That's when I said, 'We know a girl who spends her time down at those smelly docks, painting filthy sailors as they work on their stinky boats.'"

Molly added, "It was so funny when Sally said, 'How scandalous! Why would she want to put paint on a sailor?'"

After they both finished laughing, Martha continued, "And then, we said together, 'No, silly. She is painting on a canvas.' Then we laughed and I said, 'She even thinks she's a talented artist. Can you believe the conceit of that common girl?'"

"Then I chimed in and said, 'She also proclaims her granduncle is Henry Wadsworth Longfellow! How could this be? She doesn't even have one decent gown to wear.'"

The twins' laughter continued while Hannah stood fuming behind the carriage. She couldn't believe what they had just said about her. Well, yes, she did believe it because she knew they were both spoiled and conceited. They thought their status in the community allowed them to stand on all the trivial people of Portland, including her. Unfortunately, they were right about one thing; Hannah didn't own one decent gown.

If that wasn't bad enough, the twins mentioned a young man who was also at the reception, a Reginald Cunningham. Hannah knew this man as Reggie and happened to be quite fond of him. To her surprise, she had just heard he was in the girls' presence during their entire conversation. Not once did he come to her defense.

Hannah had heard enough and could not listen to the twins' maligning conversation any longer. She gathered her wits and interrupted the two deceitful girls. "Hello Martha. Hello Molly. I hope you're both enjoying this beautiful spring day."

Martha turned to her sister and whispered, "Make like you're nice for a change."

Molly jabbed her elbow into her twin's ribs. "Ow," Martha cried.

Molly turned to their expected intruder. She said, "It's excessively windy for me. I can't keep my hair in place."

Martha teased, "I hear you've been seeing an acquaintance of ours, Reggie Cunningham. Does your beau know?"

Molly giggled. "Beau know. … You rhymed and you didn't mean to."

"Did so," her sister snapped.

Hannah corrected Martha. "I've not been seeing him. Sometimes, he stops to talk with me while I'm painting down near the docks."

"Beware. He is a calculating man," Martha warned. "Reggie admires much more than your work."

Her sister piled on more. "Yes, he confesses to be a poet. We overheard him talking to a friend saying he has devised a crafty plan to use you to meet your Granduncle Henry and hopes, by doing so, he can become Mr. Longfellow's protégé."

Both girls laughed.

Hannah was stunned by the revelation but refused to give the twins any pleasure by showing her surprise. It was obvious they were hoping to see a glimpse of pain from the story they had shared. She said, "Thank you for telling me."

The twins frowned at her casual response.

"Ready girls?" shouted Mr. McLellan as he came out of the shop.

✳   ✳   ✳

Days later, I was painting by the docks again. I couldn't stop myself from seething over what the twins had shared about Reggie's devious plan to use me to get into the favorable graces of Granduncle Henry.

As he had become accustomed, Reggie strutted up behind me. "How are you today, my beautiful, red-haired painter?"

Not taking my eyes off my painting, I curtly replied, "I'm fine, *Reginald.*"

"Dear Hannah, I must make a confession," he said.

"What is it you must confess?"

Reggie placed his hands onto my shoulders. "It is my love for you, Hannah. You have taken my heart."

I turned around and stood up to face him. "Taken?" I spat. As my finger repeatedly jabbed into his chest, I said, "*Take* is what people like you do. If you don't think you have everything, you must *take* from others!"

Having backed up a few steps from my fierce condemnation, Reggie stammered, "Dear Hannah, I, I hear your words, but … I sense something is causing you distress?"

I snapped, "I am not distressed for the veil has been lifted, *Reginald.*"

"What veil is that my dear Hannah?"

Looking directly into his eyes, I said, "The veil of deceit, *dear Reginald.* You are using me to meet my Granduncle Henry!"

"Why, no, my dear Hannah," he lied. "What could ever give you that idea?"

"Do not refer to me again as *my dear Hannah*," I said. "I am not yours to have."

He pleaded, "But Hannah, I—"

Turning my back on him, I returned to my easel and picked up a brush. "You should know … Mr. Longfellow works alone. He never has and never will take on a protégé."

To Reggie's surprise, someone had exposed his secret plot. In a huff, he turned and walked away cursing his misfortune.

✶　　✶　　✶

Walking by a women's clothing shop a few days later, Reggie peeked into the window and saw Martha and Molly having a tug-of-war with a dress. He entered.

Reggie said, "Good day, ladies."

Martha grinned. "Reggie, how is your pursuit of Hannah going?"

"Not well. Not well at all," he replied. "Someone tipped her off about my plan to use her to get to her granduncle. By chance, do you know the culprit?"

"Why no," Molly lied. "Who would ever do such a thing?"

Reggie glanced at Martha. "I do have a suspicion, but I'm not prepared at this moment to say."

"Well, I'm late for an appointment." He nodded to Martha. "Good day, Martha." Then he turned to her sister and winked. "Good day, Molly."

Molly blushed.

Martha was unhappy her plan to break Hannah from her beau was not a success. On the other hand, Molly was pleased because she did not want Reggie anywhere near Hannah, nor any other woman for that matter. She had an unspoken love for Reggie and wished he would someday proclaim his love for her. Reggie's wink had confirmed in her mind her wish would come true.

CHAPTER 9

It was 1873 and Martha and Molly were in Boston completing the final weeks of boarding school. Expecting the tranquility of the McLellan mansion would be disrupted by the return of their precious offspring, their parents were in the sitting room sipping tea and reading the newspaper.

Jacob put his paper down and interrupted a moment of serenity. He turned to Minnie. "What are we going to do?" he asked.

"About what?" she inquired.

"About our girls," he replied. "Don't you think it's time they find husbands and leave us in peace?"

She smiled. "Yes, my love. It is time."

"Well, what are we going to do?" he asked, his voice showing an amount of frustration.

Minnie laughed.

"What amuses you so?"

She shook her head. "Dear Jacob, you're working yourself up into another tizzy. Why don't you have the patience to let everything play out as fate intends?"

Her husband ignored her question. He had decided he had a problem and was hell-bent to solve it. "Well, what are we going to do?"

"Our sanity must be preserved," Minnie replied. "We should approach this in the same manner as one of your political campaigns.

You could make speeches in the town square touting the fine qualities Martha and Molly possess. After all, politicians do embellish, don't they? We could have signs posted about the community with their pictures and banners waving in the wind proclaiming their availability."

"You shouldn't make light of this, Minnie. I'm serious. We must assist our little birds to fly from our nest."

"Obviously, my love, this problem of yours has been festering. Dear husband, you must have a few notions to solve it."

Clearing his throat, he said, "I suggest we hold several receptions throughout the summer to celebrate the end of our daughters' schooling. Prominent families who have sons of the appropriate age would receive invitations. Food, music, and dance will be aplenty. Our girls will love the attention, as well as the opportunity to show off the expensive ball gowns we will purchase for them."

"That's a wonderful idea," she agreed. "No matter what the cost, this investment could be one of the best we've ever made."

There was much to do for the committee of two; they began planning their daughters' exit from their home. It didn't take long until Jacob realized how much this campaign was truly going to cost them.

"Minnie," he said, "as we discussed, our summer's crusade should begin with a debutante ball. The attendees could number well over two hundred, causing a need to rent a hall. Costs would also include a quadrille band, several servants, catering, decorations, and invitations. Minnie, this one event will cost us a fortune!"

She frowned. "I, too, have concern. As Lord Byron once described a debutante ball, we don't want the event to appear as being a *marriage mart*."

He nodded. "Well noted, my love."

Silence followed while they considered other options. Minnie grinned. "I suggest an alternative."

"Praise be," Jacob said. "What do you have in mind?"

Minnie grinned. "Let's disguise our debutante ball as a charity ball."

His face brightened. "That is a devious thought. I like it. However, we …"

"What is it?" she asked.

"We support several charities," he said. "We must choose a charity all other wealthy families in Portland support. Which would be the best one to choose?"

"The orphanage?" she offered.

"Yes!" he cried. "The orphanage!"

Minnie explained, "We could enlist some of our friends to join us in forming a charity ball committee. All the while—"

Jacob completed her suggestion, "We steer the group towards inviting families with sons who are eligible bachelors. Minnie, you are not only beautiful, but you are also brilliant."

"Thank you, my love." Minnie raised her teacup. "For the children."

"For the children," Jacob toasted as he raised his teacup.

The teacups kissed, as did the scheming couple holding them.

✷   ✷   ✷

One month later, soon after the twins returned home, Jacob and Minnie summoned their dark angels to the courtyard. Tea and cakes were prepared by the servants for the occasion.

Jacob began, "Girls, what do you think I am holding in my hand?"

Gazing at the envelope their father was holding up, Martha scrunched her nose. "Tickets to the theatre?"

With nostrils flared, her sister blurted, "Could it be a monetary reward for completing our studies at the boarding school?"

He smiled. "Well, I believe you both are correct. It is a production and a reward." He explained, "Our family has received an invitation to a charity ball to raise money for the orphanage. I've heard this will be the most festive event of the year with all the prominent members within our community in attendance."

Overjoyed with the announcement, the twins leaped up from their seats. While holding hands they jumped up and down with excitement. In unison they exclaimed, "This will be so much fun!"

After the girls ceased their celebration, they said what their parents expected to hear. "Let's go shopping for ball gowns, today!"

✳   ✳   ✳

The Orphans Charity Ball was held on a beautiful evening in July. With no clouds overhead, rain would not muddy the streets nor drench the richly dressed attendees. A slight breeze from the bay kept the evening cool and offered no disturbance to ladies' coiffures and men's top hats.

The gowns chosen by the twins were made of gauze fabric and worn over a white silk slip. Martha's dress was sapphire blue with light-blue ribbon trim. Molly had chosen a ruby-red gown with pink ribbon. Each chose a white flower for their auburn hair. Both, from the shoulders up, looked as beautiful as their mother who was wearing a yellow gown with a white lace. All the women wore white gloves.

After Jacob, Minnie, Martha, and Molly boarded their family carriage, they were off to the ball. Jacob turned to his daughters. "Girls, I must remind you of the protocols and traditions surrounding a formal ball."

"You did that yesterday," Martha said.

"Father," Molly said, "you are assuming we weren't listening."

"Okay girls, what are they?"

The twins had no reply. Minnie chuckled.

Jacob explained, "Upon arrival, the men will escort their women to the ladies' dressing room where they will leave their shawls and cloaks and arrange their Victorian gowns. In turn, their companions proceed to the men's apartment to rid themselves of their boots, hats, and overcoats. When the men return to collect their ladies, they will find them in the sitting room waiting to be escorted into the ballroom."

Martha pouted. "We have no suitors."

Martha cried, "Who will be our escorts?"

"I will," their father replied. Both girls cringed.

Minnie added, "The first dance for each lady is awarded to the man who brought her. Afterwards, other men may approach the woman to sign her dance card. Keeping with tradition, no lady may dance with the same man more than four times during the evening."

Martha whined, "Mother, does that mean Father is who we must dance with first?"

"Of course," her mother replied. "As I said, that is the proper decorum."

Loud groans came from Martha and Molly.

Minnie continued, "Afterwards, you will both take a seat with your father and I standing between you. Seeing us, men will assume your dance card is ready for signing. After the first man signs his name on your card, others will follow."

With worried looks on their faces, in unison Martha and Molly said, "But what if no one signs our cards?"

Minnie replied, "They will if you are displaying your best behavior. Smiling will help, too."

Just then, their carriage pulled up to The Commodore Hotel and the coachman dismounted. With care, he assisted each passenger down from the carriage.

✳　　　✳　　　✳

The Grand Hall of the hotel was the venue for the Orphans Charity Ball. Arm in arm, Jacob and Minnie led their daughters towards what they hoped was the beginning of their daughters' departures from the McLellan mansion.

As hoped by their parents, the dance cards for Martha and Molly quickly filled. In part, by design, this was because there were far more single men then single ladies attending the ball.

The twins danced nearly every dance, and occasionally, their father individually escorted them for a break to the refreshment room. By keeping them busy and apart from each other, he hoped for a cheerful evening with no squabbles nor jealous behavior seen by others.

Keeping a watchful eye, Jacob and Minnie took note of the men who repeatedly danced with their daughters. By the night's end, the twins' parents knew who to invite to the private socials they planned to host during the months to follow.

✳   ✳   ✳

After five afternoon teas, five evening parties, and ten new pricey dresses for the twins to wear, the fruits of the parents' campaign resulted in two marriage proposals: one for Martha from a young banker by the name of Theodore Booker and the other for Molly from Reginald Cunningham.

Now that Jacob and Minnie had found potential grooms for their daughters, they turned their efforts towards planning two nuptials. Both wedding couples must say I dos before a blanket of peace could visit the McLellan mansion.

✳   ✳   ✳

Martha and Molly were out spending their parents' money while Jacob and Minnie were home enjoying a short respite from their offspring.

"My god, Minnie!" he exclaimed. "We've spent a fortune this year on our quest to find husbands for our daughters."

She nodded. "Although true, you must not say these things aloud. Hearing your words makes me feel like I am complicit to a nefarious offense."

He grinned. "It's not a nefarious offense, my dear. Consider it an offensive defense of our well-being."

She laughed. "You are such a noble politician."

"I am indeed," he agreed. "Minnie, we must try to pare back the expenses of our campaign. Do you think we could talk our girls into a double wedding?"

"We can try, but I believe it will be to no avail. You know how they are …"

✳   ✳   ✳

After the twins returned from shopping, their parents sat them down in the sitting room to discuss wedding plans. Jacob bravely offered the suggestion of a double wedding.

"No way!" the twins shouted.

Martha cried out, "A wedding is a special day for the bride. It's not one to be shared with another bride."

Molly bellowed, "How could you even propose such a thing? Father, I can't believe how insensitive and selfish you can be!"

Jacob, sitting on the sofa, retreated further into it. Minnie interjected, "Yes, my husband, how could you suggest such an abhorrent notion. Our girls are worth the expense of separate weddings. After all, they are our only daughters."

Having lost his supporting wife to an act of cowardness, Jacob sunk deeper into the cushions. He sat without saying another word while the three women planned two flamboyant weddings for the following June.

✳   ✳   ✳

The next summer, two magnificent weddings took place. Each with a reception resembling a royal ball, and each event trying to outdo the other. To their father's displeasure, both came with a price tag that significantly reduced the McLellan fortune.

Jacob was aghast when his girls approached him to contribute to their wedding journeys. In the end, he relented. While Martha and her husband left to enjoy two months traveling abroad in Europe, Molly and her husband set off to wander the Orient.

By the 4th of July, peace and quiet filled the McLellan mansion. It was truly a day of independence.

CHAPTER 10

When greed, not love, is the foundation of a marriage, misery, not bliss, is the consequence. Regrets, doubts, misgivings … call it what you may, Martha and Molly had them. Distance, rather than closeness, was the direction each of their marriages took. It was the course fated for their chosen pairings. I know this because, as I've mentioned, I know their past.

Marriage. It is the union between a man and a woman, built on the bedrock of love and compromise. If you have one, the other should follow. It is a healthy process of give and take, one which I enjoyed most of the time during my marriage. However, I must say compromise was a foreign notion for Martha and Molly.

What happened to the twins during their marriages? The answer lies within a five-year-long tragedy.

*   *   *

From the first night they laid with their husbands, the twins sought to become pregnant. Their reason was not to have a child to love, rather it was the need to produce the first grandchild. Each greedily thought the first-born would provide an enhanced birthright to the McLellan family fortune.

Meanwhile, the twins saw little of each other. One could say they needed a breather, a respite from one another. Truth be known, both women required the hostile clashes which fed their nasty souls, each starved for their nostalgic confrontations.

Martha and Molly gave themselves to their husbands; their husbands took but did not get them pregnant. This was not the silent deal they had each made when they said, "I do." Crestfallen, each twin turned on their husbands to vent their rage and to feed the void of their empty souls. In retaliation, their husbands avoided their fury by turning to personal vices.

Martha's husband, Theodore, was a wealthy banker. As bad luck would have it, there was a run on his bank soon after they returned from their wedding journey. These "runs" were commonplace during the depression. The newspapers called it the "Long Depression" as there was no sign of it ending within the near future.

By the second year of Martha's marriage to Theodore, their finances had dwindled to the point they could no longer afford the mortgage on their home. To avoid embarrassment to the Booker name, his parents purchased the property before foreclosure occurred and did not charge their son rent to live in the home. With this responsibility no longer held by Theodore, he diverted his earnings to a growing gambling habit.

One evening, in the spring of 1883, six men met for a private game of poker in a room above a seedy tavern near the docks. The entrance fee to this game of chance was one hundred dollars. The collected fees were secured in a metal box and placed in the center of the table. It was a reminder that the evening's winner would walk away with a small fortune.

As the hours wore on, each player had their share of wins and losses. When Theodore won a hand, he reached out and pulled his winnings towards him. A card fell from his long shirt sleeve, and an argument resulted with Theodore being called out as a cheater. Voices escalated; harsh words were shouted. A derringer pistol appeared, pointed at Theodore.

With a swift pull of the trigger, a bullet exploded and tore into Theodore's chest. His right hand quickly covered his heart, as his left hand opened to reveal a heart flush. If the errant card had never appeared, Theodore would have been the evening's winner. Instead, the gambler lost his life and his money. It was a poetic death for Martha's husband, Mr. Theodore Booker.

Life-changing events for Martha and Molly occurred near the same time. Whether fortune or misfortune, the twins knew if one had it the other would soon too. That's just the way life seemed to play out for them. Therefore, when Martha's husband died, Molly knew, she just knew, her husband's life would soon end as would her marriage.

After they married, Reggie moved Molly into the Cunningham manor, which also housed his parents and two younger siblings. Soon after, Reggie gave up his dream of becoming a renowned poet and turned his attention to the theatre. He believed this was a much better use of his talents and afforded him the pursuit of his vice, other women.

Theatre productions made serious demands on an actor's life for rehearsals occurred both day and night. Such burdens require sacrifice. Being the noble chap he was, Reggie collected his sweet rewards in the form of romantic interludes with young aspiring actresses. While Reggie enjoyed his life of reckless passion, Molly lived in relative solitude within Cunningham manor.

Reggie had been having private interludes with an actress in *The Pirates of Penzance*, a comic opera funded with his family's money. The unfaithful woman's husband, an actor playing the part of one of the pirates, objected to the dalliance. At the end of the first act, the offended husband improvised during a scene which included a sword fight. Unfortunately for Reggie, he caught the sharp point of his blade.

Several hundred people in the audience witnessed the dastardly deed. Most were aghast to witness the murder of Reginald Cunningham, some were pleased by the plot's interesting twist. One critic applauded the realism of the abrupt surprise ending. Another claimed the pirate did what the audience was hoping he would do. He wrote:

"Although Reginald Cunningham was a fair actor, his singing was atrocious. After having sat through an hour of his screeching serenades, the murderer blessed the audience with a quick end to it."

✶   ✶   ✶

Trials followed for both killers. This was yet again another happenstance where both Martha and Molly experienced similar occurrences near the same moment in their lives. Lending disingenuous support, each twin attended the trial for the killer of the other twin's husband. Unbeknownst to them at the time, they would soon experience another life-changing event.

Both women felt like a third wheel on a two-wheeled bicycle, unwanted and unnecessary. Within one month following the trial of their husbands' killers, Martha and Molly were forced to leave their current domiciles … on the very same day.

Two days later, Jacob and Minnie stood on the front porch of the McLellan mansion waiting to receive their daughters back into their peaceful nest. Although they loved them dearly, the last thing the aging mayor and his wife wanted was Martha and Molly retreating under their roof and protection.

✶   ✶   ✶

When Jacob spied the two carriages coming down the street, one from the east and the other from the west, he muttered, "Dear God, why must we trade tranquility for hostility?"

Both carriages pulled to a stop and both coachmen jumped down to unload. Never had Jacob or Minnie seen two men work as fast as they did to remove what they had brought. In less than a minute, both coachmen had completed their tasks, climbed back on board, and snapped the reins, leaving their daughters standing on the sidewalk next to their baggage.

Jacob and Minnie came down the steps to greet their daughters and opened their arms for hugs and kisses. Martha and Molly brushed past them, one on their left, the other on their right. They turned and watched their girls in disbelief as they rushed up the steps to the mansion.

When both reached for the doorknob at the same time, each twin finally noticed the other one had also arrived. A guttural sound came from both women.

"Truce?" they asked in unison. Each gave a nod, then both entered their childhood home.

Minnie said, "Our prodigal daughters have returned. Should we kill the fatted calf?"

Jacob grumbled. "Which one?"

She sighed. "Both. Have their bags brought into the house."

One day. Just one day is how long the truce lasted. Screams from the twins ripped through the McLellan mansion. Minnie put her head in her hands and cried. Jacob sighed as he rose from his chair in the sitting room to mediate the calamity occurring on the floor above them. As he climbed the staircase, Jacob cried out, "Dear God, why have you forsaken us?"

CHAPTER 11

It was now December 1887. Jacob and Minnie were aging, more so after their daughters returned. He was now sixty, she was six years behind him. Ailments were accumulating, as well as anxiety. Upon their daughters' return to the mansion four long years ago, their quest for peace and tranquility in their home had ceased. They just didn't have the strength to pursue it any longer.

Now in their thirties, finding another husband has become impossible for the twins. Potential suitors were few and their ability to safely give birth to children had diminished. Although the thought of marrying into wealth is attractive to most men, accepting the twins' temperament made for a distasteful acquisition.

The McLellan sisters' potential inheritance was immense. Despite their father's complaining and grumblings about all the money he and his wife had spent on their daughters, these *bribes* only took a nibble from the feast the twins expected to enjoy someday. But there were signs it would not be so after their parents died. Both Martha and Molly were concerned because their father had changed. He was always a giving man. But recently his charity had moved towards philanthropy.

In the past, the mayor had given small donations to organizations which addressed local concerns. Now, inspired by the likes of Sir George Williams who founded the first Young Men's Christian Association in

London, he decided a YMCA would be a perfect addition to the City of Portland. With a mission to put Christian principles into practice, as well as to provide activities for the improvement of mind, body, and spirit of the city's young men, Jacob believed it was a perfect choice to funnel his wealth. Martha and Molly could not let this happen.

✳   ✳   ✳

In January 1888, Jacob was sitting at his desk in the library, shuffling through a pile of mail. Minnie entered the room, tears streaming down her cheeks. He jumped up from his chair and went to her. She fell into his arms, sobbing.

"What is it, dear?" he asked.

She sniffled. "Hannah Clarke is dead."

Stunned by the news, Jacob pushed back his own tears. "How … How did she die?"

"During childbirth. God blessed Hannah with a baby boy and then … He took her."

"Hasn't that family endured enough pain? Wasn't it just seven months ago when her husband was lost at sea? Oh, dear. What is to become of the baby?"

Minnie wiped her eyes with a handkerchief and broke from her husband's consoling embrace. "I heard she named him John. Jacob, let's adopt the orphan boy."

"We're too old," he said.

"We could hire a nanny?" she offered.

"Yes, we could adopt the baby and yes, we could hire a nanny. But we shouldn't. Although his parents are dead, that baby still has two sets of grandparents. I'm sure they will do everything they can to care for him."

She pleaded, "We must do something."

Jacob sighed. "I'll send a nice donation to help them with Hannah's funeral expenses."

*   *   *

Standing just outside the room, Martha and Molly heard their parents' entire conversation. Both smiled and quietly took the stairs down to the sitting room. In a corner of the room, the twins plotted the disposition of baby John Clarke.

"This is perfect!" Martha said. In a sing-song voice, she continued, "I bet you're thinking what I'm thinking."

Her sister giggled. "I am," she whispered. "This is a perfect distraction to our father's plan to spend *our* money on a YMCA."

"Yes," agreed Martha, "let's contact the baby's grandparents and get that baby for ourselves."

Molly grabbed her sister's arm. "Wait a minute. Do you really want to take care of a baby?"

"You heard Mother she said, 'That's what nannies are for.'"

Both twins let out a big guffaw.

*   *   *

Martha and Molly enlisted the aid of a lawyer to broker a deal between themselves and baby John's grandparents. On behalf of the twins, the lawyer sent the following message:

"This money is for the privilege of raising your grandson. This token of our deep appreciation will allow you to enjoy the rest of your lives without concern about how you will meet your financial obligations."

*   *   *

Martha was in the sitting room when the family's butler handed her a sealed envelope. Having made the delivery, he hastened out of the room.

The envelope was from the twins' lawyer. She ripped it open and read the letter. "Damn them to Hell!" she screamed.

Hearing her sister's distress, Molly joined Martha on the sofa. She asked, "Care to share?"

Handing the letter to her sister, Martha replied, "They flatly denied our offer!"

Molly took a quick read. She yelled, "How can they deny us?"

"Well, they did," Martha replied. "Damn it! We need someone to help us tear that child out of his grandparents' clutches."

"Who would that be?" Molly wondered.

Martha grinned. "I know who. Seth Clarke. He's the half brother of Hannah's deceased husband."

"Ahh, yes," said Molly. "He was one of the cardplayers who witnessed the murder of your husband."

Martha nodded. "Let's request a meeting with him regarding a very lucrative business venture."

✳   ✳   ✳

Two weeks later … Sitting at a local tavern table are Seth and the McLellan twins. He raised his glass of whiskey and drank the glass dry.

Seth asked, "For what reason do I have the pleasure of meeting with you fine ladies?"

Molly began, "We have a proposal for you."

"One which will give us what we all want," Martha added.

Seth grinned. "And what is it I want?"

"Money," both women blurted.

He laughed. "I can't argue with that. What is it you want?"

"We want your nephew," Molly replied.

Seth chuckled. "How do you propose we all get what we want?

Martha explained. "We'll help you sue in court for the custody of baby John, which will include the entire estate of Samuel and Hannah Clarke. After winning the suit, you will have their money, and because you have no interest in the kid, we will adopt him."

Seth mulled over the twins' proposal for a long moment. He chuckled. "What the hell? I've nothing to lose in playing your game."

✳   ✳   ✳

Seth Clarke watched from a table in the corner of the tavern as Martha stepped into the establishment. She was bent over, leaning on a cane, and wearing a set of her father's clothes. Her hair mostly hidden under a hat and her cheeks and chin darkened with mascara. She looked around the dimly lit room. When her eyes met his, he nodded. Martha hobbled over to him.

He chuckled. "Nice beard. Same tavern? Same subject?"

Martha looked around the half-filled room of mostly men. "I didn't know where else to meet." She scrunched her nose. "Maybe we should have met at the library."

Seth raised his mug of beer. "Can't drink there. Where's your sister?"

"Out shopping." She put her arms on the table and leaned towards him. "You can't tell her about this meeting."

He laughed. "What's this about, Martha?"

She grinned. "After we win in court and you get control of the baby's inheritance, you must not give the baby to both my sister and I."

He shook his head. "I don't want the little shit."

"What I meant to say was you should only let me adopt the baby."

He winked. "Besides the baby's inheritance, what more can you offer to sweeten the deal?"

Under the table, Martha rubbed her foot on Seth's leg. The higher her foot rose, the bigger he smiled. "Me," she breathlessly whispered.

Seth laughed to himself. Just yesterday, he was sitting at this same table with Molly and having the exact same conversation with her. She, too, had dressed like an old man. He answered Martha's offer in the same manner as he did her sister's offer. "Shall we get a room upstairs where we can privately seal the deal?"

✳   ✳   ✳

A small number of people were present in the courtroom. On one side of the aisle, four grandparents sat with their lawyer. On the other, there was Seth Clarke and his lawyer. As the judge looked out over the courtroom, he noticed two spectators in attendance. Seated a few rows behind Seth Clarke were the McLellan twins. Recently, these women donated large sums of money to his re-election campaign. One of the twins winked at him.

One set of grandparents, William and Mary Clarke, were facing an evil son. He was Mary's first child and would always have his mother's love. But he was also a reminder of the pain inflicted upon her by her assailant, Seth's father, a sailor by the name of Wolfgang Stoker.

When Mary was just fifteen, an assailant pulled her into an alley and raped her. Although she was pregnant from the evil act, William Clarke stepped up and married her. Now, Mary's son was back in their lives trying to rip their grandson away from them.

Each side presented their case for baby John and described the means they had to provide for him. The four grandparents explained all they had done since his birth to make a home for the baby. On the other hand, dressed in a new suit of clothes purchased by the twins, a well-groomed Seth Clarke used their advanced ages against them. Certainly, people of their age did not possess the energy to care for a baby nor the years left in their lives to raise him.

The McLellan sisters followed with embellished statements supporting the virtuous character of Seth Clarke. Molly said, "Seth was an impressive comfort to me after my husband's death." Martha added, "Seth is a caring man who, as a successful entrepreneur, can provide the love and support John Clarke will need as he grows into an honorable citizen of Portland."

After the judge heard the lawyers' arguments, he announced the hearing would resume the following week. Each party would have one last opportunity to present additional evidence before he would make his final decision.

✳   ✳   ✳

One week later, both parties gathered to learn the fate of the baby. Except for one additional person, the same people occupied the courtroom.

The judge asked, "In the case regarding the custody of John Clarke, does either party have anything more they wish the court to consider?"

The lawyer representing Seth Clarke stood and said, "No, your honor."

"Very well," the judge said. His eyes then fell upon the lawyer representing baby John's grandparents. "And you, sir?"

"Yes, your honor," the lawyer replied. "I wish to call a witness to provide testimony related to this case." He then gestured to the old man sitting behind his clients.

The judge motioned to the man. "Please stand and state your name."

The old man rose, half bent over from years of heavy lifting. He said, "My name is Frederick Carson."

"Well Mr. Carson, for the sake of my curiosity, what do you do to earn a living?"

The old man stood as tall as his back would allow him. "I own Carson's Icehouse. I deliver ice within the city."

"Ah, yes, Mr. Carson. What information do you wish to share with the court?"

Mr. Carson stepped towards the bench. "No need, sir," the judge said. "Just stand where you are and say your piece."

Mr. Carson cleared his throat. "Last Saturday night, I was enjoying a beverage at the Bailey's Tavern and overheard a man who had too much to drink. Although my hearing might be a little worse for wear, he was only one table away from me and I heard him as clear as day."

The judge prompted, "And what did he say?"

"I heard him say he was working with two rich women to—"

Seth's lawyer jumped up from his chair and cried out, "Your Honor, I don't see what this has to do with the case at hand. I ask you not to allow this man to waste the court's time."

"Sit down. No, not you, Mr. Carson. You!" the judge demanded as he glared directly into the lawyer's eyes. "I will decide who speaks and it is not you at this time."

Silence fell onto the courtroom. The judge took a deep breath and turned to the elderly man. "Mr. Carson, please go on."

"Thank you, sir. As I said, I overheard a conversation. The drunkard was bragging to the men at his table that he was in cahoots with two rich women who wanted a baby. Once he had custody, he was to turn over the baby to the women and abscond with the baby's inheritance."

The old man took a quick glance towards Martha and Molly, then continued, "He also …"

"Finish your statement, Mr. Carson," the judge ordered.

The old man cleared his throat, again, and said, "He, he also boasted about … Oh dear, I must say this as politely as I can. He, he said he was engaged in amorous congress with both women. Ahh … Separately of course."

Martha slapped Molly. Molly slapped Martha. They growled and spit at each other. Each grabbing a fistful of hair, both women fell onto the floor.

The gavel slammed down; the judge pointed at the twins. "Control yourselves or I will have you thrown out of my courtroom!"

Martha and Molly abruptly broke from their hostility and wiped the spittle off their faces. After straightening their attire, they took several deep breaths and returned to their seats.

Seeing Martha and Molly had assumed a bit of composure, the judge turned to the witness. "Mr. Carson. Who was the man you overheard in the tavern?"

The old man pointed a finger at Seth Clarke. "It was that man," he said.

As soon as the old man sat down, the judge rendered his decision. Baby Clarke would remain in the custody of his grandparents, and they would become the caretakers of his inheritance.

While the grandparents celebrated with handshakes and hugs, the twins blamed each other for their failed attempt to adopt the baby and resumed their physical assault upon each other. Distracted by the bailiff's efforts to remove the screaming twits from the courtroom, Seth took his leave.

Seth Clarke's world had imploded. Although panic had set in, he hoped his backup plan would save him from paying his malevolent debt collectors with his life. While they waited for him on the courthouse steps, Seth quietly exited the building through the rear door while glancing at his pocket watch. He had only twenty minutes to make it to the waterfront.

Seth ran as fast as he could. Just as the crew began to pull up the gangplank and untie the ship from the lesser used moorings of Back Cove, Seth jumped aboard and was greeted by an old acquaintance.

"Mr. Clarke, you are an extremely lucky man," said the captain. "One minute more and I would have left you stranded on the docks."

Seth asked, "Permission to come aboard, sir?"

"Granted."

"Thank you, sir. Note I am no longer known by my surname. It is now Stoker."

"As you wish. Now, get to work, Mr. Stoker. Your passage to San Francisco is not without cost."

✳   ✳   ✳

The mayor's coachman was waiting outside the courthouse for his riders to appear, hoping today's trial would last several more hours.

This was not to be as the two horses attached to the carriage reared up at the sounds of Martha and Molly approaching. Dragged by the bailiff towards the carriage, one by his left hand and the other with his right, the twins hissed and clawed at each other.

"They're your problem now," the bailiff declared as he released the women, pushing them towards the waiting carriage. He turned and chuckled. "Have a nice day."

The coachman mumbled, "'Twas a nice day before you ruined it."

"It's your fault we lost!" Martha yelled. "It was your idea to ask Seth to help us get the baby."

"No. It was your fault," Molly screamed. "You knew he was a drunkard. You knew he couldn't keep out of the taverns. All we needed was for him to stay sober and keep his mouth shut. You should've done a better job of managing him."

"How dare you! This coming from a woman who couldn't control her own husband's pursuit of town whores."

Molly slapped Martha's face. Martha returned the violent gesture. A small crowd of people gathered to watch the twins' open display.

"Ladies!" the coachman whispered. "Your father and mother would not be pleased you are having this *discussion* in public."

"Humph!" both replied.

CHAPTER 12

Four years later, in May of 1892, Jacob and Minnie were in the sitting room having coffee. It was not an enjoyable experience because they could hear their daughters; the twins were engaged in another heated squabble.

He groaned. "Will this ever end? It's been four years since our girls lost their battle to get custody of the Clarke baby. Why must we continue to suffer the pain of their conflict?"

Minnie sighed. "It's because they are our daughters, and we are who they have left."

"I know, I know," he said, "they are our flesh and blood. To have peace in our home, we can't kick them out onto the street to fend for themselves. Besides, they'll just end up fighting where all eyes can see them. Then all of Portland will blame us for the hardships they endure."

Minnie mused, "One cannot be without the other. The truth be known, they hate each other as much as they love each other. This has always been since the day I gave birth to them."

"Humph," Jacob grunted. "We must do something to get them to leave our home."

She grinned. "Perhaps one will soon leave."

Jacob sat straight, nearly spilling his coffee. "You know something I don't?"

Minnie confessed, "Rumor has it, there is a man interested in Martha, Mr. Thomas Winchester."

His eyes brightened. "Really? I know this man. He's around the age of forty, which is appropriate, and he was a former business associate of Martha's late husband. Not appropriate but who can be choosy at a time like this?"

She continued, "I understand Mr. Winchester recently lost his wife and the tragedy has left him with a brood. I'll bet he's looking to find a new mother for his four young children."

"Look no further, Mr. Thomas Winchester." He laughed. "Tomorrow, I'll pay him a visit."

✳   ✳   ✳

Robert was one of the few remaining servants working within the walls of the McLellan mansion. Hearing the door chimes, he went to the front door to greet the visitor.

When the door opened, Mr. Thomas Winchester nodded to the butler who had expected his arrival. Robert turned, then led him to the receiving room to wait for Martha's arrival.

Martha bound down the grand staircase. She stopped at the base of it, taking a deep breath to suppress her joy. She had a suitor. "Mr. Thomas Winchester," Martha called out as she entered the receiving room.

The caller was a tall, slender man, impeccably dressed and fairly handsome. Fortunately, his height kept most people from seeing the growing bald spot on the top of his head. With a slight bow, he said, "Please call me Thomas. It is a pleasure to finally meet you."

Martha took measure of the man and liked what she saw. She thought, *although he is of modest wealth, he is at least a man.* "Let's go to the drawing room," she said. "We can enjoy tea and biscuits while getting acquainted."

A few minutes later, Martha was engrossed in the mostly one-sided conversation as Thomas shared what he did for a living. Soon, he was telling Martha about his children. She hid a grimace while taking a sip of tea.

Gazing into the eyes of her suitor, Martha drifted to selfish thoughts. *Yes, he has four children and would want me to care for them. But that's what nannies are for. I'm not too old to have a baby of my own; a baby who will be the first grandchild. Until that happens, a marriage to Thomas will give my parents four step-grandchildren.* She smiled. *That's far more than Molly can produce.*

During the next two months, Thomas Winchester pursued Martha. They went to parties, dances, plays, and for romantic strolls in the city's parks. This did not bode well for Molly.

✳   ✳   ✳

By July 1892, two months later, Jacob and Minnie were thrilled Martha had a new beau. There were even signs Martha's disposition was improving. On the other hand, Molly's temperament soured more than usual. To help his daughter (and himself), Jacob devised a plan to lessen Molly's bitterness.

There were several wealthy families in Portland, including the McLellans, Prebles, Tuckers, Weeks, and Moodys. Being of higher status meant associating with those like themselves. This is how Jacob McLellan knew of Lucas Moody.

Lucas was the great-grandson of Captain Lemuel Moody, who built the Portland Observatory in 1807. This signaling tower's purpose was to sight ships up to thirty miles away and to notify owners to prepare for the off-loading of their ships' cargo. Years after Captain Moody's death, the tower fell into disrepair and in the hands of Lucas's father. Jacob sent word to Lucas Moody of his wish to offer him a lucrative proposition. Lucas readily accepted; time and place was determined.

✳   ✳   ✳

It was 9:15 in the evening, the sun had just set. Jacob was sitting on a bench near Long Wharf, waiting for Lucas Moody. As he watched a couple take a romantic stroll along the pier, he envisioned Molly doing the same with Lucas. Abruptly, his fantasy ended when an unkempt man plopped down on the bench next to him.

Jacob turned and took measure of the man. He appeared to be about thirty-five and dressed for a night in a tavern. His hair matted, and a slight beard darkened his face.

"Moody?" Jacob asked.

The man nodded. "McLellan?"

Jacob nodded. "You're fifteen minutes late."

Moody wiped his nose on his coat sleeve. "So."

Jacob sighed. "Let's get on with it … I wish for you to court my daughter Molly until her sister is married."

He chuckled. "If what I've heard about her is true, she doesn't have a pleasant soul. What's in it for me?"

"I'll pay you. I'll even cover all your courting expenses." He paused to consider the man's attire. "I'll also throw in a new suit of clothes. If all goes well, a generous bonus will follow. What do you say?"

Jacob watched the man scratch his beard and then his crotch. Jacob winced. Thoughts of his suggested ruse diminished.

"Yeah. I'll do it," he said. "Got nothin' else going on."

✳   ✳   ✳

One week later, Lucas Moody paid a visit to the McLellan mansion. He was wearing an expensive tailored suit, as well as a new stylish haircut courtesy of the mayor. After Lucas entered the grand home, he sat patiently in the receiving room waiting to begin the subterfuge. Unbeknownst to his new benefactor, he had highly hoped the other sister would soon marry and then his scheme of blackmailing the mayor could commence shortly thereafter.

Minnie was not aware of her husband's underhanded plan and was surprised when Lucas Moody arrived at the McLellan mansion requesting an audience. Having been a politician and extremely good at pretense, Jacob comfortably joined in his wife's surprised expression.

When Jacob and his wife entered the receiving room, he heartily welcomed Lucas into their home. "Mr. Moody, what is the reason for your visit today?"

Lucas replied, "Mr. and Mrs. McLellan, I wish your permission to court your daughter."

"Which one?" he innocently asked.

When her husband asked the question, Minnie hadn't realized she was holding her breath in anticipation of the visitor's answer.

"Molly," he replied.

Minnie smiled; she breathed again.

Jacob looked at his wife and found she was nodding her head with approval. He turned to the young man and winked. "Let us not stand in your way. You have our permission."

✳   ✳   ✳

All was well within the McLellan household. Fights between the twins had diminished as both women anticipated a marriage proposal. Although the courting of Molly was Jacob's devious plan, in his heart, he wished Lucas Moody would learn to love his daughter and the ruse would become reality.

Lucas was waiting in the receiving room for Molly. He had arrived early to have a private chat with his benefactor.

Jacob stepped in the room. "What do you want?" he asked.

In a shouted whisper Lucas demanded, "I want more money!"

Surprised by the demand, Jacob said, "I don't understand. I pay for all your expenses to court my daughter. I even threw in a nice compensation for your troubles."

"Well, it's not enough," he snapped. "You wouldn't believe how difficult this has been for me. I want more money!"

While Jacob and Lucas were having a heated exchange, they were not aware Molly had entered the room. Having overheard most of their conversation, she stomped towards her suitor with clenched fists and a growl. Lucas saw the demonic expression on Molly's face. He pleaded, "Let me explain—"

Molly required no explanation. Her nostrils flared. With a grunt, she reared back with her fist and punched Lucas hard, sending him to the floor. While screaming like a banshee with spit spewing from her twisted mouth, she mercilessly kicked him before sitting on his chest to continue her pummeled assault.

Jacob wrapped his arms around his daughter and dragged her from the object of her discontent. She, in turn, continued to scream at Lucas as he scrambled to his feet. Keeping his eyes on her, he quickly backed away, turned, and bolted out of the mansion.

With tears streaming down her face, Molly pulled away from her father. She yelled, "I hate you!"

Jacob could say nothing in his defense as he watched Molly run up the staircase to her bedroom. A door slammed shut.

Hearing the commotion, Minnie rushed into the room. "What in heaven is going on?"

Not having the courage to face his wife, he stared at the floor. "With good intensions, I fear I've taken a path leading to Hell."

While Jacob confessed his illicit scheme, all Minnie could do was shake her head in disgust. When he was done explaining, without saying a word, his wife stood and took the stairs to their master bedroom. Another door slammed shut.

Jacob fell onto the sofa. With his head in his hands, he wondered what in God's name he could do to remedy this situation gone bad. He sighed. He could find no solution, nor could he buy forgiveness. No matter which path he chose to solve his dilemma, it always led back to where he sat. Alone and defeated.

Meanwhile, Molly was furious. She had lost trust in her father, and all men for that matter. How could her sister have happiness without her being happy, too? *This could not be,* she thought. *This will never be.* Finally, Molly accepted the fact she was destined to spend the rest of her life in the house where she grew up. She also made a vow; she would not be alone.

✳   ✳   ✳

When it is known that a man is pursuing a certain woman, it is not socially acceptable for another woman to pursue the man. Custom be damned for it was nothing more than a minor obstacle to be flagrantly discarded as Molly carried out her crafty plan.

Martha had a habit of not being ready when Thomas Winchester promptly arrived on time to take her out for the evening. While she was making the final adjustments to her makeup, hair and dress, Molly would take the opportunity to make her presence known. She'd flit into the receiving room, smile at Thomas, and say a breathless hello. Then, she would quickly exit, leaving only the memory of her and the scent of her favorite perfume.

Molly's brief encounters with Thomas became longer. The word 'hello' morphed into a phrase, and then into playful banter. Thomas enjoyed these private moments with Martha's sister. He looked forward to them, especially when Molly was wearing a low-cut dress.

After a month of Molly's play, she could sense Mr. Thomas Winchester was weakening and becoming more open to her provocative feminine temptations. *When the time is right,* she thought, *I will show my sister how distrustful her man can be.*

✳   ✳   ✳

Like most Saturday evenings, there were plays and light operas to attend. Like every Saturday evening, Thomas arrived on time to take Martha to the theatre. Like all recent Saturday evenings, Molly joined him in the receiving room as he waited for her sister to appear.

She had chosen this night for the final act of her production, and knew timing was critically important when delivering a line or when making a move on stage. It would be the same for making her play on Thomas.

"You look very handsome tonight," Molly said as she floated into the room.

"Thank you, Molly. And you—"

Molly moved in close, so close a sheet of paper was the only thing which could fit between them. She placed her hand on the sleeve of his suit, her fingers walked up his arm. "Is this a new suit?" she asked in a whisper.

"It's a—"

Molly grabbed his lapel, went up on her tiptoes, and put her nose to his collar. In a breathless whisper said, "Smells new."

Thomas, now panting, snuck a quick glance down at her ample cleavage. The sight of Molly's nearly naked breasts, her warm touch, and intoxicating perfume made Thomas dizzy.

He wanted more. *If only Martha was so bold,* he mused. Molly tenderly took his hand and led him to the sofa. With a gentle push, he fell back onto the cushions. She sat next to Thomas, making sure her dress rode up a bit on her legs. The forbidden sight of her lace stockings made his heart beat quicker.

Molly scootched closer and closer until there was no distance between them. She placed her hand on his knee and leaned in. It was then she heard Martha coming down the stairs. This was her cue, a gracious gift from her twin sister.

As Molly moved her hand up his thigh, Thomas stiffened. Pressing her breasts against him, she planted a long kiss upon his lips. As planned, Martha entered Molly's stage at that exact moment to witness Thomas's indiscretion.

Martha screamed. Molly smiled.

✳   ✳   ✳

I'm embarrassed to say I feel disheartened because I can no longer continue to visit the mortal lives lived by Martha and Molly. Simply put, I've run out of *their* time. For shortly after their parents' last attempts to find husbands for their daughters, their father had a fatal heart attack. Thus, setting the twins on their diabolical paths to kill each other.

CHAPTER 13

"God," I said. "Three months have passed; may I help Mrs. McLellan now?

There is nothing you can do for her.

"Why?"

She is with me.

"She's dead? I shouldn't be surprised. Then, what would you have me do?"

Watch. Follow the money.

✳   ✳   ✳

It was October 1893. Peter McCabe was changing the tire of a Monarch bicycle. At present, he was living a blessed life for he had everything a young man would want. At twenty-three, he was married and worked in his father's business, which sold and repaired horse-drawn transports and bicycles. If his life played out as his father planned, he would own McCabe & Son in twenty or thirty years.

Peter loved working on bicycles and was fascinated by the few steam- and gasoline-powered carriages driven about the city. These experimental toys of the rich were a symbol of wealth and power, and Peter hoped he would someday have a chance to tinker with them.

Poking his head out of the office, Peter's father shouted, "Drop what you're doing and come in here."

His father is Malcomb McCabe, known for shouting orders about his shop. When he barked, the workers quickly responded. It did not matter Peter was the boss's son because he, too, must heed his father's call with the same haste as every other employee.

Peter entered the office and, as usual, found his father sitting behind the desk. A young man, formally dressed in a grey tweed suit and blue bow tie, stood next to him. His hat in hand.

"Mr. Peter McCabe?" the stranger asked.

Peter confirmed the man's question with a slight nod.

Taking Peter's hand in his, the visitor vigorously shook it. "It's a pleasure to meet you, sir."

Axle grease from the bicycle Peter was working on soiled the man's hand. His father laughed and tossed a rag towards them.

"Sorry," said Peter as he wiped his greasy hands onto his coveralls.

With a hint of a Scottish burr, he said, "No need for an apology."

The young man took the rag and cleaned the grease from his hand. "My name is Michael Tooley," he said. "I work for a law firm which needs your immediate presence. My employer has requested I escort you back to our office."

Peter turned to his father. "Do you know what this is about?" he asked.

Malcomb grumbled. "It might have something to do with my sister."

"Aunt Minnie?" Peter asked.

With a scowl, his father turned his attention onto the papers strewn on the top of his desk.

Long before Peter was born, there had been a divide between Malcomb McCabe and his sister, Minnie. Peter had never learned why it had occurred and didn't expect an answer would ever be forthcoming from his proud and stubborn father. Despite their feud, Aunt Minnie had always remembered her nephew on his birthday.

With his father's attention now elsewhere, Peter turned to Mr. Tooley. "Well?"

Mr. Tooley shook his head. "I'm sorry, sir. That information lies with my employer." He paused, then smiled at Peter. "However," he said, "based on my experience it is likely to be good news."

Peter said, "Good news is good."

He grinned. "It is, indeed, Mr. McCabe. Now, if you'll follow me—"

"Father?" asked Peter.

Without looking up, Malcomb waved him away. "Go with him, Peter," he said. "You can finish the bike tomorrow."

Peter donned his hat and coat and followed Mr. Tooley out of the shop. Both boarded a carriage which had brought the Scottish lad to McCabe & Son.

A swift carriage ride took them into the heart of Portland's business district. After the carriage stopped, Mr. Tooley led Peter into an elegantly furnished law office. Scanning the room, he noticed all the men were dressed in the same manner as his escort, grey tweed suits. Bow tie colors were the only variation in the uniform.

Although it was cool in the room, sweat dripped from Peter's forehead. He tried to swallow, but his mouth was dry. Never in his life had he been this nervous. "Should've washed up and changed my clothes," he muttered.

Mr. Tooley approached a man sitting at one of the desks near the back of the room. His bow tie was green. He said, "Mr. Peter McCabe to see Mr. Covington."

"Of course," the man said.

Peter watched as Mr. Green Bow Tie rose from his chair and disappeared behind a closed door. A moment later, the man returned and held the door open for his boss to step through.

An elderly man entered the room and approached Peter. He was wearing the most expensive suit Peter had ever seen, this one dark blue with a gold bow tie.

With a slight bow and a click of his heels, Mr. Tooley said, "Mr. Covington, I give to you Mr. Peter McCabe."

With a quick nod of his head, Mr. Covington dismissed his young employee. He then reached out and took Peter's right hand and shook it.

"Mr. McCabe," he said. "Thank you for coming to me on such short notice. We have important matters to discuss. Please join me in my private office."

Peter followed Mr. Covington through the open door in the back of the room. Magically it closed behind them. He continued to follow the elderly man down a long hall and then into a very stylish office. Peter took a seat in one of the two leather chairs positioned opposite an ornate desk.

Peter did as the man requested, hoping none of the grease on his overalls would transfer onto the rich dark brown leather. Mr. Covington took the seat behind his desk.

Peter asked, "What's this all about?"

The lawyer replied, "For years I've provided legal guidance to Mr. and Mrs. Jacob McLellan. As you know, they have both passed, as well as their two daughters."

Peter shook his head. "Terrible losses, but what does this have to do with me?"

"Mr. McCabe, I represent the McLellan estate."

Peter cocked his head and wondered where the man was leading him.

Mr. Covington explained, "Except for a large donation to set up a foundation to establish a new chapter of the Young Men's Christian Association, Mrs. McLellan bequeathed the remaining of her estate to you."

Peter gasped. He had just been hit with a golden brick. Mr. Covington smiled, enjoying the young man's reaction.

"Sir, I don't understand. I barely knew my aunt and uncle; my twin cousins never gave me the time of day. There must be some mistake?"

"There is no mistake. Minnie McLellan was the last of the McLellans and left everything to you." Mr. Covington paused for a moment, considering how much he should tell Peter. He continued, "Mr. McCabe," he said, "Mrs. McLellan came to me shortly after the deaths of her daughters. She confessed you were her favorite nephew."

Peter leaned back in his chair and rubbed his face with his dirty hands. "This I did not know."

Mr. Covington chuckled at the sight of Peter's smudged face. "You, sir, are now the proprietor of the McLellan mansion, as well as the recipient of all financial holdings within the estate."

Peter looked down at his rough hands and began to pick at the grease under his fingernails. The room had become quiet as the life-altering revelation played in his head.

Mr. Covington broke the silence. "Sir, you must have questions."

Sir, Peter thought; his smile broadened.

With renewed confidence that his future was secure, Peter said, "I do, Mr. Covington. How much cash do I have on hand at this very moment?"

The lawyer's response caused him to gasp. Peter had just realized he had far more money than he needed for what he was about to do. He looked to the heavens and whispered, "Thank you, Aunt Minnie."

Peter wrote a figure on a piece of paper and pushed it towards Mr. Covington. He said, "I would like a bank draft in this amount to be payable to my father, Malcomb McCabe. I also require a ride back to my place of employment."

The lawyer nodded. "Of course, sir. Your request will be immediately honored. It just so happens the bank next door holds your account." Trying to be more helpful, he asked, "May I suggest you withdraw additional funds to purchase a new suit?"

Peter grinned. "Perhaps later this week."

✳   ✳   ✳

Mr. Peter McCabe returned to McCabe & Son and marched directly into his father's office. His father looked up with a start.

"Son," he said, "when I gave you permission to leave, I didn't expect you to return to work."

Peter stood tall. "Father," he said, "I no longer wish to work for you."

Malcomb jumped up from his chair. "Poppycock! Why would you not want to work here? Have I not treated you well?"

He took a step closer to his father and handed him a piece of paper. "Sir, I *do* want to work here," he replied. "But not for you."

Malcomb shook the paper in his hand. He shouted, "What is this?"

"Father, I wish to purchase McCabe & Son."

Staring at the amount written on the bank draft, Malcomb fell back into his chair. It was far more than the actual worth of his business.

"I don't understand. How did you get this money?"

"Aunt Minnie left her entire estate to me."

"My sister left everything to you?"

He nodded. "Of course, you will always be welcome here."

✳   ✳   ✳

Peter McCabe considered how his life had changed in a single day. He went to work in the morning for his father and returned home with his father now working for him.

In preparation for dinner, he washed his hands and changed into a clean set of clothes. This was one of the rules his wife, Danielle, had laid down for him soon after they had married. Putting his dirty clothes in the hamper was another one of her many decrees.

Danielle was in the kitchen fixing dinner. She was of average height with chestnut brown hair. Although she was not as pretty as some women, her deep blue eyes, warm smile, and disposition made her appear more beautiful than most. Peter walked up behind his wife and put his arms around her thin waist. He kissed her on the back of her neck. "I love you," he said.

Danielle shrugged him away. "I love you, too. Now, please set the table. Dinner will be ready in just a minute."

After the table was set and the meal served, the young couple bowed their heads. Peter prayed. "Dear Lord, thank you for this wonderful day and for all the blessings you've bestowed upon my wife and I. God, I also thank you for our new home, the one we will move into tomorrow. Amen."

Peter opened his eyes; Danielle was staring at him.

✳ ✳ ✳

It was December 1893, two months later. Peter and his wife had quickly become accustomed to living in luxury. Danielle turned her attention to managing the mansion and hired four servants. Two were a couple who took up residence in the servants' quarters within the mansion. The woman was their cook, while her husband performed the duties of a coachman and butler. Two housekeepers rounded out Danielle's household staff. With his wife in control of their life within their home, Peter attended to his new business.

Although McCabe & Son had been a profitable family business, Peter saw that change was needed to prepare for the future. While the design of horse-drawn buggies, carriages, and wagons had not changed in several years, constant variations were occurring to bicycles. This was a sign that a horse-drawn transport would soon become a relic of the past. Although bicycles would never replace a wagon or carriage, the new steam- and gasoline-powered vehicles motoring on the streets of Portland could soon take up the challenge. Peter was sure these noisy machines, which belched smoke into the air, would quickly improve in design and efficiency. When that happened, Peter wanted to be ready to meet the demand.

Seeing the need to expand the business for future products, Peter acquired several properties adjacent to his business; McCabe & Son also added the sale and service of gasoline-powered vehicles. Since only the wealthy could afford these "horseless carriages," that part of his business was slow. Peter didn't mind as he knew the future would soon come to him. By Christmastime, Peter had changed the name of the business to McCabe Motors.

CHAPTER 14

Dear God, as you've commanded, I've followed the money. The McLellan fortune is now in the hands of Minnie's nephew, Peter McCabe. What is it you wish me to do?"

Complete your mission.

"But Martha and Molly are dead. Aren't they in Hell for their wickedness?"

Not yet.

"Then, where are they?"

Although not aware of it, the deceased twins' spirits are waiting for your intervention to begin.

"But, if they're dead, how am I to fulfill my God-given mission?"

What did you and your mother collect?

"Sea glass," I replied.

How is it formed?

"What does sea glass have to do with my mission?"

Humor me, Hannah. Answer my question.

I explained, "Sailors toss empty glass bottles into the sea. Once discarded, the bottles take a journey towards land where they break as they meet rocky shores. Waves roll the glass shards in and out of the shoreline. With each cycle, sand buffs their sharp edges smooth, and the flat sides turn to a milky color of the glass itself. Finally, they litter the shoreline waiting to be collected by those who treasure the newly formed wonders."

Consider Martha and Molly are empty bottles. How would you go about changing them into sea glass?

I shrugged. "I haven't a clue."

I gave you a mind. Use it.

So, I thought for a moment, which may have been a minute, an hour, a week, or a month. "I have it," I said.

What do you have?

"Martha and Molly are empty souls, lacking any trace of compassion, grace, or humility. Upon death, they fell into the sea. Instead of allowing them to sink to the ocean bottom, You have tossed them onto the rocky shores of their afterlife. My mission, as I understand it, is to transform their broken shards into souls worth saving."

You've shown you understand my metaphor, but you haven't said how you'll buff their sharp edges.

I thought for a moment. "I will place them into people who are experiencing a tragedy in their lives. Martha and Molly will feel everything they experience. Pain and suffering, desperation, hopelessness, and so on. By leaping within these troubled people, they will come to accept that there is more to life, or the afterlife, than just their selfish desires.

"You may think I'm a vengeful angel, but I'm truly not. You've heard the adage, spare the rod, and spoil the child?"

I am all knowing.

"Well, that couldn't have described the lives of Martha and Molly any better. So, my rod will be the leap, the nudge I will use to push them towards a virtuous hereafter. Because they also possess your gift of free will, in the end, they will determine their own eternal fate."

I knew you would produce a plan.

"Of course you did. So, how do I go about choosing their compliant, oblivious hosts?"

You don't.

"I don't? But I could if you'd allow me to see the future."

That is a gift I rarely bestow. You do not require it to fulfill your mission. Let's leave it to the wheel.

"What?"

Imagine a small wheel with thirty-six numbers placed around its perimeter. Red and black will alternate for each number placed within a depression. Spin the wheel and drop a marble in the middle of it. When it stops, the marble will fall into a numbered hollow. Each number is a person who is alive and about to experience a tragic moment in his or her life.

I said, "What you've described is a roulette wheel, a gambling device. How could you use the Devil's tool to determine the twins' leaps? After all, gambling always leads to tragedy. Yes, someone wins, but always somebody loses."

Hannah, you are the one who offered the notion of using tragedies to push Martha and Molly towards redemption.

I cried, "It's now my fault?"

Your mission. You decide.

I sighed, resigned to accepting my part of what had been set in motion. "So, I need to imagine this wheel and spin it within my mind?"

Yes. However, I will make the first choice. After that, you choose when Martha or Molly is to leap. Then, you spin the wheel and drop the marble.

"Will I know what happens during each leap?"

Of course. You have the knowledge of the past, as well as the present.

"When do I stop the leaps?"

When I'm satisfied each twin has chosen her eternal path, I will place them into their final leap.

"Then, I will be done with them?"

Your mission will end.

"God bless you!"

Hannah, you make me laugh … Are you ready to begin?

"Yes, let's begin."

I thought the thought which took me back to Earth.

*   *   *

January 1894. Five senses complete an awareness that a person is living: sight, sound, touch, taste, and smell. For Martha and Molly, God changed their condition from an empty state to one where all their senses were alive.

Martha found herself in the body of an old man. Her thoughts were not only her own, but his. Both were shivering. Molly found herself in the body of an old woman. Her thoughts were not only her own, but also the woman's. The old couple huddled together, cold, teeth chattering.

Martha recognized the old woman next to her as being with the man she had pushed on the steps of the library. Molly recognized the old man next to her as being with the woman she had hit with a cane outside The Apothecary Shoppe.

"This is a horrible dream," muttered both Martha and Molly.

Twenty-one inches of snow had fallen on the streets of Portland. Although most people avoided the frigid assault by staying indoors, a few had no choice but to endure nature's brutal weather. With a windchill of ten below, husband and wife huddled together near the back door of a tavern. Warm air and the sound of people carousing bled through the cracks of its walls, both providing a bit of comfort to the aging couple.

The two were starving; Martha and Molly felt their hunger. It had been four days since their last meal. Never had the twins suffered this overwhelming weakness and fatigue. And the pain. Severe stomach cramps bent them over. Panic rose up within Martha and Molly.

The back door of the tavern burst open. The fire inside backlit an overweight man wearing a greasy apron. He threw a bucket of garbage out onto the snow. Seeing the bounty of treasure cast, the old man

(Martha) and the old woman (Molly) crawled into the small pile of waste. Both were pleased because one found a half-eaten chicken leg and the other a discarded wing. Potato peelings completed their tiny feast.

Just before morning came and the sun shined upon a new day, the temperature dropped to minus thirty. The old couple kissed and cuddled together. At forty below, they closed their eyes for the very last time.

✳   ✳   ✳

"That was sad. I assume the old couple are with you now?"

They are.

"Where did Martha and Molly go?"

Back to where I had placed them. It is a state devoid of everything except their souls.

"I've imagined this place as Hell."

Not quite. It is the place between Heaven and Hell. It is where they will wait between leaps. If you wish it to have a name, call it—

"Nothingness," I said. "To make it easier for me to nudge them towards a beneficial end, will you allow the twins to return to Earth and be amongst the living? Then, I may witness any progression they each might show towards achieving a virtuous soul."

Wise suggestion, but did not I already infer that?

"My apologies."

Let's keep their interaction with the living to certain descendants of the McCabe family.

"Which ones?"

You will see.

CHAPTER 15

Time has a different meaning in God's House. There is no clock here or other mechanism showing its passing. A second, a minute, an hour, or a year for that matter, can go by in the blink of an eye.

It is June 1894 on the earthly plane, and I am returning to the home of Peter and Danielle to observe life within the McCabe household.

✳   ✳   ✳

Danielle tightened the belt of her bathrobe which barely keeps her swollen belly covered. Pushing away from the dining table, she unsuccessfully tried to get to her feet.

"Oh, my," she said. "I just know our baby will be born today."

Peter jumped out of his chair and helped her up. He said, "Although the doctor said our baby will arrive this week, he didn't say today would be the day."

"Doesn't matter … Our baby is telling me today *is* the day."

By midday, Danielle's labor had grown painfully intense causing Peter to summon the doctor. Soon after the doctor arrived, Abraham McCabe entered this world. His cries announced his birth, as well as the second coming of Martha and Molly.

Hannah watched the scene unfold in the hallway outside the nursery and heard the thoughts held by the bewildered twins. Martha remembered having taken a hot cup of tea up to her bedroom. After changing into a nightgown, she sipped her tea, then had a fitful reaction. She recalled an urge to fly and the fragrant scent of roses. *Then there was that dream*, she thought.

Molly remembered dressing in her nightgown and taking a seat in front of her vanity. After applying an ample amount of face cream, she had trouble catching her breath. She thought: *Then nothing, until I had that dream …*

Molly panted, pointed at Martha, and laughed.

"What's so funny?" she asked.

"You!" she cried as she took a short breath. "You have a—crooked neck. And your hair … it's flattened—on one side!"

Martha moved her hands to her neck and felt up to her head. *I do have a crooked neck, and my head is leaning to one side.* Martha retorted, "Well, *you* can't say one sentence without gasping for air." She giggled and pointed. "And you have blue lips!"

"Blue lips? —What's—going on?" Molly wondered aloud.

"I'm not sure," her sister replied.

In unison, which was still a normal thing for them to do, Martha and Molly each noticed their bodies had a milky semi-transparent appearance, a faded representation of who they once were. Both fainted and fell, hovering over the surface of the floor.

Meanwhile, the doctor was in the nursery repacking his bag. Peter followed him as the doctor stepped out of the room, leaving Danielle and baby Abraham with an uninterrupted moment to bond and to rest. Both mother and child were exhausted from the miracle of birth.

Several minutes later, Martha and Molly groaned as they came out of their stupor. Slowly, each one rose to a standing position, their bare feet lightly touching the floor. The twins looked at each other and through each other. A moan escaped from both spirits.

Molly whispered, "Martha, I, —we need—to talk."

"Talk?" Martha whispered back. "You can't say a whole sentence without taking a pause."

"I can—too."

Martha laughed. "So, talk."

"Something strange—happened to me—just before I—returned home."

"Something happened to me, too. I, I had a dream," she stammered.

Molly asked, "What was—your dream?"

"Actually, it was a nightmare! I dreamed I was in an old man, starving and extremely cold. There was also an old woman who must have been his wife. I could feel everything that man was feeling. When he died, I may have, too!"

"Oh, my god. —I had the—same dream. —But, in—my dream, —I was in—the old woman!"

"What do you think this means?" Martha asked.

"I have—no idea."

The twins left the hallway to wander about the mansion. Both quietly pondered their ghostly predicament, as well as the many changes made to their home. Half an hour later, they returned to what once was their mother's bedroom. The room was quiet, dimly lit by a lone gas lamp on the wall. Light from the setting sun peeked around the window curtains into the room.

Ignoring the mother and child, Martha lashed out at her sister with a harsh whisper, "You're an idiot!" she yelled.

Molly screamed her whisper, "Am not! —You're a—fat cow!"

The quarreling women continued to berate each other with voices rising, awakening the mother. Startled, Danielle pushed herself up into a sitting position, taking in the disquieting scene.

"Who *are* you two?" she asked.

The twins broke from their squabbling, turned, and faced her.

Martha replied, "I'm sorry. Did she wake you? She has no consideration for other people."

"Look—who's—talking."

Danielle cried, "I demand to know who you are!"

Martha said, "A formal introduction is in order. I'm Martha and this crazy stammering idiot is Molly."

"I'm not—an idiot!"

Danielle sighed. "Am I dreaming or am I having a delusion?"

"If you're dreaming, so are we," Martha replied. "Molly, are you dreaming?"

"No. And—I'm not—a delusion!"

"Then, what are we?" Martha whined.

Danielle yelled, "Ladies! Get out of my house!"

"Your house?" Molly shouted.

Martha stamped her foot on the floor—which made no sound—and yelled, "This is our house!" She pointed a finger at Danielle. "You're the one who should do the explaining. Who are you? A visitor? A servant? Humm?"

"Yes. Who—are you? —And just—what have you—done with—our mother?"

Peter opened the door, giving Martha and Molly a start. Then he walked right through the twins as he approached his wife. He shuddered, then shook off the eerie, cold feeling he had just felt. "Honey, did you call for me?"

"My, my," Martha said. "He is a handsome man."

Molly went up on her tiptoes and kissed Peter on the cheek. "He tastes—good, too!"

The twins giggled.

Danielle gasped at the women's boldness. "Don't you see them?" she asked.

He looked around the room, then shrugged. "See who?"

The twins giggled.

She took a deep breath to calm herself, then said, "Never mind. Please gently place our baby in the bassinette."

Peter did as his wife asked, then sat on the bed next to her. "Do you want me to stay?"

"No. I'm going to try to get some sleep. If you please, check on me and the baby in an hour."

Peter leaned over and kissed his wife on the lips. "Sure thing," he said and quietly stepped out of the room.

As soon as the door closed, Danielle turned her attention back to the transparent women. In a forced whisper, she said, "Leave or I'll have you tossed out."

"Good luck—with that," Molly said.

The two ghosts laughed.

Martha said, "It appears only you can see and hear us. How could you think anyone would come to your aid? Besides, haven't we already established this is *our* house, not yours."

Danielle squeezed her eyes closed, wishing them gone. When she opened her eyes again, the two ghosts were still in the room.

"Welcome back!" Martha and Molly said.

With as much calm as she could muster, Danielle addressed the two women. "Explain yourselves."

Molly said, "I don't—know where—to begin."

Taking the lead, Martha said, "I'll explain."

"Humph," Molly uttered as she fell into a chair, trying to catch her breath.

"While you were asleep or nursing the baby or whatever, we—"

"Who's we?" Danielle interrupted.

"As I said, I'm Martha and that *thing* is my sister, Molly. We are the McLellan twins, and this mansion is our home."

Danielle exclaimed, "I know who you are! After you both committed suicide—"

"We're—dead?" Molly cried.

Martha frowned. She mumbled, "That might explain our precarious situation."

The twin ghosts put their heads in their hands and sobbed. After a bout of wailing, Molly lifted her head. She adamantly declared, "I didn't—commit suicide!"

"How else would you describe your deaths?" Danielle asked. "One of you was poisoned with wolfsbane in her face cream. The other had a cup of tea laced with nightshade."

Martha gasped and pointed sharply at her sister. "She murdered me!"

Molly's nostrils flared. "Well, you—murdered me, —too!"

"So, you *both* killed each other." Danielle wondered, "What are you? Demented ghosts?"

Molly frowned. "Ghosts?"

Martha scrunched her nose. "Maybe we are. While you were asleep, we found we could move about the mansion and—"

"Locked doors—are not—a problem."

"That was fun!" said Martha. "Walls and doors do not hinder us. We just float through them like they're not there at all."

Molly wailed, "Our ghastly—attire!"

"Yes, our attire … We cannot change our clothes. What a sorry lot, doomed to wear these wretched filthy nightgowns. No longer can we wear our beautiful gowns and jewelry."

Danielle laughed.

"What's so—funny?"

"Well, I can, and I do enjoy your lovely jewelry and pretty dresses. Thank you very much."

"That's not fair!" Martha screamed.

Danielle said, "Soon after you both died, your mother passed away."

"Mother is dead?" cried the twins.

"She left this house and all her other financial holdings to my husband, Peter."

"Peter?" the twins asked.

"Yes, your cousin Peter McCabe."

Both Martha and Molly whined, "Why him?"

"Peter was your mother's favorite remaining relative." Danielle glowered. "Why are you here?"

Molly pointed at her sister. "It's because—of her."

"Me? You—"

"It's because of you both," Danielle surmised. "I suppose God is punishing you for the sin of murder. Perchance you must pay for your transgressions?"

Molly blurted, "How do—we pay—"

"What is owed?" Martha asked.

Moaning, the twins put their heads in their hands again.

Danielle couldn't help but feel sorry for the twin ghosts. The two women obviously had lived unhappy lives. Since only she could see and hear them, the young mother felt a responsibility to help the poor women. But, for now, she was tired and needed rest to care for her son.

CHAPTER 16

"God, when should I leap the twins?"

Your choice, Hannah. However, I suggest you give them a little more time to show who they are. After all, they are just beginning to become familiar with their new condition.

✻ ✻ ✻

July 1894, one month later. Martha and Molly were bored. Every day since their return to the living was a repeat of the day before. With only Danielle being aware of their existence, they couldn't annoy anyone else. The twins followed her everywhere she went.

Danielle decided to give her baby a bath. "Must you hover around me?" she asked. "I can't even breathe or use the bathroom without you two watching me."

Martha asked, "What else is there for us to do? We don't eat or sleep."

"We don't—even use—the water closet," her sister added.

Martha giggled. "The servants can't see or hear us, nor can Peter. But I must say, I enjoy watching your husband reach for you at night."

Danielle sighed. "Is it too much to ask you both to stay out of our bedroom?"

"Yes," Molly said with a playful hiss. Her sister followed with a loud guffaw.

Unintentionally, Danielle dropped a washcloth on the floor. Martha leaned down and picked it up. It was a natural reflex which led to a glorious revelation. Martha and Molly could now hold items in their hands.

God had made a change to their condition. No longer did the twins just linger in the home as spectators in dirty nightgowns; they had use of their hands. At the same moment Martha picked up the washcloth, they also felt a desire to care for the baby.

Two powerful urges now gripped Martha and Molly; one pushed, one pulled. One moved them forward, the other backward. Will they help Danielle care for her baby, or will they choose misbehavior to relieve their boredom? Free will to choose would determine their future.

The twins' desire to inherit their parents' estate had been in play during their lifetimes. It was the root of their competition to deliver a first-born grandchild. This ill desire to conceive in life had changed in death to a growing need to care for a baby. Perchance God had a playful side and a peculiar sense of humor? More likely, He had given Martha and Molly the opportunity to be loved by someone who would not judge them for who they were, but for who they could become.

When no one else was in the room to bear witness to the twins' behaviors, Danielle allowed Martha and Molly to help care for her baby. She wanted to fulfill the twins' growing urge to help, but also to avoid explaining why the baby, as well as other things, were floating in the air.

Like all first-time mothers, Danielle, Martha, and Molly learned as they went. Baby Abraham grew and, as his needs changed, all three women adapted to meet the challenges. This three-way partnership, however, was often tested when the twins had a heated altercation or decided to use their hands to annoy or scare the servants.

Floaters. That's what the household staff called them. A servant would see a candy dish floating in the air, another would see a pillow.

Unexplainable and unnerving occurrences happened when no other witnesses were present.

Disarray was another issue faced by the staff. A room within the mansion would be neat and tidy; a moment later the chamber looked as if a tornado had torn through it. This created more work for the household staff.

✳   ✳   ✳

One day, Danielle stumbled upon a mess in the drawing room. Two lamps were overturned, seat cushions were on the floor, as well as every other small object within the room.

"Martha! Molly!" Danielle called out in a whispered scream.

The twins floated in. In unison they asked, "You called?"

"Yes, I called. Look at this mess!"

"My, my," Martha said. "Your servants are not doing their jobs."

Molly offered, "I suggest—you dismiss them."

"You did this," Danielle said. "Clean up this room, now!"

Martha giggled. "It's your mess, Molly."

"Isn't that—what servants—are for? —Perhaps they—are inadequate."

Danielle snapped, "Clean up this room or I'll not let you tend to my baby."

Hearing her threat caused the urges within the twins to fight each other. Since both itches needed scratching, Martha and Molly reluctantly complied.

✳   ✳   ✳

Two months later, it was September 1894. Having returned from work, Peter joined his wife for dinner in the courtyard.

"Danielle," he said. "I've received several complaints from our household staff."

"About what?" she asked.

"They are tired of it and have threatened to quit if we don't quickly do something about it."

Danielle hid her smile because she knew the answer to the question she would ask. "Dear, what is *it*?"

"*It* is disturbing," he snapped. "*It* is the mysterious things they say are happening within our home. Objects floating through the air, messes caused by persons unknown, lights flickering … Honey, they claim this house is haunted!"

Danielle disliked keeping the truth from her husband, but replied, "Oh, dear. They could be pushing to have their salaries increased?"

Peter sighed. "It could be as you suggest. Although … I've not witnessed anything they claim to have seen. But I must say, I'm beginning to believe them."

"Why is that?"

"On several occasions, this morning included, I had a strange feeling I was being watched while getting dressed."

"Damn twins," she muttered.

Danielle patted her husband's hand. "We have more money than we need. It wouldn't hurt to reward their service with a bonus."

Rising from his seat, he kissed his wife on the forehead. "I'll see to it, my love."

✷   ✷   ✷

It was February 1895, five months later. Abraham was in his ninth month of life when Molly pushed Martha aside to give him his morning bath. She fell onto the floor.

"Rest your—pretty, crooked—neck," Molly said.

As Martha rose up, she grabbed hold of the tub of water sitting on the baby's dressing table. Water went everywhere, causing Danielle to slip and she was the next one hitting the floor.

"That's it!" she cried. "Out of this room! Out of this house! Out of my life!" she screamed.

Startled by Danielle's outburst, the twins quickly exited the room through the nearest wall. Martha cried, "Now look what you've done!"

Flaring her nostrils, Molly shrieked, "It's your—fault!"

Her sister scrunched her nose. "What will we do now?"

"You're the one—who spilled the—bath water!"

"We should give her time to cool off. Let's stay away from her for the rest of the day. Surely, she will have forgotten this episode by tomorrow morning. Agreed?"

"Agreed," her sister grumbled.

With that settled, Martha noticed they had unconsciously exited the nursery through an outside wall. "My goodness!" she cried.

"My goodness—indeed."

The twins were floating outside the house. Both women looked at each other and snickered. They were now free to leave the walls of the mansion.

✳   ✳   ✳

I asked, "Another one of your interventions?"

God's will be done.

✳   ✳   ✳

Four months had passed; it was June 1895. Danielle was taking a walk with her husband and pushing baby Abraham in the buggy.

"Peter, have you heard the news? A committee has formed to resurrect the Orphans Charity Ball."

"If I'm correct," he said, "the first and last time it occurred was twenty years ago."

"Yes," Danielle said. "I'm told it was a magical evening. In fact, several of the attendees met their future spouses at the ball."

Peter grinned. "Then, I guess we don't have to go."

Danielle pulled the buggy to an abrupt stop. She said, "We must go. Now that we have the funds, we should support causes such as this. In fact, I'd like for both of us to be part of the ball committee."

He shook his head. "Sweetheart, do you really think that's possible? We are of new-found wealth, not born into prominence."

Danielle pushed the buggy forward. "Remember when we were cleaning out the old desk in the library where Mayor McLellan kept his papers?"

"I do."

"Well, I had them boxed up and stored in the basement. Guess what? Within that box are the planning documents for the original ball. We can use them to barter our way in?"

Peter kissed his wife on the cheek. "Why Mrs. McCabe, you are a devious woman."

✳   ✳   ✳

The Orphans Charity Ball occurred just one day before Abe's first birthday. With a few exceptions and help from the McCabes, it was a reproduction of the original event.

Martha and Molly were furious. They wanted to attend the charity ball wearing beautiful, elegant ball gowns adorned with expensive jewelry. Of course, they would not because the twins could only wear their soiled nightgowns.

✳   ✳   ✳

Four hundred living guests and two earth-bound spirits arrived at the Orphans Charity Ball. As the ghost twins looked around the elegant ballroom of The Commodore Hotel, everyone, including Peter and Danielle, seemed to be enjoying the evening. Hearing the beautiful music and laughter caused them to become angrier with … God?

Danielle was the only living person at the lavish event who could see them and, at all costs, the only one the twins had to avoid. *Everyone else is fair game,* the ghosts thought. Armed with shears found in a box of decorations, they set out to ensure all attendees had an evening they would remember for the rest of their lives.

Their plan was quite simple. Guests who visited the washrooms and dressing rooms would be the recipients of their acts of malicious destruction. With a quick snip of the scissors, Molly's first deed of mischief occurred when a strand of exquisite pearls fell from a woman's neck onto the washroom floor. The twins stepped back, enjoying the woman's reaction.

Danielle was also in a dressing room adjusting her gown when a woman standing a few feet from her screamed. She turned to see the woman scrambling on her knees, chasing after her pearls. Seeing a pearl roll under her dress, Danielle took a step back to where it would not be sheltered by her gown. As she bent down to pick it up, she heard familiar laughter coming from a dark corner of the room.

"Is that you, Martha? Molly?" she asked in a shouted whisper.

The lights went out and another woman screamed when the straps to her gown were severed by the twins. While she pressed the top of her dress to her bosom, two other women screamed when they felt sharp pokes in their behinds.

The mayhem continued throughout the evening. More necklaces fell to the floor, while countless straps dismembered ball gowns and brassieres.

Martha and Molly did not ignore the men. Shoelaces became divided into random lengths, as well as bow ties and boutonnieres. Except for Peter and Danielle, the twins spared no one from their evening of playful torment.

The Orphans Charity Ball was designed to be a romantic, fun-filled evening for the rich and prominent citizens of Portland. Instead, it was a catastrophic nightmare. If donations hadn't been requested and received prior to entering the ballroom, no funds would've been raised for the parentless children.

Upon returning to the mansion, Martha and Molly were pleased with the chaos they had caused. If they couldn't enjoy the ball, well, no one else could either.

When the sun rose the next morning, it did not shine on Martha or Molly. They had simply vanished, returned to the place between Heaven and Hell.

CHAPTER 17

On earth, it is now August 1896. Just as I was about to leave God's House to return to the McCabe family, He informed me that my husband is still in this earthly world.

I said to God, "It's been nearly ten years after I was told Sam died at sea. Now I'm told he lives! Why have you kept this from me?"

Sam is dead but not gone. Like you, he is a spirit. Unlike you, he dwells with the living. Therefore, he is following a path different than you, one which will eventually take him home.

"I miss my husband. Can I go to him?"

Not yet. Go now. Your mission requires attention.

"But—"

✳   ✳   ✳

I wanted to continue my plea, but God was gone. Well, not really; He is always with me. It's just that God had said what He wanted to say and ended our conversation.

I do not know what He has in store for my husband, but I do pray Sam and I can be together again. We promised each other to be together forever, and a promise should always be kept.

✳   ✳   ✳

Danielle was sitting on the floor of her son's bedroom playing with two-year-old Abraham. He loved having his mother stack blocks of wood and then slapping his hand at the tower, knocking them down. He never tired of it; over and over and over again they repeated this play.

As she placed one block on top of another, Danielle thought how wonderful her life had become. Peter had put his heart and soul into his growing business and, at times, enjoyed telling his father what to do. Abraham would soon be three and she was expecting their second child.

Danielle often wondered what happened to Martha and Molly. When her son turned one, the contentious twins had just disappeared. She wondered, *would they return when my second child is born*? That question was answered when, in late October, she gave birth to Michelle McCabe and the twins did not appear.

*   *   *

At three months, Michelle McCabe was a thriving baby girl. With no illness, little fussing, and a regular appetite, Peter and Danielle were blessed by God with another healthy child.

When midnight came, Danielle slipped out from under warm blankets and donned her robe and slippers. Being careful not to wake her husband, she quietly left their bedroom. Danielle peered into the nursery and found baby Michelle with her eyes wide open. The baby greeted her mother with a coo. Bending down, she gently picked her up. It was a sweet, tender moment between mother and child.

While sitting in the rocking chair, Danielle sang softly to her baby as she nursed. After taking her fill, the sleepy child was returned to the comfort of the bassinette. The proud mother kissed her little angel's forehead. She whispered, "I love you."

At four in the morning, Danielle rose again from her bed to care for baby Michelle. When she entered the nursery, the baby's eyes did not open to greet her. There was no coo.

Danielle whispered, "Wake up my little angel."

✳   ✳   ✳

I was angry at Him, The Lord God Almighty. I spouted, "Why did you take Michelle so soon from this world? Ugghh! Sometimes You can be so cold."

Remember to whom you are speaking.

"But, why? Why did You have to take her?"

You have much to learn, Hannah. This mission is as much about you as it is about Martha and Molly. Simply put, life is not fair. It is filled with challenges which test free will. Some are good, some are bad. Hopefully, they will lead you to become better, to raise you to a higher level.

"So, you're doing this to me, too?"

I do it to everyone.

✳   ✳   ✳

The death of baby Michelle has taken a toll on me; I require rejuvenation. Ironically, after He tires me out with His controlling and unpredictable behavior, I must go to Him to regain my strength. So, now I thirst for distraction as I bask within His grace and find myself thinking.

The expression, *Every time a bell rings an angel gets its wings,* is a nice thought, but hardly true. I do not possess wings, nor will I ever.

Why do I think that? It's because I just heard a bell ring. It was not one which signifies a blessing. It is an alarm, a nudge by God, that I must turn my attention back to my assignment.

I returned to earth; it is now May 1900, more than three years after Danielle's daughter died. Seth Stoker, my husband's half brother, has just returned to Portland.

✳   ✳   ✳

Twelve years had passed since Seth escaped from Portland, and he was confident the thugs tasked with collecting his gambling debts were no longer in pursuit. This gave him the freedom to complete the revengeful plan he had devised during his two-month passage to San Francisco. It was an evil scheme to pay back those who kept him from inheriting his half brother's fortune.

The first part of Seth's four-step plan was to amass the funds needed to commit his act of vengeance. To do this, he avoided gambling, but not the gambling houses. There was always a lucky winner destined to lose his winnings to an unlucky event. With a quick strike of his leather sap, Seth would come away with newfound wealth.

Before the gold rush of '49, the population of San Francisco was less than nine hundred. Forty years later, it exploded to 300,000. Seth knew the best way to increase his ill-found prosperity was buying and selling property within the Bay Area. After each assault on a chosen quarry, Seth converted his ill-gotten stash into property.

After five years of accumulating wealth, Seth set the second part of his plan into motion. Using his small fortune and a pretense story of an honorable New England heritage, he found a bride whose family possessed a respectable standing within San Francisco. Unbeknownst to her, she would be used as another building block to create a reputation of a devoted family man. One year later, Damian Stoker was born.

When Seth's son turned six, he began the third step of his plan. He sold all his holdings within the Bay Area, purchased passage for his family, and boarded an eastern-bound train. With his feet now planted on the Portland peninsula, he turned, reached out his hand, and helped his wife down from the train. The last step of Seth's revenge against the Clarke and McLellan families had just begun.

Two days later Seth visited Carson's Icehouse late one night. No one saw him put a match to the highly flammable sawdust used to keep the ice from melting. The fire spread quickly and soon became a raging inferno. As Seth watched the building burn to the ground, he was pleased the loss would ruin Mr. Frederick Carson. For it was the old man's damning testimony which destroyed Seth's one chance to gain control of an inheritance he believed was rightfully his.

✳   ✳   ✳

It was three years later, September 1903. Peter and Danielle were in the drawing room enjoying a cup of coffee while their nine-year-old son was on the floor coloring a picture, a drawing of a 1903 Packard Model F automobile. Eight waxed crayons spilled from the box next to a teddy bear.

His mother asked, "Which is your favorite color?"

"Red!" Abe replied as he desperately tried to stay within the lines of the drawing.

Peter turned to his wife. "I've decided to take a trip to North Carolina."

Danielle asked, "Is this for business or pleasure?"

"A little of both," he replied.

"Don't you think I deserve more than just, *A little of both?*"

"I apologize," Peter said. He explained, "As you know, McCabe Motors repairs and sells bicycles. There's a shop in Dayton, Ohio, where they manufacture and service bicycles. For the past few years, I've been receiving small shipments of their creations and selling them out of my business."

Danielle asked, "How does this take you to North Carolina? Do they have more than one shop?"

"No," Peter replied. "The owners of the business have been using their profits to fund a foray into another form of transportation. I've offered to invest some of our money in their new venture, but they've flatly turned me down. Instead, I've been invited to witness their progress in Kitty Hawk, North Carolina."

"What kind of transportation are you talking about? Automobiles? Motorcycles?"

Peter mumbled, "Ah … flying machines."

Abe stopped coloring. "Father, may I go with you?"

*   *   *

Three months later, on December 17, Peter and Abe were walking along a beach four miles south of Kitty Hawk. On a distant sand dune, they noticed two men dressed in coats and ties preparing an airplane for flight. Peter waved to them.

Eventually they caught up with the two men and Peter greeted them. "Good morning, sirs."

The older of the two men asked, "Who goes there?"

"I am Peter McCabe," he replied, "and this is my son, Abraham."

"We've been expecting you. I'm Wilbur and this is my younger brother, Orville."

Peter extended his hand. "I'm very pleased to finally meet you," he said as he shook their hands. "What do you call her, your flying contraption?"

Orville chuckled. "The *Wright Flyer*, of course."

Abe looked up to the closest man. "Mister, when did you first want to fly?"

Wilbur bent down to Abe's level. "Young man, every interest is born with a spark that ignites it. When I was around your age, my father brought home a toy for my brother and me. It was a helicopter made of paper, bamboo, and cork. Its propulsion was a simple rubber band."

Abe was puzzled by the strange word. "What's a helicopter?"

Wilbur replied, "That's a French word for a device which lifts a flying machine straight up into the air. That day, we played with the toy so much that we broke it. The next day Orville and I built one of our own. That sparked our interest in flying."

Orville added, "Someday, Mr. Abraham McCabe, I'll bet you'll find a spark to ignite an interest of your own."

With a freezing headwind gusting up to twenty-seven miles per hour, Orville took the first flight and traveled 120 feet in twelve seconds. Wilbur took the second flight of 175 feet, followed again by his brother at two hundred. During all three flights, the craft never rose more than ten feet off the ground. Around noon, after numerous minor repairs, Wilbur attempted what would be the last flight of the day.

Abe rubbed his hands together to warm them as he watched the *Wright Flyer* take off into a headwind. During the first few hundred feet, the aircraft went up and touched down several times. Then, Wilbur got better control of it and flew 852 feet before striking the ground. Although the crash landing broke the frame supporting the front rudder, the Wright brothers had proved flight was possible.

Abe asked his father, "Will you build me an airplane?"

Peter laughed, then frowned when he thought about what Danielle would say if he ever tried to do it.

Peter and son and everyone else who had witnessed the event ran to the disabled machine. Peter asked, "Wilbur, you sure you won't reconsider my offer to invest into your flying machine?"

"Not a chance," Wilbur replied.

Peter and Abe then said goodbye to Wilbur and Orville Wright.

✳   ✳   ✳

It is March 1911, eight years later. For the first time, I will spin the wheel, which I will call the "Wheel of Tragedy." I imagine the wheel for Molly and give it a spin. Then, in my mind, I dropped a marble onto its center. Round and round the wheel went as the marble danced upon its surface. When it came to a stop, the sphere fell into the hollow: 17 Black.

As soon as the selection was made by the marble, I was instantly watching Molly's leap unfold.

✳   ✳   ✳

Molly's senses had returned, and she was no longer wearing the filthy nightgown. Her outfit was an old cotton dress with leather shoes, worn and weathered. Rather than her hair being auburn and falling onto her shoulders, it was reddish blonde and tied back into a ponytail. She had taken possession of a fourteen-year-old girl.

Molly cried out to the woman sitting next to her, "Where am I?"

"In Hell," the older woman replied. "Get to work before we both get into trouble."

She shook her head. "Work? I don't work!"

"Hush!" shouted the woman. "You're already behind. I'm at least three shirts ahead of you."

With a painful look, Molly asked, "Who am I? Where am I?"

"Silly questions," she replied. "Did you hit your head? You're Kate Malone and you're on the tenth floor of a shirtwaist factory. Now, get to work and stop bothering me."

Kate (Molly) began to sew the cloth.

Again, Molly interrupted the woman next to her. "How much is Kate, I mean I, getting for this laborious task?"

The woman replied, "Same as the other two hundred ladies in this building, fifteen cents an hour. Seven hours done, only two more to go. Then we go home."

"Fifteen cents an hour?" Molly repeated. "That's absolutely ghastly!"

The woman chuckled. "Better then begging or selling yourself on the street at night."

"Speak for yourself," Molly said.

Four stations down, a woman yelled, "I smell smoke!"

Increasing cries of panic rose up from the women; the eighth, ninth, and tenth floors were on fire.

Kate followed the woman next to her as she ran to the exit, only to find the door locked from the outside. Precious time was lost as they broke down the door and discovered the rickety metal stairs had fallen away. With flames licking at their heels, they found their only escape was the roof.

From above, Kate (Molly) watched the firefighters try to save the women who had climbed on to the roof. Their hopes for rescue turned to despair when the ladders were not long enough to reach them. Kate's hair and clothes caught fire. Molly felt Kate's fear and pain as it burned the woman's flesh. Not able to stand the pain any longer, Molly jumped off the roof. In the instant that Kate's body smashed onto the street, Molly's frightful adventure ended.

✳   ✳   ✳

When Molly's leap ended, I returned to God's House. I suspect she is with her sister, floating in the realm of Nothingness. Although I am prepared to have Martha face the wheel, God has told me to wait one year.

✳   ✳   ✳

It is April 1912, Martha's turn to face the Wheel of Tragedy. Again, I imagined the wheel and spin it. After a slight hesitation, I gently placed a marble onto its center. When the wheel slowed to a stop, the marble had chosen 23 Red.

✳   ✳   ✳

Martha's senses sparked to life, and thoughts of who she was inhabiting floated into her head. She sat up on a worn mattress and looked around the … berthing area? The room rocked from one side, then to the other.

I clean passengers' cabins, make beds, and, and … A vision of her cleaning toilets burst into her head. She shouted, "My god, you people are filthy!"

Everyone within earshot snapped their heads towards her. Quick to clarify her remark, Martha said, "I'm talking about our rich passengers. They're also impolite."

Disapproving looks from the other women were daggers thrown her way. "Meagan Turner," one woman said, "you can think it, but don't you dare say it. If what you said was heard by just one of our superiors, you'd find yourself tossed into the ocean."

With Martha within her, Meagan spent the next sixteen hours cleaning up after the ship's affluent passengers. During this time, Meagan's thoughts told Martha she had led a dreary, dismal life of twenty-two years. Meagan's work on the ship was payment for passage from Southampton, England, to New York City. Upon arrival she was to live with her aunt, hopefully changing her life for the better.

At the end of the day, Meagan was so exhausted from the dreary work she fell into her bunk without eating. Martha asked her, "How do you do this every day?" She did not answer.

Panicky screams jarred Meagan awake in the middle of the night. She jumped out of her top bunk, her legs now deep in frigid water. Not understanding just what had happened, Meagan fell in line with her cabin mates as they desperately moved down passageways and up ladders towards a safer place.

After climbing onto the top deck, the frigid air stung Meagan's face. She looked about frantically, sizing up her dire situation. The ship had hit an iceberg and people were running everywhere, screaming and crying. All were desperately trying to board a lifeboat.

A crewman yelled, "Women and children first!"

Seeing this as a ray of hope to escape the sinking ship, Meagan joined a line of passengers waiting to board a lifeboat. When she neared the front of the line, the woman behind her shoved Meagan to the side. She said, "Women and children first. Not baggage."

Meagan yelled, "I am not—"

"What's the problem?" a crewman asked.

The woman pointed. "Earlier today, I saw this woman cleaning my cabin suite."

He said, "You picked an awful time to complain about her service."

"You don't get it, do you?" the woman shouted. "I paid my fare, she didn't. Shouldn't paying passengers be given preference when boarding a lifeboat?"

The crewman turned to Meagan. Although his eyes showed pity, he sent her back to the end of the line.

The line moved at a quickened pace. When it was Meagan's turn to board, she found the lifeboat could not take one more soul. Martha sniffled as Meagan desperately looked around for another lifeboat. All were gone.

Without warning, the ship severely tilted, causing Meagan to tumble towards the ship's propellers. She feverishly grabbed at anything and everything to stop her from meeting the spinning blades; she found a railing. With fingers losing purchase, loud explosions deafened her ears. The ship let out an eerie groan, ripped in two, and surrendered to its fate.

Meagan Turner lost her grip, bounced off the propellers, and plunged into the icy ocean. Martha's painful world suddenly went black.

CHAPTER 18

"God, I don't believe Martha and Molly have learned anything after their first and second leaps."

True. From now on, I will give them a memento to remind them of where they have been.

"Like a souvenir? A keepsake?"

It depends on one's perspective.

"Now, what am I to do?"

You will continue to follow the lives of the McCabe family and wait for me to return Martha and Molly to the fold. You should expect this to happen several times in many years to come.

"How many years?"

Patience, Hannah. Patience. Nine years have passed since you last visited the McCabe household. Now that the twins have each had another turn at the wheel, it is time you return to watch over them.

"Thy will be done."

*   *   *

In April 1912, Peter's business had moved from selling and servicing horse-drawn transports and bicycles to gas-propelled motorbikes and motorcars. Although the Ford Model T is his best-selling vehicle, Peter's promise to all customers was that he would deliver any car they desired. This pledge was part of the reason McCabe Motors had grown to be the largest motorcar dealership in Portland, as well as the State of Maine. For his family's personal use, Peter preferred the 1912 Chalmers Touring Car.

Peter's son, Abe, was now eighteen years old and infatuated with airplanes. The spark of his interest occurred in 1903 when he witnessed the Wright brothers' first powered flight. This spark turned into a flame after reading a story about the 1910 Air Meet in Los Angeles. There, Louis Paulhan had set a new flight record by carrying a passenger 110 miles in less than two hours.

Noting the feat was completed in a Farman biplane, Abe searched for a local pilot who knew how to fly the French-made aircraft. Without the support of his family to pursue this high-risk endeavor, he took flight lessons on the sly from this man. After only six lessons, Abe could fly the airplane without his instructor's guidance.

In addition to his passion for mechanical transportation, Abe had another love, Nettie Ross. The two had been courting since they were sixteen. Now eager to start their lives as husband and wife, the young couple were married in the courtyard behind his family's mansion.

Unlike Abe's mother, Nettie was a wide-shouldered, big-boned brunette who was very outspoken. Although not named after Nettie Sanford Chapin, the leader of the National Equal Rights Party, she endeavored to fashion herself after the activist. Thus, Abe's bride was a staunch supporter of the women's suffrage movement and often steered conversations towards her cause.

Nettie believed women should have the same rights as men, including the right to vote. Abe loved Nettie despite her rebellious thinking and hoped she would eventually direct her attention towards more traditional womanly concerns. By summer's end, his wish was partially granted. Nettie was pregnant.

✳   ✳   ✳

With their husbands busy at work, Danielle and Nettie were enjoying a morning cup of coffee in the sitting room. Gazing out the window, Danielle took in the signs of spring. The last snowfall had melted, and daffodils, tulips, and crocuses had awoken from their sleep. People out for a walk had discarded their heavy coats and scarfs, trading them for lighter, more colorful outerwear.

Nettie turned to her mother-in-law. "I can't remember when I've seen my husband this excited," she said.

"I can," Danielle said. "This always happens when a new toy arrives at the shop. They're like children on Christmas morning."

"I know what you mean." Nettie reached out to a tray of pastries. "Abe calls it his *play-day*. He mentioned a customer had requested a 1913 Stutz Bearcat and it had arrived last night from Indianapolis. After prepping the vehicle this morning, he and his father plan to take it out on a test-drive before delivering it to its new owner."

Noticing Nettie gobbling her third pastry, Danielle smiled. "Are you eating for two or three?"

Nettie patted her belly. "One baby at a time is enough for me."

Returning to the topic at hand, Danielle said, "Peter couldn't wait to get behind the wheel. Usually, I tune him out when he starts raving about a new car. This time, for whatever reason, I recall him saying …" She cleared her throat and tried to sound like him. "'In 1911, the Bearcat's racer prototype came in 11th during the inaugural Indianapolis 500 race. The following year it was converted into a roadworthy version for the public.'"

Nettie laughed. "Abe said the same to me. He added …" She also cleared her throat. "'This Bearcat is fire engine red with two bucket seats! It has no convertible top or windshield! I love the low-slung chassis! If only it had wings …'"

Both women laughed, nearly spilling their coffee.

Danielle said, "I asked Peter if he would take us for a ride in the new car. He replied with something like this … 'With Nettie bursting at the seams, the bumpy road would not be good for her. She'd have the baby right on the leather seats of the new Bearcat. I don't think the owner would appreciate that.'"

"He has a point," Nettie said. "Maybe they'll give us a honk when they drive by the house."

Danielle's tone turned serious when she asked, "How are you feeling?"

"I feel fat and look like a bloated fish," replied Nettie. "Last night, I dreamed I was a dirigible floating over Casco Bay and I exploded. Then, out of the blast came my baby. Anyway, the doctor said I should have the baby within the next few days. Do you have any last-minute advice for your daughter-in-law?"

Danielle wondered if she should tell Nettie about the ghost twins' sudden appearance after Abe was born. She quickly discarded the thought because they had not returned when her daughter, Michelle, was born. She shook her head. "No, none at all."

Loud honking from a passing vehicle caused the women to look out the window towards the street. In a quick glimpse, they saw their husbands waving as they zoomed by.

✳   ✳   ✳

God's bell rang in my head. This time the sound came with information about Seth Stoker, my husband's diabolical half brother.

✳   ✳   ✳

Upon his return to Portland, Seth learned the McLellan twins were no longer alive. The official story regarding their deaths was suicide by poisoning. He, however, sided with the rumors which intimated they killed each other. He also learned the grandparents of John Clarke had died from influenza. With the objects of his revenge no longer available, Seth turned his attention to their descendants.

Seth was not an idle man. While building a legitimate real estate business in Portland, he had gained the respected stature he had never known as Seth Clarke. Now, at sixty-seven, time was running out for him to take his revenge on the families who kept him from collecting what he believed was his due.

Seth used the early years of his son's life to build hatred for those who had hurt him. Damian, now twenty-three, is a willing accomplice to his father's vengeance. The opportune time to act had yet to be determined.

No plan of attack can take place without information about the enemy. Surveillance, or reconnaissance as the military called it, was crucial to the successful development of a plan. To accomplish their mission, father and son took turns walking the family dog through 'enemy territory.'

Seth found it surprising how people freely share information and gossip about their neighbors. When a passerby would make a comment about Seth's dog, he'd stop for the pooch to be petted. With just a little prompt from him, he'd open the person up as easily as one would open a can of sardines. Unbeknownst to them, they would become unwitting traitors to their neighbors and friends.

Seth decided the best way to punish the McLellans (now McCabes) and the Clarkes, was to kidnap their children. The ransom required would be equal to the inheritance stolen from him. Anguish felt by the parents would be considered as interest added to their debt.

Regarding the McCabes, no young child resided within their mansion. However, neighbors did mention this would soon change. Any day now, a baby would be born to Abraham McCabe and his wife, Nettie. As for the Clarkes, John (Sam and Hannah's son) and Claire had a three-year-old son and were expecting their second child later in the year.

While Seth walked the family dog past the McCabe's home, he

pondered which child should be his first victim. Honks from a passing car shook him from his thoughts. It was a 1913 Stutz Bearcat. Seth laughed. His fire engine red Bearcat had arrived.

CHAPTER 19

Nettie was lying in her bed with her newborn baby Charlie. He was content as he nursed; she was not because two uninvited visitors had suddenly appeared in the room.

Molly said, "I'm—confused."

"Why am I not surprised?" Martha said with her head tilted to one side.

In a strained whisper, Nettie screamed at the transparent apparitions, "What are you doing in my bedroom? What are you doing in my house?!"

"Well, we have questions, too," Martha replied. "Don't we, sister?"

"Yes—we do!" Molly replied.

"I'll go first. I'm Martha and *that*," she pointed at her twin, "is Molly. We're the McLellan sisters. Has Danielle told you about us?"

"What does my mother-in-law have to do with you trespassing in my home? And why is your neck crooked and your hair flattened on one side?"

Molly laughed. "She fell—"

Martha explained, "We met Danielle after she gave birth to Abe. Then, we stayed for a year to help her with the baby. I guess we're here to help you, too."

"I don't need your help," snapped Nettie.

"Whether you do or not, that isn't for you to decide," Martha said.

"We're here to stay until we're … gone." The twins looked at each other, then burst out laughing.

Molly looked around the room and saw it was decorated in a different fashion. "What year—is this?"

Nettie replied, "1913."

"Oh, my!" Martha gasped. "We've been gone for almost twenty years!"

Nettie pushed herself into a sitting position. She yelled, "Get out of here!"

Martha shook her finger at Nettie. "Ta, ta, ta. You're not getting rid of us that easily." She smiled. "Introductions are required. What is your name and who is your husband?"

Nettie sighed. "I'm Nettie; Abraham McCabe is my husband. And this is our baby, Charlie."

"Well, I'll—be!" said Molly, floating closer to mother and baby.

Martha joined her. She explained, "My sister and I last saw Abe the day before his first birthday and now, upon our return, we find he's married and has a baby boy of his own. So much can happen within the blink of an eye."

"You still haven't explained why you're here," Nettie said. "And why are you wearing those dirty old nightgowns?"

Martha and Molly told her who they were and why they thought they were ghosts. After a brief spat over which one killed her sister first, Danielle entered the room. She abruptly stopped when she saw Nettie and her baby were not alone.

With an air of disgust, Danielle greeted them, "Good evening, ladies."

Nettie asked, "Why didn't you tell me about the ghosts?"

"Until now, I had no idea they would return. Since you can see and hear them, I wonder if Abe can, too."

"Why do you say that?" Nettie asked.

Danielle sat on the bed next to her daughter-in-law. She explained, "When they appeared nineteen years ago, only my baby and I were aware of them. It goes to reason that, if we both could see and hear them at that time and I still have that misfortunate honor, perhaps Abe can see them, too."

She asked, "Should we tell Peter they're back?"

Danielle shrugged. "I never told my husband about the twins, and when he was in the same room with the ghosts, he was never aware of them. On the off chance Abe can no longer see or hear them, I think it would be best to wait until he's in the same room as the twins. If he is oblivious to their presence, we should keep it that way."

"I believe you'll find Abe in the library," Nettie said. "Please tell him to come to me."

After Danielle left the room, Molly said, "Shall we—scare him—when he steps—into the room?"

Martha cried, "Oh, yes! That would be so much fun."

"No!" Nettie snapped.

"No?" the ghosts asked in unison.

"I prefer you do not," she said. "If he can see and hear you both, I'd rather your reunion begins with a warm greeting."

"You're such—a spoiler," Molly pouted.

"Yes," Martha agreed. "You are a spoiler. How are we to improve our dreary existence if we must restrain from amusing ourselves?"

Nettie barked, "You can—"

Abe walked into the room, followed by Danielle. He asked, "What do you want, my love?"

Nettie asked, "Honey, how many people are in this room?"

Abe was taken aback by his wife's question. "I don't understand."

Nettie said, "It's a simple question which requires a simple answer."

"Four," Abe replied. "My mother, our baby, you, and I."

She had her answer. Abe could not see the twins. "Yes, and one of them has paid little attention to Charlie. I think it's time for you to get better acquainted with your son. Please take him downstairs and return him to me in an hour for his next feeding."

Abe leaned down and took Charlie in his arms. After he left, Nettie turned to Danielle. "We need to talk more about these ghostly twins."

"Yes, we do," she agreed. "Although they can be a tiresome twosome, the twins appear to be harmless."

"Tiresome?" Molly objected.

"You are!" Martha retorted.

Nettie shouted, "You both are!"

Danielle smiled as she left the room. Hopefully, Abe needed her help with Charlie.

✳   ✳   ✳

April 1913, one month later. The first month passed without any serious disputes between the twins. Both ghosts had tried, with some success, to be on their best behavior as they attempted to understand their situation.

Peter and Abe were at work, Danielle was shopping, and baby Charlie was sleeping in the nursery. In the sitting room, Nettie put her feet up and tried to enjoy a respite of solitude. A fleeting moment later the two ghosts floated into the room. Nettie let out a big sigh. "What is it now?"

Martha scrunched her nose. "Tsk-tsk, such a pleasant greeting."

Molly flared her nostrils. "Humph! —You'd think—we were—a nuisance."

"I'm sorry," Nettie apologized. "I was just …"

"We can come back later if you wish," Martha offered.

Nettie frowned. "Why are you being so nice to me? You must want something …"

"We want your help," Martha said. "Molly and I each had a frightful *experience* between the time we left and when we returned."

"It was more—than frightful!" Molly cried. "It felt—real!"

Nettie sighed. "What is it that scared you two?"

Martha took a deep breath. She explained, "When we left here nineteen years ago, everything went black for me. Suddenly, I could hear women talking. I opened my eyes and found I was lying on a bunk deep in the bowels of a huge ship! I soon discovered I was inside a young woman by the name of Meagan Turner. She, we, spent the entire day cleaning passenger cabins, making beds, and, and, and cleaning toilets!"

Molly snickered. "That's—horrible."

Martha continued, "I say *we* because I was suffering everything that was happening to Meagan. In the middle of the night, we were jarred awake by people screaming. It was a pure panic as they pushed and shoved each other to get topside. Of course, we followed the hysterical idiots up to the top deck. And what did we find? The ship had hit an iceberg, and people were desperately boarding lifeboats. Then, the ship tilted, causing us to slide back towards the propellers. There were gigantic explosions and people frantically jumped off the ship! Just before we were to fall into the spinning propeller blades, the ship ripped in two! The last thing I remember was plunging into the icy ocean. It was—"

"Mine—was a total—nightmare!" Molly interrupted. "I was fourteen—and my name—was Kate Malone."

Molly went on to describe Kate as being a seamstress who made women's blouses, which all the women were calling shirtwaists. She worked nine hours every day and was paid only fifteen cents an hour.

"Fifteen cents an hour? That's ghastly!" her sister exclaimed.

"It got—worse!" Molly cried. She further explained there were over two hundred women working in the factory, which was in the top floors of a tall building in New York City. Kate was on the tenth floor when a fire broke out two floors below. Molly recalled Kate running to an exit only to find the door had been locked from the outside. With flames licking at her heels, the only escape was to climb a ladder to the roof. Firefighters came but could not save them. When Kate's hair and clothes caught fire, Molly felt Kate's fear and pain as it burned her flesh.

Molly said, "Whether she heard—me, or not—I told her—to fly. —She did—just that. —Kate jumped off—the roof!"

Martha laughed.

"What's so—funny?" Molly asked.

"We seem to have a habit of jumping to our demise."

"Humph!" Molly said. "Like Martha—after I jumped —I appeared here—staring at you—and the baby."

"I believe you both experienced real-life tragedies." Nettie explained, "Martha, the disaster you described happened to the ocean liner *Titanic*. It hit an iceberg in April 1912, and of the more than 2200 people aboard, 1500 died. Meagan Turner must have been one of those who perished."

"Oh, my!" Martha said.

Nettie pointed at Martha's nightgown. "Is that when you got those rips?"

"Must have been," Martha replied. "I didn't have them before that leap."

Nettie turned to Molly. "You described the Triangle Shirtwaist Factory fire in New York City. It happened in March 1911; 146 women and some children died that night. That must have been when your nightgown was singed."

"Oh—my god!" Molly cried.

"Yes," Martha agreed. "It seems as if someone on high is orchestrating our life after death. We popped up when the first-born McCabe male was born and then after a time we vanished. While we're gone, we lived a tragic moment in the life of a stranger." Martha whined, "Why is He doing this to us?"

Molly cocked her head. "He? God? —Is He our—puppeteer?"

"I think so," Nettie replied.

"Do you think—it will happen—again?" Molly asked.

"I guess we won't know until after the next go-around." Martha sniffled. "That is, if there is a next time."

✷   ✷   ✷

The following day, after putting Abe down for a nap, Danielle and Nettie were in the drawing room. One floor above, the twins were bickering in the hallway.

Nettie asked, "Will they ever stop berating each other?"

"I'm sorry, you'll just have to put up with them," Danielle replied. "I suffered their tantrums from the time Abe was born until he turned one. Relief only came from their departure."

Nettie said, "It's like they can't stop themselves from fighting with each other. Is it a bad habit too hard for them to break? Or is it simply their nature?"

"It is their nature," Danielle surmised. "It's what they were born to be. However, if Martha's assumptions are correct, future interventions by God will continue to happen. Their dreadful experiences between the time they leave to the moment of their return is a lesson taught by Him. At some point, they may learn that being good will lead them to a more pleasant afterlife."

"Perhaps," Nettie agreed. "Looking to the future, I can only hope I'll live long enough to see the day when Charlie has a son. Do you think we should warn his wife of the pending torment before the baby arrives?"

"Absolutely," she replied. "Charlie's wife should not be blindsided like we were when they popped into our lives."

CHAPTER 20

I confess I've grown tired of hearing God's bell. It is loud and comes without warning. But that is the device he has chosen. So, alarmed with the directive, I will watch the Stokers, father and son, as they are up to no good. It is July 1913, three months after the last conversation between Danielle and Nettie.

*   *   *

Damian Stoker flipped the sign which hung in the window on the door to Harbor Realty. Now closed for the day, he sauntered into his father's office and plopped down into a chair across from his father who was reviewing a purchase agreement.

Seth looked up; he snapped, "What's on your damn mind?"

Damian wrung his hands, searching for the best way to phrase his question without being called stupid. He asked, "Who should be the first to pay their debt to us?"

His father opened his desk drawer and withdrew a bottle of whiskey, two shot glasses followed. He filled one glass, leaving the other empty.

"That's a stupid question," Seth grumbled. "Haven't you learned anything?"

Damian flinched. "Guess not," he muttered.

The father stared at his son for a moment. Picking up his drink,

Seth tossed the dark liquid to the back of his throat. Smacking his lips, he then slammed the glass down on his desk. Damian jumped.

Seth smirked at his son's reaction. He yelled, "Who should be the first to pay? The McCabes, of course!"

"I, I had thought it would be the Clarkes," Damian stammered. "After all, you are Samuel Clarke's brother."

His father barked, "Correction you idiot, half brother!"

Damian looked down into the empty glass and wished it to be full. "Father, I, I don't understand."

Seth shook his head, then poured another shot for himself. He explained, "The McCabes inherited a vast fortune from Minnie McLellan, whereas the Clarke assets are all buried in their home, a law firm, and a novelty shop. It's simple; the McCabes can pay the ransom in quick order."

Seth tossed back the second shot and poured a third. This time also filling the glass meant for his son.

His hand shaking, Damian took hold of the shot glass and gulped the whiskey, giving him the courage to ask his next question. "So, when do we hit the Clarkes?"

Seth smirked. "After we get the money from the McCabes." He leaned back into his chair and looked up at the ceiling. "I had a vision," he said. "A tragic one at that. The Clarkes will soon suffer great property losses due to *accidental* fires."

This time Seth refilled both shot glasses. He raised his glass for a toast. "Revenge," he said.

Both men laughed, their glasses clinked and were quickly emptied.

✴   ✴   ✴

Martha was looking out of a third-floor window, her head tilted to one side. She scrunched her nose. "Molly! Come quick!"

Annoyed by her sister's command, she yelled, "What now?"

"Come, come!" Martha said. "You must see this!"

Molly shuffled over to her sister and looked to where she was pointing. She giggled. "What about—the dog?"

"No, you moron. The men!" she said. "Don't they look familiar to you?"

"Can't say—they do," Molly replied.

*   *   *

The next day, Molly was holding Charlie in the rocking chair while Martha was looking out the window, impatiently waiting for her turn with the baby. "Molly, you must come here."

With the baby in her arms, she reluctantly ambled over to where Martha was standing. "What—is it—now? —Another dog?"

Martha said, "They're the same two men we saw yesterday."

Molly looked out the window just as the men took covert glances towards the mansion. Her nostrils flared. "I think—they're up—to no good."

"My god!" Martha cried. "The grey-haired man looks much like an older Seth Clarke. And the young man walking with him could be his son!"

"Humph! Molly said. "Much as I—despise agreeing—with you,—you might—be right."

The twins kept watching during the following three days. On each day, at least one of the men was seen walking a dog past their home.

*   *   *

"We must warn Nettie and Danielle," Martha said. "Something wicked is going to happen."

Molly shook her head. "We shouldn't—get involved."

Matha couldn't believe her sister would be so oblivious. She asked,

"What if he's planning to take revenge for losing his inheritance? I suspect he blames us."

"Now you're—jumping to—conclusions." She laughed. "What could he—do to us? —We're already—dead!"

For the first time in Martha's existence, an unfamiliar feeling of caring entered her heart. She said, "We are, but the people who live in our home are not! We must tell them, now!"

Again, Molly shook her head. "Not our—problem."

Martha said, "I believe it is. Let's find Nettie."

*   *   *

After Charlie went down for a nap, Nettie took the opportunity to relax in the sitting room with Danielle. Within seconds of putting her feet up on the ottoman, the twins interrupted her break. With far more interest than her sister, Martha shared her concern.

With her eyes cracked slightly open, Nettie said, "Just once, can't you grant me a moment's peace?"

Martha ignored her. She explained, "Several years before our deaths, an acquaintance of ours died soon after birthing a child. With the aid of the child's half uncle, Molly and I tried to adopt her baby, but we were unsuccessful. Unfortunately, we believe the half uncle, Seth Clarke, blamed us for losing his inheritance."

Nettie shrugged. "So?"

"I think he's returned to seek his revenge," Martha warned.

"Hmmm," Danielle said. "If this is true, it's impossible for him to do you harm."

Molly chuckled. "That's what—I told—my sister."

"But it is possible for him to hurt you," Martha said.

Alarmed, Nettie sat up. She asked, "Why would he do such a thing?"

Martha, more than Molly, then shared what they had learned about Seth's sordid past.

✳　　✳　　✳

That night, Nettie told Abe about the two men who did not live in their neighborhood but were always walking a dog by the mansion. She lied, "According to our neighbors, these men are dangerous and are asking a lot of questions about what goes on within our household. I worry for our child."

Abe sighed. "Honey, I think you're being overly protective of Charlie. I'm sure nothing nefarious is going on."

"I am not!" Nettie cried. "And I disagree. Something suspicious is happening!"

In an obvious effort to humor his wife, Abe said, "Okay. If it'll make you feel better, I'll hire a private detective to watch the house."

✳　　✳　　✳

Later in the week, Abe reported back to his wife. "Nettie, your concerns are unfounded. The man I hired discovered you've been seeing Seth Stoker and his son, Damian, walking their dog. Honey, Mr. Stoker is an exceptionally good customer of McCabe Motors. In fact, he recently purchased a Stutz Bearcat.

"Seth Stoker?" Nettie cried, "That's not his real name! Years ago, he was known as Seth Clarke."

"How do you know that?"

She lied, "Ah, your father told me."

"Damn it!" Abe said as he slammed his hand down onto the arm of the chair. "I can't believe he didn't tell me that when we were ordering the Bearcat."

Abe rose from his chair. Nettie asked, "Where are you going?"

"To see my father," her husband replied.

She cried out, "You can't do that!"

Puzzled, Abe asked, "Why not?"

Nettie opened her mouth to respond; no words came forth. She looked down at the floor and considered the decision she had to make at this very moment. As her eyes watered, Nettie looked up at her husband.

"Because I lied to you," she replied. "Your father didn't tell me about the Stokers, nor did I witness Seth and his son stalking our house. I'm so ashamed. …" Nettie began to cry.

Abe knelt on one knee and took his wife's hands in his. Softly, he asked, "Honey, what's going on?"

She muttered, "You wouldn't believe me if I told you."

He grinned. "At least give me the opportunity *not* to believe you."

"Very well," she said. "Come with me to the nursery."

Nettie led her husband up the stairs and stopped at the closed door to the nursery. "Your mother is in there with our baby. They are not alone."

"What?" Abe asked as she opened the door.

Danielle had just finished changing Charlie's diaper and was handing the baby to Martha. Not having the ability to see the ghost, Abe only saw his mother dropping the baby. He screamed, "No!" and dove to catch Charlie before he hit the floor.

Abe crashed into the bassinette. Rolling over on his back, he looked up. Baby Charlie was hovering in the air above him. He gasped. "What kind of magic is this?"

"It's not magic," Nettie said.

Danielle laughed. "It's actually more haunting than that."

Abe stood and turned to his mother. "What's so funny? Charlie is floating in the air and all you can do is laugh at me?"

Martha said, "Hello Abe. It's good to see you."

Molly giggled. "I'm glad—we don't—have to change—your diapers."

"I can't agree with you more," Nettie said.

Abe looked around, then asked, "Who are you talking to?"

"I'm talking to Molly," Nettie replied. "Her sister Martha is holding Charlie in her arms. They are the McLellan twins." She paused, then added, "They are ghosts."

Abe's mouth suddenly went dry. "Ghosts?"

"Yes," Nettie replied. "Although you can't see or hear them, they do exist. Why don't we go to the kitchen? I'll tell you all about the ghost twins over a calming cup of hot tea."

Abe shook his head and followed his wife out of the room and down to the kitchen. After pouring two cups of tea, both sat at the kitchen table. Nettie then told the story of Martha and Molly McLellan. Finally, she came to the moment of immediate concern.

"They are the source of Seth's background," she said. "The twins are also the ones who saw him and his son watching the house."

"Although an outlandish tale, after what I've seen, I have to consider this to be real."

"It is." She paused to take a sip of tea, which had grown cold. "Dear husband, I believe more surveillance, as well as protection, are required."

He sat straight up in his chair. "You'll have it," he said.

✶　　✶　　✶

Baby Charlie loved being outside and never fussed when his mother placed him in the baby buggy. Every morning, a walk in the fresh air had become a ritual for both mother and baby. Nettie felt safe as there were protective eyes upon them as they moved throughout the neighborhood.

Two blocks away, Seth and his son scrunched down in the front seat of a stolen Model T waiting for the moment when Nettie would push the buggy past the car. As soon as Nettie walked by pushing the baby carriage, Seth silently bolted from the car, raised a leather sap, and swung it hard towards the back of her head. At that precise moment, Charlie tossed a small toy out of the buggy and his mother bent down to retrieve it.

A swoosh of air passed by Nettie's head, causing her to glance back. It was then she saw her attacker recovering from his unsuccessful assault. She screamed. Frantically, she pushed the buggy with her baby in it away from her assailant. Seth took three quick strides, raised his weapon, and … shots rang out.

Bullets riddled Seth's body, and he fell to the sidewalk. Seeing men with guns running towards them, Damian started the engine and slammed his right foot down hard on the gas pedal. Tires squealed as they left their marks on the cobblestone. By the time the private detectives arrived on the scene, Damian had already turned the corner, having left his father dead in a pool of blood.

✳   ✳   ✳

Damian returned to Harbor Realty shortly after one in the afternoon. As he unlocked the door, he saw the CLOSED sign hanging in the window. Closed on a normal business day suggested their business on that day was not normal. Damian flipped the sign to OPEN.

Standing in the middle of the office, Damian looked around, hearing only the rapid thumping of his heart. He then sat on his father's chair; it squeaked as he settled into it.

"I must calm down," he muttered, then wiped the sweat from his hands onto his trousers.

While taking several deep breaths, Damian saw his father's picture prominently displayed on the wall. He smirked, realizing he would never hear his father's voice again. Damian chuckled. No longer would he be harangued; no longer would he be called stupid.

He yelled at the picture, "Am I not a coward for leaving you on the sidewalk? No, I say. Staying with your lifeless body would have been a stupid thing to do. I-am-not-stupid!"

Damian spun the chair until his gaze fell again on his father's picture. He asked, "Who will continue your quest, dear father?" He grinned. "I will. And I'll do it better than you."

After making his declaration, Damian scanned the office for

anything which could incriminate him. Springing from the chair, he frantically looked through office files and his father's desk. Finding Seth's calendar, he erased notations which could implicate them. When finished, he took every note his father had written regarding their planned revenge, tore them into shreds, and set them on fire in a metal spittoon.

Having destroyed the evidence, Damian took the half full bottle of whiskey and two shot glasses out of the desk. He poured two drinks, lit a cigar, and put his feet on *his* desk. Damian leaned back to enjoy the few moments he had left before the police arrived. Twenty minutes later, and the bottle empty, four uniformed policemen burst into the office.

"Damian Stoker?" one of the men asked.

Raising his glass, he slurred, "I don't believe you have an appointment."

Two of the burly officers pulled Damian from his chair, spilling his drink. Handcuffs were slapped onto his wrists.

✳   ✳   ✳

Damian was shackled to a metal chair which had been bolted to the concrete floor of a stark cold room. He was somewhere deep within the police station. That he knew. What bothered him most was his pocket watch had been taken from him; he had no idea how long he had been sitting in the uncomfortable chair.

With the passing of time unknown, Damian's mind naturally wandered. He thought about his father, he thought about the life they shared together, and he thought about the life he would have without him.

A single lightbulb dangled from the ceiling, casting a light on walls splattered with dark smudges. Were they blood stains? Signs of harsh interrogations? He wondered which empty spot on the dingy walls were reserved for him.

The sound of a key unlocking the door interrupted Damian's thoughts. He watched as a man wearing a rumpled tweed suit entered; perhaps in his fifties, he looked as if he had just stepped out of a Sherlock Holmes novel. The man took a moment to stare at him, then pulled a pipe from his mouth. He said, "I don't believe we've met. I'm Chief Detective Bevis."

Damian shrugged.

The detective asked, "Damian Stoker, where were you when your father assaulted Mrs. McCabe?"

Faking alarm, Damian replied, "Father assaulted a woman? That's preposterous!"

"It is not absurd, it's the truth," Chief Detective Bevis said.

Damian chuckled. "Just where did this supposedly happen?"

"Mr. Stoker," he said sharply, "let's get this straight. I will ask the questions, and you *will* answer them. Are we clear?"

Damian couldn't tell the truth because they would surely charge him as an accomplice to his father's crime. He couldn't confess he was the driver of the getaway car. And also that, after his father was shot, he sped off in a stolen Model T and returned it to where they had left the Stutz Bearcat. After swapping cars, he drove to Kennebunkport. Instead, he had to lie. He had to share the plausible alibi he had devised during his drive back to Portland.

Damian nodded his head.

The detective took a small notepad and pencil from his coat pocket. "Where were you this morning?"

Damian sighed. "My father told me to take his car and drive to an abandoned farm near Freeport. According to him, the owner wanted to sell the property. When I arrived, no one was there to meet me. After waiting an hour, I returned to the office to tell my father of the wasted morning."

The detective looked up from his notepad. "Who was the man you were to meet?"

"Either my father didn't give me a name, or I don't remember it," he replied. "What I do recall is I was to meet a man wearing a green jacket. As I said, he didn't show. Why aren't you asking my father these questions?"

"Because he was shot dead by private detectives when he assaulted Mrs. McCabe."

"My, my father," he stammered. "Dead?" He paused, creating a dramatic moment of grief. He shouted, "They murdered him!"

More questions followed. More lies were told. Since no one saw him at the wheel of the getaway car, the police could only try to disprove the story he had spun. After three days of investigating, Chief Detective Bevis was unable to charge Damian as an accomplice to his father's crime. He had no choice but to release him.

CHAPTER 21

I asked, "God, why do You let evil exist?"

It has a purpose.

"I miss my husband."

He is on his way home at this very moment.

"Praise be to You!"

As you should. Hannah, I must warn you not to speak with him until I allow it.

"But why?"

Sam is on his own spiritual voyage. He has made promises to you, as well as to Me. And, as you well know, promises are meant to be kept. Hannah, he is not to be aware of your presence until I am satisfied he has kept them.

"Is there something I can do to change Your mind?'

I do not barter.

"What now, then?"

Although your priority is your mission to save Martha and Molly, you may also be a guardian angel to your family.

"So be it," I said.

I smiled for God had not constrained me from contacting the other members of my family.

*　　　*　　　*

It is now March 1915. Sam has been home for quite a while now. I see him, he can't see me.

When Sam returned to our seaside mansion, he assumed the family of four dwelling within our home were squatters. Soon after my husband found out he was mistaken. The four strangers are family, *our* family. They include our son John, his wife Claire, and their two little children—Daniel and Elizabeth.

It bothers me that Sam is lonely. I wish I could help him without revealing myself. It is a quandary, which I plan to resolve.

✳   ✳   ✳

Terrible twos … It was a period in a child's life where temper tantrums, mood swings, defiance, and territorial behaviors were prevalent. Unfortunately for Nettie, this described the twins' constant disposition during their entire stay.

On Charlie's second birthday, Martha and Molly vanished. Now with the twins gone, Nettie had turned to dealing with her second bout of terrible twos. For every other word Charlie spoke was *no* or *mine*.

✳   ✳   ✳

It was June 1917; two more years had passed. Three McCabe generations were sitting around the dining room table. Charlie, now four, represented the season of spring. His parents, Abe and Nettie, were in their summer season. Falling into the season of late autumn were Charlie's grandparents, Peter and Danielle—soon to become winter.

Dinner was served, which included roast chicken, peas swimming in butter, and smashed potatoes. Charlie was being Charlie as he built a potato volcano on his plate. Gravy began to seep over its side, the spread held back by the peas fenced around his creation. The boy dipped a chicken leg into the hot gravy lava.

With a watchful eye, Nettie was sitting next to Charlie. On the other side of her was Abe. When they were married, the couple were about the same size. Now, after having given birth to a child, she is much wider than her husband.

Across the table sat Peter and Danielle. Nearing fifty, they watched their precious grandchild with great amusement. A glance at Abe gave them a pause. He was deep in thought, not having touched his dinner.

"Son," Peter said, "why do you look so glum? Last year was great for McCabe Motors, and this year should be better."

"It's not about work," he said.

Danielle asked, "What else can it be?"

"Father, you may not realize this, but … when you inherited the McLellan fortune, you set forth a McCabe family tradition. It's a heritage grounded in four principles."

Peter looked puzzled.

Abe continued, "One, if possible, all McCabe generations will reside within the family mansion."

"What's wrong with that?" his mother asked. "I love having you and your family living with us. And I do appreciate having my grandson within arm's reach."

"Nothing," he replied. "Two, family members should pour their hearts and souls into the family's business. Three, the family's politics favors the Democratic party—"

Nettie slapped her fork on the table and glared at her husband. "Speak for yourself," she snapped. "I am and always will be a proud member of the National Women's Party. Just you wait and see, the day will come when *your* party supports the NWP and gives women the right to vote."

Abe had just ignited a recurring spat with his wife and couldn't stop himself from entering the fray. He said, "And you're going to fail this fall when it's put before the voters of Maine." He shook his head. "When will you stop this silly crusade of yours?"

"When will you stop toying with that damn flying machine?" she countered.

Taking a knife, Peter clanged his glass of water. "Putting politics aside," he said, "I think—"

"I will," said Abe. "And four, patriotism to country is expected of all McCabe males."

Peter nodded. "Our family has been truly blessed. We live and thrive in a country like no other."

"God bless us," Danielle said.

Abe smiled. "Amen to that." He turned to his wife. "But unfortunately, our family's bliss will be tested."

Nettie cried, "You're not going there again, are you? Women should have the right to vote. We—"

"As you know," he said, "The Great War has been raging in Europe for over three years and recently the U.S. declared war on Germany."

Nettie asked, "My husband, what does that have to do with us?"

"Earlier today I received my draft notice."

Danielle and Nettie gasped.

Peter leaned back into his chair. He asked his son, "What are you going to do?"

Abe shrugged. "Well, I could apply for a deferment because I'm providing support for our family."

"Yes, you should," Danielle said.

Abe shook his head. "I could, but I won't."

Nettie snapped, "You must!"

Turning to his wife, he said, "Honey, I can't find it in my heart to allow other men to go into harm's way to protect our family. I just can't—"

"I don't want to lose you!" she cried. "How noble is it for you to join the fight to protect our family from the evil abroad only to be lost to us?"

Abe put his arm around his wife. "Honey—"

She pushed him away. "Don't *honey* me!" she shouted.

Hearing his mother's anger, Charlie stopped dipping into Spud Mountain, his attention now on his quarreling parents.

Nettie said, "I don't want you to go."

"Go where?" Charlie asked.

Nettie pointed to her son. "I don't want our son to be fatherless. He needs you. I need you." She looked around the table. "We all need you. I beg you, please don't go."

"I must," he said. "It's as simple as that."

Nettie sobbed; Danielle immediately went to her. Peter shook his head, while Charlie looked very confused.

Abe explained, "I don't think it will be all that bad. Yes, war does put a person's life in danger, but I believe I can lower the risk by putting my valuable skills to use. Nettie, I know how to fly an airplane, and the American Expeditionary Force is in desperate need of pilots."

Nettie muttered, "This is just another excuse for you to fly a damn airplane."

✴   ✴   ✴

Soon after reporting for the draft, Abe was commissioned as a Second Lieutenant (2LT) and sent to Kelly Field near San Antonio, Texas, to join the 4th Aero Squadron. Upon his arrival, he was caught up in a whirlwind of training and spent countless hours flying a Curtiss JN-4D Jenny biplane. One month later, he was sent to New York, where he boarded a U.S. troop transport ship headed to England. His orders called for him to join a British squadron within the Royal Flying Corps.

One month after joining the British, Abe's squadron was sent to France. Their mission: to learn the finer details of air reconnaissance before heading into battle. Knowledge of the enemy's troop movement and the spotting of artillery was critical to the Allied Powers.

✳   ✳   ✳

Every night before bedtime, Nettie and Charlie said a prayer. They asked God to keep Abe safe and for a quick ending to the war. They wanted their family to be whole again.

After Charlie had fallen asleep, he often dreamed of his father flying into battle, heroically dropping bombs and winning dogfights in the air against enemy pilots. Sometimes, the dream would become a nightmare, and he would see his father's plane being shot down with him falling from the sky without a parachute. As the earth came up to meet his father, Charlie would wake up screaming for his mother to hold him.

Charlie whimpered, "Mamma, please take the bad dream away."

Holding her child, Nettie comforted her son. "Everything will be all right. Your father will be home soon."

✳   ✳   ✳

It was Christmas morning and Charlie had not seen his father for more than six months. This was a long time for a four-year-old child, and it came with mixed feelings of joy, pride, and heartache.

Peter said, "Nettie, it's time for Charlie to open his presents."

"Yes!" agreed Charlie as he scurried under the tree. The boy grabbed a present with his name on it and tore the wrapping away. Charlie sighed. It was a new shirt from his grandmother. It wasn't what he wanted.

The next present was from his mother. When Charlie opened it, he found a pair of pants to go with the shirt. His treasure hunt was not going well.

The third present was again from Charlie's grandmother. It was heavy. When he opened it, he found a box of Clark bars. Without asking permission, he ripped the wrapper off a chocolate, crunchy peanut butter bar and shoved it into his mouth.

"Charlie!" his mother yelled. "That's the only one you'll have today."

While trying his best not to lose his mouthful of candy, Charlie mumbled, "Sorry."

Next, there was a gift from Grandpa Peter. After the boy wiped the chocolate from his mouth and licked his fingers, he lifted it and found it was also solid and heavy. Charlie smiled, as he aggressively ripped the wrapping off the present. In it he found a model 1917 Maxwell Touring Car that was also a toy bank, emblazed with the Texaco Star. His mother did not appreciate the toy soldiers sitting in the front seat of the car.

Charlie's best present was a note from his father, which included a cloth eagle wing badge. It read:

"This badge is special to me because I've worn it in several battles and returned with hardly a scratch. Until I return from this war, it'll also keep you safe from harm. Touch it, Charlie, whenever you think of me. Know that when you do, you will make your father smile."

Although Charlie loved the present, he wondered if his father had just given up the very thing which had kept him from being harmed.

*   *   *

Three months later it is March 1918, and I must spin the Wheel of Tragedy. However, this time I will do something different. I will spin the wheel for both Martha and Molly. The marble chose 13 Black.

*   *   *

"I feel awful," Martha said as she scanned the small room.

The woman she had leaped into was lying in a hospital bed and Martha was feeling the full effects of her illness. Her throat was sore, she had a horrible headache and was running a high fever. Noises were coming from a closet and Martha thought she heard a man grunt and a woman moan. She wondered if the sick woman she inhabited was also delirious.

Just as Martha's new adventure began, Molly leaped into a woman who, obviously, was enjoying a passionate moment. Within the confined space of the closet, there was the scent of sex mixed with the odor of cleaning fluids. Light filtered in around the closed door and illuminated a man. The woman straightened her uniform; he zipped up his pants.

Pushing the closet door open a crack, the woman peeked into the room. She turned to her lover and said, "Thank you, doctor, for your thorough examination. May I schedule our next appointment?" She giggled. "I do hope you can fit me in."

He chuckled. "My nurse manages my schedule."

"Hmmm," she said. "Since I happen to be her, I'll put me down for tonight."

He kissed her, then gave her a pinch on her bottom. "Mask up," he said as he snapped on his gloves.

The nurse approached the hospital bed. Martha, aka the woman in the bed, noticed a prominent mole on her cheek.

"Do you think she suspects us?" the nurse asked.

"Mary?" he shrugged. "If she does, she's in no condition to complain. Thank you for your … suggestion."

Suggestion? The answer to Molly's question instantly appeared to her. It was the nurse's silent thought behind her comment. *Oh, my. You are a clever bitch, aren't you?*

While Martha listened to the conversation between the doctor and nurse, the question of who she leapt into was answered by the dying woman. Her formal name was Mrs. Michael Merriweather. Martha found the name amusing, Mary Merriweather.

The woman had inherited her parent's fortune—amassed by her father's cattle business. Although she was married to a doctor, she was also his patient. Somehow, two days ago, she contracted a deadly virus.

The nurse asked, "Doctor, what's her prognosis?"

"Not good." Dr. Merriweather replied. "Your idea for me to visit Camp Funston to observe the carnage was brilliant. In a brief period, the damn virus had killed hundreds of soldiers. Cases are now showing up in New York; I assume the highly contagious disease was transferred by men on their way to fight The Great War."

"No, my love," she said. "You're the wily one for it was you who brought back the used tissues contaminated by the illness."

The doctor grinned. "At your suggestion, my dear."

Martha couldn't believe it. The woman's husband and nurse were not only having an affair, but they were also trying to kill Mary.

Molly smiled. The cunning couple were executing a perfect plan. She sighed and thought about her not-so-perfect plan. She thought *I should've known Martha would poison me like I did her.*

"How long does she have?" the nurse asked.

He grinned. "She won't last the day. Look at her. As you can see, heliotrope cyanosis is now present. Her skin has developed two mahogany spots over her cheekbones, and soon her entire face will be blue. As I witnessed at the military camp, black coloration will spread over her limbs and torso. Listen to her breathing. Her lungs are filled with fluids. No. She has but a few hours left."

Martha was pleased when she heard the woman had just a few hours to live. *If only I wasn't feeling her pain … this leap would pass much quicker.*

The nurse sniffed the air. "Doctor, what is that peculiar odor?"

Sex. Molly laughed.

"It is another symptom of the illness," he replied. "Yesterday, she was complaining of nosebleeds, hearing loss, dizziness, and blurred vision."

Martha glanced sideways towards a mirror hanging on the wall. She saw that Mary's hair and teeth were also falling out. Although she could not be heard, she pleaded for the woman to die with haste.

"Not a pretty sight," the nurse observed. "We must be especially careful not to contract the virus ourselves."

"We've taken the appropriate precautions," said the doctor as he gave her a hug.

Molly enjoyed the lingering kiss which followed.

During their embrace, Martha saw the doctor slip a tissue into the nurse's pocket. "He's going to kill her, too!" Martha cried. No one heard her warning.

Over the next several hours, Martha felt excruciating pain. Her existence ended when the woman died.

That evening, the nurse became feverish. Because he had a new patient, Dr. Merriweather canceled his illicit appointment.

Molly stayed three days, suffering every ounce of pain the nurse was feeling. She did not pray for the woman, she only called out for the lifetime to end.

✳   ✳   ✳

During Molly's leap, all I could think about was returning to God's House to talk to Him about an urgent request. So, as soon as it ended, I shared my plea.

I said, "God, as you know, Sam is invisible to all residing within our home. Although he can see and hear those within the mansion, he cannot communicate with them. Dear God, he is a lonely man. I need your help to help him."

What would you have me do?

"Give him purpose and allow him to be seen and heard."

So be it.

✳   ✳   ✳

His command immediately returned me to the seaside mansion I once called home. I find my granddaughter, Elizabeth Clarke, having just finished a spat with her mother.

Lizzy is four and a very headstrong child. Just before bed, she was enjoying a glass of milk and a cookie. When finished, she wanted another treat. Her mother said no, an argument ensued, followed by the child stomping out of the room.

Since Lizzy was headed in the direction of her bedroom, her mother assumed she was going to bed. She picked up her daughter's dirty glass and took it into the kitchen.

Lizzy gathered her favorite doll and a blanket from her bedroom and walked back out of the room. Just then, I appeared to her in the hallway in the form of a small ball of light and was hovering near the stairs. Gazing at me, the brave little girl did not retreat.

I moved towards the stairway leading to the third floor. Clutching her doll, Lizzy followed with her blanket dragging behind her. I then moved up the stairs. Lizzy followed. When I reached the top landing, I turned and floated to a closed door. I hovered there waiting for Lizzy. Just as she reached me, I went through the door.

Lizzy opened the door and followed me up four more flights of stairs. She smiled when I told her I loved her. When we reached the seventh-floor tower room, she pushed the door open, and I vanished from her sight.

With me no longer lighting her way, Lizzy took a step back and hugged her companion, the doll she had carried up the stairs. Moonlight streamed through the windows of the tower room, shining light onto her grandfather, my husband, Captain Samuel Edward Clarke.

With his back to Lizzy, she heard him say, "I would give all that I have in this world to feel a sea breeze, the hardness of my spyglass, and the warm touch of another human being. Dear God, not having the sense of touch makes me feel so … dead. I implore you—"

Lizzy stepped forward to confront him. "Who are you?" she asked.

He turned to the little girl, surprised by her sudden appearance. She could see him! Sam is no longer alone.

CHAPTER 22

The last time I visited the McCabes, Abe had joined the war, and the family was coping with his absence. I've since helped my husband and spun the wheel for both Martha and Molly. With concern for Abe's safety, I direct my attention to him.

*   *   *

Although the United States had declared war one year prior, Second Lieutenant Abraham McCabe had only been in the fight for two months. Abe flew a British-made Armstrong Whitworth F.K.8 biplane; it was perfect for reconnaissance missions, as well as bombing runs. This two-seater plane allowed the gunner to take the front seat while the pilot sat behind him. If the pilot was wounded, the dual controls fitted on the aircraft gave the gunner the ability to continue to fly the aircraft.

Warrant Officer Donald 'Donnie' Basher was Abe's gunner. Donnie was a Cockney from East End London whose use of rhyming slang lightened the precarious situations they often found themselves in.

When flying recon, 2LT McCabe usually took to the air unprotected by other Allied aircraft. With only his gunner for protection and company, they scanned the terrain for enemy troop movement, took aerial photographs, and radioed in their sightings. After each successful mission, Abe joined other pilots to revel in their good fortune to live another day. To celebrate, it was customary to light cigars and raise their glasses to fallen comrades of the sky.

As a child, Donnie's mother read him bedtime stories filled with supernatural folklore, which included pixies, fairies, and sprites. Playing off his boyhood memories, Hannah appeared to him as a ball of light whenever an enemy plane was nearby. With Donnie sitting in the front seat, she allowed him to see her, the light. Then, she would move in the direction of an approaching plane, thus providing a timely edge to avoid an attack.

Most of Abe's missions took him over Germany's western front, and during the past two months, it had not gone well for the Allies. All the ground they had gained in the prior year was lost when, after the Treaty of Brest-Litovsk in March, Germany moved fifty divisions from the Russian front to reinforce its western front in northern France.

Spring is known as the season of rebirth. For 2LT McCabe it is a winter of despair. Over his shoulder, Abe shouted to his gunner, "What do you see?"

"Sure as hell ain't spring," Donnie replied.

Blistered by bombs and artillery shells, the war-ravaged land beneath them smoldered with death and destruction. Deep trenches fenced with barbed wire scarred the landscape as far as the eye could see.

"I never thought I would be saying this," Abe said, "but I miss seeing grass and flowers."

Donnie yelled over the engine's constant hum, "It's not the colors you miss, old man, it's the signs of life."

"Well, I'll be," shouted Abe. "Take a look to the south and you'll see a sign of spring."

Off in the distance was an island of green, surrounded by an ocean of grey and black. It was an undisturbed piece of landscape where spring had taken hold. It was a cemetery next to the rubble of a church no longer saving the souls of the living.

Abe said, "That's a fleeting sign of *hope* my friend."

✳ ✳ ✳

During the month of July, 2LT McCabe saw the tide of the war was beginning to turn. Over 10,000 American troops were arriving every day in France to face the tired, depleted German force. When flying deep behind enemy lines, Abe noticed fewer efforts being made to send supplies and reinforcements to the German front line. Reporting his observations gave hope to his command that the soon-to-be launched counteroffensive would be a successful campaign. Abe had no doubt The Great War would soon end with a victory for the Allies.

After flying scores of missions without any bullet holes in his biplane, 2LT McCabe was unmatched by any other American recon pilot. Members of his squadron claimed he was the luckiest pilot in the war. But Abe didn't think it was luck; it was providence. His fate was destined for a safe return home, and he believed it so much he had the "Eye of Providence" painted on his airplane. This brazen act caused his airplane to be noticed and was sought after by the enemy. Word spread throughout the enemy ranks; a prize would be given to anyone who shot down the Allied biplane carrying the symbol of the all-seeing eye of God.

On August 8, Allied forces began the 'Hundred Days Offensive.' During this campaign, the Allies pushed the Central Powers out of France and back into Germany. The missions Abe's squadron flew provided critical information as they moved from one successful battle to another. For Abe, it earned him a promotion to full lieutenant, as well as air medals from the U.S., France, and England.

✳ ✳ ✳

The date was November 5, 1918. LT McCabe and his gunner were returning from another recon mission deep inside Germany. With all the success they had during the past six months, this had been a normal day in the air for them; one which would end with a safe return to base with vital recon information. With a swagger, they'd join their battle mates and receive a hero's welcome.

As LT McCabe's airplane approached the French border, a ball of light directed the attention of Abe's gunner to oncoming peril. He cried out, "Shit my knickers, two Jerry flickers!"

WO Basher had spotted two single-winged German Fokker E.I fighters gaining quickly on their slower moving biplane. Providence had finally abandoned them. Abe and his gunner were sitting ducks waiting to be plucked from the sky.

✷   ✷   ✷

On November 11, 1918, The Great War ended with an Allied victory. It was late in the morning and all pilots in Abe's squadron celebrated the end of the war and mourned the loss of their comrades, LT Abraham McCabe and his gunner, WO Donald Basher.

One week beforehand, Abe and Donnie flew on their last recon mission. An hour after radioing in their report, there was only one more communication from them. With the sound of his gunner trading enemy fire and the sputtering of the plane's engine, Abe was heard shouting, "We've been hit! Oh God, I'm bleeding." An eerie silence followed.

At 11:05, the pilots in Abe's squadron lit their cigars and raised their glasses in a toast to the end of The Great War and to their fallen brothers-in-arms. When the last hoorah was bellowed, a growing roar of joyous cheers was heard coming from outside the tent. With his arm in a sling and his gunner strutting beside him, LT McCabe paraded in to join his fellow pilots.

Abe lit a cigar and described the moment two German fighters attacked their biplane. "We were minutes from the French border when Donnie spied two Jerry flickers comin' at us like bats out of hell. Within seconds, the fighter planes were on our six."

With all eyes in the tent on him, Abe paused to take a puff from his cigar. With a slurry of embellishment, he shared details of their air battle.

Donnie added, "We were truly fortunate, my friends. Although the lieutenant had a through bullet wound to his left arm, the only other injuries we sustained were scrapes and scratches after landing in a dense grove of hardwoods."

Abe continued, "In no time, we were making our way deeper into the forest. Local farmers gave us food and water and saw to our wounds. We continued our way from one village to the next." Abe laughed. "We also sampled a lot of French wine on our way back to the base."

LT McCabe raised his glass. "To providence!"

"To providence!" toasted his fellow pilots.

✶   ✶   ✶

January 1919, two months later. Nettie and Charlie were anxiously waiting at the docks when the RMS *Olympic* pulled into New York Harbor. Eighteen months had passed with a prayer said each day. Their prayers had been answered; Abe was coming home.

Thousands of family members and friends watched in the freezing cold and falling snow as the huge British ocean liner, nicknamed "Old Reliable" for its service as a wartime troopship, tied up to its mooring.

Roaring cheers rose from the men on board as gangplanks lowered into place. With blankets wrapped around them, Nettie and Charlie watched as hundreds of servicemen began pouring off the ship, most falling into the arms of their waiting loved ones.

Charlie asked, "Where's Papa?"

Nettie pulled her son close and searched the gangplanks for her husband. "There he is!" she pointed.

Dressed in his crisp army uniform with a chest full of medals, LT Abraham McCabe appeared at the top of the gangplank and waved his right arm to his wife and child. As Nettie watched him step off the footbridge, she saw he was now wearing a thin mustache. She also noticed the lit cigar in his left hand. The war had changed him.

CHAPTER 23

September 1919. Like the rest of America, the McCabes put the war-to-end-all-wars behind them and looked to the future with hope for continued peace and prosperity. Abe rejoined his father at McCabe Motors heading up sales, Danielle managed the household, Charlie started school, and Nettie was still pushing women's rights as she entered her eighth month of pregnancy.

It is a special occasion when a father is a son's hero. This was so for Charlie. Seared in his memory was the moment his father stepped off the ship with a chest full of awards and, later, hearing the stories that earned each medal. When school began, every student had a war story to tell. Because Charlie's hero was a combat pilot, he was everyone's hero.

Soon after his return, Abe bought an airplane like the one he had flown in the war, a British-made Armstrong Whitworth F.K.8 biplane. On weekends, much to his wife's displeasure, Abe took to the air with Charlie sitting in the front seat. Often, Abe loaded several bricks in the aircraft, and while flying their mission over uninhabited islands off the coast of Maine, Charlie pretended to see enemy troop movements; brick-bombs seldom missed their mark. When Monday rolled around, Charlie entertained his classmates with stories of adventure in the sky.

*　　　　*　　　　*

One afternoon, Nettie and Danielle were in the courtyard enjoying a cup of tea. It was a pleasant autumn day when leaves were turning, some falling around them. Nettie picked a fallen leaf up off the table and twirled it in her hand. Now in her final month of pregnancy, she asked, "Do you think Martha and Molly will return after my baby is born?"

Danielle replied, "Perhaps, perhaps not?"

Nettie let the leaf fly from her fingers. "Why do you say that?"

Danielle choked back her tears. It was not fair; life was not fair. The memory and hurt of losing her daughter had left a wound deep within her. She sniffled, "The twins did not return when my daughter was born."

Nettie placed her hand over her mother-in-law's hand. "I'm sorry," she said.

Danielle wiped her tears away. "If you have another boy and the ghosts do not return, then we'll know their appearance is guided by only the first-born male in the McCabe line."

"If that's so, Charlie's wife is going to have quite a surprise if she brings a baby boy into the world."

Danielle dabbed her eyes with a handkerchief. "I guess we'll have to remember to prepare her for the possibility of the twins' surprise appearance."

Two weeks later, Nettie gave birth to another son; a stillborn.

✳   ✳   ✳

God's bell rang again. It is a sound that causes me to flinch because I know something bad is going to happen. This "bad," God informed me, will happen and I won't be able to do anything to stop it. So, I simply watch.

✳   ✳   ✳

July had been a scorcher with little rain falling on the Portland peninsula. Grassy lawns were more brown than green, tree leaves became brittle, and every house and business had a fan or two set at the highest speed. When the end of the month came, a massive thunderstorm drenched all of Portland.

During the early morning drive to work following the storm, Peter and his son were discussing sales promotion. Peter said, "Owning an automobile dealership means the boss can always drive a new car. It's useful advertising for us."

Abe asked, "Why don't I get to have a new car?"

"Because you're not the boss. Yet," his father replied.

Peter continued to drive his new white 1920 Nash Touring Car towards the dealership. When he pulled into the lot, Peter screamed, "Damn it!"

The windows of all the new cars parked outside McCabe Motors had been smashed and the interiors were soaked from the rainstorm.

∗   ∗   ∗

In 1909, John Clarke (Hannah's son) and his partner, Herbert McMillian, graduated from Harvard Law School and opened their law practice. Now, after eleven years, Clarke & McMillian was a prominent business in the Portland business community.

The rainstorm had kept John up for most of the night. Although he was tired, he had an early morning appointment with a client. They planned to begin their meeting at a local diner near the office, which was convenient for him as he needed to pick up the client's file before the meeting.

"What the hell?" John yelled as he pulled up to his law office.

The large windows facing the street had been shattered and three inches of rainwater now covered the floor.

＊　　　＊　　　＊

In November 1920, four months after the night of wet calamity, I return to the people I have grown to care about: the McCabe household.

＊　　　＊　　　＊

Soon after Maine voters sided with the women's suffrage movement and ratified the Nineteenth Amendment, Nettie joined a group of Portland women to form Maine's chapter of the League of Women Voters. Still a member of the National Women's Party, she was chosen to lead the new LWV chapter.

It was Saturday, one week before Thanksgiving. Nettie and her executive committee were at the current mayor's home attending a luncheon meeting hosted by the mayor's wife. Meanwhile, Abe was home watching Charlie.

Having just finished a bowl of clam chowder, father and son were at the dining table enjoying a slice of chocolate cake. Abe smiled as he watched seven-year-old Charlie pick up his plate and lick it clean. Abe reached for another slice and winced.

Smacking his lips, Charlie asked, "Papa, what's wrong?"

Abe rubbed his arm. "Just an old war souvenir."

"You never told me how you got shot," Charlie said as he swiped a finger into the frosting on the cake.

"Your mother prefers I refrain from sharing certain war stories. She thinks you might have nightmares if I tell 'em. Poppycock!"

"Poppycock!" Charlie repeated.

"Ahh, the vote is in. … That's two against one for poppycock," Abe said. "Okay, I'll tell you how I got wounded if you promise not to tell your mother." Abe reached his right hand out to his son. "Deal?"

Charlie agreed as he shook his father's hand.

Abe rose from his chair and moved it away from the table. "Charlie, my airplane was a two-seater. Place your chair in front of mine."

Charlie did as his father asked. "What now, Papa?"

"Sit," he replied. "You're my gunner, Donnie Basher. He sits in front of the pilot. That's me."

After both settled into their "cockpits," Abe continued, "The day is November 5th. We've flown into Germany and completed our recon. Now we're flying back to the base after another successful mission."

Abe hummed the noise of the airplane's engine. Charlie joined in. After a moment passed, his son stopped humming. "Do I just sit here? Aren't I supposed to do somethin'?"

"You're looking for enemy planes, son. See any?"

Charlie shook his head. "Nope. All I see is the light over the table."

"That's not a light. That's the sun, Donnie. Careful. Sometimes they'll attack with the sun behind them. Hides them in plain sight." More humming. Abe continued, "Just as we approached the French border, Donnie yells, "'Shit my knickers, two Jerry flickers!'"

Charlie yelled, "Shit my knickers, two—"

Abe gently cuffed his son in the back of his head. "Watch your language, Airman."

"Why?" he asked. "I'm Donnie."

"Why is because you don't want your mother to hear you say 'shit.'" Abe continued humming.

Charlie looked back to his father. "What's a Jerry flicker?"

"It's a German airplane." He explained, "What Donnie was saying is he had spotted two single-winged German Fokker E.I fighters, and they were gaining on our slower moving biplane." More humming.

"What happened next?" his son asked.

Abe replied, "Within seconds, the fighter planes were right behind us. As their guns lit up, I did a right barrel roll, followed by a loop, putting us on the rear of one of the fighters. Donnie fired the machine gun."

Charlie said, "Butta, butta, butta, butta, butta. …"

His father yelled, "You got him, Donnie."

Charlie looked around the dining room. "Where's the other German plane? I can't see it, Papa."

Abe said, "It flanked us, coming at us from the side. Shoot him down, Donnie. He's gonna strafe us with machine gun fire. Butta, butta, butta, butta, butta. …"

"Which side, Papa?" Charlie cried.

Abe grabbed his shoulder. "I've been hit! Oh God, I'm bleeding."

"What am I supposed to do?" Charlie asked.

Abe continued, "Black smoke poured from our plane's engine. As it choked its last breath, I spied a French field and pointed the plane towards it. With one hand clamped over the bullet wound, I said, 'Donnie, take hold of the dual controls.'"

Scanning the room, Charlie said, "I can't see the field, Papa."

"Use your imagination," Abe said. "With wings tipping from left to right, we landed with a jolt."

Charlie held the imaginary control stick tight. He asked, "Did we crash?"

"No," his father replied. "Steer the plane towards the dense grove of hardwoods. We'll hide under their cover."

With a wide smile on his face, Charlie said, "Done, Papa."

Abe said, "After we came to a stop, the only sound to be heard was the second enemy plane circling above us. Thankfully, the tree canopy was so thick, the only thing the German pilot could see was black smoke rising from the forest."

Charlie turned his chair around. "What happened next?"

"I passed out," he replied and dropped his head onto his knees. His head snapped up when he heard his wife come through the front door. "Put the chairs back, Charlie."

Abe dashed into the foyer just in time to take Nettie's hat and coat. "Good meeting?" he asked.

"It was," Nettie replied.

From the dining room, Charlie yelled, "Shit my knickers, two Jerry flickers! Butta, butta, butta, butta, butta. …"

Nettie screamed, "Abe!"

He shrugged.

CHAPTER 24

It is now May 1927, six years and six months after Abe and his son played out the air battle in the sky over the border between France and Germany.

"Time to spin a twin. This is for you, Martha," I said. 7 Red.

As soon as the marble dropped into the hollow, the knowledge of Andrew Kehoe's life began filling my head. Although I am unsure of the reason, he must have something to do with Martha's leap.

*　　*　　*

Andrew Kehoe's life was full of tragedy. When Andrew Kehoe was a boy, one of thirteen children, his mother lit the family's oil stove, and it exploded. To put out the flames, he threw a bucket of water at his mother, which caused the flames to fully engulf her. Everyone blamed him for his mother's death. Some said he should have known water would spread an oil fire. Others claimed he started the blaze.

After graduating from high school, Andrew left the town's persecution behind and attended Michigan State University to study electrical engineering. After earning his degree, he moved to St. Louis, Missouri, to work as an electrician. Years passed before the next tragedy in his life occurred; Andrew fell from a high perch and suffered a closed-head injury. During the next several weeks, he slipped in and out of a coma but eventually recovered from his injury. At the age of forty, he married and returned to Michigan to work on his father's farm.

Life as a farmer was not a better one for Andrew. Ever increasing taxes put a stranglehold on his ability to make monthly mortgage payments. After his wife was diagnosed with tuberculosis, medical bills piled up, adding to his ever-growing mountain of debt. To make matters worse, the bank began its process of foreclosing on his farm.

While the weight of Andrew's financial obligations was driving him further towards despair, a final tragedy occurred in Andrew's life. He ran for town clerk and was soundly defeated. He blamed the townspeople of Bath for his misfortune and promised they would pay for their transgressions.

On May 18, 1927, Andrew was satisfied that he had spent several months gathering the necessary items required for this special day and set them in place while doing minor electrical work at the local school. With preparations made, he had only a few tasks left to complete before his dramatic exit from this world.

✳   ✳   ✳

Life startled Martha. All the senses she was used to not feeling were now flowing through her like a raging river. Her eyes took in the dawn of a new day, her ears the soft breathing of the man sleeping next to her.

She reached out and lightly poked the man with a finger, then stroked his stubbly beard. She grinned. *He's real. Who am I now?* she wondered.

The door to the bedroom burst open; three children ran through it. "Mommy! Mommy!" they yelled. "We're going to be late for school."

Confused by the fact she was in full control of the woman, a condition not held before in a leap, Martha sat up and pulled the covers over her cotton camisole. She asked, "Why are you here?"

The children laughed and jumped onto the bed. "Get up," the oldest child said.

"Make our breakfast," the boy's younger sister added.

"And make our school lunches," the other sister said.

Martha was appalled. "Me. Make breakfast? Make school lunches? Why don't you ask our servant to do this?"

The children laughed. "We are," the three replied.

Instantly, Martha understood she had leaped into the mother of three children, all about five or six or seven. *My god, this leap better end quick,* she thought.

Martha reluctantly got out of bed and grabbed a robe lying on a nearby chair. After slipping her feet into a pair of worn slippers, she shuffled towards what she thought was the kitchen. While the children were dressing for school, she fumbled making coffee. *Damn it. Why couldn't I have leaped into a woman with doting servants?*

While the coffee percolated, Martha searched the room for anything which would reveal whose body she possessed. An envelope lay on the kitchen counter addressed to Mr. Eugene Hart. She mumbled, "I must be Mrs. Hart."

"Right you are, sweetheart," said the woman's husband after quietly coming up behind her. The man pecked her on the cheek.

Surprised by the loving gesture, she turned to greet him. *Hmmm, you clean up nicely.* Martha wrapped her arms around him and kissed *her husband* on the lips.

"Sorry hon. I'm running late. No time for smooching. Just need to grab a hot cup of coffee."

Martha sighed and grudgingly complied with his request; she walked him to the front door of the home. Taking the mug, he took a sip and winced. He then kissed her on the lips, then bolted out the door.

While the children ate their breakfast, Martha asked what they wanted sacked for lunch. Percy, the oldest child, told her. *Imagine …*

peanut butter and jelly smeared on two pieces of bread smashed together. What is wrong with these kids?

As soon as the children left for school, Martha roamed the simple three-bedroom home looking for clues which would tell her more about Mrs. Eugene Hart. She found nothing except for a few family photos hanging on the wall.

Martha went into the bedroom and opened the door to the closet. Three plain dresses hung neatly on a pipe, all faded from washing and wear. She chuckled. *Did I just open Hannah's closet?* She chose the pink one and thought red must have been its original color.

Returning to the kitchen, Martha noticed the clock on the wall read 8:30. According to the children, school was just starting. Her eyes then fell onto the mess she had created. Martha groaned and plopped into a chair.

After several minutes of putting off the chore of cleaning the kitchen, Martha shook her head no and walked out of the room. Suddenly, a loud boom shook the house, framed photos fell off the wall. The explosion came from the direction of the school.

Martha grabbed the woman's coat and rushed outside. While she stood in front of the house dozens of people rushed by, all heading to the scene of the blast. When panic rose up within Mrs. Eugene Hart's body, Martha lost control of the woman.

Heavy black smoke rose above the treetops a few blocks away. Consumed with the need to find her children, Mrs. Hart ran towards the school. Turning the corner, the burning ruins of the school building came into view. Martha was aghast because she saw what the mother was seeing.

Bodies were lying everywhere. Some were twisted and others were in bloody pieces scattered about the schoolyard. Men frantically searched the rubble for both dead and wounded children. It was then Mrs. Hart saw two neighbors approaching her, carrying the lifeless bodies of her little girls.

Mrs. Hart lost all control of her legs, then collapsed to the ground. She wept and wailed as they laid one daughter to her left and the other on her right. Looking up in despair, she saw her oldest child, Percy, stumbling towards her in the distance. Martha felt her overwhelming grief.

Just then, Andrew Kehoe pulled up in his truck and committed his final act of evil. He detonated the explosives he had carefully loaded into the bed of his truck. Shrapnel tore through those struggling to find their loved ones. Jagged pieces of scrap metal also tore through Percy before he fell mortally wounded into his mother's arms.

Martha cried as she felt every bit of the pain, anguish, and loss the woman was feeling.

*   *   *

Because I had spun the wheel for Martha, I couldn't help but think I had a hand in what had happened to the people in Bath. God assured me that any "fault" was His. "God's will be done," he said. I confess I am getting tired of hearing those words.

To further move me away from my dark thoughts, He asked if I had noticed any change in Martha. After considering all that happened during her leap, I realized she had taken a small step towards embracing compassion; Martha had cried for someone other than herself.

*   *   *

It is June 1929, and time for me to turn my attention back to the McCabe household. Nearing sixty years old, Peter had built McCabe Motors into one of the largest automotive dealerships in New England. He was proud of his accomplishments and knew the day would soon come for the succession of the family business. Having taught his son Abe all aspects of his business, Peter's plan was solid. However, it did have one flaw not within his control: The possibility of Peter outliving his son. Abe had an incredibly dangerous hobby. Flying.

There were only a dozen men in Portland who owned an airplane and knew how to fly the machine. To bring cohesion to this group—mostly veterans of The Great War—Abe formed a flying club with the hope of putting on air shows and hosting fly-ins at a local airstrip, Stroudwater Field.

On a warm Saturday afternoon, Abe and his son walked over to greet a young man who was preparing his 1918 British Sopwith Camel for flight. He called out, "That's a beautiful plane!"

"Yes, it is," the pilot replied as he continued his safety check.

Abe asked, "How long have you been flying?"

"Three years," he replied over his shoulder.

The young man stopped his preflight prep and turned to Abe and the boy. "Did you know the Sopwith Camel was one of the best fighter aircraft during the war, and it downed over 1300 enemy planes? In fact, this baby was in several of those dogfights."

"I do know," Abe replied. "Seen 'em in action." He sighed. "Sometimes, I wished I was in the cockpit of one of these fighters and not an Armstrong Whitworth F.K.8."

The young man stared at Abe for a moment, then recognized the older man. "You're Lieutenant McCabe! You flew more recon missions than any other American pilot during The Great War."

"That's me!" he said. "Call me Abe. This is my son, Charlie."

"I'm Daniel Clarke. My friends call me Danny." He then looked at Charlie and said, "I think I've seen you at school. You're a few grades behind me, aren't you?"

"Yeah, I'm in your sister's class. I can also fly!" Then Charlie looked down and grumbled, "But my father won't let me solo."

Abe patted his son's shoulder. "All in due time, Charlie. Danny, have you considered joining the Portland Flying Club?"

"I have, but it might be a while before I do. I'm still getting to know my plane. Besides, I plan to leave Portland soon after I graduate. I want to attend the Naval Academy and become a Navy pilot."

Abe smiled. "That's very noble of you. However, I do pray you'll not be heading to war."

Danny laughed. "Funny, that's exactly what my mother said."

"You look like you're close to being done with your preflight check," Abe said. "If you wait for us, we'll join you in the air."

He grinned. "I'd like that."

CHAPTER 25

It's November 1929, five months later, and Molly's turn to face the Wheel of Tragedy. I am hopeful because I noticed a slight movement of compassion within Martha. I pray Molly will move in that direction, too.

I imagined the wheel and used my thoughts to spin it. Then I dropped the marble with a glimmer of hope it would find the right leap to move Molly. When the wheel slowed to a stop, the marble was resting in the hollow of 24 Black.

*   *   *

On October 24, 1929, the financial world had its greatest fall when investors lost more money than was spent by all nations during The Great War. They called it "Black Thursday."

During the eleven days which followed the crash, Mrs. Hulda Borowski, a chief clerk in the bond department of Sutro Brothers & Company, spent long hours in the firm's wire room confirming the depressing news to her clients. In just a matter of hours, they had all become destitute.

Making his rounds, the security guard stepped into the wire room and saw the chief clerk with her head down, asleep at her desk. Since it was nearing midnight, he walked over to the woman and frowned.

Three times since the crash he had found her like this. The guard placed his hand on her shoulder and gave it a slight shake. "Mrs. Borowski," he said.

Hulda raised her sleepy head. "What time is it?"

He cleared his throat. "Midnight, ma'am. You should go home and get some rest."

She muttered, "Twenty-eight years … that's how long I've worked here."

He shrugged. "Long time, ma'am."

Hulda stood. "Not much longer, I think. They've already let half of us go. Can't start over if they show me the door."

He shook his head. "Doubt it will come to that, ma'am. I'll lock up and follow you out."

She nodded and walked to the door leading out of the dismal wire room.

Hours later, after a fitful sleep in her small apartment, Mrs. Borowski was still extremely tired. This was not good for her because feelings of depression always followed exhaustion. Anxiety caused by the crash added to her burden of worry. She had been warned by her doctor that a nervous breakdown was likely to follow. It was a condition she once had after receiving news of the death of her husband during The Great War.

Everyone needs a reason to get up in the morning. The reason is a purpose for a life to be lived. For Hulda, as she walked towards her dismal destination in the gloom of an overcast morning, her purpose had gravely diminished.

Hulda stopped at the street intersection and looked up at the old Equitable Building. This forty-story skyscraper had been home, not her lonely apartment. At this very moment, Molly leaped into her.

Molly gasped at the sight of the tall building. Never had she seen such a structure. The woman she was now in stepped off the curb and approached the building. Pushing the door open, Molly saw the woman's reflection. Frazzled was the word which best described her.

Hulda walked to the elevator. Before the crash, a dozen or more employees would be waiting for a ride. This morning it was just her. The operator said, "Good morning, Mrs. Borowski."

"Good morning," Hulda mumbled as she stepped into the elevator car.

The man closed the elevator door and pushed a button. Molly became excited as the car began to rise, which was a far cry better place to be than in the woman's depressive mind.

When the elevator came to a stop, the operator opened the door and wished Mrs. Borowski a good day. Molly thought the woman needed more than a wish because she was contemplating suicide. Believing her leap would stop the moment the woman ended her life, Molly offered, "I'll help you, my friend."

Hulda shuffled down the hallway and stopped at the door to the wire room. Turning the knob, she entered the windowless space. The crestfallen woman put her purse on the desk, then plopped herself into a chair. Not wanting to respond to any of the firm's clients' pleas for help, she laid her head down on the desk. A long silent moment passed before she heard the voice within her head. "On with it!" Molly commanded.

Hulda asked, "What would you have me do?"

Molly replied, "End your life in a manner which will cause you *(and me)* no pain."

"I'll jump!" Hulda cried to the voice in her head.

"Excellent choice," Molly said. Her laughter followed.

Not taking her purse, Hulda walked out of the room and then towards the elevator. *Oh, goodie,* thought Molly when the UP button was pressed.

The elevator car rattled on its way to her. When it stopped, the operator opened the door. "Leaving us so soon?" he asked.

With her head down, she replied, "Top floor, please."

When the elevator stopped at the fortieth floor, the elevator operator opened the door. Mrs. Borowski didn't get off. "I've changed my mind," she said. Molly screamed.

The man shrugged, shut the door to the car, and pressed the button for the floor where the wire room was located. Hulda returned to her desk.

Molly was furious. "How can you do this to me?"

Confused by the question from the voice within her head, the woman sat staring at the wall.

Molly yelled, "Jump!" Hulda sprung up with a start. "Jump! Jump! Jump!" Molly chanted.

Mrs. Borowski returned to the elevator and repeated her prior actions. When the elevator operator opened the door, this time she stepped out onto the top floor.

Molly continued her mantra, urging the woman towards her death.

Hulda selected a room and walked to a window inside. Once it was opened, the chief clerk crawled out onto the ledge and stood. Mrs. Borowski closed her eyes and spread her arms out. She heard the voice yell, "Jump!" Leaning forward, Hulda tumbled off the shelf.

Molly began counting the floors as Hulda passed by them head over heels. Although she lost count, Molly was happy to know the leap was nearing its conclusion. When the woman splattered onto the street, her feet met the cobblestone first.

CHAPTER 26

I am back in God's House doing what I usually do. Think. This time my thoughts are of my husband, Sam.

"God? Are you there?"

I am everywhere.

"It's been so long since I've spoken with my husband. I miss him. When may I be with him, again?"

Soon.

I frowned. "Soon? For you, soon could be tomorrow, next year, or millennia from now."

Dear Hannah, must I remind you again to be patient.

I wanted to ask Him, "Why is patience a virtue?" I did not because I knew what his answer would be. He would say, "My child, patience makes your heart grow fonder of the very things you hold dear. And, while you wait, it gives you the time to ponder if these desires are what your soul truly needs."

You know me well.

I should not have been surprised He was listening to my thoughts.

"Forgive me," I said, "but I've already waited forty-two years!"

More will follow.

God has a plan for all of us, even me. I must remember this.

*   *   *

It is August 1933, three years and nine months after Molly leapt into and out of Hulda Borowski. She has joined her sister, back into the void I call Nothingness. As they wait for God to choose their next destination, I return to Earth to follow the McCabes.

✶   ✶   ✶

For eight years, Charlie had flown in the second seat of his father's airplane. During each flight, Abe looked for moments when he could let his son take over the plane's controls. Sometimes it would be for a moment and other times it would be for most of the flight. Decisions were always guided by weather conditions.

It was the summer before Charlie began his senior year in high school when Abe finally let his son take a solo flight. Abe took the cigar out of his mouth, and he said, "Okay, Charlie, this is your time to shine. Begin your prep."

Abe watched Charlie as he walked around the airplane, checking it for flight worthiness. He looked for fluid leaks and made sure every part of the aircraft was tight and secure. Charlie then pulled the chocks away from the wheels and climbed into the cockpit.

The engine sputtered, then roared to life. After guiding the plane to the end of the runway, Charlie turned it into the wind. Abe watched the plane as it passed by him, gaining the required speed to lift it safely into the air. With the end of the runway rapidly approaching, the plane gently rose and barely missed clipping distant treetops. Abe began to breathe normally again.

He watched with pride as his son flew the airplane. After thirty minutes in the air, Charlie's final test was to land the plane.

"Damn it!" Abe cried out when Charlie did a barrel roll. "That boy is getting a bit too cocky." Abe laughed. It was exactly what he had done near the end of his first solo flight.

During the remaining summer months, Abe flew second seat while

Charlie piloted the aircraft. With each hour of flight, Charlie's skills and confidence improved. Abe believed a reward was due for his son's accomplishment. He knew it would be a wonderful surprise not appreciated by his wife.

On a mid-August weekend, Charlie's reward came in the form of a German fighter plane. It was a 1917 German Fokker Dr. I Triplane. This type of aircraft was flown by Manfred Albrecht Freiherr von Richthofen, also known as the Red Baron. To own such a plane was rare, since only 320 were built. Because Charlie planned to attend Yale College, Abe had the triplane painted the school's colors, navy blue and white. They could now take to the air together in separate planes. In no time at all, Charlie would be pursuing his father in the pretense of a dogfight over Germany's western front.

✳   ✳   ✳

Five years have passed, and it is July 1938. Much has happened in the life of my granddaughter, Elizabeth. At twenty-five, she has earned a college degree and is now married to James Nelson, the owner of a small fishing fleet of three ships. They are living in the apartment above The Maine Sail, a shop she was given to by her father, my son, John Clarke.

As I bask in the pride for my granddaughter, I hear that bell, again. It is an alarm; a warning a vengeful act will soon occur.

✳   ✳   ✳

It was a warm summer night when both Elizabeth and her husband were asleep in their apartment. Bedroom windows were open, allowing a slight breeze of cooler air to ease into the room.

As a young boy, James learned about the Great Fire of 1866. It had ravaged most of Portland and was the largest fire in the country at the time. Although it happened long before he was born, James was dreaming he and Elizabeth were desperately trying to escape its spreading flames.

James awoke from his dream when he heard his wife coughing. Because her side of the bed was next to the window, Elizabeth was first to feel the effects caused by the smoke drifting into the room.

"Fire!" James cried.

The two jumped out of bed, grabbed their robes, and ran to the door of their second-floor apartment. Stepping outside and onto the landing, they saw the pile of firewood stacked below was ablaze. Quickly they ran down the stairs.

James grabbed a fishing pike and began pushing the burning logs away from the building. With no water close by to fill a bucket, Elizabeth shoveled dirt onto the sizzling wood.

The next morning, James went down to the pier and found his fishing boats untethered from their moorings. Two were adrift out in the harbor and one was banging against another boat tied to a neighboring pier.

"First the fire and now this!" he cried. "Who's trying to ruin us?!"

✳   ✳   ✳

Before graduating from high school, Charlie McCabe's senior class selected him as the most likely to succeed. In part, this popular status was because no other classmate owned a car, as well as a plane. Charlie's popularity continued during his years at Yale, causing numerous distractions from his studies.

One distraction for Charlie was college women. Because he enjoyed dating more than one girl at a time, he had gained a reputation of being a charming campus scalawag. This rascal persona caused him to finish college without earning the love and trust of a single woman. After returning home to work in his father's business, his lifestyle continued.

Another four years passed with Charlie working at McCabe Motors and flying on weekends with his father and other members of the Portland Flying Club. This all changed when, in June of 1941, a crimson red and white biplane buzzed his 1917 German triplane.

For the next hour, the two pilots put on an airshow with their vintage warplanes. After landing on the runway, Charlie and Danny guided their planes towards the hangars. Both pilots climbed out of their cockpits, walked towards each other, and embraced like two air warriors who had just returned from a successful mission.

Danny said, "Well, look who's all grown up."

"Where've you been?" Charlie asked.

"I believe the last time I saw you was when you were flying second seat to your father. Look at you now … flying an old German fighter plane."

Charlie countered, "It'll beat your old limey plane any day of the week."

"We'll see about that." As they walked to the hangar, Danny said, "To answer your question, after graduating from the Naval Academy, I spent four years as a Navy pilot, resigned my commission, and earned a law degree at Harvard. I now work in my father's law firm. What about you?"

"Yale, then back at McCabe Motors," Charlie replied. "Still single?"

He nodded. "Yeah. And you?"

"Same as you," he replied.

Danny stopped and turned to his friend. "Honestly," he said, "I haven't found the right girl to give my heart to."

Charlie laughed. "My problem is I find too many at the same time!"

After their chance meeting in the sky, Charlie and Danny became best friends. During the next five months, they took to the air on most weekends, participating in airshows and countless mock air battles, Harvard against Yale. Then, on December 7, their lives changed forever.

✶   ✶   ✶

The day after the attack, Charlie was sitting at his desk in McCabe Motors thinking how stupid it was for the Japanese to bomb Pearl Harbor. When the telephone on his desk rang, Charlie answered, "You'll get the best deal at honest Abe McCabe Motors."

"It's me. Danny."

"I'm glad you called," Charlie said. "Since the attack on Pearl Harbor, no one's thinking of buying a damn car."

Danny asked, "Are you free for lunch?"

"Hell yes, I'm free!"

An hour later, Charlie and Danny were sitting at a local diner, ordering clam chowder and lobster rolls. After the empty soup bowls were taken away and the second course served, Danny asked, "Charlie, have you given any thought about joining the fight against the Japanese?"

"Hell yes!" He slammed his fist on the table. "I'd love to bomb those sonofabitches back to Tokyo."

"I thought you'd feel that way," Danny said. "So, I made a few inquiries with my Navy buddies this morning. If I re-enlist, I'll be given my old rank as a Lieutenant. I also learned, with your Yale degree and flying experience, you can become an officer and a Naval aviator. Do you want to fly with me?"

"Hell, yes!" was his predicted response.

That day, the two friends made a pact to enlist the day after Christmas. They would fight the Japanese together. They also agreed, if anything happened to either one of them, the other would take ownership of both planes. Like friends to the end, so it would be for the two old planes from The Great War.

✶   ✶   ✶

It was early Sunday afternoon, a week after the Japanese bombed Pearl Harbor, when the McCabe family was enjoying a traditional Sunday dinner. Seated around the table were Charlie and his parents and grandparents, as well as his sister and her husband.

After a prayer of thanks was offered, all the fabulous dishes laid out on the table were quickly passed. Abe said, "I'm going to enlist. They need pilots."

"Not old pilots," Nettie snapped.

He clutched his left shoulder. "That hurt more than the bullet wound I received in battle. Well, I *wish* I could join in the fight."

"I, for one, am not going to wish," Charlie said. "My friend Danny and I plan to enlist the day after Christmas. We're going to fight the enemy together."

"Oh, no you're not!" his mother cried.

"I must. It's my duty. Dad can't be the only war hero in our family."

Although Abe smiled when he heard his son's words, they did not lessen his concern.

✶   ✶   ✶

On December 26, Danny re-enlisted in the United States Navy and was sent directly to Pensacola, Florida, for refresher pilot training. Charlie also joined the Navy but was dismayed to discover his path to fight the Japanese would take a bit longer.

The day Danny left Portland was the same day Charlie was sent to New York City. It was there where the recruit began Midshipman School at Columbia University. The ten-week training program included boot camp where he was taught discipline and drill, as well as etiquette, ethics, and protocol required by a Naval officer. During the evening hours, he and the other officer recruits sought out the women attending the university.

✳　　✳　　✳

March 1942, three months later. After completing refresher training, LT Daniel Clarke received a promotion to Lieutenant Commander and was assigned the role of flight instructor. One week later, LCDR Clarke stood before a new class of officers who had just arrived for intermediate-level flight training. "Welcome to Pensacola," muttered Danny when he spied Ensign Charles McCabe standing among the group of new aviators.

Later that day, the two met at the Officer's Club to catch up. Charlie talked about basic training and his excitement to finally get into the cockpit of a Navy airplane. Danny explained his dilemma. He wanted to join the fight in the Pacific, but his superiors had rejected his request. They felt he would better serve the Navy by using his skills and leadership experience to train rookie fliers.

"Damn," Charlie said. "I hoped we would be fighting the enemy together."

Danny said, "The war isn't over."

When a break occurred in their conversation, Danny said, "I met a woman who is a volunteer at the USO club. I've fallen head over heels in love with her."

"Finally, the old man meets the woman of his dreams." Charlie asked, "What's her name?"

Danny replied, "Peggy Preston, and I'm going to ask her to marry me."

"Damn, you're fast." He cautioned, "Are you sure? After all you've only known her a brief time."

"Charlie, she's the one I've been searching for. If she says yes, will you be my best man?"

"Hell yes! When's the wedding?"

Danny smiled. "Very soon, I hope."

✶   ✶   ✶

Two days later, Charlie confronted his friend. "Well, did she say yes?"

When Danny nodded his head yes, Charlie hugged him and immediately realized he was embracing a superior officer. *Not appropriate.* He released his friend; a hearty handshake followed.

Charlie asked, "When's the wedding?"

"Two weeks from today. War is hell and we can't wait to enjoy a bit of heaven before the war crashes down upon us."

Charlie grinned. "When can I meet your lovely bride-to-be?"

Danny shrugged. "She's busy and I'm busy, so it won't be until next week."

✶   ✶   ✶

In early May of 1942, the Battle of the Coral Sea took place. Both the Japanese and the Allied Forces suffered heavy casualties. Many pilots and aircraft were lost. Two aircraft carriers, the USS *Lexington,* and the USS *Yorktown*, also suffered heavy damage.

Danny anticipated another battle would soon follow in the Pacific and pushed to be reassigned as a fighter pilot with the hope of becoming a squadron leader. Unfortunately, his wish was granted sooner than he thought.

LCDR Clarke's orders called him to be immediately shipped out. He had no time to see his fiancée before his departure. The best he could do was to call her on a pay telephone.

"Peg, I'm so sorry," he said. "I must leave within the hour. I'm being sent to the Pacific to join the fight. I love you. I'm sorry. I'm so sorry. I must leave now."

She sobbed. "Oh Danny, I love you, too. I'll wait for you."

"We'll be married the day I return," he promised.

When the call ended, he turned to find Charlie standing next to him. "I have to go," he said. "I've received orders to join the fight. God forbid, if something happens to me, please look after Peg."

"I promise," said Charlie. "But remember, we made a pact to fight the Japanese together. I hope to be flying with you soon."

CHAPTER 27

In mid-June, word got back to the Pensacola flight school regarding the death of LCDR Daniel Clarke. After downing seven enemy planes, Danny had flown his bullet-riddled aircraft on a low flight path towards the USS *Hornet* for a landing. During his approach, he spied a Japanese Zero which had eluded the *Hornet*'s defenses and was on a direct collision course with the carrier's superstructure. To make matters worse, a torpedo dangled from the plane's undercarriage. With grave concern for the safety of his ship and shipmates, LCDR Daniel Clarke took aim at the Zero. Within seconds, both planes collided in a massive mid-air explosion.

*   *   *

Charlie was devastated when he heard the news of his friend's death. Consumed by grief, he remembered the last words Danny had spoken to him: *God forbid, if something happens to me, please look after Peg.* Charlie vowed to keep his promise.

That evening, he went to the USO Club. He asked for Peggy and was pointed to a tall blonde woman who was talking with a serviceman. Charlie crossed the room and tapped the man's shoulder.

He said, "Excuse me, sailor. I've an urgent message for this young lady."

Seeing an officer had made the request, the sailor retreated.

Peggy looked up at Charlie. "You have a message for me?"

Charlie took a step closer. "I'm Danny's best friend from Portland, Charlie McCabe."

Peggy smiled. "Danny told me you're going to be the best man at our wedding."

Charlie took another step; he leaned close to Peg's ear. Softly he said, "Last week, Danny crashed his plane during the Battle of Midway. I'm so sorry. Danny didn't survive."

Peggy fainted and fell into Charlie's arms.

✳   ✳   ✳

"Dear God, this time You took my grandson. Why?"

It was his time to join me.

"But Danny was going to marry Peggy Preston. They could've had children and grown old together. Why deprive them of that?"

I had other plans for Peggy.

I snapped, "So, my grandson dies because you have a different path for her to follow?"

Hannah, it is August 1942, two months after Daniel died. I suggest you spin the wheel for Martha.

"Uggghhh!" I imagined the wheel, spun it hard, and threw the marble at it. It chose 21 Red.

✳   ✳   ✳

Martha was crying, the image of Mrs. Hart's three dead children playing in her mind. The mother's sorrow had filled Martha's soul, a painful feeling she had never felt. Her sobbing slowed as she noticed the sounds of the carnage were no longer heard. She closed her eyes and sighed.

When Martha opened her eyes she was in a darkened room occupied by one person; Martha resided within a new woman. With great difficulty, the woman got up from the warm bed and walked into the bathroom. When she looked into the mirror, Martha saw her. *Well, well, well,* she thought. *Who do we have here? She certainly has a shapely figure. And that diamond ring, it's beautiful. But why is it on a chain around her neck?*

The honey-blonde woman's blue eyes did not complement her for they were red and swollen from crying. In fact, every time she looked at the picture she held in her hands, the woman erupted in a torrent of tears.

The sad woman moved back into the bedroom and lovingly placed the framed photograph on the dresser. Martha caught a glimpse of the couple in the photo. The woman burst into another round of tears. Now Martha found herself crying, feeling the woman's loneliness and grief.

The brokenhearted woman fell upon the bed and wrapped herself into a fetal position. It was a similar feeling of loss Martha had suffered at the end of her last leap.

The following morning, the woman awoke with the dark cloud of despair still hovering over the blonde. Wanting the woman's mood to change, Martha encouraged her to dress for a new day.

Whether or not her message was received, the woman rose from the bed with great effort. She went to the closet, opened the door, then tried on some of her clothes. Everything colorful and dressy was much too small. The only clothes that fit her anymore were loose blouses and stretchy pants. Martha shrieked, "My god, I'm—we're—pregnant!"

The remainder of the day was spent listlessly roaming the apartment, with Martha keeping an eye out for clues to the woman's identity. When they looked under the bed and pulled out a shoebox containing letters from a man, Martha thought, *Love letters?* No. These letters concerned the remembrance of another man, one who the woman was to have married. He died before their wedding vows were shared. Martha cried again.

The woman she had possessed promised to attend a dance that very evening. However, Martha was in no mood to dance, nor was the woman she resided in. They both didn't feel well and couldn't stop crying. Martha yelled, "My god, this crying must stop!"

To escape the woman's grief, Martha thought *rays of sunshine would wash the woman's anguish away.* She reached out to open the apartment door. But Martha couldn't open it; the woman just wouldn't let her. Instead, she was pulled deeper into the woman's misery.

As the clock on the wall neared midnight, the blonde (and Martha) began to feel great pain within her abdomen. The severe cramps lasted an hour before relief came in a liquid warmth upon her bare legs. Looking upon the bloody mass, the woman gasped. For at that very moment, she had lost her last connection to the father of her unborn child. Martha left her.

CHAPTER 28

In May 1944, one year and nine months after Martha faced the Wheel of Tragedy, it's Molly's turn. I spun the wheel; 11 Black.

✳   ✳   ✳

Dolce Rico was born in 1926 to parents who had left Italy behind soon after The Great War. They wanted a new life in America; New York City's East Harlem became their home. Although not the largest Italian neighborhood, it was the poorest within the city.

Dolce, meaning *sweet* in Italian, grew up to become not so sweet. Pretty and cunning, she was driven to move out of the slum that she called home. From the time she was fifteen, Dolce latched herself to men she believed would take her away from a life of poverty. When she was eighteen, she found her savior in the form of a junior officer in the U.S. Navy. In May of 1944, Dolce Rico married Lieutenant JG Walter Caine.

Walter was attached to the Brooklyn Navy Shipyard where the USS *Missouri* was being built. In June, one month after the couple were wed, the battleship was commissioned and joined the fight against the Japanese. Following its departure, Dolce's husband received orders to report to the shipyard in South Portland, Maine.

After arriving in Portland, the couple quickly found an apartment.

Although the small rental was a bit spartan, it was far better than what she had known as a child. Indeed, life was getting better for the poor Italian girl from East Harlem.

One day, Walter came home with an announcement. He said, "Honey, I've just been made captain of a ship! It's one of the liberty ships being built in the local shipyard. Next week, I'm to sail it to England."

One week later, Dolce waived goodbye to her husband as his ship sailed out of Portland Harbor. Two days later, Walter Caine left Dolce for good when his ship was sunk by a German U-boat.

✳   ✳   ✳

Dolce had been a single woman for slightly over a year. During this time, she "prospected for gold" at local bars and the USO Club. That's what she called it as she searched for an officer with gold buttons on his uniform. It didn't matter if the man were a sailor or a soldier, what mattered was to find a man who could give her what she wanted … a better life.

Dolce was a woman with a fine figure, deep brown hair, and matching eyes. Not wanting to display any of her Italian heritage (because of the war), she dyed her hair blonde and was now going by the nickname, Candy.

Like most nights, Candy Caine went out to strike it rich. She slithered into the nightclub searching for her next hope. Her eyes set on a man wearing a yellow zoot suit with wide lapels and grey pinstripes. A purple silk tie, yellow fedora hat, and white spats completed his dapper outfit. He looked rich, and was tall, dark, and very handsome. Although not gold, she would accept yellow for tonight. With a smile and slight nod of her head, she beckoned the man to come to her.

Several drinks later, Candy had learned his name was Angelo Merino. He was in Portland looking to invest his money in a new venture. Candy considered her prospect and hoped to be his new investment. She thought, *He must have money, and a lot of it. His family's influence must be the reason he's not overseas fighting the war.*

Candy believed she had found gold and decided to take her next step to mine it. "Care to walk me home?" she asked.

Ten minutes later, Angelo Merino was taking the wrapper off his Candy.

✳   ✳   ✳

Molly found herself in a naked woman and a man was hovering over her, kissing every part of her. "This is Heaven," Molly moaned. She had just leaped into a woman who was making love to a very handsome man. *It's about time these leaps got better. Ooh, twice more? This man is insatiable!* Exhausted, Candy (Molly) fell asleep.

Hours later, the sun peeked over the horizon. Trying not to wake the woman lying next to him, Angelo slid quietly out of bed. Although pleased to have bedded the blonde, he was disappointed because her apartment displayed no wealth.

It was Sunday morning. Angelo dressed, hoping his suit was not too wrinkled for his next stop, church. He was not going there to pray for his sins. No. He was hoping to prey on wealthy divorcees and widowed women. Religion nor age mattered not to him.

Candy opened her eyes and frowned. Angelo was completely dressed. Her disappointment turned into a sly smile as she shed the covers, revealing her naked body.

She playfully pleaded, "More, sir. Please can I have some more?"

A joyful glee eluded Molly.

Angelo took in Candy's heavenly form and grinned. After a fleeting thought that he needed to be elsewhere, the man in yellow loosened his tie.

The door to the one-room dwelling exploded off its hinges as two exceptionally large men burst through the opening. One thug pointed a gun at Angelo, the other pointed his weapon directly at Candy. She screamed and pulled a bedsheet over her breasts.

"Shut up!" said the first man as he placed the tip of the barrel on Candy's forehead. Muffled whimpers replaced her screams.

Angelo raised his hands. "Guys. I know why you are here. I just need a few more days."

"Days? Already had several weeks," said the second man pointing a gun at Angelo. "Thought you could run out on my boss; thought we wouldn't find you in Portland. He wants his money now."

Angelo shrugged. "Sorry. No can do. But if you give me three more days to—"

The second man grinned. "The boss said to cancel your debt if you're not able to pay."

Angelo smiled. *Debt forgiven? Well, this is a fine turn of events.*

Church bells rang as the gunman fired three shots into the zoot suit. Angelo expired. Candy screamed. Molly had nowhere to go.

"Lady, we told ya to shut up!" said the first man. Another church bell rang as a bullet entered her brain.

As per their boss's orders, the two thugs did not leave Angelo where his body lay because he had not reached his destination. They grabbed hold of his limbs, dragged him out of the apartment, and deposited him in a stench-filled dumpster. A brief time later, as well as a short flight later, Candy landed on top of her lover.

Although the woman departed, Molly had not. It didn't take long for the rats and bottle flies to find the dead couple. God was not being kind to the leaper. Not only could she see what was happening to them, she could smell the blood and the garbage.

"I want—out!" Molly screamed, and screamed, and screamed. Two weeks later, her wish came true when the bodies were taken with the rest of the trash to the city dump.

✳   ✳   ✳

Sitting on a rotten broken-down sofa, Angelo poked his fingers into the holes of his blood-stained yellow suit. "Damn it!" he yelled.

"No. Damn you," Molly said as she sat next to the two dead bodies. "Look what—you've done—to me."

He shook his head. "Didn't do anything. Those two thugs shot Candy and me."

Molly asked, "What the hell—is going on? Why did—those men—come after—you?"

Angelo cocked his head. "Who are you, woman?"

"Don't call—me woman!" she shouted. "My name's—Molly."

He chuckled. "Well, *Molly,* you must be dead, too. Don't know of any woman who'd be caught alive wearing that filthy nightgown."

Molly yelled, "Answer my—question!"

Angelo looked down at the two decaying bodies and then at Molly's transparent condition. He guessed they must be both apparitions, ghosts, or spirits, or whatever. … "Guess time has stopped for both of us."

Molly said, "Time has stopped—for the living—not the dead. — Answer my—question. —Why did those—men kill you—and Candy?"

He sighed. "I told too many lies, lost too many bets, and owed too much money. … One night, I found myself walking alone, or so I thought. The same two thugs came up from behind me and pulled me into an alley. Their boss had sent them to deliver a message. After a few slaps to my face and a couple of punches to my gut, they had my full attention. The message was delivered. I had two days to pay for what I owed to their boss.

"Well, I didn't have the money, nor did I have the means and time to get it. But I had just enough cash in my pocket to purchase train fare. So, I bought a ticket to where I thought they wouldn't find me, Portland, Maine. What's your story?"

"I'm Molly McLellan—and I died—fifty years ago. —Once in a while—God, or whoever—puts me into—another person. —Call them leaps—jumps, or hops. —Anyway, —He dumps me—into a person—who is living—the worst day—of their life. —Guess I fell—into her. Molly laughed. "Stupid name—Candy Caine."

Angelo leaned forward on the sofa. "What in the hell is wrong with you? Can't you say a complete sentence without panting?" He shook his head. "Now what do we do?"

"We wait," Molly replied. "For Him—to make His—next move."

"Him?" he asked.

She pointed towards the night sky.

Angelo ran out of things to say to Molly, and she had nothing more to say to him. He lay back and put his feet up on one arm of the rotting sofa and began to hum.

The ghost loved tunes of the 1940s. His favorite was now playing in his head, a song made famous by The Glen Miller Band. Angelo sat up, his feet tapping the beat as his head bounced along with the vibrant melody.

Suddenly, this portion of the dump became his stage. He jumped up off the sofa and moved to the imaginary music. With a grand gesture, he announced, "Ladies and gentlemen, I give you me!"

The imaginary band continued to play in his head. The imaginary crowd roared. Angelo stepped up to an imaginary microphone and belted, "I've got a gal from Kalamazoo." The imaginary women on the dance floor swooned.

Angelo grabbed an imaginary woman craving his attention. Her name was Candy, and she was not from Kalamazoo. But she was the last woman he had made love to. Angelo spun his imaginary treat. Around she went until her delicious figure vanished into the depths of his decadent thoughts.

The ghost fell back onto the sofa and laughed. He shouted, "I loved that pipperoo!"

Molly asked, "What's a pipperoo?"

"Not you," Angelo said and put a hand up to his ear. "Do you hear that? My adoring audience is demanding an encore." Returning to the imaginary microphone stand, he leaned into it and crooned Perry Como's "Till the End of Time."

"Stop it," she said. "I can't take any more of your caterwauling."

Angelo put a hand over his heart and feigned hurt. "Although I may be a crooning cad, I'm certainly not a wailing cat." He continued singing the song.

"Uggghhh," Molly groaned.

✳   ✳   ✳

Two months passed while waiting for God's next move. Angelo continued to sing tunes from the '30s and '40s while Molly poked her fingers in her ears. Next to them, the bodies of Angelo and Candy continued to rot.

With Molly refusing to be his audience, Angelo took to singing to the rats as they scampered about the mountain of waste. Although the vermin could not hear him, he was disappointed when it got colder. The rats had moved on to warmer parts of the dump.

When frost fell upon Angelo's *burial plot,* he decided it was time for him to take a different tack; God required a nudge. Angelo stopped singing. Molly unplugged her ears. He cried out, "Hey Big Guy! I pray for You to take me!"

✳   ✳   ✳

I had been watching Molly's leap unfold. That is, until the moment Angelo called out to God. He answered the dead crooner's call by sending me, Hannah.

Angelo waited, nothing happened. Just as he was to cry out again, a bright ball of light suddenly appeared. At first it was a pinpoint in the sky. As it drew closer to Angelo, it grew to the size of a human being.

Angelo asked, "God?"

"No," I said.

Angelo rose from the sofa and took a step towards the apparition. He asked, "Who or what are you?"

I replied, "One of God's messengers."

"Do you have a message for me?" he inquired.

I said, "Mr. Merino, He still loves you despite the life you've led." I chuckled. "Bet you want to get out of here."

Angelo said, "Immediately wouldn't be soon enough."

I took that as a yes. "Good deeds will get you closer to Heaven. Agree to do them for me and you will be permitted to leave the dump and roam the city. Care to do good?"

Angelo gave a spirited nod of his head.

Molly watched as the bloodstains on his suitcoat vanished; he also disappeared from her sight. She cried out, "What about—me? Where's—my message?"

I chuckled. "What about you? Molly, dear Molly, you've already received several messages."

Her nostrils flared. "Did not!"

I vanished, leaving Molly to linger in the waste and to ponder the last words delivered by the ball of light.

CHAPTER 29

During the next few years, I watched over Charlie as he dealt with the loss of his friend. He desperately wanted to repay the Japanese for taking Danny's life, but that would not be the course charted for him. He was to stay in Pensacola and assume the role Danny performed before he was sent to the Pacific.

The summer after his friend's death, Charlie honored Danny's request; he would look after Peggy. Not able to bring himself to face her, he chose the less personal approach, letters to Peggy.

By late fall, their relationship had evolved from caring about one another to pining for each other. This was most evident in the closing of their correspondence. For both, sincerely, regards, and yours truly, had changed to always in my thoughts and … love.

When Charlie realized this change, he surprised Peggy with a visit to the USO. That evening, while dancing with Peggy in his arms, he discovered love takes its own path. It can be a short, direct one, or it can be one with several twists and turns before it reaches its destination. Either way, when love arrives, it cannot be ignored. Charlie asked Peggy to become his wife.

In the summer of 1944, marriage vows were exchanged on a sandy beach in Pensacola. It was a simple ceremony without the company of family or friends. In his heart, Charlie knew his commitment to Peggy was also a fulfillment of his promise to his best friend.

It is now September 1945, and the war has ended. Much like a farmer's plow, it had raked the earth causing furrows of destruction in its path. However, it had also created a landscape for a new life in the form of a baby. Peggy is pregnant.

*   *   *

Charlie and Peggy were ready for their trip to Portland. The car was packed to the hilt; not one inch of room left for another piece of luggage or memento of their life in Florida. Before setting out onto the highway that would take them north, Charlie pulled up to a telephone booth standing just outside a gas station.

With a dime ready between two fingers, he dialed the phone number to his childhood home. Nettie answered the call.

"Hi Mom," he greeted. "Peggy and I are leaving for Portland today."

"I'm glad you're finally coming home," Nettie said. "We can't wait to meet Peggy. When is your baby due?"

Charlie replied, "In about three weeks. Depending on how she's feeling, it'll take us at least a week to drive the 1500 miles."

"Why aren't you taking the train?" she asked.

He chuckled. "I didn't want to leave my '41 Nash 600 behind. It's a beauty and will be perfect for the trip home. Dad will love the car." Charlie paused. "How's Grandpa Peter doing?"

She sighed. "Not well. He's already passed the business to your father. I'm glad you're coming home. Before we hang up, your grandmother wants to talk to Peggy."

"Bye mom. See you soon." Charlie handed the phone to his wife.

Holding the receiver close, Peggy said, "Mrs. McCabe—"

Danielle said, "It will be much easier if you call me Grandma. There will be three Mrs. McCabes in the house soon and this will help to avoid confusion."

"Okay, Grandma," she said. "What did you want to talk to me about?"

"I want you to know the nursery is ready for your baby. Of course, you can change the décor if you wish."

"Thank you—"

"But that's not the reason I wanted to speak with you. Nettie and I must have a chat with you soon after your arrival. We have a few things to go over before the baby is born."

Peggy laughed. "Rules of the house?"

There was a pause before she answered. "Actually, it's much different than that. It has more to do with what it will be like to live in this house after the baby arrives. Old homes do have their quirks, you know."

Peggy said, "Sounds mysterious."

Danielle sighed. "You don't know the half of it."

"Charlie's giving me a signal to finish the call," she said. "We've got a lot of miles to travel today."

Danielle said, "Have a safe trip. I can't wait to finally meet you."

∗   ∗   ∗

Seven days passed before Charlie and Peggy arrived in Portland. As they pulled into the driveway of the McCabe residence, Peggy exclaimed, "It's a mansion!"

Making light of her surprise, he said, "Aww, it's just an old house; built in 1800."

"Your grandmother said it was old, but I had no idea it would be that old. She mentioned your family home had quirks. Do you know anything about that?"

Charlie shrugged. "Old houses have creaking floors, squeaky door hinges, and pipes which bang through the night. We could have a ghost, or two, wandering within its walls. Only the Shadow knows …"

Peggy laughed. "You've been listening to too many mystery radio shows during our long drive."

Once the car was parked, Charlie walked around to the passenger door. Having an urgent need to visit the bathroom, Peggy had already opened the door. As he helped his very pregnant wife out of her seat, three members of the McCabe family burst out the front door of the mansion. Without waiting for introductions, Peggy bolted past Peter, Danielle, and Nettie. "I have to pee!" she yelled.

Nettie called out, "We have six bathrooms. Take your pick."

"I assume that was Peggy," Peter muttered.

Charlie hugged his mother and grandmother and then shook hands with his grandfather. Peter said, "I am glad you are home. I missed you, Charlie."

"Glad to be back in Portland. Where's Dad?"

"He's at the dealership," Peter replied. "Should be home within the hour."

Meanwhile, Peggy had found the bathroom and freshened up. Taking a deep breath, she stepped out of the room to officially meet her new family.

✴   ✴   ✴

Afternoon tea was a daily event introduced to Danielle by the servants who had worked for Minnie McLellan. She enjoyed this custom because it allowed her to take a moment to rest during the hustle and bustle of a busy day. The morning after Charlie and Peggy arrived in Portland, Nettie invited her daughter-in-law to join her in the drawing room for afternoon tea.

Peggy entered the elegant room at three precisely and noticed three vacant chairs arranged near the fireplace. To her right, Danielle and Nettie were preparing their tea. After taking pastries from the tea cart, both turned to her and smiled.

Danielle said, "Grab some refreshments and take a seat by the fireplace."

Peggy nodded and soon joined them. An awkward moment of

silence followed before Danielle said, "Peggy, it's so nice to have you and Charlie living with us."

Peggy said, "I'm extremely grateful to you for having us." She patted her tummy. "It'll be nice to have help with the baby."

"You may have more help than you can imagine," Nettie quipped.

Danielle shot her daughter-in-law a disapproving look, then turned to Peggy. "My dear, that's the reason for this little chat."

Peggy took a sip of tea, then bit into her biscuit. Crumbs fell onto her belly, not able to find her lap. She said, "I'm not sure I understand."

"Let's start with a question," Nettie said. "Peggy, do you believe in ghosts?"

She stiffened. "Is this house haunted?"

"Yes," Nettie replied.

"No," Danielle countered.

Peggy frowned. "Which is it? Yes or no?"

Danielle sighed. "It's both. Give me a moment to explain. … Before my husband and I came to live in this home, it belonged to Mayor Jacob McLellan and his wife, Minnie. After the mayor died, all his holdings went to his wife. Then, after her daughters murdered each other—"

"Murdered?" Peggy asked.

Nettie laughed. "We'll save that story for another time."

Danielle continued, "After the death of their daughters, Minnie bequeathed her entire fortune, including the mansion we live in, to my husband. Peter was her favorite nephew."

Peggy glared. "So, who's haunting this house?"

"The McLellan twins, Martha and Molly," Danielle replied. "Soon after Abe was born, the twins surprised me when they floated into the room. I thought I was hallucinating, but quickly learned they were true apparitions. As it turned out, they're just two unhappy souls who never had a baby of their own."

Peggy asked, "Did they help you care for your baby?"

"Sometimes," Danielle replied. "Mostly they fought with each other. Until Abe turned one, I had to put up with their constant bickering. That's when they disappeared from our lives."

Nettie added, "When Charlie was born, they returned for a while, then vanished again."

"Was everyone aware of them?" Peggy asked.

"No." Nettie explained, "The ghosts can only be seen and heard by the baby and his mother. If your baby is a boy, that will be you."

Peggy gasped. "You're saying, if I have a boy, I can expect a visit from two evil spirits?"

"Can't say they're evil or not," Nettie replied. "They have horrible dispositions and antagonize one another. Although they will appear wanting to help care for your baby, be aware this is often overshadowed by their selfish desire to meet their own needs. Then, without notice, the day will come when they are gone."

"Also," Danielle added, "during the period between when they departed from this house and the time they return, the twins experienced tragedy in someone else's life. We believe God is trying to teach these two nasty women compassion and humility."

Peggy wondered, "Does Charlie know about the twins?"

"No," Nettie replied. "We thought it would be best if you told him."

"Thanks a lot," she mumbled.

CHAPTER 30

On Wednesday, October 3, 1945, ninety-two thousand babies in America were born. None were more important to Charlie and Peggy than the baby who took his first breath at Portland's Mercy Hospital. To complete the birth certificate, the doctor asked them for a name.

Wanting his son to be named after his grandfather, Charlie replied, "Peter McCabe."

Peggy's gaze went from the baby she was holding to her husband. She shook her head. "No, Charlie. We've had this discussion several times before."

"Yes, but you haven't told me why—"

"I said no." She turned to the doctor and said, "Our baby's name is Geoffrey McCabe."

With a sigh and shrug from her husband, Peggy finally won the skirmish without sharing why she had chosen the name. Unbeknownst to Charlie, naming their baby boy Geoffrey honored her former lover. During their short courtship, she and Danny had watched a movie starring Errol Flynn. He was playing the role of a pirate in *The Sea Hawk*, and his name was Geoffrey. That night two other events happened: Danny proposed marriage, and she became pregnant. In remembrance of that special night, Peggy had vowed Geoffrey would be her first son's name.

*   *   *

The day after Geoffrey's birth, he became the newest resident in the McLellan mansion and would spend the rest of his life living in the magnificent home. After nursing her baby, Peggy gently placed Geoffrey into the bassinette. Her attention then turned to the sound of a woman crying just outside the nursery door.

Understanding it was her turn to face the twins, Peggy warily opened the door, then softly closed it behind her. "Stop it! Stop your wailing right now!" she demanded in a harsh whisper.

Dressed as they always were, in soiled nightgowns, the twins were floating just above the floorboards; one was sobbing. "I can't help it," Martha cried with her head tilted to the right. "I lost my man!" She pointed at the bloody spot on her nightgown near her crotch. "I lost my baby, too!"

Peggy's scowl wavered, then turned to compassion as she recalled her own miscarriage.

Martha looked at the blonde woman, rubbed her eyes, and then saw the diamond ring hanging on the necklace around Peggy's neck. "It's me! No, I mean it's you!" she said.

"What's me?" Peggy asked.

Martha cried, "You're the woman I was in just a moment ago!"

"In?" Just then Peggy remembered what she was told about their leaps into other people. She asked, "Exactly, what do you remember?"

"I was in a very dark apartment. The curtains were drawn, and I couldn't stop crying. I was holding a picture of me … I mean of you and a handsome man. Every time you looked at it, we cried."

"That was Danny," Peggy muttered. "What do you mean when you said, 'we cried?'"

"I was in you. Whatever you felt, I felt. When I, we, went to get dressed, I saw you were pregnant!" Martha sniffled. "Then you lost the baby."

"I know," Peggy said softly, tears welling up in her eyes. "That was one of the worst nights of my life," she mumbled.

Now sobbing again, Martha added, "Mine, too."

"What about—me?" whined Molly as she tried to keep her balance. "I also—had a—bad spell."

Martha looked at her sister who had one leg three inches shorter than the other. "What about you? It's always about you," Martha said. "Can't you have a bit of compassion for others?"

Molly asked, "Where's your concern—or compassion—for me?"

Her sister rolled her eyes. "What happened to you, Molly?"

Peggy said, "My baby is sleeping. Rather than having this conversation outside the nursery, I suggest we go to the library to continue this conversation."

Peggy led the two ghosts down the hall into the library. Once they floated inside, she closed the door and turned to Molly. "What happened to you?"

Molly blurted, "I found myself—in a woman; her name—was Candy." She went on to explain the woman had met a dashing man in a nightclub. His name was Angelo, and he was wearing a yellow suit. After bedding him, she woke the next morning to the sound of two thugs breaking into the apartment. Both hoodlums were mean looking and had guns. They shot her dead. Then, she found herself with Angelo in the city's dump. Both were lingering spirits until an angel came for him. "He left me—with the—rotting bodies!"

"Oh, my god," Peggy said. "That must've been horrible."

"Humph!" Martha grunted. "You always have a better story than me." She chuckled, then poked a finger into her sister's forehead. "Is that when you got that hole in your head?"

Molly slapped her sister's hand away. She turned to Peggy. "What year—is this?"

"It's 1945," Peggy replied.

Martha exclaimed, "My, my … We've been gone for thirty-three years!"

"Who are—you? What's your—baby's name?"

"My name is Peggy, and I'm married to Charles McCabe. Our son's name is Geoffrey. Danielle and Nettie told me to expect a visit from you." She stood tall and continued, "Now that you are here, let's get one thing straight. If you two don't conduct yourselves in a civil manner, I won't allow you to touch my son."

Not understanding the word *civil*, Martha and Molly blankly stared back at her. She continued, "Here are my ground rules. If either one of you misbehaves, I will withdraw privileges from both of you for two days. Are we clear?"

"Clear?" the twins asked at the same time.

Peggy stepped forward. "Do you understand my rules?"

The twins looked at each other and then nodded their heads.

Martha scrunched her nose. "Before my leap, I also had two others."

Molly's nostrils flared. She taunted, "Tell us."

Martha said, "Well, I was in a woman who lost all her children when a school building exploded."

"Big deal!" Molly cried. "I also—had two—more leaps." She chuckled. "I may—have had—something to do—with a—damn woman—jumping off—a tall—building." She frowned and raised her shorter leg. "That bitch gave me this!"

Peggy cringed. "Martha, what was your third leap?"

"I was in a woman who was extremely ill," she replied. "I recall her husband was a doctor, and he was having an affair with his nurse. I heard them talking. … Both had conspired to kill the woman." Martha sniffled. "I felt all the woman's suffering as she laid there dying."

Molly pointed. "That's probably when you got that big mahogany stain on your left cheek."

"You have one on your right cheek," Martha snapped.

"Do not!" Molly yelled.

"Do so!" Martha screamed.

"You both do," Peggy said. "Molly, what was your third leap?"

"Well, I—was a nurse—who caught—an illness from—one of her—dying patients."

Martha pointed to her cheek. "Did the nurse have a mole right about here?"

"Why, yes—now that you've—mentioned it."

Martha jumped on her sister and screamed. "That's the second time you murdered me!"

✷   ✷   ✷

Peggy soon learned she had to treat the twins as if they were children, always testing the confines of the boundaries she had placed upon them. Her demand was simple: be considerate and respectful to everyone within her home. Several times during the past six months she had taken their baby privileges away from them.

Peggy was preparing coffee in the kitchen when she heard a bloodcurdling scream from the second-floor nursery. She bolted past Charlie, who was in search of his breakfast. Wondering what was wrong, he turned to follow his wife.

Taking the stairs two at a time, Peggy hustled her way up to the second floor. When she burst into the nursery, she discovered the scream was not one of terror, but a battle cry.

Molly had her sister's crooked head in a headlock and was doing her best to remove it from her transparent body. Meanwhile, Geoffrey was trying to poke his head out between the bars of his crib to see the melee on the floor. Clean diapers were scattered throughout the room.

Following his wife up the stairs, Charlie heard his wife yell, "Stop it! Stop it right now!" When he entered the nursery, she was on the floor picking up the mess made by the twins.

"What's wrong, honey?" he asked.

Peggy glanced over his shoulder. Molly was holding an unfolded diaper, another hung from Martha's crooked neck.

"What's wrong? I'll tell you what's wrong. It's those damn—" Peggy sighed. "I guess it's time you meet them … again. Behind you are Martha and Molly McLellan. They are twin sisters. Ghosts."

Charlie turned and gasped. Diapers were floating in the air. "What the hell?"

"Hell—is right!" Molly said. "Ever change—a diaper?"

Her sister smiled. "I'm Martha and that lazy ass is Molly. She never helps with diaper changes."

Peggy stood. "Girls, you know he can't see or hear you. Now, give me those diapers."

Charlie stared in disbelief as cloth diapers glided in the air towards Peggy. "Honey, what's going on?"

Peggy motioned for Martha and Molly to leave the room. "Get out and leave us be for a while! It's time my husband learned about the two of you. When I'm done, I'll deal with your shenanigans."

The twins left through the wall onto the second-floor balcony.

✳　　　✳　　　✳

Hannah?

"Yes, my Lord."

Don't you think now is a suitable time for an intervention? A warning?

"Yes, and I have prepared for this very moment."

✳　　　✳　　　✳

"Deal with us?" Martha asked.

Molly laughed. "There's nothing—she can do—to hurt us."

Martha pointed up to the sky. "She may not hurt us, but He can."

"Good morning, ladies."

Martha and Molly jumped in surprise when they heard the male voice. A man wearing a yellow zoot suit was sitting on the balcony railing.

Martha asked, "Who are you?"

"Hello, Molly," he greeted. "We meet again. So, this is your twin sister, Martha."

Martha turned to Molly. "You know this man?"

Molly's nostrils flared. "Let's just say—we have—a history."

"Indeed, Molly." He patted the railing next to him. "Ladies, please join me for a chat."

With reluctance, the ghost twins moved closer to him.

Martha said, "You didn't answer my question."

"I am Angelo Merino. We can see each other because, like you, I'm a ghost. But I must tell you I'm more than that. Since I left your sister rotting in the city dump, I've been a terribly busy spirit."

Martha scrunched her nose. "What dump?"

"I told you—about that leap—into Candy." She turned to Angelo. "Busy?"

He nodded. "If you remember my conversation with the light, she let me leave the dump on the condition I would do good deeds."

Martha asked, "What light?"

"What good deed—are you planning—to do—for us?"

"The deed is a message," he said. "I have it on good authority your leaps may become much worse."

Martha winced. "Worse?"

Angelo smiled. "Yes, worse. That is, if you don't change your ways."

Molly whined, "How—do we—do that?"

He chuckled. "That's for you to figure out."

"You have to tell us!" Martha cried. "We need to—"

The ghost wearing the yellow suit vanished before their eyes. While Martha considered his warning, Molly flatly rejected it.

✳   ✳   ✳

Peggy shared all she had learned about Martha and Molly with her husband. He shook his head. "You shouldn't be keeping secrets from me."

She threw a stack of diapers at Charlie. "Secrets! Might I remind you that I married into this problem? While the McCabe wives must deal with the twins' antics, the McCabe men just go about their merry lives oblivious to the chaos caused by those two damn ghosts."

Charlie flinched. "I'm sorry, honey."

"Unfortunately, *I'm sorry* is all the McCabe wives seem to get from their husbands," she said. "Although you and your father were born into the problem, it's Danielle, Nettie, and I who've had to put up with those two nitwits."

Charlie apologized again.

She sighed. "Let's go downstairs and have breakfast."

After Charlie left for work, Peggy told her mother-in-law about the incident in the nursery. Nettie replied, "I'll watch the baby while you address those awful women."

Peggy went upstairs to confront the twins. She looked everywhere, but they were nowhere to be found.

✳   ✳   ✳

Although Martha and Molly were ghosts, they were still women. Having lived during a time when people were expected to have a certain amount of modesty, as well as to honor the privacy of others, curiosity of the male body was a forbidden fruit ripe for the picking. Now that they were dead and free to wander, no barriers existed to prohibit them from satisfying their inquisitiveness.

One month following the incident with the diapers, Charlie was taking his daily shower. While shampooing his hair with his eyes closed, Martha's head poked through the shower curtain. Charlie abruptly stopped moving his fingers through his hair and opened his eyes. He had an uneasy feeling; he wasn't alone.

"Yum, yum, yum," Martha said as she picked up a bar of soap.

Shampoo seeped into Charlie's eyes, followed by a reflexive action to suddenly move towards the shower stream.

Martha reached out with the bar of soap to … "Oops," she said as it slipped from her fingers.

Taking a step, Charlie's foot found the bar of soap, causing him to slip and fall flat onto the shower floor. "Damn it!" he shouted.

Charlie toweled off and got dressed. Joining his wife for breakfast, he said, "Honey. You've got to tell those devilish women to honor my privacy. I've got a bruise on my elbow because one of them was watching me take a shower."

"My poor baby. … While you're off to work, I must spend a full day with them!"

"Well, that's not all that happened," he said.

Peggy grinned. "Did they help you dress?"

Charlie overlooked her playful taunting. "Last week, while I was enjoying a soak in the bathtub, a soapy washcloth rose out of the water and floated towards my chest. I swear one of those women was in the tub with me!"

"I bet that was Molly because she's a bit bolder than her sister." She laughed. "I'm surprised her target was your chest. Don't fret, my dear. I assume she was still wearing her nightgown."

"That's not the point!" he said. "The point is, they don't honor my privacy."

Peggy sighed. "I'll have a talk with them. But that doesn't mean they won't stop their mischief."

"Oh my god," Charlie muttered.

✳　　　✳　　　✳

Peggy and Nettie were in the kitchen washing dishes. Peggy said, "Something's up."

"What do you mean?" Nettie asked.

She explained, "It's the twins … They're no longer attentive to Geoffrey and the squabbles between them have lessened. And … there are times when neither can be found, day or night!"

Nettie laughed. "Perhaps you should count your blessings."

Peggy nodded. "You're right. But I feel something's up."

Something was up. Martha and Molly had discovered life after death had given them an opportunity to observe a whole new world. There was new entertainment, new fashions, new transportation, new everything!

✳   ✳   ✳

Often during the day, the twins ventured out of the mansion to walk among the living. More often, it was the nighttime hours which lured them away. As in their past, there were parties, dances, and theatrical performances to attend. Their most enjoyable entertainment was found in the movie houses.

Martha and Molly loved watching movies as this was unavailable to them during their lifetimes. Although they enjoyed the variety of flicks displayed on the big screen, the scary movies were their favorite.

One night in August, after having sat through a double feature, the twins were on their way to a party held at a mansion overlooking Casco Bay.

"I loved *The Jade Mask*," Martha said. "Charlie Chan was able to figure out who murdered the master of the house. I knew it was the stepson." She sighed. "I wish our home had a hidden lab and secret panels."

"It does come—with murder," said Molly, reminding her sister what they had done. "I enjoyed—*The Phantom Speaks*—more."

Martha grinned. "I can see you'd prefer that movie. The phantom is a spirit of an executed murderer who enters the body of another to kill others. Remind you of anyone?"

"You leap—too!" Molly yelled.

Martha hushed her sister. "We're here," she said.

The party was in full swing with one hundred people in attendance. It was an event to raise funds for the expansion of the city's pride and joy, Eastern Promenade Park. The mansion's décor was of a nautical nature, an elegant home much like the one where the twins grew up and now haunted.

Martha and Molly mingled among the guests and listened intently to their conversations. Eavesdropping was a naughty pleasure and provided a distraction from their paranormal existence.

Behind them, a male voice asked, "Martha, why does your head list to one side? And Molly, why are you limping and have a hole in the middle of your forehead?"

Martha and Molly turned and were aghast at who they saw, a man dressed in a vintage sea captain's uniform. The twins shrieked, "Oh, my god!"

He said, "On several occasions, my wife and I invited you to visit us in our home and you ignored every request. Now in another century, you are here without an invitation. Furthermore, you have dishonored us by wearing those filthy nightgowns."

The twins were shocked to see the ghost of Captain Samuel Clarke. Instead of responding, Martha and Molly flew out of the mansion and back to the safety of their home.

✳   ✳   ✳

It was October 1946, two months later, and Geoffrey's first birthday. To celebrate, his mother placed a small chocolate birthday cake in front of him. While the whole family encouraged Geoffrey to bury his hands into the sweet pastry, Abe and Charlie stood ready to capture the special moment with their cameras.

Geoffrey stuck his hands into the cake. Then the mischievous ghosts pushed his head down into the dessert. Chocolate icing covered his face. With his sticky fingers, he combed his hair. Snap the cameras went as Geoffrey licked his fingers and lips.

Martha said, "Isn't that delightful!"

"It is!" Molly agreed. She whined, "I wish—I could eat—cake, too."

Peggy lifted her eyes from her son's celebration to address the twins' incongruous behavior. She gasped. Both Martha and Molly were fading, transforming from their transparent ghostly figures into nothing.

It is July 1947, nine months later. God help him, the bell I have grown to dislike has rung for Abraham McCabe.

*   *   *

Peter was retired and Abe was now the manager of McCabe Motors. As the head of the dealership, he enjoyed the privilege of driving a new vehicle. This year, his choice was a maroon metallic 1947 Hudson Commodore Convertible Brougham. It was the largest and most expensive all-steel car Hudson ever made.

The luxury car arrived from Detroit and was carefully unloaded from the truck under the watchful eye of its new owner, who made sure no one scratched his beautiful baby. Abe waited like an expectant father while his team of expert mechanics checked fluids, filled the gas tank, and washed and waxed the car.

Later that day, the Commodore was ready for Abe's inspection. Except for a dried water spot on the windshield, which he promptly rubbed out with the sleeve of his suit coat, he deemed it to be perfect.

Abe usually parked his car in the carriage house after work. However, this time he left the Commodore outside as he and his wife would soon leave for dinner at Portland's finest seaside restaurant. To avoid birds dropping shit-bombs onto the car's pristine seats,

Abe carefully parked his baby away from hovering trees.

He was in his bedroom changing his clothes when a black convertible approached the mansion. The car slowed to a crawl, then came to a complete stop. The driver chuckled as he lit the cloth wick used as a stopper for the gasoline-filled bottle. With a quick toss, the Molotov cocktail flew and landed in the front seat of Abe's pride and joy. The driver sped away.

An explosion rocked the mansion. With his shirt not yet buttoned, Abe ran down the stairs and opened the front door; his beautiful baby was engulfed in fire.

✳　　✳　　✳

Just as soon as I returned to God's House for a breather, I heard Him ring the bell again. This time, the alarm came with a foretelling message. Knowing I would need assistance, I immediately sent a message to my helper.

✳　　✳　　✳

I approached Angelo Merino in the form of a ball of light. As I had directed, he was lying where I had found him, on the old rotten sofa.

"Comfortable?" I asked.

"Hey, there," he greeted me. "How ya doin'? Are you as lovely as your voice? How about givin' me a little peek under the light?"

"Hmmm," I said. "Rather cavalier, aren't you?"

He shrugged. "So, this is where I'm to receive all my assignments? Can't we meet in a more pleasant place? A dance hall would be nice."

"It's a subtle reminder," I replied. "If you don't do as I command, I will send you back to this place for what could be an eternal stay."

He snapped into a sitting position. "Didn't I deliver your message to Martha and Molly? Shouldn't I be rewarded for doing a good deed?"

I laughed. "Your reward, my dear Angelo, is for me to give you another assignment."

He sighed. "What do you want me to do?"

I told him.

∗   ∗   ∗

It was a beautiful day in Portland, warm and sunny, and everyone was enjoying the pleasant weather. Everyone except Elizabeth and Katherine because not one customer had come into The Maine Sail that day.

Katherine tugged at her mother's arm. "Momma, let's get ice cream."

Elizabeth looked down at her five-year-old and smiled. Katherine (Hannah's granddaughter) was a clever young girl who, when she saw conditions were right, did not hesitate to boldly go after what she desired. Her daughter pleaded, "Please."

"Yes," Elizabeth agreed, "let's get ice cream."

Katherine squealed with delight. After skipping to the front door of the shop, she impatiently waited for her mother to place a sign on the door: BACK IN ONE HOUR.

During the summer months, Elizabeth enjoyed dressing herself and her daughter in matching outfits. Today, both were wearing yellow dresses with black polka dots. As they strolled down the sidewalk towards the soda shop, other people walking by them smiled, then nodded to the adorable pair.

Entering the soda shop, they stood in line waiting to order their cones. When it was their turn, Katherine asked for strawberry, Elizabeth chose butter pecan.

On their way back to the shop, both mother and daughter desperately licked their ice cream as it dripped from the cones. No attention was paid to the man sitting in the big black car, a 1946 Fleetwood Series Seventy-Five.

Damian Stoker smiled when he saw the girl walking with her mother; both were laughing as they licked their cones. As they approached, he instinctively pulled the rim of his dark hat down and moved his left hand to cover the side of his face. Wearing dark sunglasses with his shirt collar flipped up, he avoided recognition.

After Elizabeth and Katherine walked by his car, Damian turned the ignition key; the powerful V-8 "L-head" engine roared to life. With the car's transmission in park, he tested the gas pedal.

Now twenty yards ahead, his targets stopped to look for oncoming vehicles. Seeing none, mother led daughter into the street.

Damian chuckled. *It's gracious of you to wear something so easy to spot.* Red, he hoped, would soon become another color to adorn their summery outfits.

He dropped the gear shift into drive and pressed down hard on the accelerator. Just as he was about to slam into them, a tall man dressed in bright yellow appeared from nowhere. He pushed the girl forward into her mother's legs; both fell onto the street.

The big black car missed both mother and daughter but drove right through the vintage zoot suit. Alarmed at first, Damian shrugged because he would make another attempt to end their lives on July 27 of the following year.

No longer visible to the living, Angelo skipped happily away from the near accident. He had fulfilled his mission, assigned by the bright white light who said she loved the mother and daughter.

With skinned knees, both Elizabeth and Katherine were helped from the asphalt by those who had witnessed the almost tragic event. A man pointed to a black car which was just taking a hard left. He cried out, "The driver of that car almost killed them!"

A small crowd of pedestrians surrounded the disheveled mother and daughter. Elizabeth comforted Katherine as her strawberry ice cream was splattered, melting on the hot street.

A police report was filed, which provided no exact description of the car, nor of its driver.

✷   ✷   ✷

That darn bell rang in my head again. This time, it comes with a warning that Damian Stoker, now fifty-eight, is up to no good and an intervention may be required. The date is May 1948.

✷   ✷   ✷

I see Damian as a lonely man, with no wife, no children, and no friends to enrich his life. His heart only holds hatred for those who had wronged his father. I know this because I know his thoughts, both past and present. As mentioned before, this is an advantage God has given me to complete a mission.

Damian was living two separate lives, one as owner of Harbor Realty, and the other as a revengeful man. The business had been a cover for the misdeeds he had done with his father, the misdeeds he did on his own, and the ones he planned to commit in the future.

Using late-night hours to perform his malicious acts, he had visited the properties of his father's enemies. A fire under the stairs leading to the apartment above The Maine Sail, car windows smashed at McCabe Motors, freeing fishing boats owned by James Nelson (Elizabeth's husband) from their moorings and spreading rumors of fraudulent behavior by lawyers employed at Clarke & McMillian were some of his vindictive pranks. Damian's favorite malicious act of revenge happened last year when he firebombed Abe McCabe's brand new 1947 Hudson Commodore Convertible Brougham.

I watched as a cool breeze blew in from the bay; Damian pulled his coat tighter around him. Hidden within the bushes near an old seaside mansion, he planned his next assault on his father's sworn enemies.

Yes, I am sure at least one intervention is required to stop Damian from hurting my descendants.

✴   ✴   ✴

Nettie entered The Maine Sail and found a woman sitting behind the checkout counter. She said, "I'm looking for Elizabeth Clarke."

"I'm Elizabeth Nelson," she replied. "Clarke is my maiden name. You are?"

"Nettie McCabe. I've come to speak with you about an urgent matter."

Elizabeth frowned. "And that is?"

Nettie took a seat on an empty stool. She replied, "Back in 1913, one of your distant relatives tried to assault me and kidnap my son."

Elizabeth gasped. "That can't be!"

"This is not a wild accusation," she said. "His name was Seth Clarke, later known as Seth Stoker. According to my sources, he was the half brother of Samuel Clarke."

"Samuel Clarke is my grandfather, was my grandfather. The other names you've mentioned are not familiar. And, as far as I know, Captain Clarke did not have a half brother."

"Well, he did." Nettie explained, "Seth was a vile man. Before I go any further, I suggest you talk with your father and confirm Seth was indeed the captain's half brother, which would make him your father's half uncle. Once verified, I know you will take what I have to say extremely serious."

Elizabeth frowned. "I'll ask him about the man you've mentioned."

"Do not delay, Mrs. Nelson, for quick action is required to protect both our families. I suggest you ask your father tonight."

Elizabeth nodded.

Nettie said, "I'll return shortly after you open tomorrow morning."

After the woman had left, Elizabeth thought about her father, John

Clarke, who was raised by his grandparents. Never had he mentioned the name Seth Clarke or Seth Stoker.

✳   ✳   ✳

It was night and everyone except for Elizabeth was asleep. Trying not to wake her husband, she carefully slipped out of bed, donned her robe and slippers, then walked down the hall to the door concealing the stairway leading to the seventh-floor tower room.

Because she had done it countless times before, Elizabeth did not require a candle to light her way. With the tips of her fingers lightly touching the wall, she climbed in the darkness towards the man who could best answer Nettie McCabe's accusation. When she reached the top of the stairs, Elizabeth was met by a closed door; she pushed it open and smiled at the man sitting at a desk.

Sitting on top of it was an old oil lamp, the only source of light casting shadows about. Pipe smoke lingered in the air.

The man stood to greet his visitor. He said, "Good evening, Elizabeth." The ghost of Captain Samuel Edward Clarke continued, "Why didn't you bring Katherine with you this evening? You know how much I enjoy seeing my great-granddaughter."

"She's asleep, as I should be. Captain, we have a matter of family history I wish to discuss with you. One I do not wish my daughter to hear."

Putting his pipe down, he asked, "What is it, my dear?"

"Seth Clarke," she said.

Hearing the name spoken, the captain fell back into his chair. This was all Elizabeth needed to confirm Nettie's claim.

"I've not heard that name spoken for over sixty years," he said. "How did you come by it?"

Elizabeth explained, "A woman came into my shop and told me Seth was your half brother. She also mentioned he was known by another name, Seth Stoker."

"Stoker?" He nodded. "Yes, I can see that. … His true father's surname was Stoker."

Elizabeth continued, "Well, the woman claimed he assaulted her in 1913, in an effort to kidnap her baby boy. She had more to say about the matter but thought I would not take her seriously until I confirmed Seth was your half brother."

The captain sighed. "He was. Seth was an evil man whose gains in life came from inflicting misery upon others. I'd love to know what he was up to."

✴　　✴　　✴

At nine sharp the next morning, Nettie arrived at The Maine Sail. "Good morning, Mrs. Nelson."

"Good morning," she greeted. "Please call me Elizabeth."

Nettie smiled. "Ahh! The change in formality confirms you believe me. Please call me Nettie."

"Your claim is true," she said. "Seth was the half brother of Samuel Clarke."

"Good," Nettie said. "Now that you know of his connection to your family, you will take what I have to say as a grave warning to you and your loved ones." She paused. "On July 27, 1913, Seth Stoker was killed by private detectives hired by my family to protect us. Seth gave them no choice when he assaulted me."

Elizabeth was pleased. "Well then, Seth can no longer hurt your family, nor mine for that matter."

Nettie continued, "Although he was never charged as an accomplice, we believe Seth's son, Damian Stoker, was the driver of the getaway car."

Elizabeth frowned. "Do you think he wants to avenge his father's death?"

"I do," Nettie nodded. "I also believe he has been the perpetrator of criminal acts my family has been victim to during the past thirty-five years."

"Really?"

Nettie continued, "These acts include arson, destruction to our home and business, and rumors spread to damage our reputation. Throughout the years, these acts have occurred on or about July 27. It happens to be the anniversary of Seth Stoker's death."

"Why have you come to me with this?"

"I share this with you because of a story I read in the newspaper." She explained, "Last year, on July 27, you and your daughter were nearly run down by a car. Coincidence? No. Damian Stoker is gathering the courage to commit more heinous crimes."

Elizabeth considered Nettie's words. "Come to think of it, there have been acts of vandalism against my family's home and businesses. All of which have occurred around the same time of the year as the ones perpetrated against your family. What can we do about it?"

"We have no hard evidence of Damian committing these criminal acts," Nettie said. "Therefore, we can't go to the police. Consequently, my family is hiring private security to watch over us and our property during the last week of July. I suggest you do the same."

Elizabeth said, "I'll share your warning with my husband. I have no doubt he'll agree we must take precautions to protect our family."

"Perhaps we can use the same agency?" Nettie offered.

"Yes, let's join forces," Elizabeth replied. "Hopefully, we'll catch Damian in the act."

As Nettie was about to leave, she said, "I wish to apologize for not extending my condolences after your brother died in the war. Daniel was my son Charlie's best friend. He was also his hero."

With sadness expressed in her voice, Elizabeth muttered, "Danny was my hero, too."

✻　　　✻　　　✻

On a perfectly clear night for stargazing in July 1948, Captain Clarke looked at the heavens through a high-powered telescope. He was pleased to see the familiar stars he had once used when navigating ocean waters.

To give his eyes a respite, he stood and walked the perimeter of his sanctuary. There was a cupola on the tower room that was at the top of the seven-story house. From this perch, he could see all of Casco Bay, as well as most of the city.

When the captain stood, Elizabeth took her turn at the telescope. It was the same one used in the Portland Observatory during the early to mid-1800s to sight ships sailing into Casco Bay.

Large windows graced all sides of the tower room. When the captain moved to the ones on the east side, he happened to look down onto the Eastern Promenade. It was then he saw a dark figure moving towards the seaside mansion.

"Granddaughter, come here," he beckoned. "I believe we have an unwelcomed visitor."

Rushing over to him, she said, "It is the night of July 27, isn't it?" When she looked to where he was pointing, she saw a man in black moving from one cover to another.

He chuckled. "For all his faults, at least Damian Stoker is a punctual man."

"Do you recognize him?" she asked.

The captain shook his head. "I have never met him before because he was born long after I died. However, it is astounding how he moves like his father. If I were able to see him up close, I would bet he even looks like him."

"What should we do?"

The captain replied, "Since everyone else in the house is down for the night, I suggest we let them sleep. I am sure your private detectives have their eyes on him. But, just in case, I suggest you go down to the study and call the agency to make sure they are aware of his arrival."

Elizabeth nodded to the ghost of her grandfather and went down to the second floor. Not turning on any lights which would alert their visitor, she picked up the telephone and dialed the number. After giving her report, Elizabeth opened the cabinet where firearms were kept, selected a 12-gauge shotgun, loaded it, and quietly walked down to the base of the grand staircase. Vowing no one would enter her home to do her family harm, she took a seat and patiently waited for the night to unfold.

Outside, the man wearing dark clothing darted from one bush to the next as he drew closer to the seaside home. A 1948 Ford F-1 truck rumbled by, forcing him to duck behind a lilac bush. As he did, the pickup briefly cast its headlights on the man and the two large cans he was carrying.

The driver of the truck smiled. "That should do the trick," Angelo said. "Another good deed is another step away from the city dump."

Crouching, Damian stealthily moved to the side door of the carriage house. He knelt, then broke the door window with a gloved hand. The sound of the breaking glass was louder than expected and caused him to retreat into the lilacs.

A few minutes passed; the intruder regained his nerve. Peeking through the bushes, Damian could see no one coming to investigate the sound of the broken window. Taking a deep breath, he carried the cans back to the side door. Setting one down, he reached in with his right hand and unlocked the door from the inside. Slowly, he pushed the door open, then quickly entered the carriage house.

Damian closed the door behind him, shutting off the outside world. He took a deep breath and was pleased because nothing could stop him from torching the place so dearly treasured by those he hated.

After removing the caps from the two gas cans, he splashed the flammable liquid about. Gas fumes filled the air he was breathing. Damian reached into his coat pocket and snatched out a handkerchief, placing it over his nose and mouth. He then pulled a second item from his pocket. With a grin, he flipped the top of the cigarette lighter open.

Meanwhile, hiding outside were four private detectives waiting for something to happen. If it had not been for the headlights of the passing truck, they would have missed seeing the intruder and what he was carrying. With guns and flashlights drawn, the men burst through the side door.

Damian turned to run but saw nowhere to go.

"Freeze!" shouted one of the men.

Damian froze, then tried to light the lighter.

Four shots rang out. One bullet tore into his right arm, forcing him to drop the unlit lighter. The second bullet bore into his right leg, spinning him out of the way of the other two bullets. Damian fell to the floor. "Son of a bitch," he whimpered.

✳　　✳　　✳

After his failed attempt to burn down Elizabeth Nelson's home, Damian Stoker was arrested and charged with breaking and entering, attempted arson, and attempted murder of multiple people. His efforts to fulfill his father's vendetta had ended and the lives of those he sought to ruin were breathing sighs of relief. Damian would spend the rest of his life in prison.

CHAPTER 32

What is it about adversity, danger, and misfortune? Can't we do without them?

We cannot, for they are the very challenges which color a person's world.

"Ah, we are back to free will, a choice between light and dark."

The dark helps My children appreciate the light even more.

＊　　　＊　　　＊

I had hoped God would have a different answer to my question. But I must admit I can see how when good is followed by bad, good can have a better outcome. It is a confusing thought, but one I see unfold after Damian's demise.

For example, strangers become allies, and sometimes, allies become friends when fighting against a common foe. This was true for Nettie and my granddaughter Elizabeth during their efforts to stop that evil man.

It is October 1948, and time for me to return to see what Nettie and Elizabeth are up to.

＊　　　＊　　　＊

During the past three months, Nettie has paid weekly visits to The Maine Sail. During their many conversations, Elizabeth often tried to get her to answer one question: How did she know Seth was the half brother of Captain Clarke? Nettie's response was either an ambiguous retort or she changed the subject of their chat.

Elizabeth took one such visit to push her friend further towards a confession. Setting her plan in place, she extended an invitation to Nettie for an evening visit to her home. She accepted and arrived at the door of the house where Hannah once lived with her husband, Sam. Nettie pressed a button causing the doorbell to chime.

Elizabeth opened the door. She said, "Come in, come in."

Nettie expected to see the usual furnishings found within the magnificent old homes in Portland. To her surprise, the home was dressed in a nautical theme. Everywhere she looked elements of the sea filled the rooms.

"You have an incredible home!" she said. "How did it become so overwhelmed by the sea?"

Elizabeth replied, "My home was built in the mid-1800s by a man who obviously loved the sea. After he died, it was sold to my grandfather, Captain Samuel Clarke."

Nettie reached out and touched one of the two brass mermaids guarding the base of the grand staircase. "When was it purchased?" she asked.

"In 1883. After my grandfather and his wife, Hannah, died four years later, it was left to my father. Eventually it became my home. It is our family's heirloom and hopefully will be enjoyed by many generations to come."

"As it is with my home," Nettie agreed.

Elizabeth smiled. "Let's go to the kitchen. I've baked a German chocolate cake for this occasion. We'll enjoy a slice and a cup of coffee before I take you to a special room in my home."

"Special?" Nettie laughed. "I thought your whole house was special."

After enjoying their dessert and casual conversation, Elizabeth said, "If you are up for a climb, I'd love to show you the tower room. From this seven-story perch, one can gaze upon all of Portland and Casco Bay."

"I'd love to," Nettie said. "Although I'm several years older than you, I believe I can still meet the challenge of all those stairs."

Elizabeth led Nettie up the grand staircase to the third floor and took a right turn, stopping in front of a closed door. She opened it, revealing a dark space. Using the light coming from the hallway, Elizabeth found the candle and matches placed on a small stand just inside the entry.

Nettie observed, "I see you have no electricity in this portion of your home."

"You're correct. I love the mystique candlelight sheds when I climb the stairs. It makes me feel like I'm stepping back into the last century. I can also enjoy it as my grandfather once did."

Nettie nodded. "Yes, I can see that. But I must say it does feel a bit ghostly!"

Elizabeth chuckled. Halfway up the first set of stairs, she turned and held the candle in front of her face. "Boo!" she said.

The two women laughed until they reached the seventh-floor landing. When Elizabeth opened the door, Nettie whispered, "This is incredible."

"You don't have to whisper," Elizabeth said. "It's not like you're going to wake the dead. Let's find better light."

Elizabeth walked over to an old oil lamp sitting on a desk adorned with nautical carvings. Once the lamp was lit, Nettie said, "This desk is one of the most exquisite pieces of furniture I've ever seen."

"My great-grandfather built it sixty years ago for the captain." Elizabeth put her hand on the desk chair. "He sat countless hours in this chair reading about adventure and looking over nautical charts before his voyages."

"Captain Clarke must've been an incredible man."

"He is … he was."

"Although amazing," Nettie said, "I have a feeling you didn't invite me into your home just to see this room. Is there something else on your mind?"

Elizabeth nodded. "To be blunt, I want to know how you came to know so much about Seth Stoker's past, and how you knew he was the half brother of Captain Clarke."

Nettie opened her mouth to reply, then closed it. An awkward silence followed.

"Obviously, you have decided not to reveal a confidence you hold dear. If I tell you a secret, will you share yours?" She grinned. "Deal?"

She paused to consider the offer. "Deal," Nettie replied.

Elizabeth pointed towards the desk. "The ghost of Captain Clarke is sitting in that chair."

"Spirit, please," he said. "You know how I prefer to be called a spirit."

Nettie laughed. "You're kidding, aren't you?"

Shaking her head, Elizabeth said, "No. I'm not, nor am I crazy."

Nettie thought, *My god, another ghost! Just how many are there in Portland?* "Prove it," she said.

"Unfortunately, you can't see or hear Captain Clarke. Only I can."

Nettie chuckled. "How convenient."

Elizabeth ignored her friend's disbelieving remark. "So, let's do this," she said. "Ask me a question set in the mid- to late-1800s which only your family could possibly know."

Nettie grinned. "Alright. Who were the husbands of Martha and Molly McLellan and how did they die?"

Elizabeth turned to the captain. "Well?"

Nettie took a step closer to her friend. "Hah, you don't know!"

"You're right. I don't know the answer to your question. That's why I'm waiting for Captain Clarke's reply."

Nettie turned to look at the empty chair and thought it slightly moved.

The captain explained, "Martha was married to Theodore Booker who died from a bullet to the heart while cheating at a game of cards. Molly was married to Reginald Cunningham. He was killed by the sword of his lover's husband during a theatrical performance."

Elizabeth repeated the captain's answer.

"My god!" Nettie cried. "How did you know?"

"From the captain's lips to my ears." She smiled. "Now, tell me your secret."

Nettie mumbled, "You have one ghost, I have two …"

"What was that?" Elizabeth asked.

She blurted, "You have one ghost, and I have two!"

Elizabeth cocked her head. "Two?"

Nettie sighed. "The McLellan twins, Martha and Molly, are my ghosts."

"Ah ha!" the captain cried.

Elizabeth asked, "Now that we know the sources for the knowledge you hold, how did you come by it?"

"I learned from the twins. … Years ago, before their deaths, they enlisted Seth's aid in a failed plot to adopt John Clarke after Captain Clarke and his wife died."

The captain yelled, "My son could've been raised by those two nitwits? With all they had, those women were never satisfied. I'm not surprised they would want what Hannah had, even if she had it for only a moment."

Elizabeth pleaded, "Please calm down, captain. You should be grateful we have answers, and the twins did not raise your son."

He apologized, then addressed Nettie. "Madam, please tell us about your encounters with the ghosts of Martha and Molly."

Elizabeth repeated the captain's request.

Nettie replied, "In an effort to avoid sharing the McLellan estate when their mother died, the twins each hatched a plot to kill the other before her passing."

"My goodness!" Elizabeth cried.

"I'm not surprised," said the captain.

"As fate would have it," Nettie continued, "they poisoned each other on the very same night. With no husband or children to inherit the McLellan fortune, Minnie McLellan left it all to her nephew, Peter McCabe. He and his wife, Danielle, had a son, who is now my husband, Abraham. When Abe was born, the twins appeared as ghosts."

"Who can see them?" Elizabeth asked. "What are they like? Are they always with you? Please tell us of their haunting."

"Us? Oh, you mean the captain and you," she said.

Elizabeth nodded.

Nettie explained, "The twin ghosts first appeared after my husband Abe was born. During their stay, they continuously bickered and fought. The twins disappeared when Abe was one, then returned when my son Charlie was born, and again when my grandson Geoffrey was born. Each visit lasted between one and two years, and only the baby and his mother could see and hear them. The twins were confined to my home unable to roam about the city."

"That's not entirely true," the captain corrected.

Elizabeth turned to her grandfather. "What's not true?"

"Yes, what is it I said that's not true?" Nettie asked.

The captain replied, "They do roam about the city. In fact, two years ago, they attended a charity event held in this house. I approached them when I noticed their presence." He chuckled. "I took them completely by surprise. If they weren't ghosts, I am certain they would have soiled their undergarments."

Elizabeth laughed.

"I then scolded the twits for wearing dirty nightgowns to the event."

Elizabeth shook her head in disgust. For Nettie's benefit, she repeated what the captain said.

"I believe you!" she cried. "I never told you the twins remain in the nightgowns they wore when they died. The twins are more ill-behaved than I thought."

Elizabeth asked, "How can they be any worse than they are?"

Nettie recalled, "I remember a story my mother-in-law, Danielle McCabe, once shared with me. In 1895, a charity ball was held to raise funds for the local orphanage. The evening started out well enough but soon turned into utter chaos when mysterious malicious acts occurred. There were even reports of shears flying, snipping everything and anything to cause havoc. Danielle also mentioned she thought she heard the twins' laughter. Many left that night believing the hall was haunted. Now that you say they were able to move about the city, it must have been Martha and Molly who caused the frenzy."

The captain laughed. "At least you have the good fortune that they disappear for long periods at a time."

"You must be on guard when they return," Elizabeth warned. "Who knows what damage they could be capable of doing to your family?"

Nettie asked, "Tell me how Captain Clarke came to be in your home as a spirit?"

She replied, "Captain Clarke died in 1887 when his ship was lost during a storm off the coast of North Carolina. For whatever God's reason, the captain became a spirit and wandered nearly thirty years before returning home. I met him when I was four years old. He has been my confidant and I've been his guardian.

"My daughter Katherine is also aware of the captain. Apparently, he can be seen only by red-haired women who are his descendants. When he's in this tower room, he appears to me as a regular living human being. When he steps out of this room, his body becomes transparent. Also, he cannot leave the mansion to wander about as your twin ghosts seem to do."

While listening to Elizabeth, Nettie had been walking the perimeter of the room taking in the sights. She asked, "Do you know why the captain remains in this world?"

"No," Elizabeth replied, "and neither does he. As the captain has said, 'God has yet to reveal why I cannot join my wife in death.' Nettie, why do you think Martha and Molly are ghosts?"

Nettie laughed. "I think if God spoke to them directly, they still wouldn't understand why they pop in and out of this world. I'd bet the entire McCabe fortune it's because God is trying to teach them the virtues of goodness. It's possible He wants them to know His grace is what they should've desired in life, as well as after death.

"Well, it's getting dark outside and my night vision for driving is waning as I age." Nettie turned to where she imagined the captain was sitting. "Captain Clarke, this has been an interesting evening and it's been a pleasure to meet you. May your earthly journey soon come to a pleasant end."

After smothering the flame of the oil lamp, Elizabeth took hold of the candle and stepped towards the door. "Our secrets and burdens have been revealed," she said. "It's time we return to our families."

Nettie followed closely behind her as they descended the staircase.

CHAPTER 33

In August 1956, Geoffrey McCabe is ten and will be eleven in October. God has told me this will be a critical year in his life. With peak interest, I now turn my attention to the boy.

✳   ✳   ✳

Charlie's passion for flying did not diminish after the war. He now had two airplanes, his and Danny's, and his father still flew the old two-seater. He enjoyed taking to the air with his father and hoped his son would also do the same. That would not happen because Geoffrey's passion was sailing.

It began when his parents took him for an afternoon sail on an old sixty-foot Brixham fishing trawler, *The Spirit of Casco Bay*. When the red sails were unfurled from two towering masts, the wind filled the canvases and gently took them gliding on the water. Geoffrey watched the deliberate moves by the crew to catch the wind; he wished he could join them.

✳   ✳   ✳

There are times when a father is alone with his son and the conversation turns towards the son's future. When asked what the child wants to be when he grows up, the answer usually is to become a doctor, a policeman, a fireman, a train conductor, or whatever his father does for a living. When Charlie asked his son, Geoffrey replied, "I want to be the captain of a ship."

On Christmas Day, five months later, Charlie and Peggy took their son to a large building near the docks. After entering the cold storage facility, Geoffrey saw it was filled with boats stored during winter months. It was then he saw a twenty-six-foot wooden sailboat with a big red bow tied to its transom. It was 1930 Dark Harbor 17. It had a slender shape, with long overhangs and a deep draft. This craft was known to be powerful, fast, and responsive under the control of a one-man crew. It also had a small cuddy cabin, providing shelter should a sudden rain squall appear.

"Merry Christmas!" Charlie and Peggy said.

"Really? Thank you!" Geoffrey hugged his parents. "But I don't know how to sail."

"All in due time," his father said.

His mother asked, "What are you going to name your sailboat?"

The boy thought for a moment, then he smiled. "I'm going to name her after you, *Peggy Jo.*"

✳   ✳   ✳

On a Saturday in early May 1959, two and a half years after Geoffrey took ownership of the Dark Harbor, he strode into The Maine Sail. It was a nautical novelty shop that also managed Casco Bay Cruises.

Katherine Nelson watched the lanky teenager as he approached; she thought his blond hair was a bit too long. She also thought of her favorite television show, *Rawhide,* and how much he looked like a younger version of Rowdy Yates.

Geoffrey stepped up to the counter, brushed his hair back with his left hand, and handed her a job application form with his right.

"Good morning," he said. "I would like to apply for a job."

Katherine snapped, "Where did you get this application?"

He replied, "My mother came into the shop earlier this week and picked it up for me."

Glancing at the form, she noticed his age. She said, "We don't need help in the shop. I'm sorry you wasted your time."

He stood tall. "I don't want to work in your shop. I want to work on your ship."

Katherine glared at the teenager. "You're way too young!"

Geoffrey pleaded, "But … but I know how to sail!"

As the two squared off, Elizabeth returned into the shop. She had been out preparing *The Spirit of Casco Bay* for another season of cruising on the bay. After joining her daughter behind the sales counter, Katherine handed her the boy's application.

Elizabeth asked, "Is there a problem?"

Geoffrey pointed a finger at Katherine. "She won't let me apply for a job on your ship," he said.

Katherine spouted, "He's only thirteen."

"Thirteen and a half," he countered.

"Why should I hire you?" Elizabeth asked.

"I can sail," he said. "In fact, I have my own boat, a 1930 Dark Harbor 17. It's berthed at DiMillo's Marina on Long Wharf."

"How big is it?" she asked.

"The *Peggy Jo* is a twenty-six-footer, and it only requires one person to sail."

Elizabeth shook her head. "Not big enough," she said. "*The Spirit* is sixty feet long and requires a crew of at least four. It's quite different than your boat." She paused. "What work experience do you have?"

"For the past few years, during weekends and summers, I've washed cars at my father's car dealership." He further pleaded his case, "Ma'am, I love the water, but I'd rather sail on it than wash cars with it."

Elizabeth asked, "Charlie McCabe is your father, isn't he?"

The boy nodded.

"Well, here's the thing," she said, "although the Fair Labor Standards Act allows you to work for your father, it does not permit you to work elsewhere until you're fourteen."

Geoffrey's eyes went to the floor and his shoulders slumped as he prepared for the pending rejection.

"However," Elizabeth paused to collect her thoughts. "If you sail on my ship as a non-paying customer, I will treat you as I would if you were my apprentice sailor."

Geoffrey grinned. "I'd like that."

"Be back here in one hour in your finest sailing attire. Also, you will need to bring a permission slip signed by both your parents."

"Thank you!" Geoffrey turned and bolted out of the shop.

Katherine sighed. "Mother, I don't understand. Why did you take him on?"

"Charlie McCabe was my brother's best friend. If Geoffrey becomes half the man his father is, I've made the right decision."

✶   ✶   ✶

Over the years, I continued to keep a watchful eye on Geoffrey because it is he who may someday meet his true love. She will bear a child, and if the baby is a boy, the twins will pay a visit to their home.

During the summers of '59 and '60, I watched Geoffrey sail on *The Spirit of Casco Bay*. Always mindful of the trust Elizabeth had placed in him, he had proved his worth and was now a full member of the ship's crew.

Sailing continued to be Geoffrey's passion during high school, and as a member of the school's sailing team, he was voted captain during his sophomore, junior, and senior years. This accomplishment led to a full scholarship to the University of Rhode Island where he joined its collegiate team.

In May of 1967 at the age of twenty-one, Geoffrey returned home with a college degree. That summer, Elizabeth made him captain of her ship.

One year later, in the month of June, God has told me Geoffrey is about to discover his true love. Since He knows the future and I do not, I take his word as gospel. So, I am off to see what God has created.

✳   ✳   ✳

Geoffrey was enjoying his second season as captain of *The Spirit of Casco Bay*. Although Elizabeth was the owner of the ship, she afforded him a wide berth so she could focus on providing historical information about Portland to the paying guests aboard the ship. He enjoyed this part of his life because, as the captain, he was in charge.

When Geoffrey was not sailing the bay, he was working for his father and grandfather at McCabe Motors. Like his father, his start in the family business was selling cars. However, unlike his time on *The Spirit*, he was not allowed to make any significant decisions; every decision was scrutinized and approved of by his elders.

On a Friday afternoon in mid-August, a group of young ladies boarded the old trawler. The cruise on the bay was part of a day-long bachelorette party. The guests wore yellow bikinis, which were a distraction to the male crew members aboard the ship. Elizabeth was not pleased as their juvenile behavior forecasted troubled waters ahead.

Terrible things can happen during a two-hour cruise, especially when the crew is not immediately responsive to the captain's orders. Wind and waves are never constant; speed and direction change without notice. To keep the sails full of wind and the ship upright, tasks had to be performed swiftly and with precision. Flirtatious banter between the crew and the scantily clad women competed with orders called out by the captain.

One party guest stood up just as a tack into the wind was ordered. A rope was loosened and the boom at the bottom of the sail swung out, catching the young lady in the middle of her back. It drove her into the chilly water.

As soon as the rope was loosened, Geoffrey envisioned the dire scene played out. Taking quick action, he cried out to Elizabeth to take the helm and dove headfirst into the bay. As he was about to break the surface, a glimpse of a yellow bikini caught his eye. Face-down, the woman was quickly sinking towards the bottom of Casco Bay.

Geoffrey desperately swam downward to the drowning woman and was running out of time to save her—and himself. Twenty long seconds passed before he could put an arm around her and swim towards daylight. When he broke the surface of the water, Geoffrey gulped in the salty air. Still cradling the young woman in one arm, he swam towards a floating life ring.

After they were safely on board, Geoffrey rolled the woman over on her back, pinched her nose and began to breathe life back into her. On the third try, she coughed water out from her lungs. It was then that he noticed not all which had fallen into the water had not been saved. Her bikini top was missing.

Elizabeth also noticed the mishap, grabbed a towel, and covered the young woman's breasts. She then took the helm and pointed the ship back to port.

Geoffrey placed his jacket on the woman's shoulders. "Thank you," she said, as she held the towel to her chest. "Thank you for saving me."

"It was my pleasure. And thank you."

"For what?"

He grinned. "I always wanted … to save a damsel in distress."

The woman laughed. "What's your name?" she asked.

"Geoffrey McCabe. I'm the captain of this ship and, for the moment, the resident shining knight." He grinned. "Pray tell, damsel, what is your name?"

She combed her wet hair away from her eyes with her fingers. "Rachel Thomas," she replied.

"Well, Rachel, it is my pleasure to meet you." He chuckled. "And to have saved, as well as seen you."

She blushed. "Cute," she said, pulling his jacket tighter.

A moment passed while he considered his next move. "May I take you to dinner tonight?"

Rachel shook her head. "Sorry. I have other plans and tomorrow I have a wedding to attend."

He countered, "How about the next day?"

She laughed. "Here's a thought … If you're not too busy saving topless women, would you consider rescuing me again? Join me at the wedding reception. I'd love to know whether you can dance as well as you can swim."

Geoffrey looked past her to his employer, who was standing at the helm. She had overheard their conversation. Elizabeth nodded.

"I would love to," he replied. "Tomorrow just happens to be my day off."

That evening, Rachel told all her friends about her hero, embellishing his selfless act. She also mentioned she had invited him to the wedding reception.

*　　　*　　　*

Geoffrey was nervous. Despite the cool breeze blowing in from the bay through his bedroom window, he was sweating profusely. As he dressed, he frantically searched for the right words to say when greeting his date.

Looking into the mirror, he wrestled with his bow tie. On the fourth attempt he finally tied it to his satisfaction. Seeing his reflection, Geoffrey tried the latest greeting to float into his mind, "Hi gorgeous! You look stunning tonight!" Geoffrey burst out laughing, hearing how lame he sounded.

Geoffrey lost track of time while practicing his words. He looked at his watch, then frantically grabbed his coat, ran down the stairs, and out of the mansion. While driving to the hotel where the reception was held, he continued to search his brain for the perfect greeting.

Pulling up to the building, he tossed his keys to the valet. "Hi gorgeous!" he said. Geoffrey's face reddened. "Sorry," he said over his shoulder, "that was meant for my …"

When he entered the ballroom, all female eyes set upon him. Pleasurable sighs were heard for Rachel's gallant knight had arrived in grand fashion, one who could grace the cover of any romance novel.

While scanning the room for his damsel (no longer in distress), Geoffrey noticed all the women were eyeing him. Feeling uncomfortable, he pivoted towards the door. In the middle of his hasty retreat, a woman took his hand.

"Leaving so soon?" Rachel asked with a smile.

Geoffrey turned to see Rachel standing before him, wearing a strapless light blue gown. Her long brown hair framed her beautiful tan face and was accentuated by freckles sprinkled across her nose. His eyes drowned in her beauty.

In turn, Rachel's eyes took in the sight of a man with broad shoulders who stood six-foot-four. His long blond hair fell over the collar of his shirt portraying a roguish playful look, a contrast to the serious one he wore while commanding *The Spirit*.

Overwhelmed by her beauty, Geoffrey's practiced words vanished from his mind. "You look beautiful!" he said.

"Thank you," she said, and pulled him out onto the dance floor.

During the evening, Rachel made sure to keep her hero to herself. Sometime during the evening, the band played "Sealed with a Kiss." He held her close as they slowly danced to the melody. Like Rachel free-falling into the ocean, Geoffrey had free-fallen for her.

CHAPTER 34

October 1969. It all started five decades ago after a recon mission. That's when Abe lit his first cigar. At the time, he had no idea this celebratory act would later cause him to pull a cart with an oxygen tank strapped to it. Abe called the tank and cart "the damn shame."

Abe threw the damn shame into the back of his brand new '69 Cadillac Coupe DeVille. *Thank God,* he thought. It had turned out to be a lovely day, which made it easier for him to throw the damn shame into the damn back seat of his damn convertible.

He put the key in the ignition and listened as the engine came to life. To clear his head of the damn shame, he sat revving the DeVille's 472-cubic-inch engine. He loved hearing the power possessed by this beautiful white behemoth for the roaring of the engine distracted him from the fact that his health was rapidly declining.

As he drove down the street, Abe considered his mission. Although it would cost him dearly, the purchase he was about to propose would provide him and his grandson with immense pleasure. *Well,* he thought as he hacked up an obscene glob of mucus and spit it into his hankie, *I can't take it with me.*

Abe pulled up in front of The Maine Sail, parked his car, and dragged the damn shame out from the back seat. Putting his breathing device on, he pulled the oxygen cart to the shop's entrance. As he struggled to pull the damn shame through the front door, it quickly closed on the cart. "Damn cigars!"

Elizabeth rushed over to help him. "Here," she said, "let me get the door for you."

"Thank you, sweetie. I appreciate your assistance."

Abe pulled the cart into the shop. "Damn cigars," he muttered, again.

"Pardon?"

"Damn cigars! They're the reason I must pull this damn oxygen cart with me wherever I damn well go."

Wanting to change the course of the damning conversation, Elizabeth asked, "May I help you find something today?"

"Don't bother, madam. I know exactly where it is."

This man is wearing an expensive suit, she thought. *Perchance I'll have a nice sale today.* Elizabeth grinned. "Is it something for your girlfriend?"

"That's cute, madam. … No. It's for my grandson. Let me introduce myself. I'm Abraham McCabe, the owner of McCabe Motors."

"I'm Elizabeth Nelson, the owner of The Maine Sail. So, you're Geoffrey's grandfather. I must say, you do have a special grandson. He has been the captain of my ship, *The Spirit of Casco Bay*, for the past two years. It's a pleasure to finally meet you."

"No, Mrs. Nelson, the pleasure is truly all mine. Geoffrey thinks very highly of you. Sometimes, he wishes he were born into your family."

Elizabeth blushed. "I must confess, he's like a nephew to me. When we're out on the water, at times I can see your banner, *Best Deals at Honest Abe McCabe Motors*, being pulled by an old airplane."

"Oh, that's my son Charlie. He'll look for any damn excuse to take to the air." He coughed. "May we sit down?"

"Yes, of course. Let's sit at the counter." Once they were both settled, she asked, "I haven't talked to your wife for a while. How is she?"

"You know her?"

"Nettie and I are good friends," she replied. "In fact, she's been a guest at my house on several occasions. I've enjoyed our private chats."

"Private, huh. What do you talk about?"

She smiled. "Mr. McCabe, I did say our conversations are private."

"Well, doesn't matter. To answer your question, Nettie is well and her volunteer work regarding women's rights keeps her busy. Can't say how many times she's said she hopes to live long enough to hold her great-grandchild." He laughed. "Poor Geoffrey. She's told him to start working on it."

Elizabeth gasped. "Geoffrey's not even married."

"Doesn't matter to her." He coughed. "Madam, although I've enjoyed our little chitchat, I must get to the reason for my visit. I have a business proposition for you."

"Well, I don't know what it could be. You're in the business of selling cars and I'm in the business of selling souvenirs and cruises on the bay."

"Madam, I'd like to buy your ship and the portion of your business which provides cruises for tourists on Casco Bay. I'm prepared to finalize the deal today."

Elizabeth was taken aback by the notion. "Frankly, I've never thought about selling any part of my business."

Abe pressed on, "I don't want to buy it for myself. This transaction would be for my grandson. I love Geoffrey and he loves to sail. Although it takes him away from the family business, it makes him happy. As long as he's happy, I'm happy."

"Well …"

"Mrs. Nelson, don't you want your *nephew* to be happy?"

She laughed. "If I decide to sell, I wouldn't even know what price to ask."

"Not a problem. I've already done the work for you."

"You have?" she asked.

Abe nodded. "Do you know only a handful of Brixham trawlers exist in the world today? It's a rare find and you have kept it in fine shape. But I have the money to make it even better. In fact, long after it's served its purpose, the ship must become a showpiece of history."

Elizabeth considered his words. She liked hearing the last thing he said, a showpiece of history. "If I did agree to sell, what offer do you have in mind?"

He pulled a check from inside his coat pocket and placed it in front of her. She was stunned by the amount written and took a moment to consider his offer.

"Well?" he said.

"I will sell Casco Bay Cruises and the trawler to you if you agree to one stipulation: the name of the ship remains *The Spirit of Casco Bay.*"

"It's a deal! That is, if you agree with my two stipulations. You removed some of the rigging and other items from the boat to convert it from a fishing vessel to one which provides tours on Casco Bay. You have them stored behind your shop. I want them included in our deal. Someday, I want it preserved as it once was when it was first launched."

"I appreciate your desire to eventually make the ship a historical keepsake. What is your other stipulation?"

"Our agreement is not to be shared with anyone before Christmas Day. I make this request as a special favor. It's going to be a Christmas present for my grandson."

"Done!" she said. "Mr. McCabe, know that I will come at you with a vengeance if you do not keep your word."

He smiled. "Although my word is golden, I'll be sure the contract includes our stipulations. I'll have it drawn up for your signature."

With their business concluded, Abe got up from his stool and grabbed the handle of the damn shame. Pulling it behind him, he walked to the front of the shop and opened the door. His cart got caught in the door again. Elizabeth heard him shout, "Damn cigars!"

✳   ✳   ✳

On Christmas Day, three generations of McCabes were in the drawing room celebrating and exchanging gifts. After the last gift under the tree was opened, Abe turned to his grandson and said, "You did not find a gift from your grandmother and me under the tree because frankly it does not fit."

Geoffrey said, "You didn't have to buy a car for me."

"We didn't. Two months ago, I purchased Casco Bay Cruises. Merry Christmas! You're not only the captain of the ship, but you're also its new owner."

✳   ✳   ✳

June 1970, six months later.

Why were weddings and funerals the main events that brought families together? This was the question that nagged Abe as he checked himself in the mirror. He scowled at the sight of himself. During the past few years, he lost weight and height. His wrinkles were more pronounced. *Well, life goes on with or without me. Thank you, God, for allowing me to be here to witness this special day.*

Abe grabbed hold of the damn shame with his left hand and rolled it out of the men's room. Nettie, who had been waiting for him, took hold of his right hand. She was his sweetheart, and wife, as well as his caretaker. Together, they entered the church's sanctuary.

A tear came to Abe's eye as he pulled the damn shame down the aisle to the row of chairs reserved for the family of the groom. *Three generations of McCabes ... perhaps four before I leave this world,* he thought. With help from his wife, he settled into his seat.

To pay homage to the swimsuit top she had lost, Rachel's bridesmaids all wore yellow gowns, and held yellow roses and baby's breath in the bridal bouquet. Geoffrey and his groomsmen all wore black tuxedos, with a boutonniere of a single yellow rose.

After the wedding ceremony was over, Abe caught up to his grandson and embraced him. He choked, "I'm proud of you, Geoffrey."

"Thanks, Gramps." A tear formed in the corner of Geoffrey's eye. "Glad you could attend our wedding."

"Made a bargain with God so I wouldn't miss it."

"Bargain? What'd you do? Sell Him a car?"

Abe chuckled, then coughed into his handkerchief. "Can't say. That's between Him and me." Abe placed the keys to his '69 Cadillac Coupe DeVille into his grandson's hands. "Treat her like the lady she is."

*   *   *

Geoffrey and Rachel loaded up the white convertible and left on a two-week honeymoon. Their first stop was on the Canadian side of Niagara Falls. Their second stop was Mackinaw City, Michigan, where they left Abe's DeVille and boarded a ferry to Mackinac Island. When they stepped off the ferry, the couple stepped back in time.

"I don't see any cars," Geoffrey said.

Rachel smiled. "That's why I picked it for our honeymoon, my love. Everyone travels on this island either by foot, bicycle, or carriage."

A coachman from the famous Grand Hotel greeted the newlyweds and assisted them aboard the horse-drawn carriage for a scenic ride to their lodging. Built in 1887, the beautiful, white, five-story hotel was perched on a hill overlooking the Straits of Mackinac.

Before their honeymoon, Rachel planned and prepared for each day they would spend on the island. With a desire to fit into the nineteenth century setting, she had packed an array of vintage gowns and dresses for herself, as well as several stylish suits for Geoffrey. Old-fashioned bow ties completed his formal attire. After one week on the island paradise, the newlyweds traveled back to Portland to begin their life within the McCabe's family mansion.

✸   ✸   ✸

Geoffrey unloaded their luggage, then looked for his grandfather. As hoped, he found him sitting at a table in the courtyard behind the home. He paused when he saw the old man had lost more weight.

Abe was taking in the sunshine, his eyes closed. Geoffrey took a seat next to him. "Grandpa?" he asked.

Abe woke with a start, then readjusted the breathing apparatus attached to the damn shame. "Ahh, you're back!"

Geoffrey placed the keys to the DeVille on the table. "Thanks for the use of your car. I can't think of a better way to have traveled during our honeymoon."

"My pleasure. So, tell me about your trip."

Geoffrey told him.

Abe grumbled, "No cars on the island?"

Geoffrey nodded. "It was like stepping back into the last century. Besides walking or riding a bicycle, the only other way to get around Mackinac Island was by taking a horse-drawn buggy, carriage, or wagon."

"Your great-great-grandfather, Malcomb McCabe, would've been pleased."

Geoffrey patted the keys on the table. "Anyway, thanks for the use of your car."

"Keep it," he said.

Geoffrey cocked his head. "What?"

Abe coughed. "While you were gone, my doctor took away my driving privileges. Appears *Old Abe* is now too old to drive."

✸   ✸   ✸

Two months after giving his grandson his '69 Cadillac Coupe DeVille, Abraham McCabe lost his fight with lung cancer. Truly a damn shame.

CHAPTER 35

It was January 1971, five months after Abe died. The door to the McCabe's library was closed for a private meeting. Geoffrey, with Rachel at his side, was facing Nettie and Peggy.

What the hell is this all about? Geoffrey wondered. *Why am I the only guy in the room?* Hoping to find a friendly ally, he took his wife's hand.

"Rachel, it's time we had this talk," said Peggy. "Because you're well into your pregnancy, your grandmother and I need to share some of our experiences."

Rachel tensed. Geoffrey relaxed, realizing this meeting was not about him. Her hand was now squeezing his hand. She snapped, "Are you going to tell me how to take care of my own baby before it's even born?"

Peggy shook her head. "We would never dream of doing such a thing."

Rachel stood. "I had a feeling not having our own home would someday become a problem. I just didn't think—"

"Honey, please sit and hear us out," Nettie said. "This is not a criticism of you or Geoffrey. Please let us explain."

The young couple nodded; Rachel returned to her seat.

Nettie continued, "This meeting is a family tradition, one which my mother-in-law, Danielle, and I began just before Charlie was born. It occurs once a generation."

Peggy said, "They sat me down in this very room when I was nine months pregnant. It was then I was given a warning should my baby be a boy."

"I," Geoffrey looked at his wife, "we don't understand. Is there a genetic defect passed to McCabe males?"

Nettie replied, "Of course not." She leaned back in the overstuffed chair and said, "I will begin with the history of this home."

Nettie talked of the McLellan family, who had owned the mansion before her father-in-law, Peter McCabe, inherited it. Leaving out no detail, she also shared the tragic deaths of Martha and Molly.

Rachel cried out, "Oh, my god! This house is haunted!"

"No, honey," Geoffrey said. "It's not haunted. No ghosts. I've lived here all my life and never saw one. You have nothing to worry about."

"Well," Nettie said, "yes, you do."

The room was suddenly quiet. Nettie took a deep breath and continued her story. Both Geoffrey and Rachel leaned forward in their seats when she told of the arrival of the ghosts. After her part of the story was finished, Peggy shared her time with the McLellan twins.

Having heard the bizarre tale of spiritual annoyance, Rachel muttered, "Everyone brings baggage into a relationship."

Geoffrey asked, "You can't be serious?"

Peggy replied, "Unfortunately, your grandmother and I are profoundly serious. As we said, they appeared after your grandfather was born and, again, after your father was born."

Geoffrey asked, "Is Dad aware of them?"

"Yes," his mother replied. "He was told soon after your birth."

"Just how did he react when you told him?" Rachel asked.

Nettie replied, "He didn't like it, of course. But what could he do? Besides, the men aren't the ones dealing with the apparitions. They only know what we've told them."

Rachel said, "I won't like it either." She turned to Nettie. "Earlier, you mentioned this meeting was to provide me with a warning, should our baby be a boy. How do you know they won't return if we have a girl?"

Nettie explained, "Geoffrey's great-grandparents, Peter and Danielle McCabe, had a daughter who died when she was only three months old. When she was born, the twins did not appear."

"Geoffrey," Peggy said, "if the self-centered sisters do reappear, I hope you are a better shoulder to lean on than your father was for me. Rachel, what are you thinking?"

"Although the twins appear to be harmless, I pray our baby is a girl."

Everyone but Rachel laughed.

Six months later, Rachel's prayers were answered when she gave birth to Maria McCabe. The twins did not return.

✳   ✳   ✳

December 1972, one year and five months later.

Despite the possibility of her next baby being a boy, Rachel wanted Maria to grow up with a brother or sister. She was an only child and felt, in some way, she was cheated out of the joy of having a sibling to share her childhood years. No threat of ghostly appearances would ever change her mind. At Christmastime, she told her husband she wanted to have another baby.

Geoffrey's first thought was of his grandmother Nettie who had died of pneumonia a few months ago. He knew she would have loved to have held another great-grandchild before she passed. His second thought was the son he wanted. Yes, the twin ghosts might return and be a bother to his wife, but he knew she could manage them. Like his mother and grandmother, Rachel was a strong woman and would not tolerate mischief caused by Martha and Molly.

✳   ✳   ✳

It was early February of 1973 when Rachel kissed her husband and said those life-changing words, "Honey, I'm pregnant."

CHAPTER 36

Two pairs of ghostly eyes scanned the darkened room. Martha and Molly were confused at first because the child in the room was not a newborn.

Molly whispered, "It's a—girl!"

"She looks to be around two years old," Martha said. "Somewhere in this house, there's got to be an infant boy. Otherwise, why would we be here?"

"Come, sister. —Let's go look—for the nursery."

The twins found Rachel in a bedroom down the hall. She was sitting in a rocking chair nursing a baby.

Martha said, "There you are."

Although she had anticipated their arrival, Rachel was startled when she saw the two apparitions floating into the room.

Rachel stammered, "I, I've been expecting you. You're Martha and Molly, aren't you?"

Martha scrunched her nose. "Peggy has ruined our surprise." She pointed. "That's Molly, the one with the limp and blue lips."

"Well," Molly said, her voice rising. "—You still have—a crooked neck—and your—"

"I know you have questions," Rachel interrupted. "So, let's save some time. Geoffrey, my husband, is now twenty-eight and the year is 1973. We have a daughter, Maria, who you may have already found in her bedroom. I assume you have returned because my baby is a boy. His name is Matthew."

Molly cried, "We've been—gone for—twenty-six years!"

Martha snickered. "Amazing … You can count."

"I can—do more—than that!" Molly yelled as she slapped Martha's head from one side to the other.

Martha screamed, "I'll kill you!"

Matthew began to cry. Holding her baby tight, Rachel stood. She then stepped between the two raging spirits.

Rachel said, "Martha, didn't you already kill her eighty years ago?"

"Well, yes. But she killed me, too. Years later, she killed me again."

"Did not," Molly snapped.

Rachel placed her baby in the bassinette, then turned to the two ghosts. "What is wrong with you two? No sooner have you come back into our lives and you're at each other's throats."

The door to the nursery opened and all eyes turned to the woman who entered the room.

"Boo!" Martha and Molly cried.

Peggy shook her head. "I see they've arrived."

"My, my," Martha said. "You're aging well. Bet Charlie doesn't stray from his blonde bombshell."

Peggy asked, "Was that a backhanded compliment?"

The ghosts snickered.

"How did you tolerate these two idiots?" Rachel asked.

Peggy laughed. "Although not invited, just think of them as shirttail relatives here for a short visit. In no time at all, they'll be gone to wherever they go."

Martha scrunched her nose, then whimpered. "Wherever is a leap into Hell."

Peggy explained, "When your grandmother and I told you about the twins, we failed to mention they leap into other people between the time they leave us and when they return."

Rachel gasped. "Like possess another person?"

She nodded. "Well, yes, sort of. … Mostly, they're along for the ride."

"And a hellish ride it is!" Martha cried. "We feel the suffering and sorrow the person is living at that very moment. We also receive a memento from each leap. Just look at the blood on my nightgown!"

Peggy sighed. "Aren't you two afraid these leaps are going to get worse? Shouldn't you think about changing your behavior?"

Both ghosts silently stared at the floor, in no mood to be scolded.

Rachel asked, "How do you endure these leaps?"

"It's easy," Molly replied. "Because—I know—they will—soon end."

"It's not that easy," Martha mumbled. Tears welled up in her eyes as she thought about her last leap. "I found myself in—"

Rachel placed her hands on her hips. She said, "I, for one, don't want to hear it. Please leave, all three of you. I'd like to spend some alone time with my baby."

✳　　　✳　　　✳

When daylight blessed a new day, Geoffrey woke to find Rachel missing from their bed. After putting on his robe, he found her in the nursery. He kissed her and baby Matthew. "Have you had a visit from our ghosts?"

She frowned. "We did."

"Where are they now?" he asked.

"I'm not sure. I haven't seen them since I shooed them away in the middle of the night."

Martha and Molly poked their heads through the wall of the nursery. They yelled, "Boo!"

"That's still not funny," Rachel said.

Geoffrey asked, "What's not funny?"

She pointed. "They are not funny. The ghosts have returned."

"Well, Geoffrey," said Martha, "we haven't seen you since you were a baby."

Molly looked at him up and down and liked what she saw. "You look—very dirty. —Isn't it—time for—your bath?"

"Cute," Rachel said. "I see you are exactly what Nettie and Peggy described. A nuisance."

Martha cried, "What do you mean by that?"

"You're obnoxious, annoying, invasive, interfering, insensitive—"

"Let's try to be civil," Martha said.

Rachel pointed at her. "You don't know the meaning of the word."

Just before Geoffrey could say anything about the one-sided conversation he was hearing, they were joined by his mother.

"I could hear you from my bedroom," Peggy said. "Oh! I didn't know Geoffrey had joined the party." She chuckled. "I'll bet you're waiting for an invitation to leave the room."

"I feel helpless because I can't see or hear them," he said. "I might as well go downstairs and make coffee."

Geoffrey kissed his wife. Even though he had been told what to expect, until now the ghosts had not been real to him. "I'll be damned," he said as he stepped out of the room.

Peggy said, "Rachel, honey, although they will continue to misbehave, the twins will not do harm to your baby. It is safe to let them hold Matthew, but changing diapers? With all the years of practice they've had, the twins just can't seem to get the hang of it."

Rachel asked, "Why would they want to care for my baby, or any baby for that matter?"

Peggy explained, "From our collective experience, Danielle, Nettie, and I, we suspect God has instilled a need within them to care for our babies."

"Need? Feels more like a compulsion," Martha muttered.

Her sister added, "Feels like—an itch—which must—be scratched."

"Damn Him," Martha and Molly said.

Rachel said, "Well, then I guess it's time to scratch that itch. Molly, come here and take Matthew from me."

Martha stomped her foot and pouted. "I should be first. She held Geoffrey last!"

"You'll get your turn," Rachel said.

"Humph!" Martha grunted.

Molly took the baby from his mother, then turned to her sister and stuck out her tongue.

*   *   *

Although Rachel tolerated the twins, by early afternoon her patience had worn thin. She found her husband reading in the sitting room.

"Twits," she said.

He looked up from the newspaper and asked, "I hope you're talking about the twins?"

She nodded. "They are silly and always taunting each other. Twit is a fitting name for them. The only time I catch a break is when your mother is watching television soap operas, which captivates them."

Geoffrey laughed. "You should leave the TV on all afternoon."

"Hmm, maybe I'll do just that."

A few hours later, Rachel asked her mother-in-law to leave the television on after she had finished watching *As the World Turns*. Sure enough, Martha and Molly stayed to watch *The Edge of Night* and *Guiding Light*. After seeing how effective the soap operas were, Rachel showed the ghosts how to change channels. The twins' favorite show became *Dark Shadows*.

*   *   *

It was June 1974, five months after the McLellan twins returned to the McCabe mansion. When alive, they were drawn to social gatherings, much like moths are drawn to a light. The two eagerly anticipated these events as they gave color and amusement to their otherwise dull, privileged lives.

Looking for an opportunity to be entertained, the mischievous spirits joined in the celebration of the second annual Old Port Festival. To their delight, thousands of Portland's citizens and tourists had gathered in the oldest part of the city where cobblestone streets were lined with nineteenth-century buildings.

Basked in excitement, Martha and Molly found the festival to be one big party. While musicians played music all day, clowns, jugglers, and actors regaled the crowd. Vendors wandered the streets selling food and drink, while local artists displayed and sold their creations. There were even aerial performances by trapeze artists high over Commercial Street.

Peggy and Rachel also attended the festival. After stopping at a table that displayed ceramic tiles with hand-painted nautical scenes, they noticed a small crowd listening to a guitar player singing "Brandy (You're a Fine Girl)." Two women in soiled nightgowns were singing along with the musician.

As Peggy and Rachel marched towards the twins, a man in a yellow suit crossed in front of them. He was wearing clown makeup and juggling several wine bottles. After a bump into another man, a flask of whiskey joined the bottles being tossed into the air.

Peggy and Rachel clapped at what they thought was a magic trick. The clown in the yellow suit winked, then juggled towards an alley. Now that the clown had moved on, the two women stepped up behind Martha and Molly.

In a shouted whisper, Peggy asked, "Just what are you two doing here?"

While floating just above the cobblestones, the twins jumped up in surprise. Martha said, "You startled me."

Molly flared her nostrils. "Have you—no decency?"

Peggy declared, "According to my mother-in-law, you two ruined the Orphan's Charity Ball with your antics. Do not do the same here."

"Did not!" the two ghosts lied in unison.

"That's not what we heard," Rachel said. "Armed with scissors, you two spoiled that charity event. Because it was never held again, who knows how many children went without because of you. You both should be ashamed!"

Molly snapped, "I'll not—confess to—something I—didn't do."

Martha muttered, "We were having fun before you showed up. Like you, we're only here to enjoy the festivities."

"Make sure that's all you do," Peggy demanded.

After Peggy and Rachel walked away, Martha asked, "How did they know? The Orphans Charity Ball happened eighty years ago."

"Doesn't matter. I hear—there's a—high-wire act—about to start." She laughed. "Want to shake—the wire?"

✳   ✳   ✳

The clown-juggler in the yellow zoot suit stood over another clown who was sitting on the ground in the alley. With his back leaning against a brick wall, the clown looked up and acknowledged the other entertainer by tipping the liquor bottle in his hand.

"Wanna join me?" the clown asked.

"Don't mind if I do," Angelo replied. "What ya drinkin'?"

The clown belched. "Courage," he replied.

Angelo slid down next to the tipsy clown. "You the one who walks the high wire?"

The clown nodded and sipped the last drop from his bottle. He shook it and muttered, "Wish I had more courage."

"Your wish is granted," Angelo said to his new friend, then passed a flask of whiskey to him.

"Thanks, mate." He belched, again.

Minutes later, Angelo stepped out of the alley.

★   ★   ★

"Shake it—again!" Molly screamed.

Martha scrunched her nose. "I did, but he won't fall!"

"Let me—try!" Molly said, pushing her sister aside.

Angelo Merino looked down from above at the ghost twins and smiled. *Another good deed done.*

★   ★   ★

The twins were in the sitting room of the McCabe mansion. Martha turned her crooked head towards her sister. "Tomorrow is Matthew's birthday. Hard to believe one year has passed so quickly."

"Can't say—I'll miss—you."

Martha frowned. "That's too bad."

"Except for—our leaps—one moment—we're here—the next—we're here." Molly laughed.

"I don't like them," said Martha.

"Well, I—don't either. —But it's—a small price—to pay—to have a—life after death."

Martha said, "I want them to stop. Molly, why is this happening to us?"

Having just stepped into the room, Peggy had overheard some of the twins' conversation. She said, "Good question. So, why do you think your afterlife is the way it has been?"

"Because God—is bored. —He's playing—with us."

Martha shook her head. "Although I don't think it's that, I just can't put a finger on it."

"If this—is Hell—it's not all—that bad."

"It can't be," Martha said. "Everyone knows Hell is all fire and brimstone."

Peggy offered, "Maybe it's something else altogether."

"Like what?" Martha asked.

"When you're not with us or leaping into another life, you both have told me your existence is empty. You are in a void where you have no sight, no sound, no smell, no taste, or touch." Peggy paused. "If it were me, I would think that was Hell. On second thought, what you've described could be what Catholics call purgatory."

"What's that? Molly asked.

"Roman Catholic doctrine states it is a place or state of suffering inhabited by the souls of sinners. While there, the dead atone for their sins; it is a place for cleansing or purifying." Peggy smiled. "Makes sense, doesn't it? After all, you are sinners and you're dead."

"Humph!" the twins grunted.

As Peggy walked out of the room, she called out over her shoulder, "Atone, ladies, atone!"

*   *   *

Peggy and Rachel were in the kitchen decorating Matthew's first birthday cakes. One was a large cake for the family to enjoy, the other for Matthew. His small cake would provide plenty of priceless moments to be captured by the camera when he dove into it.

While decorating the cakes, Peggy shared the discussion she had with the twins the previous day.

Rachel asked, "So, if you're right, the twins' afterlife is meant to give them the opportunity to atone for their wrongdoings." She sighed. "Why does God make the McCabe women suffer their visits?"

After placing one candle into the large cake, Peggy replied, "I've been thinking about that. Yes, we've had to deal with their antics, but we have also benefitted. Remember, it was the twins who made us aware of the Stokers. If it weren't for them, who knows what would have happened to our family?"

Rachel asked, "If that was all there was to it, why is God continuing to place Martha and Molly into our lives?"

Peggy sighed. "There's more to God's plan or it's over. It's possible we may never know in our lifetimes. Let's pray our ghost twins soon leave us and don't return when my grandson has a boy of his own."

Rachel lit one candle. "It's time to bring the cakes into the dining room."

When Peggy and Rachel entered the room, everyone began to sing the birthday song. The two women noticed the absence of Martha and Molly. They said, "Good riddance!" with a chuckle.

CHAPTER 37

It is July 1975, one year and a month after the twins disappeared from the McCabe household. Although God seems to have unlimited patience, I do not. It's time to push, perhaps shove, Molly towards her redemption.

As before, I imagine the wheel with thirty-six numbers set in depressions alternating red and black. I spin it, round and round it goes. Over the center of the wheel, I imagine a marble in my hand and move to drop it.

I pause as a thought occurs to me: *Has God rigged the wheel? I laughed, wondering if the number the marble randomly chooses will make no difference. Does every number result in the same leap? Can He be that controlling?*

"Yes," I said as I dropped the marble. 25 Red.

✳   ✳   ✳

Although Molly could see nothing, she sensed she was no longer in the void where she was kept between visits to the living world. Her clue was the overwhelming odor of rancid grease.

The man she found herself in, reached out his hands and immediately hit a solid barrier. It was slippery, sticky, and slimy. He understood where he was because he had done a hellish thing to others. He was trapped within a small cylindrical prison.

His thoughts were now Molly's thoughts. In fact, at this precise moment, he wanted to kill the men who had locked him in a steel drum.

Shortly after being released from prison, Jimmy Hoffa attempted to regain the power he had lost during his incarceration. *Damn Kennedys.* His troubles all began with John Kennedy and his younger brother, Bobby. He muttered, "I would send an assassin if they weren't dead already."

Before regaining consciousness in the 50-gallon container, Jimmy had dinner in Bloomfield Hills, Michigan, with his right-hand man, Frank Sheeran. After dinner, he and the "Irishman," that's what everyone called Frank, left the Machus Red Fox restaurant. When they got to the limo, Frank opened the rear door and Jimmy leaned over to get into the car. That was the last thing he remembered before he awoke in the greasy drum.

Jimmy heard highway traffic and knew he and his small prison were in the back of a pickup truck being driven to his grave. Where? It didn't matter. He knew his life was over for that's how it ended up for the people he had ordered to be killed.

Molly disliked the confines of the dirty, stinky container. Whenever the truck hit a bump in the road, Jimmy's head slammed the wall or the lid of the steel drum. She felt his pain and joined Jimmy in his hatred for the men who put him into the barrel.

Hours passed, then a day or two before the truck turned onto a gravel road. When it stopped, the vehicle was put into reverse and slowly backed up.

A few moments later, Jimmy heard two men talking as they climbed into the back of the truck. One voice was familiar, the other he did not recognize.

The lid of the steel drum was removed to reveal a hot, steamy night in late July. Because he had been cramped in a tight position during the trip from Michigan, Jimmy couldn't stand. All he could do was squint up at the stars.

Jimmy was weak, thirsty, and hungry, and could not resist the men as they pulled him up into a standing position. As they held him, he recognized his new permanent residence. It was a toxic waste dump in New Jersey. Several years ago, he had visited this site to rid himself of an enemy. He was pushed back down into his steel casket. Before the lid was secured back onto the drum, he heard the Irishman say, "Teddy Kennedy sends his regards."

God enhanced all of Molly's senses to the point where she could see in the dark. She didn't care, for this leap would soon end … so she thought.

During the first day in the dump, Jimmy screamed, cried, and whimpered. On the second day, he lost control of his bowels and bladder. His waste now competed with the rancid stench inside the barrel. Molly wasn't happy with Jimmy because five more days would pass before he died.

✶　　　✶　　　✶

It has been four years and ten months since Molly fell into Jimmy Hoffa. Now, May 1980, it is Martha's turn at the wheel. 15 Black.

✶　　　✶　　　✶

From nothing to something, a new leap happened to Martha. As soon as she said happy birthday to Matthew, she was sitting on the front porch of a lodge in southwest Washington. This all occurred within the blink of an eye. *Who am I now? Where and when am I?* She wondered.

A moment after her leap began, Martha found she was not in a she. *Strange,* she thought. In the past, Martha had to slowly learn who, what, and where she was. This time, she immediately knew everything about the man.

His name was Harry R. Truman, and he was born in West Virginia 83 years ago. In 1917, Harry enlisted in the U.S. Army Air Service, served two years during The Great War, and survived an attack by a German U-boat when it sunk the troopship on which he was traveling. After the war, the lure of cheap land brought Harry to Washington state where he was unsuccessful as a gold prospector. He then became a skilled bootlegger, smuggling alcohol from San Francisco to Washington. Once Prohibition ended, Harry became the owner of an automotive service station, married, and had a daughter.

After two divorces and the death of his third wife, Harry's life changed once again as he became the owner and caretaker of Mount St. Helens Lodge on Spirit Lake. For years, he was known as the old codger who cleverly avoided being caught poaching by the local forest ranger. Now, because of his defiance of authority, he had gained the status of a local folk hero.

Harry was enjoying the sunrise while sitting in his beloved rocking chair on the front porch of the lodge. Through his eyes, Martha watched the dawn break as he sipped from his coffee cup. Smoke rose from the mountaintop.

The Native Americans called Mount St. Helens 'Louwala-Clough' or Smoking Mountain. It was a suitable name for it had been smoking ever since it erupted 4500 years ago. During the past two months, a series of earth tremors had occurred beneath the northern flank of the mountain resulting in steam and ash slowly being released through its crater and vents. In April, when an intrusion of magma caused a bulge to appear, authorities evacuated hundreds of people living in the sparsely populated area. Harry, and a few photographers, refused to leave.

When giving interviews to reporters, Harry was quoted as saying, "They don't have any idea when it will blow. Until they do, I refuse to pack up and leave. Hell, if the mountain goes, I'm going with it. That mountain has shot its wad before, and it hasn't hurt me a bit. Those goddamn geologists with their hair down to their butts ..."

Law enforcement officials tried one last time to remove Harry from his lodge. He screamed at them, "You couldn't pull me out of here with a mule team!" Some people would say Harry was a proud man. Most, however, believed he was a foolishly stubborn old codger.

At 8:32 a.m., Mount St. Helens was shaken by an earthquake of about 5.0 magnitude. Deep inside Harry, Martha was terrified as she watched the entire northside of the summit slide down the mountain. As the mass of rock and ice began to move, it was overtaken by an enormous explosion of steam and volcanic gases. The lateral blast surged northward towards the lodge, stripping millions of trees from the hillsides. Spring Lake began to boil before the 680-degree pyroclastic flow touched the water.

Martha's last warning of what was waiting for her in Hell was given when she lingered for a time amongst the smoldering ashes of the old man. Martha screamed.

✳   ✳   ✳

It is now August 1989, nine years and three months after Mount St. Helens erupted; I prayed Martha's taste of Hell had changed her. Expecting it to be Molly's turn, I was surprised when God wanted her sister to have the next leap. Martha's eyes snapped open after the ball chose 2 Black.

✳   ✳   ✳

Running a brush through her hair, the smallish blonde girl gazed at her reflection in the mirror. Her crooked smile showed excitement; Kristine O'Connell was going to the Dairy Queen.

As with other leaps, Martha was aware of this girl's thoughts. She was thirteen and her sister Karen was exactly one year younger. People often mistook them for twins.

Kris joined her sister who was sharing roasted, salted pumpkin seeds with her twin cousins, Gary and Cary. The only difference Martha could see between the two boys was one parted his hair on the right side and the other on the left. The cousins were from a small town up north and were nearing the end of their visit.

Karen was the youngest and the boldest of the four. She happily led them all out of the house, skipping in the direction of the ice cream store. Then, one block from the DQ, Karen launched into a sprint. Ten minutes later, after spending twenty-five cents a cone, the four children were licking their way back home.

Curiosity and the need to play drew Karen to a pile of logs, each weighing more than a thousand pounds. Without missing a lick, the leader of the small gang of kids ran into the vacant lot and climbed to the very top of the stack.

Making a line, Karen's three followers prepared to follow. With the cone in her mouth, she carefully placed one foot in front of the other, balancing her way across the top of the pile. Before she jumped down, Karen turned and beckoned her cousin Gary to duplicate her acrobatic feat. Accepting the challenge, he climbed onto the pile and began his dangerous trek. When he was halfway across, Cary repeated his twin brother's move.

Kris, having just taken the last lick of her cone, shoved the rest of it into her mouth. Just as she had climbed to the top of the stack, she saw Cary jumping off to join her sister and cousin. Now it was her turn.

As Kris looked down on her playmates, Martha wished she had shared a pleasant outing such as this with her twin sister. But that was never in the cards because their playfulness was always intertwined with selfishness.

Kris took a tentative step, then another and another. With her arms stretched out and face forward, she continued to cross the pile. Halfway through her nimble stunt, the logs shifted. Kris screamed when they dislodged from each other; she fell into the mass of rolling timber.

The three children watched in horror as Kris was lost in the tumble. All was still after the final log rolled away. Kris lay on the ground, broken. Martha screamed. "Oh God, please help her!"

Gasping for a breath of air and not able to move her arms, she struggled to sit up. With all her might, the small blonde girl slowly stood. "Help me," she whimpered, then collapsed onto the dirt.

The next several minutes passed in a blur as Gary, Cary, and Karen stood helplessly watching as adults came to the rescue of their playmate. Kris was placed onto a gurney, then moved into an ambulance. During the ride to the hospital, Martha didn't feel the child's pain. When compared to other leaps, this was an unusual experience.

When they arrived at the hospital, doctors, nurses, and technicians came to the aid of their new patient, Kristine O'Connell.

While the girl slept, Martha heard them talk about the girl's injuries. Both collarbones were broken, as well as several ribs. One arm, dislocated from the shoulder, was now back in place hanging in a sling. Both lungs had collapsed and were now inflated. The scariest injury was that the girl's heart had shifted from her left side to the right.

Days, then weeks, then months passed while Martha stayed with Kris. However, this little girl did not wallow in her pain, instead she embraced her maladies. Kris relentlessly questioned her doctors and nurses, seeking to understand how each part of her was injured and the efforts the medical staff were making to remedy her situation.

For the umpteenth time, Kris asked to see her medical chart. As she reviewed her progress, Martha said to her, "I think you should become a doctor."

Kris heard what Martha had said as being a thought of her own. At that very instant, Martha's leap abruptly ended.

CHAPTER 38

I began my mission to save Martha and Molly one century ago and have watched several generations of McCabes live their lives. What I've noticed is, in 1893, Peter McCabe began a family tradition. It was a heritage grounded in four notions.

One, if possible, all McCabe generations will reside within the family mansion; two, family members will pour their hearts and souls into the family's businesses; three, the politics of the family favored the Democratic party; and four, patriotism to country is expected of all McCabe males.

Matt and Maria are the children of Geoffrey and Rachel McCabe. As they entered their teen years, I saw both were inclined to veer from family tradition. I've heard it was the generation in which they were born where young people were influenced by shifting societal values.

*　　　*　　　*

With one exception, Maria chose to follow the traditional path trodden by McCabe women. As expected of her, she worked part-time in her father's office at McCabe Motors during her high school years. Tradition then called for Maria to attend a liberal college in New England. Instead, she chose Hillsdale College, a small, rural, conservative school in southern Michigan.

In early September 1989, a few days before her first semester began, Maria met her college roommate, Diane Sinclair. It didn't take long for the two college freshmen to become best friends.

David Sinclair, Diane's older brother, was attending college about two hours north of Hillsdale. Like Maria, he also leaned towards conservativism. He was pursuing a degree in Automotive Marketing and Management. In October, David came for a visit during Hillsdale's Homecoming Weekend. As his sister hoped, he and Maria fell in love. Setting their political beliefs aside, this was a match made in heaven for the McCabe automotive dynasty.

✳　　　✳　　　✳

Two years passed and Matt's life-changing adventure began when his father took him out on the *Peggy Jo*. As the son of the owner of *The Spirit of Casco Bay*, he could help his father by coiling ropes and picking up trash left by paying customers. On the smaller craft, because it was only the two of them, he was treated like a junior member of the crew. By the time he was fourteen, the boy had acquired the skills and experience required to sail the *Peggy Jo*.

In 1989, at age sixteen, Matt became a member of the local sailing club. That year, he also joined the Portland High School's sailing team. Although he could drive a car, his father's rule of not sailing without another experienced sailor aboard the *Peggy Jo* stood fast. Geoffrey knew the dangers of sailing alone and did not want to lose his son to an errant gust of wind or lack of judgment.

After graduating from high school in 1991, Matt continued to follow in his father's footsteps by attending the University of Rhode Island and was a member of their collegiate sailing team. He welcomed reliving this part of his father's life as it aligned with the one he wanted for himself. However, in his heart, he knew once he had completed college he would wander further away from the McCabe tradition.

✷   ✷   ✷

Having shared the paths Matt and Maria chose to follow, it is now time for me to turn my attention to an important event soon to come. God has told me it will be about Charlie McCabe's friend, my deceased grandson Danny Clarke.

✷   ✷   ✷

It is mid-October of 1991; Charlie has just received a call from the White House. It was an invitation to attend a special ceremony to be held in the East Room. The event was to honor his best friend, Daniel Clarke, who he had last seen alive fifty years ago.

Over the years, Charlie often wondered what his life would have been like if Danny had survived the war. Peggy would have married Danny, he would have stayed single, and, at the age of seventy-five, he'd be a lonely bastard. He thought, *Oh Danny, by saving your shipmates, you saved me.*

One week later, Charlie and Peggy flew from Portland to the Washington National Airport where they were met by a man dressed in a black suit. After introducing himself as their chauffeur, he led them to a limousine and drove them across the Potomac River to the White House. Once through security, they were escorted to the East Room and seated in the second row.

Charlie looked around the room and saw it was filled with high-ranking military officials, politicians, reporters, and cameramen. Then, he noticed someone familiar to him. Charlie leaned over to Peggy and whispered, "Honey, seated in front of us is Danny's sister, Elizabeth."

Peggy said, "I thought I recognized her. She was at our son's wedding. I regret not getting to know her better."

"No time like the present," he said as he tapped Elizabeth on the shoulder.

Elizabeth turned and immediately recognized Charlie. "Thank you for coming." Tears trickled down her cheeks. "I'm sure my brother sends his love from Heaven above."

Charlie said, "If there was anyone who earned the right to enter Heaven, it would be Danny. Elizabeth, this is my wife, Peggy. You met her at Geoffrey's wedding."

"My lord. It's hard to believe the wedding was twenty-one years ago. Peggy, you look as lovely now as you did then." She asked, "How is my Geoffrey?"

"My son is fine and his wife, Rachel, is also doing well. As for their children, our grandchildren are both in college. Maria is a junior and Matt just started. It's remarkable how time passes."

"Yes, it is," Elizabeth agreed. "My goodness, where are my manners? Sitting with me are my daughter, Katherine, and her husband, Erik. Next to them is my grandson, Adam. Katherine, this is—"

Their conversation was interrupted when a woman at the podium announced the ceremony would begin with an introduction from Admiral Thomas B. Hayward, Chief of Naval Operations. After he said a few words, the admiral stepped aside for President George H. W. Bush.

President Bush began the program by sharing Daniel's love of flying. He then talked about his service to the nation during his first enlistment and followed with his act of patriotism when he re-enlisted after Pearl Harbor was attacked. The President also described the moments which led up to the split-second decision Daniel made to sacrifice his life to save his ship and fellow seamen.

The President closed the tribute to Daniel by saying, "The selfless act of giving one's life for others is the greatest expression of love a person can bestow on his fellow man. It is an honor for me to award Lieutenant Commander Daniel Clarke the Congressional Medal of Honor. The courage and bravery of this man should never be forgotten. On behalf of my hero, this award is being accepted by his sister,

Mrs. Elizabeth Nelson, and her daughter, Katherine Nelson-Scott."

As they made their way to the podium, Charlie saw Elizabeth was having difficulty walking. *It's nice Katherine is here to support her,* he thought. Then, he quietly chuckled when he remembered the time when she told his son, Geoffrey, he was too young to work for them. *Where have all the years gone?*

Charlie's eyes watered as he watched the ladies accept Danny's award. He missed his best friend and recalled the numerous hours they had spent pretending to be ace combat pilots before the war. *Life is so unfair. It was you who deserved to have Peggy, not me.*

Charlie's trip down memory lane was brought back to the present when he noticed his wife's soulful tears had turned to uncontrolled sobbing. Putting his arm around Peggy's shoulders, he pulled her tight to him. Looking up, he whispered, "Danny, thank you for the life you've given me."

✴   ✴   ✴

Seven months after the ceremony—May 1992 to be exact—Maria returned home and told her family she would not complete her final year in college and would soon marry David Sinclair. An afterthought was thrown into the mix; Maria was pregnant.

By mid-summer, the newlyweds had moved into the McCabe mansion. Geoffrey hired his new son-in-law on one condition: David's political persuasion was not to be shared at McCabe Motors. Soon after, political signs to re-elect President Bush and for his opponent, Bill Clinton, littered the front lawn of the family's home.

As for Matt, he was in his second year at the University of Rhode Island. He was pleased that his family's attention was directed away from him and towards his new brother-in-law.

✴   ✴   ✴

Maria was eight months into her pregnancy when she was asked to join her family at the dining room table. Except for her brother, all the McCabes living within the mansion were present.

Rachel began, "This meeting is a family tradition called for the benefit of our new soon-to-be mother and her husband."

Maria and David sat up in their seats.

"Don't be alarmed," she said. "It's time for you to be aware of what the rest of us know may happen shortly after your baby is born. That is, should you have a boy."

David laughed. "Circumcision?"

Maria kicked David under the table.

Rachel was not amused. "Perhaps … however, this meeting is to tell you of a visit you may have from two women who died in 1893."

Maria stammered. "You're kidding. Ghosts?"

Except for David, everyone else at the table nodded.

Rachel then told the story of the McLellan twins, their deaths, and their visits as ghosts when a first-born male McCabe was born. Since Charlie and Geoffrey never actually saw the ghosts, they had nothing to add.

Maria shook her head in disbelief.

Peggy said, "It's all true."

"Why wasn't I told about this when I was younger?" Maria asked.

"Because, until now, it wasn't necessary," Rachel replied.

David chuckled. "Is it too late for a divorce?"

Seeing no one was laughing along with him, David turned to his wife. "Honey," he said, "maybe we should move out of the mansion."

Maria nodded. "That's the most appropriate thing you've said during this meeting."

"I don't think that'll work," Peggy said. "Because they're not bound by the walls of this home, I'm sure they will find you."

Turning to his mother-in-law, David said, "Okay, you've told us about their visits, but you haven't mentioned why."

Rachel explained, "I believe God is trying to give them a chance to change their wicked ways."

Maria sighed. "How many of their *chances* does our family have to endure? They've come after the birth of Abraham McCabe, Charles McCabe, Geoffrey McCabe, and Matt McCabe. Now, they'll return if I have a son! Will this never end?"

David put his arm around his wife. "Honey, they can't be that bad. After all, all the McCabe mothers before you were able to deal with their mischief."

Maria brushed her husband's arm off her shoulder. She snapped, "That's easy for you to say! Like the other McCabe men, you won't be seeing or hearing them."

"Perhaps God is testing us?" Peggy interjected. "When I was younger, my fiancée died and I lost my baby, causing my belief in God to diminish. Because of Martha and Molly, I have changed."

Maria asked, "How have you changed?"

"I now realize there is a higher power. If He tries to shape those who are no longer living, I'm convinced He also shapes the lives of the living."

"I get it," David said. "The test, His test, is having them choose between good and evil."

✳   ✳   ✳

While everyone waited for the newborn to arrive, I turned my attention to Martha. This time it is her turn to be plucked from the void. On a Friday in December 1992, the wheel chose 6 Red for Martha.

✳   ✳   ✳

It was very cold, the sidewalks slippery, as darkness set upon Portland. City lights brightened the night, while colorful strings of lights announced the Christmas season. Snow was falling adding three inches of whiteness that already covered the city.

Julie McGuire sat in the driver's seat of her family car. She looked up at the electronic sign on the top of the building next to the People's United Bank; it displayed 5:00 P.M. and thirty-four degrees. Due to the gusty winds coming off Casco Bay, anyone walking the streets would swear it was twenty degrees colder.

Julie's twelve-year-old son, Michael, sat next to her in the passenger seat. His younger sisters, Mandy and Mindy, sat behind them. All were hovering under wool blankets, each member of the family of four wearing three layers of clothing. Five minutes from now, it would be time for their mother to start the car's engine. All eagerly waited for the warm blast of air to fill their home, the 1981 Ford Escort.

Julie turned the ignition key after the required time passed. Nothing happened. One gauge in front of her read 237,391 miles. The needle on the fuel gauge did not waver from E. Julie cried. Her children shivered.

She looked across the parking lot and wondered what she could do to warm up her children. Steam was rising out from a grate behind the Public Library. Although it had just closed for the day, the library could still be of service to them. Quickly, Julie ushered her brood of three towards the heat rising from the depths of the building.

The workday had ended, and employees from both the bank and library had left the buildings. All were headed home to enjoy a delicious dinner, as well as the warmth of a cozy home.

A man dressed to the nines stepped out of the bank, locked the door, and walked briskly towards his 1992 Cadillac Eldorado. Halfway to his car, he glanced over to see a mother and her three children. He wanted to castigate her for putting her children in harm's way for everyone in Portland knew the indigent congregate in that exact spot after dark. But he had a dinner date with his wife and didn't want to keep her waiting. The man continued his walk towards the car.

Martha, now within the man, enjoyed the warmth of his expensive winter coat. "I'm in a man," she said. "Huh. … So, you're Mr. Gerald Jeffries, as well as the president of the bank."

With a slip and a slide, Mr. Jeffries fell onto his back. He slowly sat up. Placing his left gloved hand onto the wet snow, he started to rise. As he did, Martha saw the family of four huddled around the steam coming out of a metal grate. Immediately, she wanted to help them.

Mr. Jeffries brushed the snow off his clothes and proceeded towards his car. Martha looked back at the bleak sight of the shivering family. "Have you no compassion?" she asked.

The banker did not reply because he could not hear Martha's question.

Martha was steamed at the man for not wanting to offer help to the family. "Turn around," she said. The man did not stop. Martha shouted, "I said, turn around!"

Mr. Jeffries stopped in his tracks.

"Hmmm," Martha said. *For whatever reason, God has just allowed me to control this man.* Testing her power, she commanded, "Stand on your right foot."

The banker stood on his right foot. Martha giggled. "Now go help those people behind the building."

Mr. Jeffries turned and walked towards the family hovered around the grate, causing the mother and her children to flee. "Stop," he called out. "Please don't run away. I want to help you."

Julie ceased running. Seeing their mother had stopped, the children also ended their flight. Her lips trembling, she asked, "What … what did you say?"

"I want to help you," he said. "Why are you standing around the grate?"

"I, I ran out of gas," she stammered, "and could no longer keep my car heated. So, my children and I had no choice but to huddle around the steam coming from the library. It's not against the law, is it?"

He shook his head. "No. But it's not safe for you to be here."

Julie looked towards the back of the library and then towards her car. "What choice do I have?"

Martha gave Mr. Jeffries another command, "Give her money."

The banker reached into his pocket and pulled out his wallet. After extracting $1000 from a secret fold, he handed it to Julie.

She shook her head. "But I can't—"

"Yes, you can. Take it," he said. "Find a hotel for the weekend. Here's my business card. Call me on Monday and I will make sure you and your children don't spend another night out in the cold."

Julie embraced the banker. Martha smiled.

Mr. Jeffries turned and walked towards his car. Martha stayed within him, and suspected the leap was not over for all prior leaps had ended with a tragedy for the person she was within.

While the banker drove away in his luxury car, Martha thought about what had just happened. Because of her, the man had shown compassion to a needy family and had also committed an act of grace. *Or was it she who did these things?*

Martha considered the leaps she had experienced during her afterlife. On the sinking ship, after being outed as a cleaning woman, Meagan Turner was turned away from boarding the lifeboat. Surely, she would have lived if the wealthy passengers had shown humility. It would have been a humble act to allow Meagan to board. Upon reflection, Martha was sure she would have acted just like the wealthy woman who sent Meagan to the back of the line. *Shame on me,* she thought.

When she was within the patient dying from the Spanish Flu, Martha had not felt one ounce of compassion for the suffering woman. She only wanted Mary Merriweather to die quickly so that she, herself, did not have to endure the pain any longer. Then there was Peggy Preston who miscarried her baby. Same thing … no compassion.

Then, at the end of her leap into Harry R. Truman, she had lingered within the ashes of the man after he had been incinerated by the blast from Mount St. Helens. She was now sure God was punishing her for not understanding what she should have known during her lifetime.

Martha heard herself say, "Committing acts of compassion, grace, and humility during one's life, or afterlife, will lead to a better tomorrow."

As soon as she had said those words, Martha ceased to be within Mr. Gerald Jeffries.

CHAPTER 39

It is one month after Martha's leap, January 1993. Expecting another leaf has been added to the McCabe family tree, I have returned to see if Martha and Molly have made any change in their ways.

*   *   *

On a winter's day, the snow was melting as a brand new 1993 Chrysler New Yorker pulled up to the hospital entrance. Its driver, David Sinclair, was careful not to splash his wife and newborn with the icy slush. She was sitting in a wheelchair; their son cradled in her arms.

After placing the gearshift into park, David helped his wife and son into the New Yorker's expansive back seat. Baby Nathan fussed as he was secured into the child safety seat, his mother buckled beside him.

After closing the passenger door, the proud father took his place behind the steering wheel. David turned to his wife, a pensive look on his face. "Are you ready for them?" he asked.

"I am," Maria replied. "Instead of dwelling upon what a nuisance these ghosts can be, I've decided to help them move on. I don't want them bothering our son's future wife."

David frowned. "You'll have your hands full," he said. "I just wish there was something I could do to help you." He sighed, moved the gearshift into drive, then pressed his right foot on the accelerator pedal.

✴   ✴   ✴

Martha clamped her hand over her sister's mouth and yelled in a strained whisper, "Stop it. Stop it right now!"

Molly, who was sobbing, panted, "You won't believe—where I've been."

"From the grease on your hands and nightgown, I'd guess—"

Molly abruptly stopped crying when she took note of the filth covering her sister. She pointed. "You've been—cleaning fireplaces?"

To no avail, Martha tried to brush the volcanic ash from her hair and nightgown. "It doesn't matter anymore," she said.

Their attention turned to the sounds coming from the floor below. A minute later, David entered the nursery. With their new baby in her arms, Maria followed.

"Surprise!" Molly shouted.

Maria shook her head. "We've been told to expect you." She turned to her husband, placing the baby in his arms. "Please bear with me for a moment. I expect the one-sided conversation I'm about to have will be dreadfully awkward for you to hear."

He nodded, then took a seat in the rocking chair.

Molly pouted. "He knows?"

"Yes, he knows," Maria replied. "In fact, Peggy and Rachel have enlightened the whole family of your on-and-off-again visits. They've also advised me on what I should do during your stay. So … you behave, and I'll treat you in a gracious manner. If we work together, I think it's possible we can get through your visits with no complications."

"I would have it no other way," Martha said.

Maria thought *that was easy*. She said, "Because my younger brother Matt has not yet married nor has a son, I have the unfortunate privilege of you popping into my life."

Molly giggled. "It is—an honor—isn't it?"

Martha, her head still tilted, threw a disapproving look at Molly.

She said, "I apologize for my sister's mockery."

"I did no—such thing!" Molly snapped. "Where's Matthew?"

"As I said, you're stuck with me."

"Who are you?" Martha asked.

"I am Maria. I'm sure you saw me as a toddler during your last visit." She pointed. "This is my husband, David, and our son, Nathan. Now, listen to me. … During the next three days, you two are to leave us alone. Our baby needs to get used to both his new home and his parents. Will you do that for us?"

Martha smiled. "Yes, of course," she replied.

"Humph!" Molly grunted.

Maria gently took Nathan from her husband, then she placed him into the bassinette. She turned to the twins and said, "You should also know the year is 1993, and you've been gone from the mansion for nineteen years. Like my mother, I've no interest in hearing about your leaps. Now, please leave us."

The twins left the room, floated down the grand staircase and wandered silently throughout the first-floor rooms, mindful of the changes made since their last visit. The final room they entered was the sitting room where they took a seat near the fireplace. Although heat was coming from the hearth, neither Martha nor Molly felt the flame.

As they took in the ambiance of the room, tears rolled down Martha's cheek. She mumbled, "I had an awful leap."

Molly smiled. "Tell me, sister."

"His name was Harry R. Truman," Martha began, "and he owned the Mount St. Helens Lodge at Spirit Lake. As he lived his last morning on earth, a volcano erupted. The blast consumed him … and me! Instead of leaving him right away, I lingered in his ashes. Oh, God …"

Molly laughed. "Hot as—Hell?"

"As a matter of fact, it was. I don't ever want to do another leap." Martha looked up to the heavens. "Dear Lord, please forgive me for the bad things I've done."

Molly laughed. "Forgive you? —You've got—to be kidding. —He's playing—with your mind."

"Perhaps He is," she said with a whimper. "Molly, I forgive you for what you are doing to me right now and what you've done to me in the past."

"How precious," Molly mocked. "I'll never—forgive you—for taking my—chance to inherit—mother's fortune. —Rot—in—Hell!" She continued, "I was in—Jimmy Hoffa. —It took that—inconsiderate bastard—seven days—to die. —Christ almighty—the stench—I had to—put up with."

"You shouldn't say things like that."

Martha has changed, Molly thought. Usually, her sister's temper was as hot as the month of July. Not once since they returned had she challenged her.

✴　　　✴　　　✴

Four months later, May 1993. In the wee hours of the morning, Maria had just finished warming a bottle in the kitchen and headed upstairs to the nursery. About halfway up the staircase, she heard a commotion behind her and turned to see the twins stumble through the closed front door. Martha and Molly froze when they saw Maria.

"Peggy said you could leave the mansion," Maria said.

Molly snapped, "You're mistaken."

"You've caught us," Martha confessed. "Yes, as you can see, we do leave this house. Every time we return from only God knows where, there are so many new things to see. It's a wonder how the world changes after one's death. You mustn't hold our curiosity against us."

"I don't," Maria replied. "In fact, I find your time away a blessing."

As Maria continued to climb the stairs, she wished the twins would roam about Portland twenty-four hours a day, every day during their stay.

*   *   *

Three months later, Martha decided another apology was needed. It wasn't to her sister, nor was it to any member of the McCabe family. It was to a man she had wronged after his death. She knew Molly would not agree with what she planned, so she needed to find the perfect time to escape from her sister's prying eyes.

The musical play, *Phantom of the Opera*, had come to the State Theatre in Portland for a week-long run. On opening night, 1870 live people and two dead sisters found themselves spellbound by the haunting musical love story. Martha and Molly were especially enchanted by the opening scene of Act II, "Masquerade." The ball gowns worn in the scene were exquisite!

The ghost twins vowed to attend every production while it played in Portland. Knowing how captivated Molly was during the costume-ball scene, Martha decided this would be her opportunity to separate from her sister.

Martha chose the third night of the production to escape. Midway into the "Masquerade," she backed away from her twin and melted into the crowd. Martha left the theatre and made her way to the ghost she wanted to see. Since he could not leave the place he haunted, she had to come to him.

Upon her arrival, Martha walked through the front door of the seaside mansion. She searched the first, second, and third floors of the home, but was unable to find the captain. With only one more place to look, she took four more flights of stairs and entered the seventh-floor tower room.

"Martha, what are you doing here?" the captain asked.

Her voice quivered as she replied. "I've come to apologize to you."

Captain Samuel Edward Clarke came out of the shadows and into the dim moonlight shining into the room. "Where is your sister? You two are usually bound at the hip."

Martha trembled with fear. She stammered, "M-M-Molly doesn't know I'm here. N-n-nor would she ever agree with my reason for coming."

"Martha, just what is it you have come to say to me?"

"I'm terribly sorry for being disrespectful to you and your wife, Hannah. And I'm sorry for trying to take your son away from his grandparents." She cried, "I'm such a sorry lot. Please forgive me."

He stepped closer. "What do you know of forgiveness?"

Martha paused to ponder her reply. She said, "Although I love my sister, I also despise Molly for her treatment of me. When I forgave her, I felt the release of a great burden I've been carrying during my entire existence."

The captain nodded. "Did Molly forgive you?"

She looked away from him. "She did not."

He asked, "What do you hope to gain if I forgive you?"

Martha turned back to him. With a sheepish grin, she replied, "Bygones be bygones?"

"Ahh, I know what you want. You wish us to make an agreement that certain hurtful things said and done should remain in the past. Dropping this weight, you hope we can both more forward."

"I guess so."

The captain took hold of her hands and looked directly into her eyes. It was not an easy thing for him to do as her head was tilted to one side.

"What I have learned in life, as well as death," he began, "is that it is never too late to apologize for misdeeds nor to seek forgiveness. Martha, I accept your apology. Know I forgive you, as well."

As the captain's forgiveness washed over Martha, her eyes changed. No longer cold and heartless, they had softened. Revealing a soul moving towards the light.

"That's very gracious of you," she said. "I see why Hannah loved you."

Martha hugged the captain. After releasing him, she continued, "I believe my heartfelt apologies to you, to my sister, and to God are necessary. Perhaps I can now be allowed to move on to whatever He has planned for me." She asked, "When do you think it'll happen for you?"

"When will I join my Hannah?" The captain sighed. "God only knows. Like you, there must be something He is waiting for me to do. When that moment comes, I believe my voyage in this world will end. Until then, I'm enjoying what no man has ever experienced. I have the privilege and the pleasure of knowing my descendants."

"I must confess, the blessing you speak of never entered my mind." She smiled. "I've also enjoyed meeting my shirttail descendants."

Martha walked towards the door; she turned to him before floating through it. She said, "Captain, what is it that seafarers say? Oh yes, I remember. … I pray your final voyage is filled with fair winds and following seas."

"Thank you, Martha. May God be with you."

Martha smiled. "I believe He is."

✴　　　✴　　　✴

Martha returned to the theatre and joined Molly just as the musical play was ending. While both were clapping with the audience, Molly leaned to her and inquired, "Where have—you been?"

Martha knew her sister would chide her if she knew the truth. She replied, "I went to watch the play from a different vantage point."

Vantage point? Molly remembered what her deceased husband Reggie said many times: *The best vantage point to see a play is from the stage.* She chuckled.

✴　　　✴　　　✴

It was the final night of the production, and the play was about to begin. Molly said, "Martha, like you did the other night, I'm going to find a better vantage point. Do not follow me."

Martha nodded. *It'll be nice to enjoy the play without hearing my sister sing along with the actress playing the part of Christine Daaé,* she thought.

Unknown to the twins, two couples had, at the last minute, bought tickets for the final night of the play. After arriving at the theatre, Geoffrey, Rachel, David, and Maria took their balcony seats.

The play began with a public auction in Paris when an auctioneer presented a music box with a cymbal-playing monkey attached to it. After it was sold, the chandelier was hoisted up to the roof for display. Once in place, the story shifted back in time to 1870 when Carlotta Giudicelli, a famous soprano, prepared for the performance of the grand opera, *Hannibal.*

As the play continued, both Rachel and Maria were surprised how much their husbands enjoyed the music and the story. Never had they seen Geoffrey and David experience a more enjoyable night at the theatre. Unfortunately, Rachel's and Maria's enjoyment abruptly ended when the actress playing Christine Daaé began to sing. Molly floated in, joining the soprano in song.

And so it went for the entire production. Every scene Christine was in, Molly was, too. Whether she was chasing her dream of being an opera singer or simply being pursued by her suitors, Christine was never alone because a ghost was always with her.

Nearing the end of the play, Molly finally disappeared from the stage. As Rachel and Maria began to enjoy the reprieve, they heard a bloodcurdling scream. They were aghast to see Molly riding the chandelier as it fell from the ceiling and crashed upon the floor of the stage.

CHAPTER 40

It was January 1994, nearly one year after the birth of Nathan Sinclair and the return of Martha and Molly. At present, both were in the entertainment room watching a soap opera, *The Bold and the Beautiful.*

Both twins were on the edge of their seat as the handsome lawyer began to disrobe his beautiful assistant. The romantic scene abruptly ended, followed by a commercial about a pill which was guaranteed to enhance a man's sexual prowess. Martha grabbed the remote and turned the television off.

Molly yelled, "Why'd you—do that?"

"We need to have a talk," Martha replied.

"Can't you—wait?"

"No. Nathan will turn one tomorrow and it's possible I will not see you again after tonight."

"So, poof—we're gone," Molly said. "Poof—we leap. Poof—we're back—again."

Martha said, "I don't think that's going to happen for me."

"Why—is that?"

Martha shrugged. "I just feel it."

"I just—*feel* it," she mocked.

"Molly, please forgive me."

"Over my—dead body!"

"Oh Molly. I fear it may be over your dead soul. Look at us. We are a sorry lot. The night of my death, my hair got flattened on one side of my head and I've a broken neck. There's a crushed rose in my hair and grass stains on my nightgown. To make matters worse, I've accumulated several mementos from my leaps. My gown is ripped from when I crashed into the ship's propeller, and I have a mahogany spot on my face from the Spanish Flu. I've numerous blood stains on my nightgown, and my hair is grey from all the volcanic ash clinging to it."

Molly shrugged. "So?"

"So, look at you! Your death gave you blue lips, tea stains on your nightgown, and you can't complete a sentence without taking several gasps of air. Your gown is simply filthy; it's tattered, singed, and greasy. My god, Molly. Your right leg is three inches shorter from the fall off a building. Every time I look at you, I can't help but stare at the bullet hole in your forehead."

Molly stuck a finger in the hole and shrugged. "I can't see it."

"Dear sister, we look more indigent than the old couple we first leaped into. If they were to meet us on the street, they would offer us—"

"Nothing!" Molly shouted. "They—had nothing—to give."

"Dear sister, they would have offered us compassion."

"Humph! —I'd rather have—a warm bath and—a clean nightgown."

"I will miss you, sister."

Molly stuck out her tongue and grabbed for the remote. "Gimme that!" she yelled.

✳   ✳   ✳

It is June 2016, twenty-two years and five months after the twins vanished again from the McCabe household. As I hold the imaginary marble in my hand, I must confess I'm afraid to drop it. My fear is that

Molly may be in for a horrific ride. Truth be known: I'm also concerned for myself. You see, when she leaps, I must watch what happens. God forbid, I may witness an event more gruesome than I'm prepared to handle. All that said, God's will must be done.

I take a breath to calm myself and spin the wheel. The sphere falls from my fingers. 11 Black.

✳   ✳   ✳

"Here we—go, again," Molly said. "Pop in—pop out—leap. … Pop in—pop out—leap. … Around and around—God's merry-go-round."

Hmmm, since prayer is the accepted communication with God, I should pray to Him. She bowed her head. "Dear God—let me stay—in this world—so I may—enjoy the—city's nightlife." Molly laughed.

"Who have you—popped me into—this time?"

In less than the blink of an eye, Omar Mateen's past and present thoughts filled her mind. *Oh my,* Molly thought. *He is a terribly angry man.*

Consumed by hate, Omar calmly approached a building were several Latino men and women had gathered. Blaring music assaulted his ears as he considered his sacred mission. Molly felt the man's repulsion but didn't understand it. *No matter. Whatever he does is of no concern to me.*

Omar believed he was a righteous man who, by doing God's will, would be rewarded in paradise. Hiding his weapon under his green, blue, and white plaid dress shirt, he pushed through the crowd and muttered, "Sick animals. God has sent me to end your sinful frolicking."

Molly chuckled. "Sinful frolicking? —Ooooh. This leap—should be—exciting!"

Omar entered a nightclub called The Pulse. Through his eyes and ears, Molly could see and hear the gaiety. She gasped; this merriment was far different than anything she'd ever witnessed. Men were seductively dancing with men and women were dancing with other women. She cried, "Oh my! They're groping and kissing each other." Molly closed her eyes to shut out their behavior; Omar's hatred forced them open.

Mostly Latinos, three-hundred and twenty strong, filled the club when the last call for drinks was heard. *Last call?* Omar chuckled. *An appropriate name for your final night on earth.* He raised his rifle, a SIG Sauer MCX semi-automatic, and began to randomly shoot the club's decadent patrons.

Rather than being appalled, Molly was entertained by Omar's slaughter. "One, two, three," she counted as each hedonist fell to the floor. "Four, five, six," she continued as each victim's joyfulness ended.

The loud music in the darkened room confused the Latin lovers as they tried to escape their nightmare. Omar smiled as people screamed and hid behind any barrier they could find. Steadfastly, he walked throughout the building shooting everyone he saw. Leaving nothing to chance, Omar put another bullet into the still bodies he stepped over.

Although Molly continued to count, her amusement waned. At number thirty-three, the loud gunshot was followed by blood and human tissue splattering on Omar's face. He grinned. Molly flinched for the disagreeable odors of blood, feces, sweat, and urine had displaced the pleasing fragrances of perfume and cologne.

For thirty minutes, Omar emptied his rifle, reloaded his weapon, and continued firing. When his gun momentarily jammed, he took out a handpiece, a 9mm Glock 17 semi-automatic, and shot anyone he thought was still breathing.

Warm liquid cooled on the barroom floor as it oozed from his slaughtered victims. Blood was splattered everywhere, making it difficult for those who were trying to flee the mayhem. All had trouble finding their footing in the wet and sticky gore.

At first, Omar was infuriated by the infidel blood sticking to the soles of his shoes. Then, seeing his new plaid dress shirt defiled with blood, he gained a new perspective. Indeed, God will accept the stains as badges of honor. Omar smiled. *I am truly an honorable and righteous man.*

Molly's counting of the dead and wounded reached Omar's ears. Hearing the count of ninety, Omar let out a boisterous laugh. He had reached the "gay nineties" and was still going strong. Molly didn't join his laughter.

Having wreaked havoc in the barroom, Omar entered a restroom and found more patrons waiting to be delivered from their evil. Omar fired sixteen times into the group of fifteen sinners crowded together, killing two and wounding several others.

A woman broke from the pile of victims and dragged herself across the floor. When she reached out to help her wounded lover, she found Omar standing above her. Pulling his Glock from his belt, he placed the barrel's tip onto her forehead. She looked up in terror and screamed, "Why?"

"God sent me to deliver a message to you." He pulled the trigger.

"One hundred—and two!" Molly cried.

Taking a short respite from the carnage, Omar made a call on his cell phone to his second ex-wife. Because of repeated beatings and isolation from her family, she had taken their three-year-old son and fled to California. Omar's call to her was to say a final goodbye to his son; he could only leave a message.

Time was running out for Omar. Because his god required him to tell the world his reasons for the holy deeds, those still breathing were taken hostage. Omar dialed 9-1-1.

For the next two hours, Omar spoke with the hostage negotiators. He confessed he was a Mujahid, a Soldier of God, and pledged his allegiance to the Islamic State of Iraq and the Levant (ISIL). While Molly listened to his confession, she knew it to be false. *If he were truly an honorable man, as he considered himself to be, Omar would have mentioned he was bisexual and had often visited gay clubs prior to his marriages.*

By the end of Omar's blessed mission, forty-nine lay dead without a pulse at The Pulse. Another fifty-three were severely wounded. Molly didn't feel sorry for these people; she felt nothing for them. Her only interest was an end to this uncomfortable interruption to her existence. Finally, shortly after 5:00 a.m., a SWAT team of heavily armed officers breeched the building and put round after round into Omar's body. Molly was counting, again.

∗   ∗   ∗

Darkness set upon Omar's life when the eighth projectile entered him. Molly was pleased; God was not. He commanded me to spin the wheel again for Molly; 19 Red.

∗   ∗   ∗

Six months later, Molly opened her eyes expecting to be welcomed by her sister. That was not to be for she had leapt into another man.

"Oh God—not again. —Can't You—be more—creative?"

Three men joined the seriously ill convict in the back of the ambulance, two were armed corrections officers and the other was a nurse. Molly wished she had leapt into one of the three handsome men and not into the suffering old man strapped to a gurney.

"Stay with me Charlie," the nurse pleaded. "It won't be long before we arrive at the hospital."

"What does it matter?' the prisoner mumbled. "What does it matter if I die in a prison or a hospital? What does it matter?"

"It matters to me," the nurse replied. "I've never lost a patient en route to Mercy Hospital."

With tires screeching to a halt, the ambulance stopped in front of the emergency entrance. The back doors to the vehicle burst open; a gurney quickly rolled out and into the building. While the doctors examined the old man, Molly sensed the evil dwelling within him. She gasped for she was not alone in Charlie; the Devil made three.

The nurse asked, "What's the prognosis?"

The doctor replied, "Presently, among other maladies, Mr. Manson is suffering from gastrointestinal bleeding. He's too weak to survive surgery, therefore I'm releasing him back into your care. To be honest, I hope he dies in a lonely cell instead of in my hospital. Get this piece of shit out of here."

Every second, every minute, every hour, and every day after being carried back into his prison cell, Molly felt Charlie's agonizing pain from colon cancer. She yelled, "Damn it! —You—did this—to me!"

The Devil chuckled. "As much as I want to, I cannot take credit for what I've not done. Molly, you should know by now … you did this to yourself."

"I did—not!" Molly screamed. She turned to the man she was in and yelled, "Die—you bastard—die! The sooner—you do—the sooner—I can escape—this torture."

"Molly," the Devil said, "I fear you do not know the meaning of torture. I can help you with that."

One week passed, then two, then three. Although the pain Molly felt was excruciating, it never came close to the assault Charlie's thoughts were having on her. They were tearing her mind apart.

After one month in this horrible hell, Molly wished for a leap into another dying soul. *Bad as this is, it couldn't be any worse. Could it?* Molly closed her eyes as tight as she could. "Let—me—go!"

"Molly, my love."

Molly opened her eyes and was greeted by the warm smile of her departed husband.

"It is I, Reggie," the Devil lied. "Come with me. I'll take you from this misery."

"I—"

A man wearing a yellow zoot suit appeared. "He's lying to you."

"Angelo?"

The ghost chuckled. "You chose Reggie once before. How did that turn out for you?"

Molly sobbed. "He cheated—on me."

He nodded. "It is his nature. He'll cheat again."

Molly turned to Reggie and shook her head no. "He's right. —I can't go—with you." Turning back to Angelo, she said, "And I—can't go—with you. You—abandoned me—too."

Angelo explained, "I had to make a choice. Now it is your turn to choose."

"I never abandoned you," said the voice of an older man.

Molly turned to Reggie to find he was no longer with her. Mayor Jacob McLellan had spoken the words. She cried out, "Father!"

He whispered in her ear, "Molly, my dear, I was always there for you and I'm here for you now."

A bright ball of light suddenly appeared. She proclaimed, "He's not your father."

The woman's voice coming from the light seemed familiar to Molly. She asked, "Who—are you?"

"Listen to Angelo," she said. "You have a choice to make. Now, make it!"

"You must come with me," her father pleaded. "You were always my favorite."

"He's not your father," the light repeated. "You know your father never favored one daughter over the other. He loved you both, equally."

Molly finally recognized the voice. "You were—always kind—to me—and to my sister. You—never lied—to me."

"Choose!" shouted the voices in unison.

"I, I choose … Dear God—I want—my sister."

Jacob McLellan's face filled with fury. "Damn you!" he screamed. "Damn you, you little shit!"

When Charles Manson's heart exploded, Molly prayed to God for the gift of seeing Martha again.

✳   ✳   ✳

"My God!"

I agree.

"I don't think I can bring myself to spin the wheel again."

Hannah, your mission is not over. She has not yet been saved.

"Another spin?"

For the prodigal twin.

I sighed. "May I take a short break from this mission? A respite if you will?"

Granted. Call out to Me on Christmas Eve, 2018.

CHAPTER 41

I didn't take the next two years off because guardian angels never rest. They continue to work on their primary mission, which is to watch over their loved ones.

I called out to him, "God? Are you there?"

I am.

"It's Christmas Eve. Should I spin the wheel on this hallowed day?"

Not yet. First, I have a gift for you.

"A Christmas gift? Whatever could it be?"

What do you want most?

I laughed. "You already know my answer."

I do. But I want to hear you say it.

"I want my husband to hold me in his arms."

So be it.

✳ ✳ ✳

I went to my husband, just in time to see him fulfill his promise to God and our descendants. Now free from his Earthly restraints, we share our love as we had promised each other; to love one another forever and ever.

It is now April 2019, four months after God allowed me to join Sam. Although my husband has completed his mission, I have not. With renewed vigor, I spun the wheel for Molly—35 Black.

✳   ✳   ✳

"What? My God!" Molly cried. "What have—You done—to me?"

The disheveled and shackled man looked much older than his twenty-four years, his chains rattled as he shuffled into the brightly lit room. Large muscular hands pushed down on his shoulders, forcing him to sit on the cold metal chair. Using the last bit of his strength, the man pulled on his restraints as every part of his body was being strapped into the chair.

The prison guards stepped away from what they had done and were pleased their prisoner had not spit on them during the process of preparing him for his execution. Then, the man's thoughts became Molly's thoughts, and she knew the punishment to come was well-deserved.

John William King was a white supremacist who, with the aid of two friends, had dragged a Black man behind a truck until several parts of his lifeless body had been torn away from his torso. What was left of their victim was dumped in front of a Black church as a message to all who worshiped in this God's forsaken house—not even The Lord God Almighty can protect you from our hate.

John had waited ten years on death row for this moment. The window curtains were pulled back, revealing a small group of people who were there to bear witness to his end. Needles were poked into John's arm; a deadly fluid flowed through his veins.

Molly whimpered, "I miss—my sister." She prayed, "God—please—forgive me. Please—forgive me. Please—"

✳   ✳   ✳

"Tell me I am done."

You are finished. Hannah, what have you learned?

"Me? I thought all this was about the twins."

Remember? I said your assignment was as much about you as it is about them.

"I remember. I just hoped you forgot. Silly me …"

What have you learned?

I gathered my thoughts, as well as my courage. I replied, "The powers of good and evil are real. They pull and push everyone, including me. It is a game of tug-of-war on our very souls."

Do you recall how the twins' unruly behavior improved your life?

"I confess I do. When I visited the twins at their home and, just as I was about to leave, they taunted me in front of their art tutor. It was that day I discovered I had the talent to paint."

Were there other times?

"Yes, several more … but the one I appreciated most was when they tried to destroy my love for Sam. It was after their plot was exposed, I realized just how much I loved him. It was then I decided, should he ask, I would marry Sam.

So, can there be a benefit to the existence of evil?

"I believe there is."

What else have you learned?

I was silent as I looked back at my afterlife journey. Then it came to me. A revelation which should not have been a surprise.

I said, "Both Martha and Molly required forgiveness. Until they asked for the gift, no one could truly give it." I took a deep breath. "Lord God, please forgive me for I have held an anger towards you for cutting my life short, as well as my husband's."

Granted.

I felt the magnificent warmth of His embrace. I asked, "May I go, now?"

Yes, you are done.

"I wonder … Was I successful? Did I save Martha and Molly?"

Hannah, did you forget? I have the final spin of the wheel.

My shoulders drooped. "So, it's not over for them. Will I ever know what You have in store for them?"

You will be summoned before I take the last spin of the wheel. Until then, be with your husband.

CHAPTER 42

It is now February 2022. God has just spun the wheel for both Martha and Molly. I watch as the marble falls. It chose 14 Red.

✶   ✶   ✶

Lying on her back with her hands caressing her bloated tummy, tears trickled down the young woman's cheeks. She reached out and shook her husband awake. "Honey."

The man groaned. "It's the middle of the night."

She whimpered, "There's something wrong with my babies."

He rolled onto his side to face her. "You're just being silly."

"Silly?" She sniffled. "That's not a comforting thing to say to your wife."

Realizing his words were unwisely chosen, he sat up to atone for his mistake. "I'm sorry." Taking a more reassuring tone, he said, "The last ultrasound showed the twins are doing well and you were in excellent health. Remember what the doctor said?"

"She said my emotions will run wild. But I don't think it's that. Something's not right with our babies."

He reached out to hold her, she snuggled in his arms. "But your water hasn't broken," he said. "Are you having contractions?"

She shook her head. "No. But I feel something is wrong with my babies."

He knew her concerns could not be dismissed. He said, "I'll make an appointment for you to see the doctor later today."

She pulled away from him. "It's two in the morning and I don't think I can wait for an appointment." She pleaded, "I need to see a doctor now."

He sighed. "Okay, let's get dressed and go to the ER." Before getting out of bed, he kissed her tummy and felt two kicks hit his lips. He chuckled. "I think they're fighting with each other."

She scowled. "That's not funny. Now, help me out of bed."

✶　　　✶　　　✶

The woman was lying in an ER hospital bed, her husband at her side. As they waited for the doctor to arrive, she continued to worry about her babies. On the other hand, he was thinking about a story his mother had told him. It was a story about two peculiar twin ghosts, Martha and Molly McLellan.

For one hundred years, the ghosts had popped into the lives of the mothers who lived within the walls of the McLellan mansion, always after the first-born male was born. Now that he and his wife were living elsewhere and they were having twin girls, he assumed the conditions for the return of the unwanted specters were no longer present. Therefore, he had every reason to believe his wife would not be bothered by the ghosts.

The doctor entered the room holding the patient's chart in one hand and leaning on a cane with the other. She was a small blonde woman in her mid-forties. When she looked up, her eyes fell onto the husband. "Lieutenant?" she asked.

A look of shock came over the man. "Captain O'Connell?"

"Not anymore," she said. "Last year I retired from the Navy. You?"

"I recently transferred into the reserves. What's with the cane?"

She sighed. "My childhood afflictions have caught up with me."

He recalled the incident the doctor had shared in the ship's mess. She was thirteen when several huge logs had rolled over her. Crushed her.

The woman lying on the bed couldn't believe her husband and the doctor were having a casual chat while she and her babies required immediate attention.

"Doctor," she said, "I fear for my babies. I know something's wrong with Lizzy and Katie."

Dr. Kristine O'Connell turned to the woman lying in the bed. "Please accept my apology. I didn't expect to run into your husband after leaving the Navy." Approaching her patient, the doctor said, "So, I see you've already chosen names for your girls."

"Please save my babies," she pleaded.

"Don't you worry," she said. "Let's see if today you will meet them."

Minutes later, everyone within the examining room watched the screen as a foreboding image commanded their attention. An umbilical cord was wrapped tightly around the neck of one of the baby girls.

✶　　✶　　✶

Martha could scarcely make out her surroundings. Try as she might, she couldn't discover the identity of the person she was in. The thoughts held by this tiny person were of contentment and a powerful desire to be born. Embraced within the warmth of a mother's womb, Martha sensed they were not alone. She could hear voices filled with great concern coming from outside the woman's body.

During her lifetime and after her death, Martha had collected countless memories. Like leaves falling from a maple tree on a cool autumn day, her fond and not so fond recollections were being scattered about, quickly fading from her mind.

Martha looked to one side and saw another baby, this one in distress. The umbilical cord around that baby's neck was choking the life out of her.

✳   ✳   ✳

One minute Molly was enjoying the warmth of a liquid world, the next she was not. Her hands went up and felt the cord around her neck. She frantically thought, *Is it time for my execution? Oh, God! Please save me!*

A pair of little hands reached out to Molly; tiny fingers gently unraveled the cord. As each wrap untangled, knowledge of Molly being Molly dissolved from her mind. Before all her memories had vanished, one final thought was sent to her from the other baby within the womb.

There, my sister, now we can both be born again.

✳   ✳   ✳

After having witnessed God's miracle, I stepped out of the hospital to find a fresh blanket of snow had fallen on the Portland peninsula. Hours ago, dawn had broken, and a blazing warm sun was now melting the snow. It was an unusual occurrence as it was late February, and the temperature had risen to a pleasant sixty-five degrees.

As I stood basking in the sunlight, two people walked by me discussing the reason for the abrupt change in the weather. Both said it was due to global warming.

I chuckled for it was God's proud smile which had caused the climatic change. His efforts—and mine I should add—had saved the souls of Martha and Molly, the newest members of the McCabe dynasty.

ABOUT THE AUTHOR

Cary Vajda worked for forty years in the field of higher education where his focus was nonfiction. Reports, evaluations, regulations—his work was important, but was a poor outlet for his creative side. With encouragement from his daughter, a fiction writer, he has immersed himself in the world of fantasy—and found his passion. Residing in Midland, Michigan, with his wife, Sally, the two enjoy the bounty of nature from their home on the high banks of the Chippewa River. In addition to repurposing antique furniture, Cary now writes in his free time. *Saving Martha & Molly* is his first published novel. Three others are waiting in the wings, all part of a series named Ghosts of Casco Bay.

9 781965 278857